Y9 Box 6

(36)

Heart to heart

HEART TO HEART

Ten love stories
edited by Miriam Hodgson

MAMMOTH

First published in Great Britain 1996
by Mammoth, an imprint of Reed International Books Ltd
Michelin House, 81 Fulham Road, London SW3 6RB
and Auckland, Melbourne, Singapore and Toronto

ISBN 0 7497 2641 5

A CIP catalogue record for this title
is available from the British Library

Printed and bound in Great Britain
by Cox & Wyman Ltd, Reading, Berkshire

Contents

Hump and Son

Anne Fine

'You're fired,' he shouted at her when she finally came through the door.

'Oh, Ned,' she said, handing him a bag full of vegetables to carry. 'It's only Wednesday.'

'I know it's only Wednesday,' he stormed. 'And this is the third time this week you've taken over two hours for lunch, so you're fired. Hump and Son can't afford to keep you.'

'Hump and Son can't afford *not* to,' she said, and sailed up the stairs.

Ned sighed. She was right. He couldn't fire her. She was the only secretary in Greater London who could read his father's writing. Weighed down by his worries and her shopping, he fell in behind.

'Marry me, then,' he wailed.

'No,' she said, reaching the landing.

'Why not?' he asked, as he always did.

Laughing, she shut the door to the Ladies in his face.

He trailed disconsolately into the cramped and cluttered office where Edward Hump, curled like a malignant owl over a jumbo-sized pad, was composing his eighteenth whodunnit that year.

'She's getting worse,' Ned told his father. 'She'll have to go.'

'Go away yourself,' said Edward Hump. He was wondering whether, just for a change, he might let the butler be the murderer after all. But then the vicar should have attended Miss Phipps's tea party in chapter two for an alibi, and she had already printed those pages. If he rewrote them now, she would be furious. Feeling art thwarted, he wiped his pen on the curtains she had chosen. It would have to be the vicar, as usual. He promised himself that next time he would work the plot out fully before he began.

Ned was astride the swivel chair now, fiddling with the keys on her word processor, and grumbling softly. 'She's *never* been this bad before.' Irritably he drummed his fingers on the keyboard, and a series of strange and unaccountable letters suddenly appeared on her screen.

Yet another victimpf*q!?!

'Two whole hours and a quarter,' he muttered, freshly outraged. 'For *lunch*.'

He tried to delete his small contribution to his father's work, stopping only when he noticed line after line on the screen rapidly melting away. 'She's been awful since the last time I proposed to her.'

Edward Hump toyed with the notion of a torrid affair between the vicar and Miss Phipps in chapter seven. Sales might rocket, solving Hump and Son's financial problems; but finding the idea rather distasteful, he discarded it again. After all, money wasn't everything.

'When *did* you last propose to her?' he asked his son.

Ned looked at his watch. 'About six minutes ago,' he

said. 'But I really meant the time before that.' He took another look at the empty screen. She would be furious. 'I know she'll marry me sooner or later,' he said mournfully. 'I just wish she'd hurry up.' He spread his hands. 'What's *wrong* with me?'

Edward Hump despaired of his son at times and this was one of them. He placed his pen on the jumbo pad, where it lay, leaking gently.

'Forgive me if I trample,' he began courteously. 'But perhaps she would view your suit with more favour if you were to refrain from thrusting a week's notice in her face with one hand as often as you offer her the other in marriage.'

His son did not look up. He was making a chain from her paper-clips.

'Perhaps there are finer points to your policy of courtship,' Edward Hump kindly suggested. 'But steeped though I am by trade in the machinations of warped minds, they escape me.'

His son was rooting for more clips in the corner of her desk drawer.

'Your bearing strikes me as odd,' pursued Edward Hump. 'Not calculated to engage a young lady's confidence in the long-term prospects for any normal relationship. You take her out to lunch and detain her, proposing, for over two hours. On return, you fire her for being late.' He rescued his pen from the ink flood that threatened to submerge it. 'In her less flighty moments, she may have doubts about you.'

Ned held up his chain of her paper-clips. Although it was nearly a metre long, it did not cheer him appreciably.

'*I* don't take her to lunch,' he said.

'Pardon me,' said his father. 'You used to. I thought you still did. It seemed to fit nicely. Each day this week, for example, she has risen from her seat promptly at one o'clock, planted a kiss on my cheek and said happily: "Heigh-ho. Off to see Ted." Or Ned. I forget which. But it's all the same thing.'

Ned tore the paperclip chain to bits in his fury.

'It's not the same thing at all!' he snapped. 'Not at all!'

The next day, at one o'clock, he followed her. She set off at a brisk pace down the High Street. Ned shambled behind, hands sunk into trouser pockets, staring morosely at the back of her long legs. At one point she shot into a chemist's shop. Intrigued by a display of greying trusses in the window, he almost lost her.

Emerging, she jaywalked across the road, and a tanker driver braked to let her pass, whistling appreciatively. Ned jaywalked after her, and the same driver speeded up to cut him off, with a nasty oath. Loftily, Ned ignored him. The end of the enormous tanker finally rolled clear, and Ned saw her legs disappearing into the museum's revolving door. He hared up the steps, but the foyer was empty.

The museum was vast — three floors with numerous offshoots, two exhibition halls and an outdoor annexe. Ned was not a systematic man. It took him an hour and three-quarters to find her, and it was his third time around.

She was standing in a huge, vaulted chamber, half-hidden by a trio of walruses, stroking the snout of a large stuffed seal. She seemed to be telling it something.

Ned leaned, panting and bemused, against a large elk. He felt a little cheered. Perhaps Ted had stood her up. Perhaps she would marry Ned on the rebound.

A polite cough startled Ned from his pleasant thoughts. A museum attendant was at his side.

'Would you mind?' the attendant said. 'Them elks is precious.'

Ned pointed across to the walruses. 'What about *her*, then?' he demanded peevishly. 'She's stroking that thing's *nose*.'

'That's different,' the attendant said. 'That seal's been condemned.'

Accepting this explanation, Ned took his own weight.

'Besides,' the attendant went on. 'She's gentle with him. *Leptonychotes Weddelli* don't come to no harm from her.'

'Who don't?'

'*Leptonychotes Weddelli*.' After a pause he added loftily: 'Weddell's seal to you.'

Knitting his brows, he, like Ned, stared across the room. 'Odd, though. *She* calls him Ted.'

Ned's large mouth fell open.

'Or Ned. One or the other. It's all the same thing.'

'Only to the hard of hearing and the half-witted,' Ned muttered unpleasantly.

Deeply hurt, the attendant made to go. Ned caught his arm. 'I'm terribly sorry, truly I am,' he pleaded. 'I'm a little overwrought.'

Mollified as much by Ned's obvious misery as by the apology, the attendant once again became expansive. 'Comes here every day,' he said. 'Strokes that there seal's nose and talks to him for hours. Even brings sandwiches sometimes.'

'For the seal?' asked Ned, astonished.

'For her lunch,' the attendant said, eyeing Ned narrowly. 'The seal is dead.' He rocked proprietorially on his heels. 'Strange that she should choose him from all this lot.' He made a generous gesture which took in all his finer specimens, himself and Ned.

'Very,' Ned muttered bitterly.

'And downright unsanitary, when you come to think. That seal must be thirty years old if he's a day. Stuffing's *pouring* out. That's why he's been condemned. Only yesterday I told her, "You ought to choose someone else to talk to, dear. How about a nice moose," I said. But she wouldn't have it. Oh, no. Women are like that, though.' He scratched his chin. 'Said he reminds her of someone she loves.'

Ned went all cunning.

'Did you ask her why she hasn't married this man who looks like a seal and whom she loves?' he asked, casual to a degree.

'No,' said the attendant, and wandered off to prise a small child from the knees of his nice moose.

Ned glared, dispirited, at the elk against whom he had been forbidden to lean. The elk glared back, looking a bit like she did when she was in one of her moods. Finding the odds against him intoxicating, Ned tried to stare the elk out. The elk won, and Ned looked round again.

She had gone.

He approached the seal warily, from the rear. Horny

hind flippers led up into threadbare fur, mottled cream and fawn, and blotching into silver on the back of its head. The taxidermist's seam spiralled from one end of the seal to the other, like a stocking gone awry. The seal smelled of mould and mothballs, shed stuffing in places, and had no neck. And it reminded her of someone she loved? Ned was not a vain man, but it crossed even his mind that to kindle a love so unflattering might perhaps be worse than kindling no love at all. He poked the seal's paunch experimentally, and a whiff of decaying fur rose up and hit him full in the face. Ned decided that there must be another man in her life, not noted for personal freshness, and by name of Ted. He walked round to the front of the seal to inspect the stuffed facial likeness of his rival for her hand.

It was only then that he saw the seal's eyes. They loomed up at him, set wide above bristled cheeks, large and chocolate brown, and a little bloodshot around the edges. Ned stared at them, appalled. He had seen both of them before. They were his eyes too. There was no possibility of his being mistaken. He recognised them from shaving.

Panicking, Ned looked away.

The elk had brown eyes, too. He supposed, thinking about it, that most animals did. Feeling calmed by this reflection he looked back at the seal. His shock was again immediate. No other animal had eyes like these eyes, and these eyes were like his. This seal's eyes brimmed with memories so forlorn, the cool elk and his brothers could not guess at them. Ned found these eyes worse than harrowing. They told of all the pitiful hours this seal had passed, vigilant and alone, on drifting ice floes, longing for better days. The bleak Antarctic twilight had brought this seal to such desperation that he had lumbered off towards his very hunters, prepared to hazard life itself for the sound of a muffled voice, or the sight of two eyes that were not his own, gazing back reproachfully from an ice looking-glass.

Ned swallowed, near to tears. He stretched out his hand, as she had done, to comfort the seal with a caress. But he could not bring himself to touch it. It would, he thought, be like saying 'There, there' to a shipwreck.

Ned began walking round and round the seal, thinking. Could it be that he looked like that (give or take a few whiskers) to her? Could it be that she felt this shattered each time he turned his own eyes on her, imploring marriage? Then small wonder that she always refused. No one could live with that seal, and stay sane. Why should she take such a risk with him? There was no hope.

Ned stopped circling the seal, and began walking up and down the chamber in straight lines.

Of course there was hope. The seal was stuffed, and must always look as it did now; whereas Ned was alive, and could possibly look different on occasions. He was not forever shaving or proposing, after all.

Ned wandered off to the sides of the chamber in search of his own reflection. Stationing himself four-square before the dark furry tummy of a conveniently encased bat, Ned stared at himself in the glass. His own eyes looked, if that were possible, a shade more woebegone even than the seal's. Ned gulped and began his experiment.

He smiled at himself warmly, unconscious of the attendant's curious stare. The face crumpled up, as smiling faces do; but the eyes remained tragic – two islands of suffering in a sea of good cheer.

He tried a knowing, man-to-man look. The eyebrows played their part with enthusiasm, but the eyes refused to be drawn.

He told himself a short joke, and chuckled at the punch line. The eyes were unamused.

Sympathetic understanding and swashbuckling arrogance fared no better. Ned made one last attempt – a depraved leer. The bat seemed quite taken, but the eyes were indifferent. Ned lost his temper.

The eyes lit up, transformed. Ned hardly recognised himself. He sighed with relief, unguardedly, and the eyes wavered. So he thought of how she made him carry her vegetables all the way up the stairs, and then slammed doors in his face. The eyes rallied. He recalled the sneaky way in which his father had for years postponed all increases in his salary. The eyes became positively frenzied.

A rare feeling of exhilaration swept through Ned as he stood, seemingly riveted to the bat's tummy, remembering one affront to his pride after another, and watching his eyes flash. The attendant, lurking behind the walruses, thought it was odd, the sort of creatures people took fancies to, nowadays. He wondered momentarily if the bat reminded Ned of someone he loved.

Ned, taking one last look in the bat, thought it was

astonishing just how much he had brooked from them both. He strode from the museum, a new man.

The slamming of the office door caused Edward Hump to catch his funny bone on the *Dictionary of Acids and Poisons*. A large blot of ink fell from his pen on to the inspector's explanation of the fiendish way in which the vicar, with the help of Miss Phipps, had disposed of all nine bodies overnight.

'You're back, then,' he said, testing the small ink pool for depth with the tip of his finger. 'Would you be so good as to pass me some blotting paper?'

In answer, Ned swung the door open once more, and slammed it shut with even more force than before. Edward Hump looked up.

So did she. Indeed, she went further. She stopped typing and, pushing the keyboard forward a few centimetres, rested her elbows comfortably on the desk, and her dimpled chin on her cupped palms.

He waved a banker's order threateningly in her direction.

'How much does a normal person earn?' he demanded of her. 'Someone normal, my age, like me. How much?'

She told him. His eyebrows shot up in astonishment. He glared venomously at his father. Then he snatched up a pen from the marmalade pot full of them on her desk, and filled the amount in on the order. 'I'm not earning a penny less than a normal person any longer,' he muttered fiercely.

He slammed the order down in front of Edward Hump.

'Go on, then,' he said aggressively. 'Sign it.'

Edward Hump peered with interest at the amount Ned had decided to earn.

'I can't pay you that much,' he said. 'It's as much as I earn myself.'

'That's quite all right,' Ned told him. 'You're retiring at the end of this month.'

He pulled his father's resignation from a trouser pocket and uncrumpled that, too, upon Edward Hump's desk.

'Go on, then,' he repeated. 'Sign them both.'

Edward Hump wished his son would go away. He wanted to get the vicar defrocked and safely imprisoned by the weekend, so that he could get on with some gardening. Laboriously, he stained a dotted line at the foot of the banker's order with his spidery runes.

With unaccustomed adroitness, Ned whisked the precious slip of paper away and pocketed it. 'Now the other,' he said firmly.

Edward Hump turned his flagging attention to the other foreign body on his desk, and made a big effort.

'Much as the notion of resignation from Hump and Son appeals,' he began, 'and, Lord knows, the shrubbery could do with some sustained attention—'

'Blast the bloody shrubbery,' shouted Ned. 'Sign it!'

Edward Hump made a little scratchy mess on the spot his son's finger indicated. Almost immediately, another drawback struck him. He nodded in the direction of the only secretary in Greater London who could read his writing.

'What about her?' he said. 'If I retire, it's curtains

for her. She'll have to go. There'll be no work for her. Possibly she'll starve.'

'She won't starve,' said Ned.

'She may well,' his father disagreed. 'Her filing is dismal. No one else would employ her.'

'*I'm* going to employ her,' said Ned. 'I'll feed her. I'll feed her lots of milk. We'll be needing another "and Son". Or "and Daughter". She can have them. She can have lots. Bloody cotfuls.'

'I see,' said Edward Hump. 'It's all clear to me now. You're planning on altering the tone of the books we produce. Hump and Son is moving from murder into romance.' He waggled a finger at the two of them. 'I warn you, the outcome is generally much the same.'

'We'll be all right,' Ned said, turning to his beloved. 'Won't we?'

She turned on him that cool, elk-like look that drove him wild. 'Will we?' she said. 'Oh, will we really? And suppose I don't choose to have your mangy babies, Ned Hump?'

'I warned you,' Edward Hump muttered. 'Romance is dead.'

But Ned didn't hear him. He was beside himself with rage.

'Choose? *Choose?*' He was shouting to make the light bulbs tremble. 'You're going to choose. You're going to choose right *now*. You're going to choose between that disgusting old mothbag seal in that crumbling museum, and that malevolent old mothbag, my father, in that ink-swamped desk over there, and this fine strapping person, myself, standing before you. And you are going to choose *me*!'

He thrust his face, scarlet with rage, over the word processor at her, and they glared at each other.

Suddenly she smiled, and kissed him wetly on the nose.

A few days later, while his father was engaging the registrar in a bit of light chat about the Brides in the Bath, Ned Hump signed his name with a flourish wherever his new wife placed her dainty, freshly manicured finger.

'There,' she said, pointing. 'And there and there and there and there.'

It seemed an awful lot of places to have to sign your name, just to get married. And his father, appending his name as witness whilst explaining to the registrar how best to chop up a body, said much the same.

Then the three of them ambled happily through the doors into the sunlight, arm in arm, and as the photographer stepped forward to greet them, Ned Hump honoured his bride with his first sweet nothing.

'*Now* you're fired,' he whispered in her ear.

She smiled imperturbably. Pulling a slim roll of legal papers out of her bouquet of lilies, she lifted her face for her first married kiss.

'Don't be so silly, Ned,' she said to him sweetly as the photographer took his first picture. 'You've only just this minute made me a partner.'

Romeo and Juliet, Act VI

Geraldine McCaughrean

Forget what you've read of twin suicides, tragic misunderstandings, star-crossed lovers. Everything went exactly to plan.

The friar's unholy potion worked perfectly. His letter explaining the plan reached Mantua without delay. Romeo arrived at the appointed hour, entering the graveyard and levering open the Capulet vault just as Juliet stirred. He was in time for his face to fill her waking vision: the sweetest sight her eyes had ever beheld.

There was one moment's danger, when Count Paris confronted them at the gates. Banished from Verona on pain of death, Romeo knew he must draw his sword and kill Paris, if they were to make their getaway. Fortunately, the count's reactions had been slow, his eyes still full of tears at the thought of Juliet's untimely death. Seeing them both standing there, in the twilit river mist, he seemed to freeze, overpowered by uncomprehending fear: perhaps he thought he was seeing ghosts. Romeo, on the other hand, was keyed up, on his mettle. Moving among all those coffins, tombstones and bones had heightened his appreciation of life. He was young; he was in love; he was alive. One quick thrust under the count's heart, and he and Juliet were safe. They rode to Mantua by moonlight, breaking their journey to make love and to sleep under a fusillade of stars.

Not that the thing had gone entirely in accordance with Friar Lawrence's plan. The priest who married them, then arranged for their elopement, had nursed sentimental notions of family reconciliations, happy endings, the Houses of Capulet and Montague united by the love of their offspring, and so forth.

Paris's death had put paid to that. Romeo and Juliet could never return to Verona. But what did that matter? What did they care? They had each other. They needed no one and nothing else. They were grown up. They prided themselves on being more grown up, in truth, than the sentimental friar. After all, they knew mysteries that he would never know in his cold, celibate cell, reading his dusty Scriptures. Romeo and Juliet had discovered the alchemy of love, and that had showered down on their heads whole constellations of dazzling insight.

Still, finding a post was difficult. Because of Paris dying, Romeo feared he might be a wanted man the length and breadth of Italy. So he did not dare give his own name or state his background when applying for positions. His clothes marked him out as a nobleman, but his lack of beard also marked out his extreme youth. And what, after all, could he actually do? There seemed no call for secretaries in Mantua that summer. He was quick with his sword, but not so quick as to teach fencing. He could pick flowers, but not grow them. He could versify, but that is not a paying trade. He could climb walls but not mend or build them. He could ride horses, but not shoe or groom them.

An aged countess called him 'the very man she had been searching for'! But then, when he mentioned that he was newly married, and in love, she suddenly found that she had mistaken: he would not suit her needs at all.

They laughed about it, he and Juliet, in their comfortable inn room, eating cutlets and drinking out of each other's wine cup. They laughed and laughed about the ugly, antique, amorous countess until their foreheads and fingers touched across the table. Then they stopped laughing and they stopped eating, their throats too tight for food, their stomachs too shrunk by a different hunger. They wrapped themselves in one another, as though vying each to be the most inward layer. They tunnelled to the molten centre of the earth, and re-emerged from it like volcanic lava splattering the sky with hot new constellations.

Then suddenly the money was gone. The landlord's smiling face froze over like a pond, losing its colour. He threw their baggage out into the street. Even to afford cheaper lodgings, they had to sell the silver crucifix Juliet wore round her neck.

He refused to sell his sword.

The lodgings they found were cheap and jumping with fleas. But they had each other. What more did they need? They lived on bread and fruit, and had too little to wear when autumn turned to winter. But to combat the discomfort they invented a game: they were Adam and Eve, returned secretly to paradise, living in perfect simplicity, simple perfection among the fruit trees of wisdom.

Sitting cradled between her husband's knees, his arms circling her from behind, his chin resting on her hair, Juliet considered how she might be of more practical help than just inventing games. She loved dresses, but she could not sew. She could speak Latin, but not the language of the market-place, haggling for a good price. She liked to eat, but she could not cook.

She would have made a good lady-in-waiting, or so she believed, but the marquesa in the crumbling palazzo on the corner of the square did not seem so sure. She opened the shutters, the better to look Juliet over – walked her round like a museum exhibit, then flicked her forefinger at the taut laces of her bulging stomacher. 'That is *not* precisely what I meant when I advertised for a lady-in-waiting,' she said, with haughty sarcasm.

Romeo was full of wonder at the thought of being a father. His eyes filled with stars, his hands reached out to feel the wonder of it, then stopped, in loving parenthesis, not quite daring to touch her swollen stomach. 'Our love. The living proof,' he said. 'Our child.' Then he saw the fright in her eyes, and he took fright too.

Juliet loved children – after all, a year ago she had been one herself – but she did not want to give birth to one. The thought of something growing inside her was terrifying – more terrifying than the friar's potion which she had so eagerly taken into her body to achieve a likeness of death. This likeness of life in her little, immature womb might very well kill her by its arrival. Besides, it made her not lily pale and lovely so much as cabbage green. For a while, she was violently sick every day, something which disgusted Romeo so much that his solicitude came only from the other side of the door. Later sympathy hardened into disapproval.

'You know, I suppose, I've no money for a new dress, if you soil that one,' he said.

As the baby quickened and began to kick, the need for money kicked just as violently at Romeo's guts. One day he went out and, without asking her opinion, attached himself to a private troop of soldiers. He brought the news home and flung it at her feet, along with a dead, unplucked chicken: a celebratory dinner. The bird's dangling claws, shrivelled and clenched, caught in the hem of her dress. His belligerent face dared her to find fault with his choice of profession.

'Will you have to fight?' she asked, her eyes round with fear.

'I can do that well enough,' he said, with a touch of swagger. His livery was too big for him; it made his neck look scrawny and stretched, like the chicken's. 'I have to sleep at the barracks, naturally.'

How could she complain? His sacrifice was huge: to sleep on a hard bed among snoring, stinking, brutish soldiers. How could she complain? And yet they had not been apart before – not since Verona. She had never slept with only the fleas and mice for company, the drip of the leaking roof, the noise of the woman coughing in the room downstairs. Juliet was sick after dinner.

'All that chicken. Wasted,' he said, bundled up his belongings and went to the barracks then and there.

*

She did not know how he could bear it, being among coarse fighting men all day, every day. He so sensitive and tender and loving and gentle. But oddly, the separation refurbished some of Juliet's sweetest feelings towards her husband. She longed for his company now, whereas, looking back, she could see how they had begun to grate and chafe against each other in the oppressive confines of their single tiny room. Now she longed for him.

Now she loved the idea of him so dearly that she went walking down by the barracks so as to glimpse his dear face. The soldiers whistled and miaowed at her from behind the iron grilles on the windows. Fists curved out into the sunlight in obscene gestures. The interior was dark: she could not see in. Romeo could have been any one of them.

'Please stay with me,' she said, when he next came home. 'What if the child comes and I'm all alone?'

'You can call a friend.'

'I have no friends. Not here. Not in Mantua.'

'And that's my fault, I suppose.'

'I didn't say that. I didn't say it was anyone's fault.'

'That's what you meant, though. If we had stayed in Verona. All your smart Capulet friends. All those simpering, tight-kneed virgins could have come cooing over your big mistake. Congratulating themselves it wasn't them.'

'*Mistake?*'

She did not ask him again to come home more often.

The child was born with the help of the woman downstairs. And Juliet did not die, though she thought she was going to. The baby, wizened and blue, did not seem greatly to resemble either Juliet or Romeo. If anything, it most closely resembled the woman downstairs, especially when it began to cough — a little, tiresome, feeble cough. Within a week it was dead.

'Shall I send word to the barracks, child?' said the woman from downstairs. 'He ought to know. These things change a man.'

'He will come when he can,' said Juliet, imitating the serenity she had seen in other, grown-up women, mimicking poise and composure.

'And what's to stop him coming, I'd like to know?' the woman carped shrilly. 'They don't *have* to sleep at the barracks. If you ask me, they only do it to be nearer the whorehouse . . .'

When he came at last, he had been drinking. His breath was sour with Rhenish and cheap beer. His eyes could not, or did not, focus on hers.

'I thought I might write to my father,' said Juliet. 'About the child.'

Perhaps that smacked of betrayal. Perhaps Romeo was jealous that a man other than he had found room to lodge inside her head. Besides, drink had never agreed with him. He hit her across the mouth with the back of his hand. It was the kind of thing that happened all the time at the barracks — every time a word was spoken out of turn. Fists, swearwords, a brawl.

He was sorry afterwards. He went to embrace her. But she pulled away from him, trembling like a captive rabbit.

That's his answer to everything, she thought. He was banished for killing my cousin Tybalt, wasn't he? In a fit of temper? Wasn't he? And he killed Paris, didn't he? For no good reason.

And all of a sudden she remembered what had happened at the graveyard gates. She saw it as if for the first time – as though it were happening in front of her. She had shut it out till now. She had shut her eyes at the time, but not soon enough. She had witnessed the look on the count's face: the shock, the fresh tear stains, the confusion, the pain. He had come to mourn her supposed death, and Romeo had killed him for it. Romeo and his temper. From that everything bad had stemmed. From that had come one disaster after another. From Romeo's filthy Montague temper, his childish Montague spleen.

'If I had married Paris, like my parents wanted . . .' she began to say.

She did not need to say any more, for he was far ahead of her. If he had not killed Paris for love of her – to make good their getaway – he might have found employment in Mantua, escaped poverty, degradation, lice and a soldier's barbarous, bloody life. He might have been a poet, harboured poetical thoughts towards a poetical world, kept alive his boyhood belief in everlasting love. But instead, Juliet had decided to love him, to rely on him, to burden him with her devotion, to saddle him with obligations and guilt.

'I should have married Paris,' she said, this time with more certainty.

'Yes,' he said, as he ran her through with his sword.

Sweet Caroline

Berlie Doherty

Caroline trailed behind her grandmother. The road was full of rubble and yellow dust. On either side diggers and bulldozers were throbbing like huge insects. Daily the honey-coloured shells of new hotels seemed to spring out of the earth.

'Gran, how can you stand this racket all the time?'

'You get used to it,' her grandmother said. 'And it can't go on for ever. Think how lovely it will be when it's finished.'

'It was probably much nicer before they started.'

Caroline thought longingly of England, with its cold, wet, wintry streets, but she kept her thoughts to herself. Her grandparents had paid for her flight over to stay with them in their winter apartment in Malta. The day after she left hospital after having her tonsils out they'd sent a telegram: 'Send Sweet Caroline. We're missing her.' Even then she hadn't really wanted to come. But it was only for a week, and half of it had gone already. She'd be free to go back home soon.

'I'm really sorry we can't take you out today,' Gran said for the tenth time. Grandad had sprained his ankle tripping into a pot-hole. 'You'll enjoy exploring on your own, though. And the public transport here is so simple. Nothing can go wrong.'

Disorderly queues of holiday-makers chatted in the bus-terminal square. They were all on winter sun holidays. There wasn't a young person in sight. Caroline stood with her head down, hoping no one would notice her. Gran was looking at the map.

'Where would you like to go? Valletta? Rabat?'

The names meant nothing to Caroline. She stared at the row of little snub-nosed green buses. Another was just pulling up to join the line. It was gleaming with green and eggshell-blue paint. The round headlamps looked just like eyes, wide awake with surprise and fun.

'I'll go on that one.'

'Number 51.' Gran peered at her timetable. 'I don't think I know that route.'

'It's a lovely bus,' said Caroline. 'I'd really like a ride on it. I don't really care where it's going.' The bus began to rev up. Caroline ran to it. 'Bye Gran!'

It was the first time Caroline had shown any enthusiasm for anything since she came. 'I do believe,' Gran told her husband later, 'that our little Caroline has fallen in love with a bus!'

That was the day Caroline met Victor.

When she was paying her twenty-cent fare Caroline noticed two things. First, that the driver was only a few years older than she was, and second, that there was a passenger seat at right angles to him, facing him across the narrow front of the bus. All the elderly people crowded down to the back in a giggling huddle, sharing horror stories about the state of their hotels and apartments. She'd heard it all before. A woman in matching flowery shorts and T-shirt tapped her on the arm. Caroline recognised her from Gran's apartment block. 'On your own today?' she asked Caroline. 'You can come and sit with me if you like.'

The driver nodded to the seat alongside him and Caroline sank down into it, blushing slightly. He glanced across at her. She noticed that his eyes were the colour of walnuts.

'You like Malta?' he asked her.

Caroline nodded. She hoped he would think it was sunburn that was making her face glow.

'English girl?'

She nodded again. She tried not to look at him. The floor and the ceiling of the bus were painted the same shining eggshell-blue. On the wall next to her face was a little brass fire extinguisher, gleaming like sunshine. She could see her reflection in it. Festooned around the driver's cab were colourful badges and holy pictures, and there was a glass case on a shelf above his head. It was edged with a fringe of golden tassels, and inside that was a blue-robed statue of the Virgin Mary, lit by a bulb that looked like a candle.

'You like my bus?'

'It's beautiful!' Caroline said. 'It's like a little house!' She dared to look at him at last. As he drove he flicked smiling sideways glances at her.

'You are London?'

'Sheffield.'

The driver fished in a box underneath his seat and

brought out a handful of striped scarfs. He released a red and white one and draped it across the windscreen shelf.

'Sheffield United!'

She didn't tell him that she wasn't interested in football, or that her brother supported Sheffield Wednesday. She just smiled at him and felt warm.

'Your name?'

'Caroline.'

'My favourite name,' he said, instantly.

'Is it?' She was surprised. 'I'm named after a Neil Diamond song. My dad used to sing it when he was in a rock band.'

'I know it.'

And there he was, the driver of the most beautiful bus in the world, singing her song at the top of his voice. At the back of the bus a choir of white-haired, sun-flared holiday-makers sang out the chorus. Outside the window the sea was a deep, glimmering blue. The prickly-pear hedgerows glowed with flowers, and lemons like yellow moons blazed in the trees.

The journey ended in the square of a little village near a sandy bay. The holiday-makers piled out, as noisy and light-hearted as a class of children on a school trip. Caroline was the last to leave the bus.

'*Ciao*, Caroline,' the driver said.

'Chow,' she said awkwardly.

'I am Victor,' he told her, raising his hand to her as he drove away.

She watched his bus until it was out of sight. The woman in the flowery shorts and T-shirt called out to her and she followed her up a lane. She stood gazing over a wall at a heap of stones which, the woman told her, were the remains of Roman baths. 'See that square there?' the woman said. 'That's a Roman toilet. And it seats fifteen at a time! Three on each side!'

Twelve, thought Caroline, but she kept it to herself. The woman reminded her of her gran. The backs of her hands were flecked with brown freckles, and she had a gold ring on every finger. If she was in England now she'd be wearing boots and dark woolly clothes, scuttling to the shops between icy showers.

'All sitting there in their togas, having a good old gossip in the sunshine! Just imagine.'

Caroline went back down to the beach and ate the picnic lunch of salty cheese and dusty tomatoes that Gran had bought for her on the way to the bus station. She dipped her toes in the cold sea and then fell asleep, and dreamed that she had put on a blue robe and climbed into a glass box, a candle in one hand and a brass fire extinguisher in the other. She was shaken awake by the woman in the flowery shorts.

'You'd better hurry, love,' she was told. 'The last bus goes in ten minutes. Wouldn't do to miss that.'

Caroline was flustered. She had promised herself she would only go back in Victor's bus, and now she had left herself with no choice. All the holiday-makers flocked to the square, calling out to each other like seagulls. Caroline closed her eyes as she waited with them. She could hear the bus coming. She could feel the heat from it as it pulled up alongside her. When she opened her eyes she saw her bulgy reflection in the bumpers and knew that it was his bus. She took it all in:

the car badges on the radiator grill, topped by a shining jaguar, and over the split windscreen the word FORD in big red letters. She snapped up every detail as if she were a camera. She would write it all in a diary when she got back to the apartment. She would borrow Gran's watercolours and paint a picture of Victor's bus.

On the journey home Caroline told Victor about her school and her tonsils operation. He told her he had always wanted to go to England, to Sheffield in particular. Yes, he said, really, Sheffield was where he wanted to live.

'Why?'

'It must be a very beautiful town.'

Caroline imagined the little bus weaving in and out of the Supertram tracks along West Street. She saw all the sunny-faced passengers beaming out at city pedestrians. She saw herself in her front seat, waving at her school friends.

Victor leaned across and broke into her daydreams. 'What is your boyfriend called?'

'I haven't really got one.' She was blushing now, all round her neck and inside her ears. Victor laughed. She couldn't help joining in.

When they arrived at the depot Gran was waiting anxiously. Caroline stepped off Victor's bus without giving him a glance.

The next morning Caroline said, as casually as she could, that she wouldn't really mind exploring on her own again.

'Our Caroline is growing up,' said Gran, with an air of great secrecy.

'You could go to Popeye Village, as they call it,'
Grandad suggested. 'They built a set there for the film,
and you can walk round it. You'd enjoy that.'

Caroline was careful not to commit herself.

'You can get the 47 bus and it drops you off about a
mile away.' Grandad scanned his bus-route map. 'Or,'
yawning slightly, 'get the same number bus you caught
yesterday and do a six-mile hike to it along the coast.
But I shouldn't think you'd fancy that.'

'No,' said Caroline, not looking at him or at her
smiling gran but at the filmy curtains of their apartment
billowing out over the view of half-built hotels and
rubble. 'I don't suppose I would.'

Half an hour later, and still breathless from running,
she was sitting on the bus. She narrowly beat an old man
to her seat. She knew Victor was pleased to see her.

'I'm going for a long walk today,' she told him. 'Right
along the coast.'

'Mind they don't shoot you.' He laughed at her
startled look and put out his hand towards her. 'They
might think you are a beautiful dove in your white dress.'

'They don't really shoot birds, do they?'

'Of course. Or trap them if they sing.' He shrugged.
'We all do.'

She bit her lip and looked away from him. He stopped
the bus sharply and pulled down the leather strap that
opened his window. He leaned out, shouting something
in his unfamiliar language, sharing a joke of some sort
with a fruit seller on the kerbside. A few minutes later
he turned back to Caroline, holding towards her a large
red apple.

'You are my apple's eye,' he told her.

She carried the apple in her rucksack all day. By the time she reached Popeye Village she had blisters on both heels and the soles of her feet ached from walking on the crinkly rock path of the cliff-tops. Nobody had been shooting birds but she had found lots of shooting butts with blue cartridge shells scattered round them. She saw a man carrying half a dozen tiny cages of singing birds, and watched him laying nets for traps. She wanted to run to him and set the birds free. Had Victor really said 'we all do it'? She felt clouded and bewildered, her throat ached. 'People are different, that's all,' she tried to tell herself. 'People think differently.' After all, her father caught fish, didn't he?

She enjoyed looking round Popeye Village. She imagined Victor coming out of one of the tipsy houses with an anchor tattooed on his arm. She took some photographs to show her brother, and that gave her a wonderful idea. She asked a tourist if he would take a photograph of her with her camera. She smiled shyly at the lens. It was for Victor. She would send it to him when she got back to England. She wouldn't even have to say who it was from. He would pin it up among his badges and holy pictures for everyone to see. She was so pleased with the idea that she asked every tourist who came along to take a picture of her. She would send the very best one to Victor.

By the time she'd used up all her film she knew it was too late to walk back the way she'd come. The last bus home was at five. She followed the other tourists down the country lane to the 42 bus stop. Maybe Victor would change buses just for today. He knew where she'd gone. Maybe he would drive his number 51 round to this stop, just to pick her up.

As she waited at the bus stop she took his apple out of her rucksack, polished it lovingly, and put it back. She was never going to eat it. When it had shrivelled up to nothing she was going to plant the core in the garden, right over the spot where Ginger Tom was buried. She would gather its blossoms into an envelope and post them to Victor.

The bus that came was scruffy and dinted. Its seats were threadbare and it was driven by a young man with a shaved head. He had three noisy friends sitting behind him. He drove with his hands waving in the air and his head twisting round like an owl. He shouted abuse at pedestrians and other drivers out of his window, and hurtled up and down lanes as if he was in a racing car. Caroline clung on to the seat, her knuckles white, her stomach in her throat. She wanted to die. She wanted Victor to soar up to the bus like Superman in his blue vest, push the driver out of the window and take over the wheel. But he didn't. Behind her the elderly tourists chortled, 'He always gives us a thrill for our money, this one!'

Just as she was stepping off the bus she saw the 51 pulling away. She ran towards it, and just caught a glimpse of Victor's face. The day bloomed again. She sang to herself as she ran back to the apartment. She would be on his bus again tomorrow.

Her grandparents were delighted to see her looking so cheerful.

'We'll spend the day together tomorrow,' they promised her. 'We'll take you to Mdina. After all, you've only got two days left.'

Two days left!

Desperately Caroline tried to find ways of spending the day on her own, but her grandparents were insistent.

'You can't possibly leave Malta without seeing Mdina,' Gran said. 'It's the ancient capital. We can go to the catacombs – think of that! And seeing as you like painting so much, we can take the watercolours and do some sketching. We'll spend the whole day there!'

Misery like a grey skin wrapped itself round Caroline.

It was the bleakest day of her life. She trudged behind her grandparents through the quiet streets of Mdina, and couldn't raise a smile or a word for them. She stood in the dimly lit passages of the catacombs and knew how Juliet had felt, alone in the cold darkness. She heard a party of schoolgirls shrieking with laughter and wondered how they could be so frivolous, so soulless. She felt edgy and strange. It was almost as if she was shedding her old skin, and there was a new self inside her urging to be let out.

It was late afternoon when they arrived back at Buggiba terminal. It was her last full day, and she hadn't seen Victor. Her grandparents had given up trying to cheer her out of her mood. Then, just as they were turning up the side-street to home, Grandad said, 'I hope you've taken a photo of those old buses for your dad.'

That new self began to soar inside her.

'What a good idea,' said Gran. 'You nip down to the buses, Caroline. We'll go back and start the dinner off.' She and Grandad held hands and walked slowly up the pitted street.

Caroline felt as if she were flying as she ran back to the terminus. She would have a photograph of her bus, with Victor at the driving wheel. No one would know. Every time she showed the picture of the little tubby bus she would see Victor again.

But the 51 wasn't there. People were all coming home from their days out, tired and sunburnt. The green buses were lining up like snug peas in a pod. She took a quick snap and turned away. A sudden toot made her jump. There was her bus, its headlamps flashing hello at her. Victor laughed down at her and pointed at her seat and without a second thought she stepped on to the bus and sat beside him. He had one more run to do, he told her. He had missed her.

They hurtled along the coast road, and she spilled out for him all the events of the day. All of a sudden it had been a day of delights. They laughed and joked as passengers clambered on and clambered off at their stops. Every now and then he sang snatches of her song. She leaned back and looked along the length of the bus. It was as familiar to her now as the apartment room. She would never forget how the red cables threaded their way across the eggshell-blue ceiling to the brass bell near the cab. She loved the way they made it chime. She loved the posters of gaily painted fishing boats and domed churches and knights' towers. She imagined living in the bus, polishing the fire extinguisher and the bell, scrubbing the painted floor to keep it spick and span. It would make a wonderful home. She and Victor would drive round in it to the end of their days.

If her grandparents noticed how her eyes were sparkling when she came back, or wondered how it could have taken her an hour and a half to take a photograph, they said nothing. But she couldn't sleep that night. Tomorrow evening she would be flying home again. When she had told Victor this she had promised to ride on his bus again the next morning. It would be very special. Maybe he would abandon his route and drive her round and round the island. She wouldn't mind if she missed her plane.

To Caroline's utter misery her grandparents decided to have a run on the bus with her. She didn't even look at Victor when they climbed on. They squashed up next to her in the long seat alongside Victor and chatted to him about the local racecourse. Caroline said nothing at all. She kept her head down and her hands clasped across her rucksack. She could feel the apple inside it.

They got off at a place called Mosta. They wanted to show her the church. Caroline hated churches. She hated her grandparents. She turned quickly round to Victor as they climbed off the bus ahead of her. 'I may never see you again,' she blurted out.

He leaned across, took her hand, and kissed it. 'Come back to Malta.'

'I will!' She could come back at Easter. She could spend the whole of the summer there. When she was old enough to leave home she would live there.

'*Ciao*, Sweet Caroline.'

'Chow, Victor.'

And when she jumped off the bus her gran put her arms round her shoulders and gave her a little squeeze, just as she used to do when she was about six years old and hopelessly unhappy about something. 'How about a cup of hot chocolate and a date slice?' she suggested.

When her bags were packed and she was waiting for the taxi to take her to the airport her grandad said, 'I hope you've enjoyed your little holiday, Caroline. It's no big deal really, being stuck with a couple of old fogies like us.'

Gran smiled at her.

'I've had a wonderful time!' said Caroline. 'It's the best holiday I've ever had in my whole life!'

She stepped into the taxi with a light heart. As soon as she lost sight of her grandparents' waving hands she opened her rucksack and took out the apple. She blew on it softly, her lips almost touching it. She breathed in its sweet, delicate scent.

She couldn't believe it when she saw the bus coming towards her. For a wild moment she imagined that Victor was about to hold up the taxi and kidnap her. She craned forward to wave to him. But the number 51 sailed on past her taxi, and Victor didn't even see her. He was too busy looking at the girl who was sitting beside him on Caroline's seat. They were both laughing out loud. Across the dashboard was draped a black and white scarf. The 51 bus roared past and away, away in a drizzle of yellow dust, away and out of sight, like a dream.

It was not until the taxi driver opened the door at the airport that Caroline realised she had eaten the apple. She paid the driver, walked into the departure lounge, and threw the core into the bin.

Regine, Regine

Jan Mark

He noticed the rug because they had one like it at home in the garage; slate blue with lean yellow stripes that divided it into squares. It was spread out in the alcove between the end of the library railings and the corner window of Crackers bistro. There were similar rugs spread out on the pavements all over town, little rafts of territory with one occupant, occasionally two; sometimes a dog as well, always a plastic margarine tub.

'Have you got any spare change, please?'

Some of the rug-rafters played musical instruments, like the guy with the recorder outside the covered market. Others, having nothing to offer, could only ask 'Have you got any spare change, please?'

This girl said it mechanically, as if triggered by a photo-sensitive cell when someone passed between her and the light; a neutral, impersonal voice, asking not for herself but for the body that must be fed. Not even her head moved when she spoke. She sat like a stone, like a conglomerate of stones adhering in a single lump; cracked leather coat, tartan wool wrappings, matt-black boots. Like mica in granite, little rings shone in a spiral

up the rim of each ear, the only shining thing about her.
'Have you got any spare change, please?'

The man in front of Robert stooped slightly to one
side and dropped coins into the margarine tub without
slackening speed. But he was not walking very quickly.
Robert, having no spare change, was about to accelerate
around him on the offside, thereby avoiding the robot
request, when his lowered eyes took in a second head
emerging from the corner of the rug.

It was a dog's head. He saw the round brown eyes
gleam in a coat as pale as limed oak and as slick as an
otter's. The animal arched its neck and from under the
rug came a long pointed muzzle like a dagger drawn
from beneath a cloak; more beak than muzzle, more bird
than dog. An impossibly slender limb was extended,
trembling.

'Have you got any spare change, please?'

He had not meant to stop. He carried only a five-
pound note and a five-pence piece, the one too large, the
other too small. But now that he had stopped he could
not simply walk away.

'It's beautiful, what is it?'

'It's a dog, isn't it?'

He crouched by the rug. 'I meant, what breed?'

'Lurcher.' She did not look at him, keeping the photo-
sensitive cell trained on the pavement.

The word conjured up smoky fires and caravans,
poached rabbits. 'I thought they were hairy.' And hard.

'Yes, well, the hairy ones are, aren't they? She'll be a
retriever cross.'

'Where did you get her?'

'Got given her, didn't I?' A shadow skimmed them. 'Have you got any spare change, please?'

It was no tinker's bitch. The lurcher stood up and stretched on tiptoe. She was tall and serpentine, from the beaked head to the quivering curve of her tail, and seeing his shoulder at a convenient height, rested her chin on it, very gently. He felt her breath on his ear like a shy kiss.

'Siddown. Have you got any spare change, please? Siddown.'

The dog sat.

'She's so slim.'

'I feed her, don't I? I always feed her first.'

The girl looked at him for the first time, with very blue eyes. At the roots of her stiff orange hair she was as blonde as her dog.

'I didn't say thin. She's like a dancer.'

'Look, I don't want to sound rude, but people won't give nothing if you're here. They'll think I'm enjoying myself.'

'I'm sorry.' He stood up.

'Skint, are you?'

He felt the five pounds in his pocket. He had kept his hand on it since the moment he first saw the rug; the five pounds and the five pence. He held out the note. She took it without looking at him. 'Thanks.'

'What's her name?' The dog was sitting upright but as he watched she slid forward, crossing one foreleg over the other, lowering her tapering head on to the folded paws, like a swan; like a ballerina at the end of *The Dying Swan*.

'Everyone says that. "What's her name?" They never ask *my* name, do they?'

'What is your name?'

'Q.'

'Q?'

'Q for question. No answer.' There was a short silence. 'Have you got any spare change, please? Are you still here?'

He said goodbye to the dog, not to Q. Q was watching the margarine tub, but the dog was looking at Robert. When he glanced back, a few paces farther on, she was still watching him.

'Have you got any spare change, please?'

He had hoped that with his five pounds she might pack up and go somewhere warm. Without his five pounds he would have to walk home. No, he would not, he could go to the cash point outside Natwest and get some more; but he walked home anyway. To replace the gift from his own substantial account would make it an insult. He wished he felt generous, but all he had paid for was guilt.

Usually he cycled to and from school but his father had given him a lift that morning because of the rain; calling him a wimp, although he had not asked for the lift and had twice refused it. The streets were still wet but the sun picked out droplets on the bare branches so that they looked like buds. Where did Q go when it rained? Where did she sleep? In a doorway, curled up with her beautiful dog for warmth or company or protection? He did not imagine that Q's dog would offer much in the way of protection and he remembered how she had responded to him, a stranger, perhaps a danger-ous stranger, by lowering her trusting swan's head on to his shoulder.

The guy with the recorder by the covered market had an Alsatian. It was stout, elderly and affable, but still an Alsatian. No one would take any liberties with it. There had been an Alsatian at home once – Duke – before Dad decided that Duke was a threat to his supremacy. Mum had left shortly afterwards, but she came back. It seemed that there was nowhere else to go.

She was out, though, when Robert arrived home in the outskirts of a fresh rainstorm. He thought of Q and her dog. Some of the rug-rafters sat it out through rain and wind, but not the ones with dogs. Q would surely take her under cover, she was so unprotected in that fine pale hide, beside Q under her layers and bundles of cloth and leather.

Dad came home at six. His mother continued to be out. Where did she go? When she was at home she seemed always to be in one of their many other rooms. Robert could just remember an earlier time, a much smaller house, when they had had only one living room and all three of them had lived in it, in the days when Mum and Dad both went to work, and came home, and Robert went to Riverview Primary, in the days before St Luke's College.

St Luke's considered itself liberal in the matter of uniform. Senior boys could wear trousers and sports jackets of their own choosing, its having gone unnoticed that very few people of any description wore sports jackets these days. It made them all look about thirty.

He put down Q's hostility to the sports jacket; she must have known where he came from. The dog had not known.

He saw them both next morning as he cycled along the High Street, recognising the orange hair first, then looking at once for the swan dog, pacing gravely elegant into the entrance of the covered market. He called out, 'Hello!'

Q, already walking away, did not turn back. Why should she? There was no reason to suppose that the voice was calling to her. But the dog turned, her soft ears lifting hopefully. She remembered him.

At half-past four they were outside the library again. Long before he saw Q he had spotted the dog's profile. She was sitting upright on the edge of the rug, gazing towards the road. He pulled up alongside the kerb and before he had dismounted saw the ears lift. She was not an eager, grinning, panting dog, but she let him know that he was no longer a stranger.

Robert put two pounds in the margarine tub. Q had not said, 'Have you got any spare change, please?' She too admitted that he was not a stranger.

'I saw you this morning,' he said. 'Going into the market.'

'They don't throw you out of there, not like the Avedon Centre. Can't even walk through that without some security guard sniffing up behind you. Anyway, the café opens early, for the traders. And they don't mind her.' She nodded towards the dog which was staring up at him along the length of her nose.

'Do you want to go there now and have a coffee?'

'No, I only just got here. I stop for an hour. There's a stall round the corner, you could bring me one. White, three sugars. It's outside the church.'

'And can I bring her anything?' He had just felt a gentle, reminding touch against his knee. 'What *is* her name?'

'Regine.'

'That's beautiful, that's perfect.' He looked down at the lurcher's regal head. 'It's from the Latin for queen.'

'I know.' Q sounded bitter, as if the dog had somehow got hold of something it was not entitled to. 'What about that coffee?'

'I saw you today,' his father said, at dinner. 'While I was driving down Haymarket. You were outside the library. Talking to that street girl.'

Robert knew better than to make any kind of an answer at this stage. The pauses between Dad's statements were there to impress the enemy, not to give anyone a chance to reply.

'You didn't give her anything, did you?'

'No. I was just talking. About the dog.'

'That's what the dog is for. Pity. People with too much sense to give to beggars feel sorry for the dog. If they had any sense at all they would work it out that if you can afford a dog you can afford somewhere to live. How much did she take you for?'

'I didn't give her anything.'

'Ran away from home, I suppose.' Dad did not look at Mum, but at some point about twenty centimetres to her left.

'I didn't ask.'

It was not the kind of thing you asked anyway. All he did ask, next afternoon, was, 'Where are you from?'

'Aylesbury. Why?'

He put another two pounds in the margarine tub, his fee for the consultation. He had also brought the coffee in advance, white, three sugars. Regine had left her corner of the rug to sit beside him as he crouched at the fringe of it.

'Look, what are you after?'

'I'm not after anything, just talking, like I talk to anyone. Why did you leave?'

'Are you Social Services?'

The sports jacket. 'I'm still at school. And I didn't mean, why did you leave Aylesbury, I meant, why did you come here?'

'It's as far as I got when the money ran out. I had two hundred saved. It seemed like a lot till I started spending it.'

'Would you go back if you had the money?'

'You going to give it to me?'

'Would you?'

'If you won the lottery and gave me the lot I wouldn't go back. Well, I might, just to trash the place.'

'Aylesbury?'

'Our house. Have you got any spare change, please?'

Evidently his time was up. He stroked Regine's head, fondled her ears in farewell. The dog stood up, as if to follow him.

'Siddown. Have you got any spare change, please?'

He put another pound in the tub. 'If you had the money, would you get a flat?'

'You asking me to move in with you?'

'*No.*'

'Don't worry, only joking. If I had an address I could sign on. Then I'd get a job. Don't look at me like you're wondering who'd employ me. I don't *have* to look like this. Only, I don't know if I could take *her*.' Regine's ears lifted. 'A lot of places don't allow pets. Anyway, her sort needs exercising.'

As he left he felt two eyes on him, not Q's.

He had eleven hundred pounds in the bank, his safety net. At nights he rehearsed the conversation that was going to trigger the moment when he jumped, the moment when Dad said once too often, 'Gutless, that's what you are. If you had any guts you'd have decked me by now.'

That had started when they both noticed that Robert had become the taller of the two. When he was a kid the insults had been random, indiscriminate, simply intended to goad him to tears. Now he was beyond weeping the tone had altered unsubtly. If he had any guts he would be a man, he would strike down his own father. But he had to be gutless because there was not room for two men in the house. All men were enemies. Women were tolerated for, being obviously inferior, they offered no kind of competition. But they had to be kept in their place. Mum's friends no longer visited the house because Dad would stand around, killing conversation with his silent contempt. He had a specially developed belch for driving women away.

The eleven hundred pounds was the latest total of a slowly growing secret hoard, the money that one day would enable him to walk out of the house and never come back. At first he had thought of simply doing a runner, but the sight of the rugs, the dogs, the margarine tubs, reminded him of what would happen.

He worked at the yard on Saturdays because he dared not refuse, despite knowing that the drivers automatically disliked the boss's son and suspected him of grassing. In the office – there were only women in the office – they looked at him with pity, but never with sympathy.

He was meant to start at eight thirty, but when he saw Regine and Q at the market gates, waiting for them to open, he pulled into the kerb.

'You following me?'

Regine was too refined to tug at her string but she leaned towards him until the string became taut. The iron gates began to clash open.

'Do you want a coffee?'

'Aren't you going somewhere?'

'No rush.'

There would be a price to pay for arriving late, but that was only part of the greater price.

The earliest customers, they took a table in the window, the first time that they had been at the same level. Regine went under the table with the smoothness of habit. Presently he felt a companionable warmth and weight against his leg.

'You won't go home?'

'I said so, didn't I?'

'Why did you leave?'

'Why d'you want to know?'

'Just interested.'

'You thinking of leaving too?'

'Not yet. I'll be going to university next year.'

'If I had a place to live I'd do part time. City and Guilds, or something.'

'Would you stay here?'

'You trying to get rid of me?'

'Yes, that's why I asked you to come for coffee.'

Still she did not smile. 'What *do* you want?'

'I could give you the money. To get somewhere. To live.'

'What's in it for you?'

'Nothing. You need the money. I've got it.'

'You a Christian or something?'

They were all supposed to be Christians at St Luke's. Daily prayers. 'No, it's just sitting in the bank, doing nothing. You could use it.'

'I'd never be able to pay you back.'

'It doesn't matter.'

'And what about her?'

Regine stirred, under the table. 'I'd look after her for you. She likes me.'

'Yes.' Q stared across the table at him. 'She doesn't like me. I mean, she's never settled. She was grown up when I got her.'

'How long have you had her?'

'Only a couple of months.' There was a long silence. 'I stole her.'

'Who from?'

'I don't know. She was tied to a post outside a pub.

For hours. It started sleeting so I untied her and walked off. In Reading.'

'Wouldn't you miss her?'

'I'd get a cat. I like cats.'

He would not go to the yard this morning. The price rose again. Instead he went to the bank and wrote a withdrawal slip for five hundred pounds. Then he screwed it up and wrote another for a thousand and went to the towpath where he had arranged to meet Q. On the way he called at a pet shop and spent nine pounds on a leather leash.

'I don't know why you're doing this,' Q said. 'I don't see what you're getting out of it.'

'I'll think of you in your room, with the cat. Signing on. City and Guilds.' For all he knew she had a habit and the whole lot would be gone in days.

She handed him the string. Regine looked from one to the other and then shifted her forepaws in his direction.

'Just one thing – what does Q stand for? It's not really for question, is it? I can't think of any girls' names beginning with Q. What's your real name?'

'Regine.'

'That's *your* name? You called her after you?'

'No, I gave her my name to get rid of it. Stupid sodding name.'

'No, it's lovely—'

'Not for me, it isn't. People like me always get names like that. Haven't you noticed, on the news and that, these little kids and babies that get beaten to death, they've all got fancy names, like that was the only thing

their parents could be bothered to do, give them some
fancy name and then bash them about because they
didn't know what else to do with them. My sister's in
care. Shandrelle.

'I shan't see you again. I shan't stay here,' Q said.

'You could come back some day – visit us – let me
know how you get on.'

'No, leave it like this. You can still hope. Don't walk
with me, I'll go up to the roundabout, hitch a lift.'

'Don't do that, it's not safe. Get a train, or a coach.
You can afford it.'

'Yes, I can, can't I?'

He sat on a bench with Regine and watched Q set out
back to the town centre, tote bag in hand, rug over
shoulder, boots kicking up spray from the puddles. She
was taking his safety net with her.

He walked home slowly, steering his bike with one
hand. Beside him Regine paced her elegant dancer's
steps, never deigning to trot. He had to slow his stride
to hers; she would not hurry to keep up with him.

The car was in the drive. Dad would be in the lounge,
having spent the afternoon planning what to say to his
gutless offspring, prepared only to bawl him out for not
showing up at work.

When Robert and Regine looked in at the door the
first person to see them was his mother. The glass in her
hand tilted dangerously as she took in the figure at his
side.

His father followed her gaze and adjusted his tirade.
'You can take that back where you found it.'

The safety net had gone. He jumped, without looking at the drop. 'No.'

Dad turned his back. 'I said, get rid of it.'

'This is Regine,' Robert said. 'I just paid nine hundred and ninety-one pounds for her, and there's no way we can get it back. Sorry I didn't come to work this morning, I'll do double time next week. We're going for a walk, now.'

Right up to the corner of the street he could hear Dad shouting, from the cocktail bar, the hall, the front door, then the gate, oblivious of what the neighbours would think. The only reason he was not pursuing them up the road, Robert guessed, was that his mother was clinging to his arm like a mud weight.

He did not want to risk letting Regine off her leash just yet, so when they reached the rec he ran beside her, and when they stopped she stood on her toes with her slender paws on his shoulders, looking up at him with love. He might be too gutless to defend himself, but he would defend her to the death, for now he had no choice but to stand his ground and fight. The safety net had gone, but all the same, he had been saved.

Triads

Garry Kilworth

Lee Tam Cheung was an illegal immigrant, and he lived in the massive slum known as the Walled City. Cheung had come to Hong Kong at the age of fourteen, not on a traditional junk, but on one of the smugglers' craft: a sleek launch with three huge outboard engines designed to outrun the customs' boats. He had at first stayed with an uncle in Kam Tin, a Hakka village in the New Territories, but when it became too hot for him there he fled down into Kowloon and entered the Walled City.

Inside the Walled City an *eye-eye* was safe, since this piece of land in the centre of the colony still belonged to China, though too far from Beijing to be administered or policed. Only when he left the slum did Cheung risk being stopped by the police and sent back to China. Not that the risk prevented him from going outside the Walled City.

Actually, there was no longer a wall around the ancient city of the Manchus, but it was still just as impenetrable to strangers. An area the size of a large football stadium had filled with boxy slums, built haphazardly, side by side, one on top of the other, until it was now a single unit, a labyrinth of dark tunnels and stinking corners. People within had to call to those with dwellings on the edge to find out if it was night or day, raining or fine. It was said that the 'ghost children' born in the gloomy tangle of tunnels and cells asked the eternal question of all oubliette prisoners: 'Who stole the sky?'

Bundles of electric wiring ran in tangled loops alongside dripping hosepipes carrying the city water supply, to junction boxes with no lids and silver paper in place of fuses. There were people living in cupboards, running fish-ball businesses. There were large families in tiny single-roomed flats. There were over thirty thousand people, crammed in a place without natural light, with fetid air, and crawling with rats and cockroaches.

Cheung didn't mind the darkness, dirt and squalor. He expected them in a place where the Hong Kong police could not enter and lawlessness flourished. The Walled City was a place run by the Triads of which Cheung was a member. Cheung was a *tin-man-toi* for the 14K, a watchman for one of the most notorious of the Triad gangs. He had a tattoo on his left shoulder to prove his allegiance, for the members of a Triad gang are not all known to each other on sight.

Cheung, at sixteen, was a strong youth, good-looking and as yet unscarred by the knives or choppers of rival gangs. Cheung enjoyed his privileged position as a Triad member, the camaraderie of his friends. Cheung thought he was satisfied with his lifestyle.

Then he fell in love.

It had been on a balmy evening in November. The last of the typhoons had swept through the colony and had gone its savage way up into China. Cheung and two friends were sitting on the harbour wall, Kowloon side, watching the light-encrusted craft weaving in and out of each other – the banana-shaped junks bobbing high on the water, the innumerable ferries, the lighters, the barges, the sampans, the jetfoils – laughing and joking, when an expensive white yacht passed with a young girl on the deck. She looked up from a magazine she was reading and stared right into Cheung's eyes. The two people, youth and girl, were only a couple of metres apart at that moment.

Cheung was immediately smitten by her beauty. She looked so clean he could have licked her hands like ice-cream. Her thick, black shiny hair hung down her back and as she turned shyly away from his glance he could see that it was cut in the straightest line he had ever seen, just at the point her tiny waist met her small hips. Her eyes were like black gems; her teeth as delicate and white as eggshell porcelain; her nose a neat button on her perfectly heart-shaped face. She was, he guessed, seventeen or eighteen years of age.

Without saying a word to his companions, Cheung stood up and began running along the harbour, keeping pace with the boat. The girl looked up once, and then down at the deck immediately, but he could see she was smiling. Once, Cheung had to dash out into the busy streets because his way was blocked along the edge of the harbour, but he shot back to the water's edge again as soon as he was able. Then the yacht pulled away from Tsim Sha Tsui and began to cross the harbour to Hong Kong Island.

Cheung ran to the Star Ferry, managed to pay his sixty cents and jump on a boat that was just leaving. The yacht was slightly faster than the ferry, but still it had only just berthed at Queen's Pier when the ferry docked. Cheung raced down the gangways and reached Queen's Pier just as the girl was getting into a Rolls-Royce. He hailed a taxi. When he could not get it to stop, he jumped out into the road in front of the next one. The driver leaned out of the window.

'What are you doing, you little fool? Get out of the way.'

Cheung said, 'I need to ride.'

'Go to the taxi rank then,' screeched the driver, an old man with a dark patch of skin down his cheek.

Cheung wrenched open the back door. 'Follow that Rolls,' he said. 'Don't worry, old man, I'll pay you your fare.'

The driver seemed to relax after that, only occasionally glancing into the rear-view mirror at his passenger.

Once out of the fast-moving traffic of Central, and on the winding roads of Midlevels, the taxi managed to keep in touch with the Rolls. Finally the Rolls stopped outside a block of luxury flats. Cheung heaved a sigh of relief. At least she didn't live in a house with high gates and dogs. He paid the taxi driver and ran towards the Rolls, stopping and slipping into the shadows of roadside bushes when a man got out of the driver's side.

After a few more moments, the girl got out. She was wearing a tight black dress, a single string of pearls, and smart leather shoes. She carried a Gucci handbag. She could have been any one of ten thousand Hong Kong girls. Even the Gucci bag did not need to be real: there were copies to be had of designer bags and watches all along the Nathan Road.

The man got back in the Rolls and manoeuvred it slowly down the ramp below the block of flats. Cheung came out of the shadows and ran up to the girl.

'Do you like me?' he said, startling her. 'I like you. Can I meet you? Where can I meet you?'

She stared at him with round eyes for a moment, then she said softly, 'Saturday – I'm going to the theatre with some friends. Meet me in the interval, in the Cultural Centre coffee shop . . .'

'I'll be there,' hissed Cheung, fiercely, and then he was gone, back into the shadows of the foliage. A few seconds later the man returned. He was smart, slightly corpulent, wearing a business suit. He carried a black briefcase. Cheung could see he was a successful man. Her father, no doubt. The pair went arm in arm up the steps, into the hallway of the flats, to be greeted by a watchman. Cheung stared at them, visible through the glass doors, as they took the lift. She looked back once, blindly, into the night.

On the way back to the Walled City, Cheung told himself stories about his future.

'I could be successful too. I could be a businessman, if I got the chance, later on. What I would like to be is someone like Jackie Chan – a film star – or Andy Tam – a pop singer. People have said my voice is good. Yes, I could be a pop singer. You have to be an old man like her father, to get respect in the business world, but pop singers need to be young. She won't marry me yet, I know that, especially if she finds out where I live and what I do, but if I get to be successful, then she'll think about it, I'm sure. I'm good-looking. She likes me, I can tell. All it takes is a little money.'

When he arrived back at the Walled City his *daih-lo* asked him where he'd been.

Cheung studied a rat that was crawling into a crevice while searching his mind for a reply. It would not do to lie – he had been with two of his gang when the yacht passed. But they would laugh at him, maybe even be angry, if he talked about *love*.

'Following this rich girl,' said Cheung. 'I – I can get some money out of her.'

'That's dangerous,' said his Triad big brother. 'It's better to stick to shopkeepers and tradesmen.'

Cheung nodded. 'This is a sure thing though. She likes me. There won't be any real trouble, you'll see.'

She was not there on Saturday. Cheung was furious and went to her block of flats. He waited. When she did not appear, he kept going back. Finally, when he saw her, she was going *into* the flats, carrying a small suitcase. She had obviously been away with her father, who accompanied her up the steps to the building as before, carrying the rest of the luggage. Cheung used a pair of binoculars to watch the lift lights and discover which floor she lived on.

He waited until she came out again, then followed her on a stolen motor bike. This time she was driven by the chauffeur. The car went to Kai Too, where she got out and entered a department store. Cheung ditched the bike and followed her.

He caught up with her in one of the aisles, in the perfume department.

'You promised to meet me,' he said, grabbing her arm. She looked frightened and about to scream, so he let her go again. 'You *promised*,' he said with grief in his tone.

'I – I don't know you,' she faltered, looking around at a counter assistant who was watching them.

'Yes, you do, you promised to meet me,' he said, helplessly. 'Why didn't you keep your promise?'

He waited for her answer, a little giddy with the cloying fragrance of the perfumes.

'I – it's – it's very difficult,' she murmured, looking down. 'I do like you.'

Suddenly, he was elated. She *did* like him, after all. It was going to be all right. She was just a bit shy, that was all, a bit scared of her father. Once she knew how he could arrange things, meetings and things, and give her a good time, then she would trust him more. They would have a fine time together, and he would work towards becoming more respectable, so that they could eventually marry.

They spent the rest of the day together, in the park, at a cinema, finally at a coffee shop. He held her hand. She allowed him once to touch her hair. They behaved like ordinary couples. In the dark of the cinema she had kissed him and her lips had been astonishingly soft, like the petals of flowers. Cheung fell desperately in love with her and asked her if she loved him. She had smiled sweetly into his eyes.

'Yes,' she said. 'I can't deny it.'

He was ecstatic. 'Don't *ever* deny it,' he said. 'I can't stand that.'

'I'll never deny our love,' she replied.

A little later he asked, 'Do you like Andy Tam?'

'I *adore* him,' she said, her eyes sparkling. 'I met him once, you know.'

'Really – you really met him?' He was a little crestfallen by this news.

'You're a lot like him,' she said. 'I think. You look like him, only tougher. Tough like Bruce Lee.'

Cheung's heart immediately swelled in his chest.

'My name's Lee too. I can do martial arts,' he said. 'I've done that.'

'I could tell,' she smiled.

They ordered coffee and cakes, and she questioned him all the time, about how he came to Hong Kong, where he lived, what he did. Cheung answered her with a mixture of lies and truth, trying to hide the worst of his background, but bringing out some truths, making them sound more romantic than they actually were. She was such a delicate girl, so well formed, so beautiful.

'How old are you?' he asked.

'Seventeen.'

'I'm eighteen,' he said untruthfully, wanting to be older than her, instead of younger.

He looked at her hands. They were slim and tapering – smooth, unblemished. She had led a closeted life. She hadn't had to sell fish or frogs in Sham Shui Po live market, or skin snakes with a razor blade before boiling them in fat, or spend hours binding the claws of green crabs with raffia. Her hands were made to lift bone-china teacups to her rosebud lips. Her cheeks had felt nothing but soft pillows. The clothes she was wearing looked flimsy and needed to be handled with care. She was a fragile doll, made by an artist with an eye for perfection, dressed in diaphanous silks and satins.

'Eighteen,' he repeated. 'Almost . . .'

She accepted his lie without a murmur, though her eyes were full of amusement. He wanted to challenge that amusement, tell her this was serious, that he was in love with her, but he knew that would be a mistake. He was balancing on a wire at the moment. Once he got to know her better, then would be the time to argue with her over such things.

'I have to go,' she said, suddenly getting up.

'I'll pay,' he said. Then he remembered something. 'What's your name?'

'Sophy,' she replied, pulling on her lace gloves. 'Goodbye.'

'Wait,' he cried. 'When will I see you again?'

'I'll find you,' she said.

She fluttered a gloved hand at him and smiled, then walked quickly from the room without looking back. Cheung paid the bill, then rushed out after her, but she was gone, lost in the crowd. Still, it didn't matter, not that much. He knew where she lived. One step at a time. He was progressing. He had never had a girl with a *gwailo* name before. That was posh. Well, just once he had been with a girl called Celery Woo, but she was a fishmonger's daughter and that didn't really count.

The next two weeks were long ones. Cheung's duties as a *tin-man-toi* kept him busy at the Walled City. A big deal was in progress which the Big Circle Triad wanted to be part of, but the 14K had rejected the partnership. This meant that Cheung was needed as a watchman almost twenty-four hours a day, to warn of any attack by the Big Circle. He sat in the dark, damp recess of the alley which led to the 14K's section of the vast warren which formed the interior of the Walled City and reflected miserably on the fact that *she* was probably out with her friends, laughing and having a good time.

Cheung looked around him in disgust, at cobwebs dripping from the mass of dangling wires; at cardboard, corrugated metal and boxwood rooms around him; at the rats around the rubbish; at a dripping hosepipe joined with sticky tape. Was this his destiny, to live and die in this place? To breathe the trapped, stale air of this sordid ghetto? And the smell? Was he supposed to live with the smell of damp rot, cooking and sewage for ever? The only people who were probably worse off were the Vietnamese refugees, in the various camps around the colony.

There had to be an end in sight, when he would be able to wear expensive clothes, walk around without worrying about the police, go into a classy restaurant . . .

Something moved in the net of shadows at the end of the alley.

Cheung leapt to his feet.

'Attack!' he screamed. 'Attack!'

The Big Circle came out of the darkness then, yelling and shrieking, their faces contorted.

When it was all over, and the Big Circle had fled,

there was the sweet smell of blood in the gamy confines of the tunnel. Cheung and his comrades laughed and joked with each other as they made their way through the wormery of the Walled City to one of its illegal doctors.

'Did you see Cheung?' cried Small Ng, the third member of Cheung's cell of three. 'He was a real warrior!'

Cheung felt like a giant. His feet seemed to float over the flagstones of the lower-level alley. He had fought a battle and had emerged victorious – not *only* victorious, but a, *hero*. He was a bandit from the water margin, a freedom fighter who had vanquished the foe! Mandarins would tremble at his name. Warlords would beg him to fight at their side. Mystical mountains would whisper his deeds.

He knew from experience that his part in the fight would be exaggerated, until it reached legendary status.

The doctor stitched his wound and Cheung told his friends he was going outside.

'What for?' asked Fat. 'Aren't you going to stay and drink beer with your friends? We should celebrate our victory.'

'Later,' Cheung said. 'I have something to do first. I'll meet you in Kowloon City – in the Korean Bar.'

Cheung was risking his newly earned prestige by not following the rituals of a victorious battle, but he had to see her, he *had* to see Sophy, while the lustre of achievement still shone from his form, while he still felt omnipotent, godlike, immortal. He just had to see her, *now*.

'Well, don't be late,' Fat warned. '*Diah-lo* will want you there.'

'Tell Big Brother I'll be there,' he assured his friend. 'Don't worry about me.'

Cheung drifted like a phantom out of the Walled City, into the streets of Hong Kong, his arm a throbbing pleasant reminder of recent events. First he went to a hardware store in Kowloon City and bought a length of nylon rope. Then he took a taxi all the way to Midlevels. Once outside the block of flats where she lived, he waited for a car to arrive – any car – hiding close to the garage. When one came, he slipped into the garage while the electronically operated door was open. He let the car's driver use the basement lift. When it returned, he used it himself.

He knew that the garage lift would go to the tradesmens' entrances to the flats. The door to Sophy's flat, like all Hong Kong flats, would be protected by a metal gate. The front door, reachable only through the lobby lifts, would also be reinforced by protective steel cage doors difficult to force without a great many tools and a lot of uninterrupted time. There was another way in though, via the balcony.

Cheung went all the way up, to the roof.

Once on the edge of the roof he counted the balconies downwards, until he was sure he had the right one. Then he tied one end of the nylon rope to a TV aerial support post and abseiled down to Sophy's balcony. He still felt like an emperor, a wild emperor of the north: invulnerable.

Using a screwdriver he forced the balcony door open

and stepped inside the flat. The lights were on and he stared about him in amazement at the opulence.

The size of the room was the first thing that impressed him. It was as large as the foyer of a big hotel. There was a huge chandelier hanging from an elaborately decorated ceiling. Around the walls were expensive-looking paintings and tapestries. One of the paintings was of Sophy, in a ball-gown, with a necklace of diamonds around her lovely throat. On the floor were Chinese silk rugs, covering highly polished hardwood tiles. Much of the furniture was rosewood, with silk cushioned seats on the chairs, but an enormous leather suite dominated the far side of the room. Around the edge were various display cabinets, filled with china, marble and jade ornaments. On one or two small carved tables stood other objects: ceramic bowls, statuettes and heavy ash trays.

While Cheung stood engrossed in the scene around him a figure entered the room by the main door and gave a startled cry.

Cheung whipped round to see a man standing there, caught in an attitude of indecision.

'You're her father,' said Cheung, stepping forward. 'I am pleased to meet you, sir. Is Sophy here?'

At the mention of the name, the man seemed to collect his wits, and he drew himself up. 'What are you doing here? How did you get in?'

'My name is Lee Tam Cheung, sir,' said Cheung. 'I wish to marry your daughter.'

At that moment, Sophy herself came into the room,

by another door, and gave out a little gasp when she saw Cheung.

They stood there, a loose group of three, for a few moments.

Then the man found his voice again. 'Sophy, do you know this boy?'

Cheung waited for her to acknowledge him as her boyfriend.

'He – he delivers the groceries sometimes,' said Sophy faintly. 'You must have seen him, Father, surely? He's the grocery boy, from the Welcome Shop, aren't you, Cheung? Poor boy, he's a little touched in the head.'

Touched in the head? Cheung felt physically sick. She had denied him. She had denied him. He felt utterly humiliated. He wanted to die.

'I have to go,' he said.

'Yes, yes, go home to your mother, Cheung,' said Sophy quickly. 'Let him out, Father.'

Something occurred to Cheung then, which made him feel hot and angry. Her words had stirred something unpleasant in his blood: something murky and unclean. His *honour* had been stained by this encounter. He needed to wipe out that stain before he could leave the flat. Otherwise she could laugh at him for the rest of her life, and he would hear her in his dreams.

He reached out and snatched a statuette from a nearby table.

'I'm taking this,' he said, fiercely. 'It's what I came for – this.'

'You are not,' said the man. 'You . . .'

Cheung took up a martial-arts stance and Sophy screamed.

'You get out of my way,' snarled Cheung. 'Let me out of here. If you try to stop me the 14K gang will come to you. They'll wreck your precious Rolls-Royce. I'm a chief in the 14K — we don't mess around, you understand me?'

The man started to say, 'Now look here ...' but stopped on meeting Cheung's burning eyes. He turned then and went through a hallway to the front door. He opened it, and the steel cage door beyond it, and held both of them wide for Cheung.

Cheung turned to Sophy and said, 'I know you — if you ever say my name again I'll kill you,' then he ran through the hallway and out of the flat. He did not bother with the lift, but took the fire-escape stairs, four at a time, down to the ground floor.

Cheung hailed a taxi and took it to Kowloon City.

Once in the streets of Kowloon City, Cheung felt safe again, but he was depressed and still angry. He glanced at the greenstone object in his hand, under the still neon lights of the restaurants and shops. He was astonished to see that it was a jade representation of Sophy herself: he recognised her immediately. Some artist had faithfully captured her face and form in this small sculpture in his hand.

The anger swept through him again. It was the *real* Sophy he had wanted, not a cold jade statuette. They were not the same thing, were they? He stroked the mottled green figurine. A beautiful work of art: perhaps even more perfect in form than Sophy herself? A perfected Sophy. Perhaps they weren't so different? They both had hearts of cold stone. And he had one of them. Maybe he had the finest one? He would have liked to believe that, but found it hard.

A jumbo jet roared low over the rooftops of the city, following the approach lights attached to the eves of the buildings. It seemed to miss the roof tiles by only a couple of metres as it thundered over, rattling doors and windows.

He walked up to the swing doors of the Korean Bar and pushed them open, stepping inside. His friends were all there. They looked up and cheered, waving bottles of beer. He waved the figurine.

'A trophy,' he yelled. 'To honour our victory!'

They cheered again, wildly, and he walked among them, receiving the backslaps, feeling like a prince who has stolen a kingdom, but found it to be a wasteland.

Mr Right, Where Are You?

Andrew Matthews

Francine isn't talking to me. I know we're supposed to be best mates and everything, but right now I couldn't care less if she never spoke to me again.

She's offended. Francine doesn't need to talk to let you know she's offended. She just stands with one hand on her hip, raises one eyebrow and gives you a glare that would melt pound coins into butterscotch sauce.

It's not *my* fault she's offended. It's because of Mark. Well, her and Mark . . . well, Mark and me too. Actually, now I come to think about it, it's all our faults.

You know how girls knock round in pairs – one pretty and the other a reject from Crufts? Well, Francine is drop-dead gorgeous and I'm the copping-partner. You know, the dumpy one with the muddy complexion. The one who always has change for the loos and a never-ending supply of hair-ties. The one at the disco who gets talked into asking some spotty Neanderthal to dance so that Gorgeous can come on to his hunky friend. That's a copping-partner. That's what I used to be to Francine – but not any more! If she tries to treat me like that again, I'm going to hand her a hairbrush and invite her to make a bottom/bristle interface.

Then there's Mark. Brown-haired, clean-jawed Mark. Mark whose eyes crinkle when he smiles ... Here's an experiment for you. Get a slice of really cheesy pizza and take a bite. Look at all the gooey, cheesy bits that make strings between your mouth and the rest of the slice. That's what happens to my insides when I look at Mark.

I've always been that way about him, ever since he rescued me from a spider in biology when we were in year seven. He was cute then. He went on being cute until we started year ten last September. Mark returned to school after a holiday in Greece, with a fantastic tan and a new haircut and suddenly he was a lot better than cute. Girls took one look at him and it was Hormone City.

Not long after, the first bit of graffiti appeared in the girls' loos in Main Block. 'Mark Curtis 4 Me.' By half-term, all the cubicle doors were covered with 'Mark Curtis 4 Me's. Every one was in a different handwriting.

Like every other girl, I ate my heart out. I cried about Mark one night and rushed over to the mirror to look at myself. That's the face of a girl with a broken heart, I thought. That's the face of a girl whose dreams will never come true. It was deeply sad.

Then it got worse, because Mark started dating Francine. Only in the privacy of my bedroom did I sometimes admit to myself that I was jealous. That's 'sometimes' as in 'every night'. I thought, why Francine? Why should she have everything? Why should she get all the best boys? I had a yearning, poetic soul that longed to soar on wings of romance, but boys seemed more interested in pretty girls with big boobs.

Mum would give me a look when I was feeling down like this and say, 'Never mind, Ruth. Mr Right will come along one day.'

If I thought hard enough about Mr Right, it almost made me feel better, but I could never picture his face. Sometimes it was nice, looking out of my bedroom window and knowing he was out there in the world somewhere.

Anyway, I swallowed my envy and my broken heart (*can* you swallow a broken heart?) and concentrated on being a best mate to Francine. Only I made too good a job of it. On the evening of her first row with Mark, she came round to my house and cried.

Mark wanted to see a film that Francine didn't fancy. He said that was fine, he'd go on his own. Francine took that as meaning Mark cared more about some manky film than he did about her. Mark told her not to be stupid and Francine said, 'Oh, so you think I'm stupid, do you?' After that, it developed into a full-scale barney.

Ever tried comforting a friend when she's playing silly Bs with the boy you'd most like to get your grubby mitts on? Not easy!

I played the copping-partner again – the girl who stuffed her shoulders with blotting paper so her friend could cry on them. I told her it was just a silly argument. If what she and Mark had was real, they'd soon kiss and make up. I said, 'He's probably trying to ring you right now.'

Francine lifted her tragic, tear-stained face and said, 'But he doesn't know I'm here.'

I said, 'I don't mean here. I mean your house.'

Francine said, 'But I'm not there! He's probably rung and rung and thinks I don't care about him enough to answer the phone.'

They made it up eventually, but that was the first of many tearful evenings. You see, having a totally wonderful boyfriend isn't enough for Francine. She plays mind games. Like, she'll pretend to be huffy with a bloke, and if he gets upset about it, she'll know how much he really likes her. She tried the mind games on Mark, only he wasn't having any. Result? Tears before bedtime, and guess who provided the tissues?

They broke up and got back together so often that I was like – Hey, it's Wednesday! Any minute, Francine will come over for a hearty boo.

And then they *really* broke up, because Mark told Francine she was immature. Everybody's got a word that makes them blow their stack. It might be a swearword, or a nickname, but when they get called it, they freak out totally. Well, Francine's word is 'immature'. It's what her dad says when he wants to wind her up.

'I'm never going out with him again!' she sobbed into my shoulder. 'He really hurt me this time!'

I said, 'Don't you think you're overreacting just the teensiest little bit?'

'No!' said Francine. 'Anyway, Scott Hawkins is going to ask me out tomorrow, and I'm saying yes.'

I thought, You'd rather go out with *Scott Hawkins* than Mark?!!

Don't get me wrong, Scott Hawkins is nice, but if boys were ice-cream, Mark would be chocolate fudge with pecans, and Scott would be vanilla. Still, who was I to criticise? I couldn't even get a date with a frozen yoghurt.

Days of deep gloom ensued. Francine bit my head off at the least little thing. I knew she was hurting about Mark and that she'd made a mistake, but getting Francine to admit it was impossible. Every time I tried, the words 'stubborn' and 'cow' slipped into my mind. In the end, I just let her get on with it.

A fortnight passed. Mark went out with Sophie Salamon, Tina Jenkins, Jessica Hargreaves, Charmain Khan and Debra Thomas – though not all on the same night. You'd think that going out with so many gorgeous girls would make Mark happy, but it didn't. He moped round school with slumped shoulders and a miserable expression.

It was a Thursday when it happened. I'd just started a bit of French-into-English, when Mum tapped my bedroom door and said, 'Phone.'

I went downstairs thinking, don't tell me, I know – another chapter in the continuing saga of Francine, but when I picked up the phone, the voice on the other end said, 'Hi, Ruth. It's Mark.'

My insides went on a white-knuckle ride and a flock of bluebirds circled my head going 'tweet, tweet, tweet'!

I said, 'Mark! Hi, how are things?'

He said, 'Cool. Look, are you doing anything tonight?'

I thought, what is this guy *on*? It's year ten assessments in three weeks, I'm up to my armpits in coursework and he's asking me if I'm *doing* anything?

I said, 'No, not really. Why?'

Mark said, 'I thought you might fancy meeting up.'

I waited as long as it takes light to travel two millimetres before I said, 'Yes!'

Mark said, 'D'you know that take-away near Haston's Garage?'

I said, 'What, Chicken Licken? Sure!'

Mark said, 'See you there about seven.'

When I put down the phone, I had a smile I didn't think anything could wipe off.

He'd noticed me! After years of pizza goo and crying into the mirror, Mark Curtis had noticed me. I was on his list — after Francine, Sophie, Tina, Jessica, Charmain and Debra, admittedly — but at least I was there.

Mum appeared in the hall and clocked my grin. 'Who was that?' she said.

'Mr Right, with any luck,' I said.

I suppose I ought to have lost my appetite, but I got stuck into beefburger and hash browns, no problem. I spent ten minutes cleaning my teeth in case my breath smelt, then slipped into my best jeans and baggy white top, figuring that no one dressed up on a Thursday night, not even to go out with Mark. I told Mum and Dad that I had a date and I'd be back before half-ten, and I left them with their chins on the floor.

It was a wonderful evening. It was still light, and the

few clouds that were in the sky were fluffy and edged with gold. I was feeling pretty fluffy and gold-edged myself, but I tried hard not to do that thing where you look forward to something so much that it's a disappointment when it actually happens.

Mark was waiting for me. He was next to the litter bin outside Chicken Licken, with his hands in his pockets. He saw me and smiled.

That smile! It was the first smile I'd ever had from Mark, and it did to me what an eye-level grill does to marshmallows. I widened my grin, walked up to him and said, 'Hi!'

Mark said, 'Hi, glad you could make it.'

I said, 'I'm glad you're glad.'

Mark laughed and said, 'I'm glad you're glad I'm glad.'

I thought, you made him laugh – good sign!

'So,' I said, 'where shall we go?'

Mark said, 'I thought we might hang out for a bit.'

'OK,' I said. 'What say we walk to the End of Civilisation as We Know It.'

Mark said, 'Where's that?'

I said, 'Peel Park.'

Mark said, 'Why is that the End of Civilisation as We Know It?'

I said, 'Have you seen what goes on there after dark?'

Mark laughed again because Peel Park is where the rebels go to drink warm lager and smoke interesting cigarettes. 'Yeah,' he said. 'Why not?'

We turned to go and I saw Merilyn Sutton. She was waiting to be served in Chicken Licken, and she was gawping at us through the window. That meant it would be all over school the next day – RUTH PEARSON GOES OUT WITH MARK CURTIS!

I thought, brilliant!

We walked along Walpole Drive, and talked, and it went well. I looned a bit to make Mark laugh, and he looned back. Then he said, 'I can talk to you.'

I said, 'That's good, because you *are* talking to me.'

Mark said, 'I don't always find it easy, talking to girls.'

I could believe it. When you have to beat girls off you with a stick, there isn't much time for idle chit-chat.

I said, 'You just open your mouth and let words come out.'

Mark said, 'With most girls, I don't know what to say.'

Which meant I wasn't most girls. I trod carefully, in case I ascended bodily into heaven.

We walked on, and then Mark said, 'I knew it'd be good to talk to you. I've always been able to tell what you're thinking – just by looking at you. I can't do that with most people.'

I grabbed his arm to stop him walking, looked him straight in the eyes and said, 'What am I thinking now?'

My mind was going: snog me! Snog me until crowds gather and cheer!

Mark did his crinkly-eyed smile and said, 'Well, I don't know *now* exactly, but . . . remember that time in year seven when that spider was in the biology lab?'

I said, 'Oh yeah! You were really good about that.'

Mark said, 'You didn't say anything, but I could tell

you were scared. That's when I started wondering about you.'

'Wondering what?' I said.

Mark said, 'Wondering if I could really tell what you were thinking, or if I just thought I could. That's why I was afraid to ask you out.'

'Afraid?' I said.

Mark said, 'I always imagined that you and I would sort of understand each other. I thought if I ever asked you out, we might not, and I'd be disappointed.'

I said, 'And are you?'

Mark said, 'No.'

We started walking again. I looked down Walpole Avenue and I could see a glittering future at the far end.

Mark said, 'I needed to talk to someone who understands. Someone I can trust.'

I shot him a sideways glance, and he was staring straight ahead, as though he was looking at the future too. He said, 'Ruth, I—!' then he turned and grabbed hold of me. Mark Curtis fell into my waiting arms, just like I'd always dreamed.

It was good inside that hug. Mark was as warm as a teddy bear, and he smelt nice. I could feel his breath on my neck. I thought, this is it!'

And then I noticed that his shoulders were bouncing up and down like a kangaroo in a sack, and I realised he was crying.

I said, 'Mark?'

He said, 'I'm sorry! I'm really sorry!' His voice was hoarse, like he was forcing the words out. 'I miss her so much. I've never felt like this. I don't know who I am without her. I want to talk to her, but I don't know what to say. Tell me what to say, Ruth.'

I didn't have to ask who he was talking about. The air was filled with the tinkling of my broken dreams. Mark was the only honest-to-goodness lovely thing I'd ever held, but it was no good. I had to let him go. He wasn't mine.

I said, 'I'll talk to her for you.'

Mark wiped his eyes with the back of his hand. 'Will you?' he said.

I said, 'Ooh, yes!'

And I did. Next morning, before registration, I walked straight up to Francine, ignoring her glare.

Francine said, 'How was the date with Mark?'

I said, 'I—!'

Francine said, 'You might have told me! We're supposed to be friends! Or are you just hanging round to pick up my leftovers?'

I said, 'You're an idiot, Francine! You're still crazy about Mark, and he's still crazy about you. If there's anything sensible keeping the sides of your skull apart, you'll ring him tonight and talk.'

Francine went red. 'Who asked you about it?' she said. 'What gives you the right to mess with my private life?'

I said, 'Friendship.'

Francine said, 'Well, thanks, *friend*,' in the sarcastic voice she does so well. 'Next time I'm thinking about slashing my wrists, I'll ask you round to hold my hand.'

I said, 'Oh, stop being so immature, will you? You don't deserve someone like Mark.'

That did it. I'd used the word. Francine flounced off like a busy feather-duster and left me standing there, angry, with an ache that still hasn't gone away.

She must have rung him, because next day it was all over school that they were an item again. And have I had any thanks from Francine for my part in it? No way. I'm not expecting any, but it hurts a bit that Mark hasn't said anything. He knows my number, after all.

So, they're back together, and I'm on my own, which is OK, because I'm used to it, only ... Look, I know you're going to come along sooner or later, but couldn't you make it sooner?

Mr Right, where are you?

Birthday Love

Michael Hardcastle

'You've got to forget him, Toni!' Laura insisted. 'Just forget him, *please*. Otherwise this trip'll turn out to be a total disaster. You won't have seen anything, you won't have experienced anything, you won't have *lived*. You're even looking half-dead already!'

'Oh, thanks,' Antonia murmured, closing her eyes to the horror of that description and leaning back against Sophie's drawn-up bare knees. 'Actually, it's true, I do feel only half-alive. I hope Kevin feels just the same. If he does, then that just brings us closer together, doesn't it?'

Affectionately, Sophie ran her fingers through Antonia's long auburn hair and then gently squeezed her rigid shoulder muscles. 'Laura's right, you know. You've got to enjoy yourself. I mean, you might never come to Brussels again in the rest of your life, so—'

'But it's all right for you, Sophie, you've got Warren here with you, haven't you?' Antonia pointed out. 'Everything's *perfect* for you. You're not thinking of somebody in another country all the time. You—'

'Oh sure!' Sophie laughed, still trying to release Antonia's tenseness. 'And where precisely is Warren?

Over there, telling dirty jokes with the rest of the lads as usual, all ganging up together until it suits them to rejoin the rest of us. Or planning how to get more cans into their rooms tonight. They think more of that sort of thing than anything else. Honestly!'

Antonia didn't know what to say to that because all she could feel was the emptiness within her, the longing that possessed her for a boy she'd fallen in love with three weeks and two days ago. People were forever saying real love didn't happen like that, deeply and instantaneously and with no doubt in the mind at all. But it had happened to Antonia and she no longer cared what anyone else said about it. It was simply true, in every sense, and that's all that needed to be said about it.

'You want to be glad Kevin isn't one of them,' remarked Laura, always willing to follow Sophie's lead. 'He'd be just as bad as the rest. Ignoring the things that matter in life – us! So what was he doing this evening when you phoned him? Or is that a secret, another secret, between you?'

'He – wasn't there.'

'But – but you said he *knew* when you were phoning, you'd fixed the times *specially*,' Laura reminded her, her tone a mixture of amazement and, Sophie thought, triumph.

'I know, but, well, plans change sometimes, don't they? I mean, we'll talk later, I know we will. It's no big panic. Kevin just had to be out, that's all. Honestly, why're you going on about it, Laura?'

'But—'

Soaring notes of music drowned whatever she was

going to say and green and red searchlight beams flashed across the barely darkening sky. And the 'ooooo-ohs' from hundreds of spectators crammed together in Grand'Place rose as if from one throat.

'Is it – oh, I don't know, Beethoven?' Laura asked. Facts to her were always sacred and nothing was allowed to get in the way of them.

'Who *cares*?' Sophie expelled a breath she hadn't known she was holding. 'Who cares? I mean, just look at all that gold on those buildings. Is it real?'

Antonia stared at the dazzling scene, the buildings now bathed in white – and then red and then green – and white again. She looked but she didn't see because her mind would reflect only images of Kevin Glasgoe, Kevin who'd promised *faithfully* that he'd be hanging on the end of the phone when she rang at the promised time. But wasn't. Unimaginably, he wasn't there. So where could he possibly be?

A sudden thought entered her like a dagger: could he be out with Sandra? She'd meant a lot to him not so very long ago, he'd admitted it. 'I'm a romantic,' he'd said and laughed. 'I love travel – going to exciting places. I love surprises – romance. I love you, darling Toni, I love you.' Remarks like that were what made him so special. But, did he still really care for Sandra? Did he tell her he loved her still?

'Got to get up, getting cramp,' Sophie hissed in her ear. So Antonia, too, had to get to her feet. They'd been sitting for ages on the cobbled square, waiting for the free music and light show to uplift them, to 'enchant every tourist who witnesses it in the medieval splendour of this unforgettable setting', as the publicity leaflet oozed.

'Hey, watch it!' Laura protested as a black-T-shirted boy practically knocked her over while jinking away from a surging pack of revellers. He turned, grinned and made a gesture that was surprisingly elegant and gracious.

'Must fancy you,' Sophie said, surprise and sudden envy in her voice. Then, to their astonishment, another boy, red-haired, athletic, handsome, was standing in front of Antonia, his hands on her shoulders, smiling beguilingly into her eyes and saying: 'You look wonderful, *wonderful*. Made for love. Come and drink with me now, this minute. Come. Please say you will.'

'You're crazy,' Antonia told him, because she had to say something. Madness really was in the air, she decided: music and searchlights and old buildings. Is that what they did to people? Well, it wasn't for her. All she wanted—

'You'll be safe with me, I promise. I just can't resist you, can't you see that?' he went on, his hands sliding down her bare arms to link his fingers with hers. She shook herself free but there was a tingling somewhere in her veins. Sophie and Laura, she saw, were staring at them, transfixed.

'You're wasting your time,' she snapped. 'I've got a boyfriend – better than you in every way. He—'

'So where is he, then, this *miracle* guy? Why isn't he here, dancing madly with you, loving you like crazy, like—'

'Oh, get off!' Antonia somehow managed to disentangle herself from him. 'He can't get away, that's why I'm on my own.' It was the wrong thing to say and she knew it the moment she saw his eyes re-ignite (though the glow had hardly faded anyway).

'Well, I'm here and he's not and you need somebody. You need me.' He took hold of her again, running his fingers tantalisingly, tinglingly, down the inside of her arms, from elbow to wrist.

'You're just — just an opportunist,' she replied, wrenching herself free once more.

'So what? What's wrong with that? I like you — like you a lot. You've got gorgeous skin. It feels like warm silk. You—'

She plunged away, thrusting herself even between linked couples, and so heard no more of the pleas he intended to make. And he, with a very Gallic shrug, sauntered away in another direction, searching afresh.

'Honestly, wish he'd tried it on with me,' Laura told Sophie. 'You'd think she'd've been knocked out by a boy like him, grabbed him and never let go. I mean, what's Kevin got compared to him?'

'Beats me,' Sophie admitted. 'Beats Kevin and Warren by a million miles! Life's really rotten sometimes, isn't it? Still, the music's good, and the lights. Beats Bonfire Night at home — and the weather's better!'

Antonia sank down on to a corner of a wooden platform that supported tables for open-air drinkers outside a boisterous Greek taverna. Her mind couldn't really cope with anything but her concern for Kevin. Had anything happened to him, something so awful he couldn't get to the phone to call the hotel?

Umpteen times she's warned him not to fool around with his brother's motor bike, the superbike, Eddie called it. Kevin hadn't a licence, he wasn't used to it at any speed and it wouldn't be fair to her if anything happened to him. He laughed off her fears as he laughed off almost anything that really mattered. Had he, this time, laughed her out of his life? Had he given her up just because she'd gone away?

They'd met in a baker's shop, of all places, choosing identical cakes for the lunchtime walkabout picnic. That was only four weeks ago but the magic that was supposed to embrace couples only when they truly fell in love had seized them almost immediately — and simultaneously. Antonia had no doubts at all about her feelings for the boy with the smile 'as wide as a farmer's gate', as Sophie had enviously described it. And he'd kept all his promises to her, she was positive of that. Until ... until ... until now.

'I'll be in, hanging on to the phone like a drowning man clutching at a lifebelt,' he had grinned, employing a phrase she suspected he hadn't minted for her. But the first time she'd rung him his mum answered disapprovingly, complaining *she* didn't know where he was; and tonight — tonight was silence. No one at all picked up the Glasgoe phone. So there was only one more planned phone call before the school trip ended. That was in Strasbourg on Saturday, the night before her birthday. She hadn't wanted to come on this visit to the twin European capitals in the first place; only the certainty they'd be in touch with one another by phone would make it tolerable. No, not *touch*: that was the worst torture to be endured in their separation. But they would be in contact. And they'd have a record-breaking, bank-breaking conversation just one minute into her birthday. 'Midnight magic, that's what it'll be,' Kevin promised, eyes alight with the latest excitement in their day-glo new life together.

But, after tonight's second successive failure to make contact, what hope was there that he'd be at the other end of the line on Saturday? Birthdays had always been important to her; he knew that because he said they were just as important to him, too. 'The one day in the year you can call your own,' he enthused. 'So it has to be special. And yours will be, I swear on my life, darling Antonia.' She believed him. Then. But now . . .? Was he lavishing money on a night out with Sandra again? After all, money was no real problem to him because of what his grandmother had left him in her will.

'Oh, there you are!' Laura broke in on her, grabbing her shoulder so fiercely that Antonia felt she was being attacked. 'We were afraid some foreign agent for a Turkish harem had spirited you away! I mean, you never know your luck, do you?'

'I know *my* luck,' Antonia said darkly. 'I—'

'Oh, for goodness sake stop glooming the night away!' Sophie broke in. 'Listen, I'd better tell you that I know about Kevin, something anyway. Should have told you before but I didn't want to spoil things. Won't be the first time he's let a girl down. He was having a high old time with Trish Grant until he dropped her like a stone. Just chopped her off, like that.' She demonstrated a fearsome cut with the side of her hand that could have broken whatever was in its way.

'Oh, he told me about her,' Antonia replied, almost gaily. 'Said she was playing a different game with another boy and just using Kevin as, well, as bait. He wasn't having that – or her!'

She saw the defeated yet doubting exchanges of glances between her friends and somehow that cheered her up. Why couldn't they understand what an honest person Kevin was? He'd never two-time anybody or allow himself to be used in that way. Maybe later on she'd ring again, catch him *this* time.

'Hey, I'm hungry,' she announced to their amazement. 'Why don't we grab some French fries, sorry, Belgian fries? I mean, they are supposed to be the best in the world, aren't they?'

Flowers filled the Grand'Place next morning in place of floodlights and Mozart and guzzling, gaping tourists. Flowers for sale – and wholesale weddings. Glamour, shining beribboned cars: new-suited families in conspiratorial huddles; brides glowing on the balcony of the city hall, focus of a frenzy of cameras. A Brussels tradition on Saturdays, it seemed.

Marriages, Antonia knew, were all about promises, keeping promises. Well, Kevin had made promises, too: 'I'll be in touch, I promise, darling Antonia,' he said, practically his last words to her before they left England. Some promise!

'I thought Paris was supposed to be the capital of romance, not Brussels,' joked Sophie who wished that she were officially in one of the bridal groups. 'Must be an amazing feeling,' she was about to say when she saw that Antonia was trying to hide tears. Not, she could sense, of shared happiness.

'He still wasn't there?' she had to ask.

'Don't talk about it, I can't,' Toni told her. And for the rest of the day she said scarcely a word to anyone about anything as St Gregory's pupils and staff moved on sleekly by coach from one country to another. Not much seemed to change, though, as Belgium became France for once again they were regaled by coloured lights and music filling the night sky. In Strasbourg, however, fountains played brilliantly on the roof of a covered bridge and lasers pierced high clouds and pictures were flashed on to walls like murals. And nothing at all changed for Antonia. Kevin's silence was going to sabotage the celebrations for tomorrow, the last full day of their trip but, above all, her sixteenth birthday.

'Hey, look who's here!' Laura suddenly exploded in Antonia's ear as they all huddled together at the end of a tiny bridge overlooking the river basin where the lights and music show was being staged.

Antonia spun round, eyes ablaze with expectation, desperately seeking the longed-for face. 'Where, where, oh where?' she cried. Then she saw him: the French boy with the red hair, the one who'd tried to enchant her in Brussels; and, in the same instant, he caught sight of her, too.

'What're you doing here? You're following me, aren't

you?' she challenged him. 'I've told you, I'm not interested, so—'

'I *live* here, I live in Strasbourg,' he declared, arms spread wide as if in surrender. 'So I can't be following you, my pretty English girl. We meet again. That is fate. You must believe in it. You must—'

'I believe in nothing, nothing, nothing!' she shouted, startling everyone within metres of them. Laura and Sophie reached out to try to calm her but she eluded them as she backed away. 'Promises mean nothing, you mean nothing, nothing matters any more.' And she fled, fled to the hotel, luckily close by, where all St Gregory's pupils and staff were staying, fled up the stairs and locked herself in the room she was sharing with Sophie.

It was after midnight when everyone else returned and Sophie, sympathetic as ever to anyone in pain, simply said she'd share with someone else when Antonia failed to respond to her gentle knocking on the door. 'After all, it *is* her birthday now, so she might as well enjoy this bit of it. Kevin's silence will be sure to spoil the rest of her day.'

'Happy birthday, dear Toni, happy birthday to you!' they carolled, standing around her bed, letting cards cascade down all over her. Her waking thought was that everything must be all right and that Kevin had telephoned or sent a special delivery letter: and that's why they were all so happy for her.

'How d'you get into my room?' she asked, trying to fasten her pyjama jacket discreetly and then immediately remembering she'd gone to the bathroom during the night and probably hadn't relocked the door.

'We'd've broken the door down if we'd had to,' Laura told her. 'Can't hide away on your birthday, you know. So come on, get up and enjoy yourself. We'll give you two minutes to get decent and then we'll be back.'

The moment the room emptied she whipped through the pile of cards and packages and knew there was nothing from him. She didn't cry because it was what she'd realised would happen. Why should she care when he so obviously didn't care a scrap for her? As she flicked through her hair she rationalised that the extra cards meant that everyone, absolutely everyone, on the school trip was trying to make up for the predictable disappointment. Sweet Sophie must have worked on the rest of the gang like mad to persuade them to contribute.

'So that's it, Kevin, you're *dead*,' she told herself as she went downstairs to the breakfast room. 'My heart is just as cold as yours.'

To her astonishment, they all stood up to greet her, boys as well as the girls, and watched avidly as she opened presents: romantic novels, her favourite hair spray, a left-handed hairbrush from joker Daniel, stationery for love letters from Sophie, inevitable shower gel and, biggest surprise of all, a silver alarm whistle from Laura ('I mean, with *your* looks you're always at risk, so, be prepared').

'Aren't you hungry?' somebody asked and she realised she 'could eat a horse'!

'Well, the French do, so I'm sure the cook here could

provide one,' remarked Daniel to mixed reactions of horror, disgust and disbelief.

'I'll settle for eggs and bacon and fried bread and tomatoes, can't manage on just flaky French buns and tasteless jam,' Toni declared to an aggrieved-looking waiter.

'If you can put all that lot away you *must* be feeling better,' whispered Sophie, and Toni, sipping superb coffee, nodded.

'I know I've got to get on with the rest of my life,' she announced. 'I've decided—'

Without warning, the door burst open, and he was coming towards her, coming unstoppably through the straggle of other late-breakfasters and hotel guests wanting to book out, coming like a vision produced by the miracle of rubbing a genie's magic lamp. His smile had never been brighter and she hardly noticed the tabloid-sized birthday card and the cellophane-wrapped roses and red-ribboned parcel.

'But how – how—' she stammered while everyone else fell silent, mesmerised by such an impossible reunion. She felt so weak she could barely get to her feet.

'Told you I'd see you – and you didn't believe me, did you? Told you I'd be in touch whatever it cost – and it cost a fortune, just the plane ticket alone, first flight of the day. *Brilliant* planning, started before you even left England. I daren't answer the phone 'cos I knew you'd guess I was up to something.' He paused, wreathed in triumph, gazing into her eyes. 'And it worked, every bit of it worked! And all because of you,

Toni, just you. Look, I brought you this and this and this.'

Kevin held his gifts out to her but, discovering her balance again, she moved towards him, pushing them aside.

'All I want is you,' she murmured as she flung her arms around him.

Together

Steve May

Tasha never does things by halves. Falling in love was no exception. She did it in a big, big way. Tasha is a big, big girl: not fat, but tall, and well built, like she should be throwing javelins. For the love affair, she picked on Tim. I've known Tim since we were at junior school. Tim is a nice boy, but shy. He's big too, and a brown belt at Tai-something, but he wears glasses, and he stoops so you'd think he was scared of treading on you.

Tasha said, 'Tell Tim I want to go out with him.'

'Why do you want to go out with him?'

'Because I fancy him and he's the only boy in our year who's taller than me.'

'Tasha wants to go out with you,' I told Tim. Tim went white.

'Don't you like her?'

'Yes, I suppose,' he said, 'but she's scary too.'

I said, 'Come on, it's not scary going out with someone, it's nice, and fun.'

How wrong can you be?

At first, they're like Mr and Mrs. They go everywhere together, holding hands. They stroll by the river feeding ducks. They stare into each other's eyes. They even send me a joint birthday present: 'With thanks and love for bringing us together.' Taking it in turns to write one word each.

'What a pair of wallies,' goes Nathan. Nathan is in the year above us, and smells like a rabbit hutch. He smokes with the fag hidden under his hand so no one can see it, and he hisses the smoke down into corners and behind tables. He's got ginger wispy bits of beard, and he's always staring at your legs.

'Those two make me feel sick,' he goes. And all his mates go, 'Yuk!'

But, he kept staring. And he had a good laugh two weeks later, when Tim and Tash fell out. Or, Tasha fell out with Tim. Of course, it's got to be immense, falling out from a great height. Suddenly, she hates him like poison. She screams at him, she chases him across the road after school, kicking him.

'Wimp!' shouts Nathan, and all his mates snigger.

But Tim, he won't fight back.

So, they're not speaking to each other. Who *do* they speak to? You guessed. Tim rings up. He's been standing outside Tasha's house in the pouring rain for two hours, hoping to catch a glimpse of her.

'Why didn't you knock on the door?'

'Because she said she never wanted to see me again.'

'She's just doing it to show how much power she's got over you.'

'No, she's not. It's my fault. I must have upset her.'

And so on. When I hang up on Tim, the phone rings straight away. It's Tasha.

'Who've you been speaking to? You've been on the phone for ages.'

'Tim. He's been hanging about outside your house.'

'I know, I saw him. I wanted to go out and ask him in.'

'Why didn't you?'

'I didn't want to be the first one to give in and now he's gone away and I'm never going to see him again.'

And she starts crying.

This gets seriously tedious. And it's ongoing, like a TV soap. They're on and off, off and on, and it's always Tash who calls the shots, and Tim who blames himself. They use me like a cross between Marriage Guidance and Postman Pat.

'I don't know why you let her treat you like she does,' I told Tim. 'If it was a boy, you'd stand up for yourself, tell them where to get off, but with her, you're such a wimp.'

But he just looks away, all sheepish. Makes you want to hit him, or scream, or something.

I told Tash she was treating him like a doormat.

'You always stick up for Tim,' Tasha said. 'I expect you fancy him yourself.'

I told her I've known Tim for years and years, since we were in the junior-school nativity play together.

'And I bet you were Mary and he was Joseph,' and she starts crying again, and when I try and comfort her she takes a big swing at me with her elbow so I nearly go flat over on my back off my stool. This is happening, by the way, in the middle of science, with Mr Petherton.

Mr Petherton is a hundred and thirty-six years old, and deaf, and a very slow talker.

'You can either mark the woodlice with nail varnish,' he's going, 'or just count them up each day.'

I was so mad, I pulled Tash's hair and gave her a slap on the face. Whack! That shocked her! She punched me on the shoulder and I grabbed her arm and pulled her off her stool, and there we are on the floor, biting and kicking and hissing. Mr Petherton keeps on talking.

'Plot your figures on the left side of the graph for each weekday, and use red for the weekend.'

Then we rolled into another stool and it crashed over, and he stopped, and we stopped, and he peers over the bench and says, 'I warned you about rocking back on your stools, girls. You'll hurt yourselves.'

Tash and me weren't talking all that day, not even on the bus home, but sure enough, come six o'clock, the phone rings. It's her, and she's blubbering again.

'I'm so sorry, I don't know what came over me, but I love him so much, and I thought you were trying to take him from me, and I'm jealous 'cos you're like a friend to him, and he likes you much more than he likes me . . .' and so on and so on.

I said, 'If you love him so much, why don't you show it a bit more?'

'I can't. When I'm with him I keep having to hurt him, I don't know why. But as soon as he's not there I'm so guilty and I want him back again.'

Which is like word for word from this soap that's just been on the telly twenty minutes ago.

And then another hour later, she rings up, and says in this creamy voice; 'I just thought I'd let you know, Tim and me, we're *together* again.'

This was all very bugging, but quite funny, till Nathan put his oar in. He'd been staring more than usual lately, and mostly at Tasha.

'What's she like, then? Bit of a goer, is she?'

'She wouldn't go anywhere with you.'

'No?' He's got yellow eyes with a red line round the lid bit. 'We'll see about that.'

And off he slinks, with his mates.

That evening on the bus, Tasha was bubbling over.

'You'll never guess what,' she goes.

'Nathan Ellis asked you out.'

'That's right. I couldn't believe it!' She's got her hand up by her throat like she's choking. 'I mean, Nathan Ellis, he's so totally naff. And he's always cheeking the teachers, and smoking and stuff, and he's always got loads of money. I bet he steals it.'

And she keeps giggling and talking about him all the way home. Even after I got sick of it. When we got off, I asked; 'Are you and Tim *together* today?'

She sniffed.

'I suppose so,' she said. 'For the moment.'

The next day, the rumour started. I heard it first off Jess. 'Did you know? Tim, he's gay.'

I swallowed, went a bit hot in the face, said, 'What makes you think that?'

Jess is bursting with it. 'I don't think it, I know it. He

was out on cross-country and he asked Dave Jarrett to give him a kiss.'

Dave Jarrett hangs around with Nathan Ellis.

'If you believe what Dave Jarrett says, you'll believe anything.'

Jess tuts, like I'm stupid. 'It's not just Dave Jarrett. Anna Cummins saw Tim follow Will Themen into the toilets. It's true.'

I shook my head, walked off. But I heard the same stuff and more from Julie, and Hannah, and Tracey Brain. It was like everyone had a Tim story, and it spread like wildfire. Worse, because Tim was off school.

'I expect he's got Aids,' Tracey said, all solemn, like she was an expert.

Surprise, surprise, Tasha corners me at dinner-time.

'I feel so betrayed!' she goes. 'I trusted him and he's let me down, and I feel soiled.'

I led her out of the hall, because everyone's listening, and we walked round the field. I said to her, 'Have you talked to Tim about it?'

'How can I? He's hiding from me. That's why he's off school.'

I took a deep breath. 'Tash, this is just a rumour. I bet it's Nathan Ellis who started it.'

She goes shifty, flushes up. 'Why would Nathan Ellis want to start a rumour like that?'

'Because he fancies you himself.'

She looked away, but you could see she was trying to hide a smile. That made me mad.

'And you fancy Nathan, do you?'

'Don't be stupid.'

'Yeah, I know it's stupid, and so are you, because you haven't got the sense to see that Tim's a really nice bloke, but Nathan, he's just a dirty little ferret—'

She turns on me. 'Maybe you're the stupid one. After all, you've never been out with Tim. You don't know what he's *really* like.'

Back home, the phone kept going every five minutes, and everyone wanted to know about Tim, and my mum and dad kept asking what it was all about, and in the end I said, 'You know Tim? Everyone says he's gay.'

My mum said, 'Well, what if he is, what does it matter?'

That bugged me. I shouted, 'It doesn't worry me at all, why should it?'

And my dad said, 'Maybe the lady doth protest too much,' which really made me see red, so I told him to mind his own business.

'Sorry,' he goes, 'but I've always liked Tim. And his father's pretty well heeled. You could do a lot worse in the marriage stakes.'

'Do shut up, Les,' hissed my mum.

I slammed the kitchen door so hard the chopping-board fell into the sink, and the chimes in Gran's broken clock went tinkling.

Then I sat in my room.

When the phone went next time, I knew who it was going to be, so I stayed where I was, but two seconds later Dad sticks his head round the door.

'It's for you-oo. It's *him*. Tim.'

When I got in the kitchen, my mum does this silly whisper, '*Gender bender*.'

When I picked the phone up, it was dead.

I was mad, I tell you. Mad at Mum and Dad, but mad at myself, too, for telling them anything.

'I expect he's going to kill himself, now, you wallies. You're so tolerant and everything and then when it comes down to it all you can do is make stupid comments.'

And I grabbed my coat, and pulled my boots on, and off I went.

When I got to Tim's house, he wasn't home. His mum was in a real state.

'He had a temperature of a hundred and two this morning, and then that girl rang up, and next thing I know he's disappeared. I expect he's gone to see her.'

She tuts. She doesn't like Tash.

'I was going to ring up and check he's all right, but it seems so silly.'

I said I'd do it.

Tash was home. She sounded peevish. Tim hadn't been there.

'How should I know where he is? Ask one of his boy-friends. Now, if you don't mind, I'm expecting a call.'

'Any luck?' Tim's mum asked.

I pretended it was no big deal, but my heart was pounding and my blood was boiling up inside.

'I expect he's gone for a walk. I'll go and see if I can find him.'

I tried the park, but there were only toddlers there, so I went down to the river. It's nice there, and quiet, with trees all along, and I was just sniffing at the smells, and calming down, when I saw him. He was on the bridge, leaning on the parapet.

He didn't look up. I stood next to him.

Silence.

'Don't jump,' I said.

'I might as well,' he goes. He's looking very sorry for himself. His nose is red, and his eyes.

I said, 'I mean, if you are, it doesn't matter.'

Tim looked up at me. His glasses are steaming up where he keeps having to blow his nose, so he takes them off.

'If I am what?'

'If you are gay.'

The word stuck in my throat.

He looked away, shaking his head.

'So you believe it too?'

I pulled at the sleeve of his jacket.

'I didn't say I believed it, I said I don't care. You're my friend. That's what matters.'

'Even your mother thinks so.'

'She was just being stupid.'

'Yeah, everyone's just being stupid.'

And he turned away so he had his back to me. That bugged me! I grabbed his arm again, and tugged him round, and he didn't want to come, but I forced him, I was so mad. I had him by both his sleeves.

'For God's sake, stop feeling so hard done by all the time. Who cares what people say? It's what you are in yourself that matters, and sometimes, I reckon you're the biggest wimp in the entire universe.'

He's staring at me. His eyes look bigger without the glasses. His voice is croaky, with the flu.

'Tell me what *you* really think.'

I couldn't answer. There was a brick throbbing in my throat. I'm angry and I feel tears getting hot round my eyes, he's such a wuss!

I started to say, 'I don't know what I think.'

But he leaned forward and he kissed me on the cheek.

Then he put his glasses back on.

My face was hot and my lips and all up my chest, like a rash. I put my arm round him, felt him, big under the jumper.

He wanted to hold hands walking back home, but I wouldn't. Not once we got on to the main road. Felt stupid. But I kept glancing up at him, and he's got this little smile. His mum, she smiled too when she opened the door. Made me go hot again.

I told him, 'You go to bed and keep warm and I'll call round tomorrow.'

And I kissed him on the cheek. In front of his mum.

I didn't want to, but I thought I'd better go straight round to Tasha's house, and get it sorted out. All the way there I was working out in my head what I was going to say. When I turned into her road, I stopped. There was Tash, walking towards the bus stop. Bouncing along beside her on the tips of his toes so his head just came up to her shoulder, was Nathan Ellis. Tash was giggling. Nathan had a big smirk on his face.

They were arm in arm.

Together.

The Inkpond

Joanna Carey

Handy with a knife, and perfectly at ease skinning rabbits, gutting fish or threading wet pink worms on hooks, I was an obliging child, always ready to help my big brother. He and his friend Ian were tireless hunters and gatherers of almost anything nature had to offer in the leafy glades of our post-war Home Counties village. Really, it was Ian I did it for — my brother gave the commands, but it was for Ian that I obeyed.

Ian was sandy-haired and soft-spoken. I worshipped Ian, not exactly from afar, but from the distance created both by the few years between us, and the fact that I was a girl. And, of course, Ian was my brother's best friend — his private property. Uncomfortably aware of my adoration, Ian seldom spoke to me directly, but, unlike my brother, he did occasionally acknowledge the fact that I was a faithful and uncomplaining servant.

Although I kept a bunny of my own, safe and snug in a hutch, most Saturday evenings I'd be out in the yard with a sharp knife and an enamel basin, skinning the wild rabbits the boys had caught and lining them up, headless, moist, mauve and veiny, on the kitchen step, ready for the pot. The skins I nailed flat against the garden shed with a view to curing them; my brother had plans for a fur-lined waistcoat.

'Doesn't she mind doing that?' Ian would ask, but my brother, he'd just laugh.

'She's tough as old boots, my little sister. Not exactly silk-purse material, if you know what I mean.'

I was tough, it was true – and I chose to take his words as complimentary, though I wasn't sure what he meant about 'silk-purse material'. For reasons of economy I was often dressed in my brother's outgrown clothes, and the pockets of my grey flannel shorts bulged with catapult elastic, air-gun pellets, split shot, swivels and other odd bits of fishing tackle. I even had my own disgorger, for getting hooks out of the fishes' throats. I would happily spend my own pocket-money on a tin of maggots, just so I could offer them to my brother – and Ian – for bait. The fish they caught, anything from gudgeon to pike, weren't always edible but not much was wasted. I was kept busy with all kinds of projects. I had problems with a prize-winning tench they caught. It was a big green fish and my brother wanted it stuffed and mounted as an entry for the 'hobbies' exhibition at their school. I slit it open, removed as much loose matter as possible and dried it out with talcum powder. Then I stuffed the cavity with sawdust and cotton wool soaked in Dettol, and stitched it up with buttonhole thread. I gave it a coat of yacht varnish to firm it up but, even so, we had to bury it quite soon after.

Worse still was the dead fox they found near the main road. Hit by a car, I suppose, but it looked all right –

beautiful really. The boys wanted to preserve the skeleton intact, so we took the body, in my old doll's pram, to the place up in the woods we called the Inkpond — a dark lake overhung by trees. Using my skipping rope, we tied it up securely and hung it in the water from a branch.

'It'll decompose,' said my brother, 'the flesh will drop off and there'll be creatures in the water that'll pick it nice and clean.'

It was my job to hoist it out now and again to see how it was getting on. I would poke at it with a stick to get the bits off, and then lower it back to let the inky black acid water finish the job. I found it hard to stop thinking about that fox under the water.

Everyone could see that I was keen on nature study and one year I was given a butterfly net for my birthday. It was a beautiful net, green and swishy with a polished wooden handle.

'A girl with a butterfly net. Now there's a pretty sight,' said my grandad who was visiting. And with uncharacteristic generosity my brother discreetly offered me a few drops of cyanide (procured with some difficulty by Derek, the son of the village chemist) so that I could make my own 'killing bottle' — a screw-top jar like the one in which he and Ian regularly snuffed out the brief lives of countless brimstones, red admirals, peacocks and pearl-bordered fritillaries.

On one occasion the boys had sent off to London for the chrysalis of a swallowtail butterfly. They'd nursed it lovingly in a special box until it began to wriggle and split. We'd watched spellbound as the butterfly emerged, stretching its wings to dry. Then, without so much as a test flight, it was dispatched to the killing bottle and pinned to a cork table mat in a cigar box.

Some creatures miraculously escaped the boys' grim harvest. They always tried to care for fledglings that had fallen from their nests – the success rate wasn't high, but there were some survivors. Then one day they found a fully grown kestrel with a damaged wing. They brought it home, and I was told to keep it in a cage in my room and look after it. I fed it with worms and dead mice. I loved that bird. I loved the way it would stand on one foot and grab with the other, and the way it would tilt its head to look at me. Ian, whose father was the local butcher, would sometimes bring it scraps from the shop. My heart would lurch when he'd pedal up the lane to our house specially to give me little paper parcels of pig's liver, perhaps, or giblets, still warm from his pocket. Soon the bird's wing was better and one morning – it was Coronation Day, a school holiday – I opened my bedroom window on an impulse and set it free. It soared up and away over the trees and out of sight. My brother was furious, but Ian quietly told me that I'd done the right thing. I glowed in the warmth of his approval.

As they grew older, the boys' hunting instincts altered and diverged. Ian became more of an observer. He'd stay out all night in the hope of seeing badgers, and he was a keen birdwatcher. But he still seemed compelled to hang around with my brother who was now after the grey squirrels with his air gun. Squirrels were a pest; there was a price on them. You could get a shilling each for the severed tails if you took them up to the County Council office. Taller now, and stronger, I was expected to go on these expeditions — often as not carrying the gun, or the long pole with which to poke the dreys. We'd cut the tails off with secateurs. Disconnected, they were stiff, mangy things. I had the job of tying them up in bundles. I'd then dip them in Jeyes Fluid to disinfect them, wrap them up in pages from the *Exchange & Mart* and keep them in my sock drawer until we had enough to make it worthwhile catching the bus in to town to get the money. Twenty-five tails meant we'd come home with one pound five shillings, though I'd be lucky to get so much as half-a-crown for my trouble.

Secretly I felt a bond with Ian in that he too was more and more uncomfortable with this wholesale slaughter, but I could see that, like me, he was too scared to speak his mind. But he did argue, as fiercely as he dared, against my brother's increasing use of snares for rabbits.

'At least with a gun,' he said, 'you can see what you're doing. But a snare — that's barbaric.' Then one day we found Winkle, our neighbour's ginger cat, dead in one of the snares. The wire noose had caught him by the leg and he was half-eaten by foxes. We were all upset. I cried, and I could see my brother was confused — and he was annoyed when Ian tried (rather awkwardly) to comfort me. Mum said we had to explain to the neighbour what had happened to Winkle. She insisted. In the end we went round there and mumbled something about finding Winkle's body in the woods. We didn't tell the truth of course. After that our hunting days were numbered.

A rift grew between me and my brother. Ian still came to see him, but they'd no longer plan fishing trips, or examine their collections of butterflies. They'd talk or listen to records on the Dansette. Ian would always give me a bit of a nod as he passed through our kitchen. I'd station myself there with a book if I knew he was coming. But if I so much as smiled at Ian, my brother, silently, behind Ian's back, would make a vivid gesture of throwing up. Then he'd usher Ian into his room. There'd be laughter and I'd hear the click of snooker balls, or the thud of darts on the back of his door. Repeatedly humiliated like this, I wept at the kitchen table.

'Leave them be,' said my mum. 'That's boys for you. They're awkward buggers. Don't push in on them. They need each other just now. They grow up slowly, boys do, in fits and starts. Ian'll surprise you one day, you mark my words.'

At times like this I'd get my rabbit in from his hutch, watch him hop and quiver round my room. I'd lie on the floor beside him and blow soft whorls in his silky fur or I'd hold him tight, feel his sharp little rabbit bones and think about the fox in the Inkpond.

There was an odd, uncomfortable atmosphere in our house which didn't begin to lift until the autumn of the year my brother went off to college.

I saw Ian sometimes when I went shopping in the village; he was now working in his father's shop. Buying sausages one day, I was staring at the old-fashioned enamel shop sign. 'Family Butcher', it said.

'Frightening, that sign, if you think about it,' said Ian, looking up from the pig's head he was splitting. He dropped the ears in a bucket and put down his cleaver. It was nice – whenever I went in there, he'd set aside what he was doing, wipe his hands on his apron and come over and talk to me. He'd never have done that with my brother around. He was still a bit shy, but working in the shop had made him a little easier to talk to. And he seemed these days to take me a little more seriously. I wondered if he'd noticed the Autumn Glints I'd rinsed my hair with.

'We should get together,' he said one day, looking away as he spoke, one foot awkwardly tracing a pattern in the sawdust on the tiled floor of the shop. I blushed.

'We could go up the Inkpond one evening,' he went on. 'Remember that fox?' We both laughed. The skeleton plan was long forgotten, the rope itself had rotted away and the fox was most likely decently buried by now in the silty mud at the bottom. But Ian's invitation thrilled me; somehow I felt it was what I'd been waiting for all my life. Really though it was a vague, insubstantial invitation and as time went by I realised that probably nothing would come of it.

Even so, I boasted a little at school about a romantic entanglement and I dreamt about Ian. Night after night, swotting away at my O-level revision, learning off chunks of Wordsworth, reading *Wuthering Heights*, perfecting my diagrams of how to dissect frogs, I'd recall Ian's words. I'd imagine him standing beneath my window – perhaps in the moonlight – calling me to come down. But nothing happened. I'd see him in the shop or at the bus shelter, but always, just as he was about to speak, a customer would come in, or the bus would arrive. And that's as far as we got.

The year wore on. My brother came home for the

Christmas holiday. He brought a girl with him. She had sharp stiletto heels and long red nails. One night, when it was beginning to snow, Ian came over and they all went off to the pub together. It was late when they got back. They were leaning this way and that, laughing and talking too loud. Ian was still with them. I was in the kitchen, reading.

They were all freezing cold, so I made some cocoa and took it into my brother's room, thinking I might join them for a bit. 'You've brought one cup too many' said my brother, handing me the tray. Ian pretended not to notice as I left the room with my cocoa. The girl said nothing.

I went up to my room. I looked out. It was snowing quite heavily now. I put the cocoa down on a chair and switched on the electric fire. Out on the hill I could hear a fox barking.

I got into my nightdress and then, leaving the door not quite closed, I wrapped myself in the eiderdown and lay on the bed. I was half-asleep when, about an hour later, the door opened. It was Ian. I sort of knew it would be.

'I'm setting off home,' he said. 'Just thought I'd . . . well . . . I'm sorry about . . . well . . . It's just that your brother, well, you know what he's like . . . anyway, *she's* got her claws into him now . . . I've left them to it . . . I just thought I'd see if you were all right . . .'

I thought about it.

'Oh, I'm all right,' I said. And suddenly I was. I was cross, but I was all right.

'Come in,' I said. I didn't give him a chance to say

no. I hauled him into the room and shut the door firmly. Ian was startled. He stumbled, crashing into the chair and knocking over the forgotten cup of cocoa. He fell, all anyhow, on to the bed. 'Shh,' I said. 'I don't want Mum waking up.'

He sat there like a rabbit – not a limp dead rabbit, not a comfy pet rabbit – but a trapped rabbit who fears that any minute he'll be gutted and skinned.

It was a long, awkward encounter. Really, what I remember best is the sweaty smell of his pullover, steaming away in front of the electric fire, on the chair where he'd flung it, and the dark damp mess on the floor where the cocoa had seeped into the carpet. I felt a deep dark sense of disappointment. It made me think of the pond in the woods.

I sat up suddenly. 'Why don't we go up the Inkpond?' I said. 'That's what you said we'd do, when we got the chance.'

He wasn't keen but he seemed almost transfixed, powerless to disagree. So we went, even though it was past three in the morning. We crept out of the house. It had stopped snowing. We made sharp tracks in the new snow. We walked for a long time in silence. We reached the woods. It was easier to walk here. Ian stopped.

'There's something I should have told you,' he said. 'It's what I came round to tell your brother. I'm going up north next week. I'm going to work in my uncle's shop in Newcastle. I'll not be seeing you for a bit.'

I don't really know what I felt. I just walked on till I reached the Inkpond. Frozen over, it looked entirely different – clean and smooth in the moonlight. Then, as

I stood there, one of the huge overhanging branches began to creak and groan under the weight of the snow it had collected. With a slow shriek it split from the trunk and fell like an axe, leaving a jagged hole in the ice. Suddenly you could see the twinkle of the inky dark water underneath. It was frightening. I stepped back from the pond, looking around me to see where Ian had got to. He was way back among the trees.

Something made me turn back to the pond. A vixen was standing on the ice, not far from where the branch had fallen. She could see me but she seemed preoccupied with something beyond. She lifted her head, sniffed the air and then set off at a trot across the pond. She leapt on to the bank, silently dislodging a spray of powdery snow from a brittle clump of reeds. She stood again for a moment and had a little shake, just a metre or two from me. After a moment's thought she set off, confident and decisive, along the narrow woodland path that led to the open fields and the hill behind our house.

I followed her. She never once looked back.

And neither did I.

Claudine

Robert Westall

When I first saw Claudine, I thought she was ugly. And stupid. How was I to know she was just lost?

Yet I should have known. Our parish hall was full of lost children, sixty of them. Little bundles of misery with a brown label tied round their necks, giving name and address. Bundled up in their best coats, far too hot for the May sunshine. Carrying all they had in the world in tiny suitcases, or carrier bags, or cardboard boxes done up with coarse string.

Few cried; it takes energy to cry. We didn't even notice the ones who were crying till we saw, close-to, the shine of tears on their cheeks. They didn't make a sound, just sat there in rows on every table-top and windowsill like little parcels, waiting to be collected.

We tried to be kind, to speak softly, to smile at each one. But we were hot and tired too. This was the third lot we'd had today. Evacuees from London. So easy to treat them as parcels, to forget the homes and fathers and mothers that had been torn away from them so swiftly.

My mother was wonderful, holding their hands, taking them to the lavatory. This was important, because they were so afraid they would sit silent till they wet themselves, if you weren't careful. But few smiled back at her. Most just raised huge eyes, asking the fearful silent questions – who are you, what are you going to do with me? Some did not even raise their eyes, but just stared into space.

If they were parcels, my father was the postman. The vicar of this parish. The man who dealt with those villagers who had come to collect themselves an evacuee, as you might collect a stray dog from the dogs' home. Could you blame them for wanting the pretty ones and leaving the ugly ones, the ones who smelt or had greasy hair and running noses? Could you blame them for wanting the older girls who might help with the cooking and washing-up, the sturdy boys who might join in the farm-work? Even if it meant splitting up the tiny families who clung together? My father did not blame them, but he was strict with them, and a vicar could be strict in those days. He knew all the families, the mean families who only wanted a useful pair of hands; who might starve the children. The families where the husband came home drunk and beat his own children. And he knew the kind ones too, the women who were poor, but made up for it with warm hearts and many cuddles, who would take three or four, even of the ugly ones. I can see him now, dashing from group to group with his notebook in his hand, little and quick with combed-back Brylcreemed hair and sharp eyes behind his horn-rimmed spectacles.

And I was the clerk, sitting at my trestle-table till my bottom ached; like the Recording Angel, writing down where they had come from and where they were going to. I must not make a single mistake, even if I was just fourteen, nearly fifteen. My father relied on me; and I loved him. I would have died rather than let him down. That feeling is not so common now. I often wonder if any still feel it.

In the end, they all went. Our gallant Boy Scouts and Wolf Cubs began to clear up the half-drunk mugs of milk, and sweep up the crumbs and crushed pieces of cake off the floor. Doing their bit for the war effort; every crumb swept up, a poke in the eye for Adolf Hitler. And I smiled at my mother and father, sharing our weariness. And old Jack Hawkins came in to lock up the hall, and said had we heard the news on the radio – that the Germans were still sweeping across Belgium as if nothing on earth would stop them, and our brave boys were retreating just to straighten the defence line, and the French 75mm guns were taking a terrible toll of the German tanks . . .

We smiled again, with our bitter new-found cynicism, and it was then that I saw the older girl sitting in the corner, with her head down. I thought, till then, she was an adult who had come with the children, in charge of some of them. But now she made no attempt to move. She had high-heeled black court shoes, but no stockings. It was considered vulgar, even in those days of shortage, not to wear stockings; it was what tarts did. Her long raincoat was fashionable, but dirty. Her hair had been done up in a grown-up style, but was now escaping from its hairpins and falling over her face in greasy strands.

'Who is she?' asked my father, in a low voice.

'She is French,' said my mother. 'She doesn't seem to know much English. That's why I left her to the end . . . refugee.'

I felt wary. I never spoke to girls in those days, not even English girls. Girls would suddenly burst into giggles without warning; or even slap your face if you made the wrong joke. They seemed to be constantly on the lookout for a chance to giggle or slap your face. They were like living land-mines. And though the French, as everyone was always saying, were our gallant allies, the French were odd. Their soldiers wore sky-blue uniforms, instead of sensible khaki. Their airplanes and guns and tanks were funny shapes, even funnier than the Germans. They were far too interested in love and food and drink, even in wartime. And they had strange toilets, where you could not pull a chain . . .

My father went across to the girl, and gently tapped her on the shoulder. She looked up wearily, as if for the thousandth time, and reached into her handbag and produced an envelope and gave it to him. I don't think she even saw him; giving the envelope was just a habit, and her eyes stared at the beams of the ceiling.

My father shook out the contents of the envelope. A passport, and some papers, official papers. My father said, 'She crossed the Channel on the Dover ferry four days ago. Since then she has been to Canterbury, London, Guildford, London again, and now here. They've been passing her round like a lost parcel . . . What has she had to eat? Where has she slept? The poor child is worn out. Nobody would take responsibility for her, because she was French.'

'But we don't speak French either!' said my mother.

'To hell with that,' said my father. 'She's a human being. She needs a bath, a meal, a bed. We'll worry about speaking French afterwards. Anyway, our Ronnie can speak French.'

He looked across at me, expecting miracles. Even though I had given up French at school a year ago, to take up shorthand and typing instead, because I wanted to be a journalist. My last mark in French had been seventeen per cent; I was the despair of the French teacher. But for my father, anything.

I plunged in and shook her hand, which was long and slim, with long nails, which I thought very wicked, especially as they were painted red, and the red had chipped.

'*Je suis* Ronnie Cafferty,' I said, after long thought. '*Voici mon père! Voici ma mère!*' I couldn't remember any more of the French I had learnt at school, except *la plume de ma tante est dans le jardin* and that didn't seem very appropriate to the present event.

A faint ghost of a smile dawned on her pale lips. Even in her weariness she was laughing at me.

'*Je m'appelle* Claudine Deschamps,' she said, and then I remembered that was the right way to say it.

'Take her up to the vicarage, Ronnie. Give her the spare room. We won't be long clearing up here. Carry her suitcase for her. She looks all in.' Then my father and mother turned away into more discussion about tea urns for the next day, with old Jack Hawkins.

We were a long time getting to the vicarage. Her case seemed to weigh a ton, and she was so weary she tottered on her high heels and almost fell several times. She kept having to grab for my arm. What made it worse was that several of my schoolmates were about, tearing up and down on their bikes, no doubt supervising the war effort.

'Who's your lady-friend, Caffers?' shouted Alan Jones, who was my worst enemy, as she staggered into me and clutched my arm again.

'She's French,' I shouted. 'A refugee.'

'God, Caffers has picked up a French tart. Ooh la-la!'

'When you getting married, Caffers?'

'You don't *marry* French tarts, *do* you, Caffers?'

'Faff off!' I yelled.

That only made things worse. They nearly fell off their bikes laughing, and some of the things they said, I was glad she was French and couldn't understand.

Then, to cap it all, she bent down and took off her shoes and walked on in her bare feet.

'Ooh la-la!' Alan Jones shouted. 'Cabaret! Strip-tease! Better than Gypsy Rose Lee!'

'I'll kill you when I catch you!' I shouted.

'Go on, you won't have the strength. You don't know what French tarts are like!'

My face burned like a furnace. And the unfair thing was all the time I was blaming *her*.

After a million years, we turned in at the vicarage gate, and they left us alone. Our front door was open; we never locked it in those days. I didn't know where to put her. In the kitchen? In the sitting room? She was leaning on my arm all the time now, and she was pretty heavy. Her eyes were blank, and her mouth hanging a bit open. Perhaps she was ill, really ill.

I suddenly thought that if she collapsed, we'd have to *carry* her upstairs. And that would be *embarrassing*. Best get her up to bed while she could still walk.

I'd never realised our stairs were so steep. Or the handle of the spare room so stiff. But I got her in there at last. A plain little room. Just a narrow bed, a chest of drawers with a bowl and ewer, and an embroidered picture saying 'God Is Love'. It was where we put visiting curates, when there were other people staying, and the house was full.

But her eyes opened wide, as if it was the Kingdom of Heaven.

'*C'est jolie,*' she said. '*Très jolie.*' And fell on to the bed and then fell on to her side, and pulled up her long legs and was instantly snoring. At least, I thought she was asleep. But then she might have fainted, like the women who came to early service without eating any breakfast . . .

I hovered, uncertain what to do. I'd never in all my life seen somebody fall asleep that fast. Maybe she was really ill. She smelt funny, foreign.

But as I watched, to make sure she was still breathing, a change came over her face. The stupid look faded; her cheeks grew rosy in sleep. She suddenly looked like a little kid, like my cousin Monica when she was asleep with her teddy bear. And she suddenly looked . . . beautiful. Except that her right hand kept groping as if it wanted to hold something. It fingered the edge of the turned-down sheet, the bottom corners of the pillows, but they didn't seem satisfactory. I felt a great pity for that groping hand. I desperately wanted to comfort it. It seemed so terrible that the hand should be hungry, still wandering about, when the rest of her was asleep.

In the end, I went to my own room and got my old teddybear. Not that I'd touched him for years; but I hadn't the heart to get rid of him, so he just sat on top of a pile of books in one corner of my room, getting dustier and dustier. I got rid of the worst of the dust by banging him gently, and making a great cloud of dust motes that hung in the last rays of the setting sun, coming in through the window.

Then I went and offered the dusty bear to the hungry hand. The hand felt him; then closed tight round him. The bear would do.

I felt I had achieved something great. I felt as if I suddenly *owned* her. I surveyed her slender clutching hand; the stray lock of hair that moved across her rosy cheek with every breath she took; her long slim bare feet. Such joy was mine. The joy of a fish that closes its mouth on the bait.

The moment before it feels the pain of the fisherman's hook.

She came down for the nine o'clock news, washed and changed. She had put her hair up in some beautiful arrangement, and she wore no make-up. Anyone could see she was a lady, not a French tart. She ate the sandwiches my mother had made for her with a daintiness that could not conceal her hunger; she gathered the last of the crumbs together on her plate, and ate them from the end of her finger. And she stiffened every time

the newsreader mentioned a French town. As if someone
had stuck a pin into her body. '*Les Boches*' she would
mutter. '*Sales Boches.*' Though she definitely didn't have
much English.

'Ask her where she's come from.' said my father.

'*Où est ton maison?*' I stumbled. Was it *le maison* or *la
maison?*

A stream of French flooded from her, that I was
instantly overwhelmed by. But my father thought he
caught the word 'Passy' and also the word 'Paris'. Not
hard, since her address was in her passport.

'*Où est ton pere?*'

We caught the word *soldat* and *armée blindé* and *char
de combat*. Her shoulders went back, her back straightened and her eyes shone, though with a hint of tears, I
thought. She was obviously proud of her father; and
very afraid for him.

'I think he's a soldier in the tank corps,' I told them.

'Ask about her mother!'

'*Où est ta mère?*' I blundered on. But all I got was a
flood about *mère* and *grandmère* and *bateau* and 'Calais'.

'I don't know how we're going to cope,' wailed my
mother. 'I don't know anyone who speaks French. What
about your French master at school, Ronnie?'

'He's just joined up,' I said.

'She'd better stay with us,' said my father. 'Better the
devil you know! If we give her back to the bureaucrats,
they'll probably shove her round till she starves to death.
Ronnie can cope. Meanwhile, I'll write to the French
embassy. God help them.'

*

Cope? How do you cope, fourteen hours a day, with someone who doesn't speak your language, and who's worried out of her mind for her father, her mother, her grandmother, her home, her dog and cat, and last of all her country? Somebody who can't understand what she hears, or what she sees, somebody who can't help weeping with the very strangeness of it all; however hard she tries to sniff back the tears, and wipe her eyes when she thinks you're not looking at her?

Well, you cope because you have to. We spent hours teaching each other words like knife and fork, bus, toilet, garden, field, cow, horse ... You let her play the old wind-up gramophone till the needles wear out and you haven't got any more and can't get any more because there's a war on and all the steel is going on munitions to beat the Nazis. You dig out your sister's old bicycle because your sister is in the ATS and doesn't need it any more, and you mend punctures in both the tyres, and then you take the French person out on it, and she nearly gets flattened by lorries ten times a journey, because she keeps worrying about her father and her mother and her country and keeps riding on the right-hand side of the road instead of the left.

And you take her to your favourite places, and it just doesn't *work*. I mean, there's a stream flowing through a little wood near home, and the sun shines down in a little glade, and you can sit with your feet in the stream with the water running between your toes and you can watch the minnows nibbling at your toes and the sun on the ripples and pebbles and forget about the war ... and the first English sentence she ever manages is 'Why are we do this?'

And all the time the war is going so wrong, with the British and French armies being pressed back and back to the Channel ports, and the retreats going on and on, and you are being told, 'Our troops are in fine spirits,' till you could *scream*.

My last trump-card was the old aerodrome at Chancely. I used to have so much fun at that aerodrome before the war. It was just a big flat grass field, with one rusty metal shed, but rich blokes used to come there to fly their planes and you could hold their toolbags while they fiddled with their engines, and fetch things for them, and if you helped enough, they might take you up in the back cockpit for a little spin, if nobody more important was available . . . Of course it was abandoned now. But there was the wreck of a Tiger Moth, and the stripped fuselage of a new Gull you could sit in the cockpit of, and pretend you were a fighter ace. And locked in the hangar were the remains of a Gypsy Moth that might be coaxed one day to fly again. The hangar was locked with a big chain and padlock, but you could see it inside, if you peered closely through the grimy oily cobwebby window.

All this I showed her. She managed to ask if the Nazis had wrecked the two planes, and when I said no, she lost interest and started her damned brooding again, sitting on the grass with her knees up in front of her, and her arms tight round her knees, and her chin on her arms . . .

I walked off; I was sick of the brooding. I mean, if we

were all going to be slaughtered by the Nazis anyway, why waste what time we had left while the sun shone?

It was then that I found the new stuff. Pits dug round the edge of the field, with a heaped wall of sandbags round each. Over one pit, somebody had raised an army tent, and when I cautiously looked inside, there was a table in the dim light, and on the table a telephone. The army sort, with a little handle at the side that you whirl round and round.

Well, I went in. Wouldn't you? And I picked up the handset, like they did in the movies, and whirled the handle.

Then it *worked*. A voice came through, and I was so scared, I nearly dropped the whole thing. A man's voice that said, 'Stutely Fighter Control.' I was so paralysed that I couldn't say anything. The voice said again, 'Stutely Fighter Control. Do you read me?' Then after a silence, another voice said, 'It must be kids mucking about,' and then the first voice said again, 'Stop mucking about, whoever you are. You are interfering with Air Ministry property and harming the war effort as well, and if you don't stop it, we'll send the RAF police to sort you out good and proper. You wouldn't want to go to prison, would you?'

And I dropped the handset back as if it was red-hot, and went back to Claudine, and suggested that we get away quick. She shrugged, and we got on our bikes and went.

Part of our road home lay alongside the railway line that runs from Dover through Ashford and Headcorn. As I

was cycling along it, with Claudine trailing limply
behind, I heard a train starting to overtake us. What
caught my attention was that it was overtaking us so
slowly; trains normally do that section like a streak of
lightning. I glanced sideways, as it came level, and saw
it was full of soldiers, coming from the port of Dover.

As the slow speed of the train was odd, so was the
behaviour of the soldiers. Normally they hung out of the
carriage windows, waving to all and sundry, and whistling at any girl they passed, especially girls on bicycles
who might be showing a bit more of their legs than
usual. But these soldiers just sat, motionless, staring
blankly at the passing countryside. And many were still
wearing steel helmets, which normally soldiers never do,
as they're so heavy. And these men looked . . . dirty.

Uneasy, somehow, I waved to them, trying to stir
them into life. One or two waved feebly back, but they
soon stopped. For some reason it worried me deeply.

And then came a carriage full of men in uniforms of a
different colour. Sky blue. None of them waved at all.

But suddenly, behind me, Claudine went beserk.

'*Français!*' she shouted. '*Français!*' Then she shook
my shoulder, nearly knocking me off my bike. '*Où est la
gare?*'

I nodded ahead, bewildered. Then she was off like a
rocket, pedalling like a fiend. I had a rare job keeping up
with her. We whizzed through the little village of
Headcorn, and up the ramp to the station. The train of
soldiers was still standing there; women were handing
them sandwiches and mugs of tea and handfuls of
cigarettes through the carriage windows. Claudine ran

through them, knocking them left and right in her haste to find her Frenchmen. I followed, apologizing to the women, saying, 'Sorry. She's French,' as if that would explain everything.

I reached the French carriage just behind her. The French soldiers looked different from the British. The British had looked very weary, but glad to be here. The French had that same lost look that the evacuee children in the village hall had had. Lost in a strange land . . .

Until Claudine began jabbering such a stream of French that would have swept the strongest dam away.

What a change came over the Frenchmen. They suddenly crowded to the windows, all jabbering away just as hard, falling over each other in their eagerness. They opened the carriage doors and flooded the platform with pale blue – very filthy oily pale blue. They embraced her and kissed her on both cheeks, one after the other. Some wept unashamedly, but most grinned as if it was Christmas. One or two even whirled her off her feet and carried her up and down the platform on their shoulders. The women who were giving out sandwiches had a hard time getting through, I can tell you. I couldn't make out a word of it, except them saying *jolie, très très jolie* and *comme Marianne*.

And then the whistle blew, and the engine hooted, and all the Frenchmen bundled back on board, and waved frantically as the train drew out, cramming every window. And Claudine stood so upright on the platform alone, like a soldier, with her hand to her forehead in a stiff salute, until the train was just a speck.

Then she turned to me. Her face was blackened with

their oily fingerprints, like a stoker's. Her dress was stained where she had been held in their oily embraces. But her eyes were huge and shining like stars, and at the same time full of tears.

'Dunkirk,' she said. 'From Dunkirk. But they will return. To fight the Boche.' It was the longest speech in English she had ever made.

'*Ton père?*' I asked 'Had they seen him?'

She shook her head, and suddenly she wilted. Then she straightened up again. 'I shall await every train. It is my duty. *Pour la France.*'

I tried to argue with her, but I knew it was useless. I cycled home alone.

For a week, she lived on Headcorn Station. I think the women must have fed her. They soon spotted how she cheered the Frenchmen up. And by now, in a blundering way, she could explain what the Frenchmen said; what they wanted. Where she slept, if she slept, I don't know. My mother kept on driving up there in our car, with a change of clothes for her, towel and soap. Only one thing she asked for: a piece of red, white and blue material. My father found a piece, rummaging among the bunting left over from the Coronation in 1937, when we had a celebration tea on the village green. Claudine twisted it into a sash, which she wore across her shoulder. Somehow she made it look French red, white and blue, not English.

She did meet every train, even those that came through in the middle of the night. A few times I went up to see her, but I found it too painful. Her mounting excitement as a train became due was awful to behold. She could not sit still, but paced the platform like a caged tiger. Then, if the Dunkirk train contained only British, or if the train was not a soldiers' train at all, she would wilt like a flower, and have to sit down and rest. And if there were Frenchmen, they mauled her so, in their joy, and she gave them all, with shining face, and none of them knew how exhausted she was. Afterwards, she would fall asleep on a porter's trolley, still sitting upright.

And never a word about her father . . .

And then the wonderful thing happened for me. One afternoon, I was digging my father's flowerbeds up, so we could plant vegetables for the war effort, when six aeroplanes flew overhead. I looked up with great interest at all aeroplanes in those days; we all did. And I knew they were Spitfires, from their oval wings. I stood leaning on my spade to watch them out of sight, feeling cheered and proud. And then I saw the sun flash on their wings, as they banked and turned and started to descend.

From the way they vanished behind the trees, one by one, I suddenly knew they were landing. And they could only be landing at the old aerodrome.

All thoughts of vegetables forgotten, I leapt on to my bike and cycled like the wind. And when I reached the aerodrome there they were, lined up as neatly as guardsmen on parade, with the pilots in their flying jackets gathered in a little group, smoking.

But there were more wonders. A row of khaki tents had sprouted like mushrooms. A flag-pole had been raised, from which fluttered a yellow windsock, and the pale blue ensign of the RAF. There were several lorries, and a stained petrol bowser, and crowds of ground crew.

But it was the Spitfires that drew me. They looked like great sharks, with their pointed noses. I could see the little patches on their wings, that covered the mouths of their eight machine-guns. I shook with pride and joy and desire, creeping as close to them as I could, without crossing the fence that bounded the field.

The pilots took no notice of me. They were laughing and shouting at each other, and waving their arms to imitate the flight of planes. And they were at the very far end of the row of Spitfires . . .

Greatly daring, watching them carefully out of the corner of my eye, I crossed the fence. Tiptoed up to the first great plane. The shining red propellor boss, the neat tyres on the wheels, their every tread outlined by the bright sun. The shine of the open cockpit hood . . .

Then I heard a shout, and turned and saw one of the pilots running towards me. I thought he was angry, and turned to run. But he was too quick for me, and caught me.

'Sorry,' I gabbled. 'I just wanted to look . . .'

He was not angry. He grinned.

'Ronnie Cafferty! Little Ronnie Cafferty! Still crazy about aeroplanes, I see!'

I looked at him. He looked so strange in his flying helmet with the radio leads dangling.

'Don't you remember me? You held my toolkit enough, in the old days!' He pulled off his flying helmet and said, 'Bunny Beaumont, you old idiot!' and raised his hand and ruffled my hair. And it was the same old

Bunny who'd taken me for flips in his old Tiger Moth, before the war.

Now he dragged me towards his friends. 'Chaps, meet Ronnie Cafferty, the best holder of toolkits in the business!'

And they made a great fuss of me, ruffling my hair, and giving me punches in the ribs, and asking me where the nearest pub was. They were all very young; they didn't look much older than I was.

At last I was able to gasp out, 'What are you doing here?'

'Just a practice, old son,' said Bunny. 'To see if we could turn this old aerodrome into an emergency fighter station. In case the Hun gets too keen on Manston, and makes things too hot for us there. He'll never notice a forgotten old hole like this.'

'How long you staying?' I gasped, still lost in wonder.

'Only half a day, and then home to Manston for grub! Piece of cake! But we'll be back on Thursday. These beggars need more practice avoiding the cowpats while they're landing. Mucks up the tyres so. Drives the ground crews bananas. But we'll be here all day on Thursday, God willing, and we'll be bored out of our minds. We look to you, old lad, to lay on the dancing-girls. Or at least a decent spot of cricket. Got a bat and ball? And a map reference of where all the best beer is? That so, chaps?'

They all grinned and nodded.

'And,' said Bunny, 'if you're a good lad in all this, I might give you a flip in my new kite. Bit of a change from a Tiger Moth, eh?'

I waited and watched them take off, one by one. Waited till they had dwindled into dots on the horizon, heading for Manston. Even waited while the ground crew packed up their tents and lorries and drove away with a respectful wave.

Then I cycled home in a dream.

The trains from Dunkirk stopped coming through Headcorn on the seventh day. The miracle rescue of Dunkirk was complete, and, filthy and weary, Claudine came home. Still without news of her father.

But she was a different Claudine. Tired out though she was, she carried her shoulders back and her head high. She had been of use to *la France*. She also seemed to have got a lot more English suddenly. Perhaps memories of old schoolteaching had revived, because they were needed so much. She still spoke jolly odd English, but she kept plugging away till she was understood now. And she was as determined as me to push on the war effort. She began going round with my mother in her car, helping with the evacuees. My mother said she worked very hard, and the children liked her.

To me she was different too. She called me her first little English teacher, and ruffled my hair when she passed my seat at table. I think she was grateful for the trouble I had taken over her, those first few awful days. She came for bike rides in the evenings, quite willingly. And when I showed her my favourite places now, she understood, and enjoyed them. We went to my stream and dangled our bare feet in the brook, wriggling our toes and touching them together under water, which had a funny feel which made her giggle, because the water was cold, even in summer, and our feet were half-numb. I kissed her twice by that stream and she let me, and ruffled my hair again afterwards, with a rueful teasing grin on her face. I say 'she let me' because I can see now she didn't take me seriously. She was more than two years older than me – seventeen. But I was taller than her (though she was tall for a girl) and she wore no make-up, and her arms grew brown with the sun, and her face freckled, and she, as strangeness left her and happiness returned, I suppose she looked and seemed younger than she was.

Of course, by this time, I was secretly but madly in love with her. Because, as the French soldiers had said, she was beautiful, with her long straight nose that just tilted at the end, and her huge green eyes that tilted up at the outside tips, to echo the upward tilt of her lips. A beautiful French witch who stole my young heart quite away.

So, between the French witch, and the English wizard at the aerodrome, I was happier than I have ever been in my life.

I kept the aerodrome a secret from everybody. For one thing, I was cutting school to be with the pilots and take them to the pub and play cricket. With the Germans sitting in Calais and Boulogne, just across the Channel, it seemed far more important to keep our pilots happy than to do maths and geography. I don't know what my poor father would've said, but he never knew. And besides, I was jealous of other kids finding out that the fighters were there sometimes. The aerodrome was three miles from anywhere, and hardly anyone went there, except the farmhands who mowed the surrounding fields. And I wanted the pilots all to myself, especially Bunny Beaumont. To me, Bunny Beaumont was a god. They were all young gods, always laughing and making jokes, but Bunny was chief god. He had taken me up in his Spitfire.

Of course it was illegal. At Manston it would never have been allowed. But at this aerodrome, Bunny himself was in charge, and nobody was going to split on him.

And you can fly two in a Spitfire, if the pilot leaves off his parachute, and sits on his passenger's knee. It helped that Bunny was small, of course. He was smaller than me, with his hair thinning in front and the little moustache he worked so hard on with so little success, that was one of the squadron jokes. They were always suggesting he put cow manure from the field on it. Little he was, nearly as small as a jockey. But a young god to me . . .

Anyway, on my knees he sat, and off we went, him swinging the Spit's high nose from side to side, so he could see where he was going, so that he almost made me airsick before we left the ground. I couldn't see a thing. But then the tail wheel came unstuck from the field, and the plane levelled, and I could see ahead, over Bunny's shoulder, the line of trees tearing straight at us. He gunned the engine till it roared like a waterfall of sound, and then we lifted with a surge that nearly betrayed my stomach again.

After that, it was quite wonderful and I didn't feel sick any more, even when the sky above turned into green fields, and, looking out of the side of the cockpit, I saw the shining sun nestling among clouds beneath my feet.

When we landed, he stopped the engine, and pushed back the cockpit cover, and we just sat. It was funny, in a way, having your hero the young god on your knee, when I hadn't even had a girl there yet. The engine began to make clicks as it cooled, the rooks were cawing in the trees, it was sunlit and peaceful and I felt able to ask the great question.

'Can you beat them, Bunny? The Luftwaffe? The Stukas?' I was mortally afraid of Stukas, having heard what they had done to our army in Dunkirk.

'Stukas?' He laughed. 'Flying dustcarts. Knock 'em down like flies if we catch 'em. Piece of cake. Only got one gun and as slow as the Isle of Wight ferry. Not worried about Stukas. It's the ME 109s we have to watch out for.' He turned and saw the worried look on my face. 'Don't you worry about ME 109s either. They're twenty miles an hour slower than this little kite, and they can't turn as fast. And if you push them too hard, their wings break off. And we've got armour behind us there, and a bullet-proof Perspex windscreen in front.' He tapped it softly with his gloved hand. 'Piece of cake.'

As I said, I lived in a daze of happiness, with the Hun sitting just across the Channel. I look back now, an old man, and know that fortnight was the happiest of my life.

And then came the day that France surrendered. A bright fine day. We listened to the radio all day. They kept playing a tune called 'The Trumpet Voluntary' an old seventeenth-century tune, by someone called Jeremiah Clarke. Its harsh bitter tones put strength into you, between the terrible news bulletins. It made you feel strong and bitter and brave, even though your stomach fluttered at the same time.

'Ah, well,' said my father. 'We're alone now.'

I looked across the table at Claudine. Her head was down, her long hair, unbraided for once, hiding her face. But her hands were clenched into folds of the table-cloth. The folds of the cloth stretched in a great arrowhead right across the table, under the plates and dishes. The knuckles of her hands were whiter than the cloth. I had an awful feeling she was going to pull the cloth right off the table, and all the plates and dishes with it. She spoke with her head still down.

'You abandoned us,' she said. 'You left us to fight the Boches on our own. We would never have given up, if you had not left us alone.'

Nobody said a word. Then she rose and walked up to her room.

'Better go after her,' said my father. 'You understand her best.'

She was sitting on her bed, with an open penknife in her hand.

'God,' I said, 'you aren't going to cut your wrist or anything?'

Her lips twitched, but it wasn't any kind of smile. 'The knife is for the Boches,' she said, 'but it would not even kill a Boche rat ... I must fight, I must fight.

I will not surrender. But there is nothing to fight with . . .'

'Come downstairs and listen to Mr Churchill,' I said. 'It will make you feel better.'

'What is Churchill to me? He would not give Daladier fighter planes, when Daladier asked for them.'

But she came down just the same. It was the night Churchill said that the Battle of France was over, and the Battle of Britain was about to begin.

'What is this Battle of Britain?' she asked.

'It will be in the air,' I said. 'At first.'

'Oh, what can I do about such a thing?' Her shoulders drooped again.

I took a deep breath. I would have died for her at that moment. Instead, I offered her my most precious thing, the secret I had told no one, not even my father.

'I know some fighter pilots. They sometimes fly from near here. They have Spitfires.'

She gazed at me with empty eyes.

'Bunny Beaumont might even give you a flight in his Spitfire. He took me.'

Light came into her eyes. 'Beaumont! It is a French name. He is a Frenchman.'

'Sorry, he's as English as I am.'

'*Merde*. It is a French name. We have a village called Beaumont-Hamel. He must come from there – or his family. In French the name means 'beautiful mountain'. I will talk to him.'

I didn't disillusion her. Anything to get that hopeless look off her face.

*

The next time the planes came, I took her. She dressed in her best, with her hair up in its most beautiful style, and her red, white and blue sash across her jumper. I had a hard time keeping up with her, and I was twenty metres behind when she dropped her bike on the grass, and ran across to the little group of smoking pilots.

They stopped talking, and watched her come. To them, she must have looked quite something. And RAF pilots had an eye for pretty girls.

'Squadron Leader Beaumont?' she asked.

Bunny pushed out a hand, smiling appreciatively. 'Honoured to make your acquaintance,' he said. I think he'd spotted she was foreign, and a real lady.

'You are not French?' she asked, puzzled.

''Fraid not, ma'am. But anything else I can do to oblige you ...'

'But your name is French. It is a place in France.'

Bunny pushed back his officer's cap and scratched his head.

'Well, they do say we came across with William the Conqueror in ten sixty-six, but it's a very long time ago.'

'Then you are *really* French?'

'Anything to oblige a lady ...' Then he looked across at me, gentle, baffled.

I told them the whole story. Gabbling so fast in my embarrassment I don't know if Claudine understood half what I said. But all the pilots were very interested. They were bored, and with her eyes shining like that, she was beautiful.

'Must do something about this, Bunny,' said Taffy

Lloyd. 'Can't leave a lady with only a penknife to fight old Hitler with.'

Bunny frowned, and then seemed to come to a decision.

'Mademoiselle, we will fight in your name, and in the name of France.'

'Then why are you not fighting now?'

'Good bloody question,' said Taffy Lloyd. 'One I ask myself ten times a day. We're not even allowed to cross the coast and fly over the Channel. Bloody orders from the top brass.'

'Mademoiselle, the time will come,' said Bunny gently. 'Meanwhile, would you care to inspect your new squadron?' He led the way to his own aeroplane.

She noticed the two swastikas painted on the side of the fuselage, below the cockpit.

'You are an ace?' she asked.

'Knocked down a couple of Huns in France,' said Bunny diffidently.

'In my name, and with the blessing of God, you will knock down many more!'

All the pilots cheered.

After that, she was filled with energy. She sought out a Roman Catholic church in the nearest town. Having gently told my father than his was not a proper church, and he was not a proper priest. It was there that she prayed for the pilots, and lit candles on the gaunt wrought-iron candelabra to keep the pilots safe. I picked up that habit of lighting candles from her, and have kept it all my life. She even persuaded the English Catholic priest to come out to the aerodrome and bless the planes. The pilots shuffled uncomfortably, with their hands clasped awkwardly in front of their groins, but I think they liked it really. Pilots in war are very superstitious.

She also made sure that when they came, they would have hot coffee and something to eat; somehow my mother and she arranged it between them. In all this, I followed her around like a little dog. For school had finished for the year by then.

But still the Germans did not come. Instead, she learnt to play cricket with the pilots, who much appreciated the flash of her long beautiful legs as she ran after the ball. They also took her to the pub with them. They took me too, of course, but I had to sit on the wall outside, while they sent me out a half-pint of cider. *She* went inside.

I protested to Bunny, told him she was only seventeen.

'She's a young woman, Ronnie. People grow up fast in a war. Anyway, she'll soon be eighteen. And she's good for morale. You wouldn't grudge the lads would you?'

Of course, I said no. But I was jealous, hideously jealous. They were taking her off me; I was the child left outside. Laughing and flirting with the pilots, she had no time for me any more, except to fetch and carry for her. To her I was a child too. I thought of ringing up the police and reporting her for under-age drinking. But I had not quite descended that low; even on the day I watched them through the pub window, and saw Bunny holding her hand under the pub table.

It was obscene. She was only seventeen, and Bunny

must be twenty-three or four, really old. He was going bald in front. For all I knew, he had a wife, though he had never mentioned one. He was a cradle-snatcher. But far from being disgusted at his age, her face was lit up as I have never seen it. And so was his.

It was so much worse because I loved them both. Bunny was still my god, even if he was growing feet of clay. And she was still my precious one, who I had saved by giving her my most precious things. The very English words she was saying to him, I had taught her.

I did not know what to do with myself. I walked away up the road, wishing that I was dead. Till I heard a shout.

It was an airman from the field, one of the ground crew on a bicycle. His face was very red, and he was panting.

'Are they in the pub, Ronnie? There's something up. Something big! Yellow alert. Five-minute readiness. The Jerries are coming!'

There was such a scramble. Both Claudine and I, back at the field, helped them into their flying kit, which made them look strange, like Martian monsters, great bears clad in fur and kapok. The ground crew were starting up the engines. Before they scrambled aboard, Claudine kissed each pilot for luck.

Then a short wait, while the pilots kept nervously revving up their engines, till you could have gone mad with the noise. Then the telephone in the tent rang again, and a man ran out and fired a green flare into the air. It landed in the hedge, belching masses of grey smoke. It set the hedge on fire.

And then they were off, in pairs, bouncing across the rough field until they suddenly smoothed out in flight, and their wheels began to retrace.

We listened until their engine noise was lost in the song of the birds.

A long long wait. We did not know what to do with ourselves, except to walk across and across the field. We were so pent up, we could not even bear to walk side by side. The ground crews twitched around, moving the petrol bowser, checking their strange equipment, the long boxes full of shining belts of machine-gun cartridges. Then they sat down and tried to play cards. But at the least sound of an engine, their heads would swing up towards the south.

The engines were always car engines, moving along the main road in the distance . . .

And then there were engines that were not car engines, that got louder and louder. Tiny dots to the south. One . . . two . . . three. And then no more.

'*Mon Dieu*,' said Claudine, and crossed herself. 'Where are the others?' Her face was as pale as a marble tombstone. There wasn't anything left about killing the *sales Boches* now. She was terrified . . . for Bunny?

But we had not long to wait. There were now two tinier dots, behind the three large ones. And then, one by itself. They were all coming home.

The first Spitfire touched down and taxied up to us. There was a hole in its tailfin. Just one little hole, but we both spotted it. The next four seemed untouched, but none of them was Bunny. You could tell from the numbers and letters on the side.

Then Bunny swept across the field, and rolled his plane over high in the air, once, twice, three times . . .

'Three,' I shouted. 'I think he's shot down three!'

And then we were overwhelmed by a mass of pilots shouting, laughing and throwing their arms round Claudine and giving her great smacking kisses.

'I got one for you, princess! A bloody Stuka, over Portland Bill. Hit him right up the arse at fifty yards spitting distance and he just blew up. Nearly singed my moustache off!'

'Two. I swear I got two of the sods. They're rubbish. Slow as Teddy's old motor car. I don't know what we were worried about.'

'Even old Taffy got one . . . like shooting fish in a barrel.'

They acted like men drunk, punching and slapping each other. Bunny kept on saying, 'Steady down, lads, steady down. The war's not won yet.' But even he could not keep still for a moment.

And behind them, the ground crews worked like fiends possessed, getting the aircraft ready to fly again. Silent, absorbed, frightening.

Then the telephone in the little tent rang again. And every man froze where he stood, and I suddenly saw fear on their faces . . .

But the only message was that the Huns had gone. The pilots were to return to Manston, and report their kills.

Each of them embraced Claudine again, before they left. For luck. She *was* their luck now. Bunny embraced her last; and it was different. It lasted much longer, and when they broke apart, there were tears in her eyes. And she stood waving till he was out of sight, a mere dot. Though he could not have seen her. I knew that something had grown between them that was so big that I was no more than a pygmy, an ant.

I left her, and cycled home alone.

That was the last we saw of them for a long time. The time for practices was over; the time for cricket and drinks in the pub and giving flights to kids. They stuck to their home base, Manston, now.

All but Bunny. He drove over to see Claudine in his little Singer sports car, and they would go off alone together. They had eyes for no one but each other.

I raged at my father. Claudine was too young, only seventeen. He stood in place of her own father. He must put a stop to it!

My father took me and sat me down in his study, with a solemn face. 'Bunny wants to marry her, as soon as she's eighteen, in October. I am trying to contact her father, to get his permission, through the International Red Cross. Though I'm not getting very far.'

It was like having a spear driven through my chest. It was as if she had died. It was as if I had died.

'She's too young,' I said at last.

'It is you who are too young,' he said. His voice was sympathetic, but stern. 'Your time will come.'

'What does age matter?' I said. 'Age doesn't affect what you feel for someone.'

'That's what I'm saying. Age doesn't affect the way she feels, either.'

'Life's not fair. If I'd been five years older, I could have shot down a lot more Jerries for her than Bunny Beaumont.'

'It's not a matter of shooting down Jerries, old lad.'

'It's not *fair*.'

'Life isn't fair,' said my father, and sighed.

One evening Bunny turned up when nobody was expecting him. My father and mother had driven across to an important ARP meeting at Canterbury, and taken Claudine with them. So there was only me to open the door. I put Bunny in the sitting room, and then felt I had to sit with him.

'Got a whisky, old lad?' he said, in a strange muffled voice. As if he was ashamed.

Contemptuously, I fetched him a small whisky from my father's precious store. All the more contemptuous because my father had hardly any left.

'Thanks,' he said, but his hand shook so much as he took the glass that he spilled half the whisky over his hand and the chair. 'Sorry. I'm a bit tired.'

I switched on the light, for it was starting to get dim in the room, though it was nothing like time for the blackout. I sat looking at him. The bald patch on the front of his head was bigger. His face was very white, and there seemed to be new small lines all over it. He looked older than my father. He looked nearly as old as my grandfather. I was sickened at the idea that anyone as beautiful and young as Claudine should marry an old drunkard like this. I really hated him. But I had to say something to him.

'How's Taffy?'

'Taffy?' He seemed to come out of a daze. 'Taffy who?'

'Taffy Lloyd.'

'Oh. Poor old Taffy bought it three weeks ago. A flamer, poor old sod. No chance to get out of the cockpit at all.'

'How's Russ, then? Russell Taylor?'

'Got the chop as well. About a week ago. And for Christ's sake don't go on asking. All the ones you knew are dead but me. And the kids that came after them . . . there's only me left of the old lot.'

The flesh below his left eye kept quivering. And he kept looking at his watch every two minutes. You could see he was having to make himself sit still.

'Is there another whisky?'

Silently, I got it for him.

Then he said, head down, to no one in particular. 'We're all shot to hell. No matter how many we knock down, there's always more tomorrow. Manston's bombed flat – useless. The ground crew won't come out of the air-raid shelters any more . . . look, how long is Claudine going to be at that meeting? Where are they holding it?'

'They could be hours. And I don't know where it is.'

Both lies. But I didn't care. I just knew he was going to die, and then Claudine would come back to her senses. And I wouldn't have to think of this old drunk touching her face and body any more. And having wished him dead, I wanted rid of him.

He got up. 'I'll be off then. You don't like me any

more, do you, Ronnie? What the hell have I done to you?'

'Nothing,' I said. How could I ever have told him? I hated him more because he couldn't even guess what he'd done.

'Good night, old lad.'

I let him see himself out.

I felt a hand come down on the bedclothes, and shake my shoulder. I came out of a dream of Claudine laughing in the sunlight, and saw Claudine serious, in the dim light of dawn in my bedroom.

'Hurry up, Ronnie, get dressed. The planes have come back – Bunny's planes. I heard them, and I've just watched them land. You must help me. I must get coffee and sandwiches up there for them.'

I got up, grumbling. I'd thought I hated her now nearly as much as I hated him, but when it came to it, I didn't. Love's a funny thing.

We had a terrible battle to load up the bicycles, but we rode off into the sunlight with my parents waving goodbe in their nightclothes.

'Be careful now,' shouted my mother. She hadn't wanted me to go. Airfields got bombed, even little harmless airfields like ours.

Claudine looked so young that morning. As I followed her she looked very young because she was wearing white ankle socks. As if she was still a schoolgirl, as if she might still fall in love with me.

The airfield was very different now. There were nine Spitfires, brand-new and shining with paint. Some had not even fired their guns yet, for there were no long soot trails beneath the wings. There were no less than three petrol bowsers, and a lot more trucks, and a lot more men, and even three Bofors guns for airfield defence. There were sentries, who wouldn't let us through, until Bunny came over and sorted things out.

Sunday 15 September was the day in my life like no other. I suppose my dear father ran his church services as usual, and prayed for victory just a little harder. I suppose my mother cooked and washed up as usual with uneasy glances at the low hills that hid the airfield from her eyes.

But I was in a world apart. One look at the faces of Bunny's pilots told it all, as he introduced us. Six of them, the old hands, were weary to death, could hardly keep their eyes open. The other two, new boys, looked rested but scared, kept licking their lips. But they all smiled as Claudine handed them coffee. Young men will smile at smiling young women, even on the edge of the grave.

The telephone rang well before nine o'clock, and they were away in three lots of three, bouncing over the rough grass. We watched them climb, and even before they were finished climbing, the waves of German planes were on top of us. Never so many before. Neat patterns of fifty and a hundred heavy bombers, so neat and precise they might have been drawn on the sky with a ruler. And the tiny crosses of enemy fighters, flying far above them. All heading for London.

Then the sound of machine-guns, like a distant boy running a stick along distant iron railings. Hundreds of

boys running hundreds of sticks . . . little swirling breaks
in the German formations, as our fighters went in like
mad dogs among sheep. Many trails of smoke falling
down the sky so slowly, so small we could not tell if
they were German or British. And then the massed
formations redrew themselves with precision, and ground
on inexorably towards London.

We cheered our heads off, as we saw nine of our
planes coming back. All were safe!

Until the wheels of one collapsed on landing, leaving
it sliding along the turf like a screeching plough, digging
up great heaps of soil, with its propeller bent into
horseshoes. The pilot was pulled out safe, with blood
streaming down his face. And one plane would never fly
again.

Another pilot, having landed his plane, was carried
off on a stretcher to hospital.

Seven took off, when the telephone rang again. Then
the Germans were returning from London.

They did not look so neat now. They flew at all
heights, some so low we could see their pilot's heads,
and the numbers on their sides. We saw smoking engines
and stopped propellers, and one bomber, that had no
nose left, and slipped and yawed like a landed fish, and
we watched as it crashed on a hill nearer the coast, and
cruelly we cheered the distant explosion as its crew died
in a tiny puff of smoke.

Five of our fighters came back that time. Bunny came
across to our dugout for a coffee, while his groundcrew
sweated half-naked to refill his petrol tanks and rearm
his guns.

'Charlie Hill baled out,' he said, talking to the empty air between our heads, a man far away. 'But Billy didn't have a chance. He hit a Jerry head-on.'

And the ground crews were having trouble with one of the remaining fighters. Its engine kept coughing and sending out great clouds of black smoke.

Four took off, when the phone went after lunch. Nobody was smiling now, not even Claudine could manage it.

That afternoon, there seemed twice as many Germans. They stretched as far as the eye could see.

'*Mon Dieu*,' whispered Claudine, pressing close to me without even knowing she was doing so. 'It is the end of the world!'

Again the flurries high in the sky: the vapour trails on the blue, crossing each other out, the slowly falling flamers. They meant little to us now, whether they were British or German. Again, the Germans passed over towards London. And over the low hills to the north, low clouds of dark blue that were not clouds. London was burning.

Two of ours came back. One was Bunny. Halfway across the field to us, he bent down and was sick. We ran to him. Claudine embraced him, in front of all those who were watching.

'It is enough. You have done *enough*!' In spite of all her control, terror was in her voice.

'Must get some more *sales Boches* for you, princess!' He took hold of her chin, and lifted her face from where it was pressed into his shoulder. 'Chin up!' He gave a weak grin. 'I think I got three Boches for you.'

'I do not want Boches,' she said. 'I want *you*.' Then he turned on his heel and walked away, and went and sat in his cockpit and remained there.

The other fighter was no longer fit to fly. Its gun controls had been severed by enemy bullets.

When the telephone went for the last time, Bunny flew off alone.

We saw few Germans returning. They say they took a route further east, a quicker route to the coast.

But we saw this one fighter coming. The sound of its engine was rough and strange; it kept on coughing and failing, and then starting up again. It flew with one wing lower than the other, and there was a long white plume of glycol smoke, trailing from its engine.

'*C'est Bunny*,' whispered Claudine, clutching me. '*C'est Bunny*.'

'He's damaged,' shouted somebody. 'He can only get one landing-wheel down.'

We were watching so close, with bated breath, that we never heard the Germans coming. We only heard our own Bofors guns opening fire, like a man slowly hammering on a wooden plank. They were fighter bombers, coming in low from the north. I don't know how they had at last discovered our little airfield; maybe it was the three wrecked planes on the runway.

But they blew those three planes apart, in a hail of bullets. One of the petrol bowsers exploded with a blinding flash and roar, then another, and another. Ground crews were running for their slit trenches in all directions.

I grabbed at Claudine. 'Get down, get down.'

But she clung to the sandbags and would not get down. 'Bunny. Bunny.'

And in his plane came, amidst the bursting bombs and bullets that tore the turf into fountains. He kept it upright, even on one wheel. Then it pitched down on one wing, and began to spin in cartwheels across the grass towards us. I watched it fall apart like a daddy-long-legs caught in a lampshade. The propeller blades bent up, the tail fell off. Then it stopped a hundred metres away. I saw quite clearly that Bunny had pushed back the cockpit canopy.

And then he just sat there, grinning like a fool. He made no attempt to move.

And then I saw an evil lick of yellow flame, under the engine.

He was going to burn before our very eyes!

I heard the roar, as the German fighters came in again.

And then Claudine was out of my arms, and out of the slit trench, and running towards that plane. I saw her long legs running, her white ankle socks, against the pall of black smoke belching from the burning petrol bowsers. Running through the hail of German fire, towards a plane that was going to blow up at any second.

My Claudine! I would not have run for Bunny Beaumont, but my Claudine was different.

I overtook her as we reached the plane, as another evil flare of yellow flame licked from under it.

I was on the crumpling wing, which crushed under my feet. I grabbed the stupid grinning Bunny under the armpits. Thank God he had pushed his cockpit canopy back. Thank God he had undone his safety harness.

Thank God he was little, smaller than Claudine, smaller than me. I felt a surge of triumph as he lifted in my hands. I felt another, as I threw him across my shoulder, as if he was a child.

'Run!' I screamed at Claudine, and then I was running, harder than I was ever to run in my life again.

The Spitfire blew up, and knocked me on my face.

I saw Claudine lying in front of me, with her lovely hair on fire. Then she raised her hands, and beat the fire out. And all three of us crawled into a heap, as the German planes came in for the last time, and the turf boiled around us, and truck after truck blew up, and even the old rusty shed where lay the Gypsy Moth that would never now fly again.

Total ruin. Our airfield was gone. In one day, never to return.

But we three were alive, laughing and crying and hugging each other.

Just for one brief moment, Bunny and Claudine and I were one. For the last time.

'You're a funny sod, Ronnie,' gasped Bunny weakly. 'Can't stand me one minute, save my life the next. I don't figure you at all.'

And then the ground crew came running.

They were married in the Roman Catholic church that December. It was snowing. My father gave the bride away, and I was groomsman. Charlie Hill, who had bailed out, was best man. And Bunny limped up the aisle with a leg whose knee would never bend again. That was the reason he had not moved from his cockpit when the plane was burning; he couldn't move. He said it had hurt so much when I lifted him that he had nearly fainted. He said he would never be able to fly again.

So you might have thought they would have lived a peaceful married life. But I doubt it. We lost track of them, over the war years, as people did.

But when I was doing my basic training in the RAF in 1944, I saw a film of the recapture of Paris, by the armoured Free French forces of General Lattre de Tassion. And there, on the leading tank, amidst the snipers the Germans had left behind, sat a young woman in the black beret of the Resistance I swear was my Claudine. I mean, she was still wearing that ridiculous old sash, wasn't she?

The Authors

Anne Fine has written of love with wonderful insight in THE SUMMER HOUSE LOON. Her most recent novel is STEP BY WICKED STEP.

Geraldine McCaughrean's most recent novel was GOLD DUST, Winner of the Beefeater Award.

Berlie Doherty has written most eloquently of love in DEAR NOBODY, Winner of the Carnegie Medal.

Jan Mark's most recent novel was THEY DO THINGS DIFFERENTLY THERE, shortlisted for the Beefeater Award.

Garry Kilworth's most recent novel was THE BRONTE GIRLS.

Andrew Matthews has written funnily and poignantly about love in WRITING IN MARTIAN and its sequel SEEING IN MOONLIGHT.

Michael Hardcastle's most recent short stories are to be found in DOG BITES GOALIE.

Steve May's most recent novel is CLOSER, CLOSER.

Joanna Carey's most recent short story is published in IN BETWEEN.

Robert Westall's novel FALLING INTO GLORY is a superb love story.

Also edited by Miriam Hodgson

MOTHER'S DAY

Telling stories about the special relationship between mothers and daughters by ten of today's top authors.

Laughter, tears, misunderstandings, anger, frustration, discovery and loyalty are only some of the feelings these stories uncover in the power and complexity of the relationship between mother and daughter.

'Mothers and daughters are like loving hedgehogs; full of warmth and prickles.'

Vivien Alcock

Including stories by Vivien Alcock, Annie Dalton, Marjorie Darke, Berlie Doherty, Anne Fine, Jamila Gavin, Gwent Grant, Monica Hughes, Jean Ure and Jacqueline Wilson.

'Right on the button for 12-year-olds upwards.'

Daily Mail

'Commendable variety of material . . .'

Junior Bookshelf

A Selected List of Fiction from Mammoth

While every effort is made to keep prices low, it is sometimes necessary to increase prices at short notice. Mandarin Paperbacks reserves the right to show new retail prices on covers which may differ from those previously advertised in the text or elsewhere.

The prices shown below were correct at the time of going to press.

☐	7497 0343 1	**The Stone Menagerie**	Anne Fine	£2.99
☐	7497 1793 9	**Ten Hours to Live**	Pete Johnson	£3.50
☐	7497 0281 8	**The Homeward Bounders**	Diana Wynne Jones	£3.50
☐	7497 1061 6	**A Little Love Song**	Michelle Magorian	£3.99
☐	7497 1482 4	**Writing in Martian**	Andrew Matthews	£2.99
☐	7497 0323 7	**Silver**	Norma Fox Mazer	£3.50
☐	7497 0325 3	**The Girl of his Dreams**	Harry Mazer	£2.99
☐	7497 1699 1	**You Just Don't Listen!**	Sam McBratney	£2.99
☐	7497 1849 8	**Prices**	David McRobbie	£3.50
☐	7497 0558 2	**Frankie's Story**	Catherine Sefton	£2.99
☐	7497 1291 0	**The Spirit House**	William Sleator	£2.99
☐	7497 1777 7	**The Island and the Ring**	Laura C Stevenson	£3.99
☐	7497 1685 1	**The Boy in the Bubble**	Ian Strachan	£3.50
☐	7497 0009 2	**Secret Diary of Adrian Mole**	Sue Townsend	£3.50
☐	7497 1015 2	**Come Lucky April**	Jean Ure	£3.50
☐	7497 1824 2	**Do Over**	Rachel Vail	£3.50
☐	7497 0147 1	**A Walk on the Wild Side**	Robert Westall	£3.50

All these books are available at your bookshop or newsagent, or can be ordered direct from the address below. Just tick the titles you want and fill in the form below.

Cash Sales Department, PO Box 5, Rushden, Northants NN10 6YX.
Fax: 01933 414047 : Phone: 01933 414000.

Please send cheque, payable to 'Reed Book Services Ltd.', or postal order for purchase price quoted and allow the following for postage and packing:

£1.00 for the first book, 50p for the second; **FREE POSTAGE AND PACKING FOR THREE BOOKS OR MORE PER ORDER.**

NAME (Block letters) ....

ADDRESS ....

....

☐ I enclose my remittance for ....

☐ I wish to pay by Access/Visa Card Number ⬚⬚⬚⬚⬚⬚⬚⬚⬚⬚⬚⬚⬚⬚⬚⬚

Expiry Date ⬚⬚⬚⬚

Signature ....

Please quote our reference: MAND

All characters and events depicted are entirely fictitious; any resemblance to anyone living or dead is entirely coincidental

SLAVES OF IRONTOWN

by

Adriana Arden

CHAPTER ONE

'Now take everything off,' Constable Colter told Melanie Paget briskly: 'clothes, boots, watch, jewellery, the lot.'

'We've got to have some full-length photos of you undressed for your criminal record,' Constable Mattock explained.

The three of them were standing in a small brightly lit room within Shackleswell Central police station. In front of Mel was a digital camera mounted on a tripod, while the wall behind her was marked with a big "X" of lines and circles like a target that incorporated a graduated height scale. The other furnishings comprised a metal locker, a small table on which rested a desktop printer, a couple of hard chairs and a large flat screen TV on a hinged frame folded back against one wall.

Mel was scared and miserable enough having just had her fingerprints taken without being confronted by this totally unexpected additional humiliation casually linked with the phrase: "criminal record." She gulped as fresh concern creased her pretty face, hoping she had misunderstood. 'You want to take pictures of me… naked?'

'That's way we process offenders like you in Shackleswell, girl,' said Colter, who was sandy-haired and of beefy build. 'Every physical detail gets recorded now so there's no chance of mistaken identity later. Those are the rules and you've got to obey them.'

'If you don't like it you shouldn't have done anything to get yourself arrested, should you?' Mattock, who was taller and darker, pointed out.

'But it was only for vagrancy,' Mel protested, thinking even as she spoke that it sounded such an old fashioned charge. 'I didn't know it was wrong. I was just looking round the town. I'm not a real criminal.'

'You were letting your own life go to waste,' Mattock said scathingly. 'That's criminal enough as far as we're concerned.'

'We take that sort of thing seriously in Shackleswell,' Colter added. 'This is a clean, efficient town. All waste gets collected up and properly recycled.'

'And it's all got to be recorded in the process,' said Mattock, tapping the camera meaningfully. 'Every detail.'

Mel felt sick and confused. Were they talking about picking litter off the street or people like her? Whatever it was it seemed they still expected her to strip-off, which she could not possibly do in front of two strange men even if they were in uniform. 'Can't you get a woman officer in to take the pictures?' she pleaded.

'There aren't any available,' said Mattock impatiently. 'Now hurry up. This isn't the time or place to come over all shy. You haven't got anything we haven't seen before. You're not the first foolish girl we've handled, you know, and you certainly won't be the last, so let's be having those clothes off.'

Mel chewed her lip nervously. They kept calling her "girl" as though she was a child when she was actually nineteen, and now they wanted to photograph her naked. This was not the way they did things in TV police series. But then what did she know? After the terrible mistakes she had so recently made how could she trust her own judgement any more. Perhaps there were new procedures in place because of the threat of terrorism or differences between police forces. She felt the return of the brooding misery her arrest had briefly displaced. Did it matter? She had made her choices and this was where they had brought her. Any further shame she suffered was her fault. Perhaps after all she deserved it...

Taking a deep breath Mel shrugged off her anorak then stooped to untie her boots. As she handed over each item

~ 8 ~

the officers examined it and then put it in a plastic bag. Why were they bagging it up? It was hardly evidence. Would they give her some sort of prison clothes to wear instead? Blushing furiously she had to take another deep breath and screw up her eyes before stripping off her bra and panties, leaving her naked and trembling in front of them with her thighs squeezed together and hands clasped across her breasts and pubes.

The policemen looked up from examining her underwear with mild seen-it-all-before interest.

'Stand with your back against the chart, hands by your sides and look straight ahead,' said Colter. 'And don't cover yourself up again.'

Mel shuffled backwards. There was a step up onto a kind of low podium built against the chart wall. She climbed onto it and slowly lowered her hands, exposing herself totally to their gaze.

Her face was heart-shaped with rounded cheeks, a neat softly cleft chin, a well-shaped mouth, pale eyebrows, intense dark blue eyes and a firm, straight nose slightly turned up at the end. Her hair was an urchin-cut pale blonde mop. Milky breasts, caped by light pink areolae with darker nipple crowns, stood out prominently from her chest, despite being a shade on the heavy side for her height. She had a tight waist, feminine but not over-full hips and strong, girlishly shapely legs. Her buttocks were well rounded and a light fuzz of honey coloured curls covered her pubic cleft.

They took pictures of her from the front, both sides and rear. Then they had her clasp her hands behind her neck and took another set. She was uncomfortably aware that this posture lifted her breasts higher, as if she was showing them off, and that her nipples were swelling and hardening. That was too much. How could she respond like that in such circumstances?

'Back right against the wall and spread your arms and legs along the cross lines,' Colter commanded and miserably Mel obeyed.

There were sharp clicks as spring-loaded clamps snapped out of slots in the wall panels and closed about her wrists and ankles. Mel gave a yelp of alarm and tried to pull away but the clamps were rubber-lined and she could not slip out of them.

'Hold still,' Mattock said, snapping off another picture as if nothing strange had happened.

Mel twisted and squirmed helplessly, tasting the rising swell of fear in her mouth. Maybe they did need nude photos for criminal records but this was going too far. She fought to keep her voice steady. 'Please let me go… I want to put my clothes on now.'

'You don't need them anymore,' said Colter briskly. 'You stay as nature intended. That's how girls like you go up before a judge in Shackleswell.'

'What? No, I…umphh!'

Colter had pushed a sponge rubber ball into Mel's mouth. It expanded behind her teeth, pressing her tongue down and stifling her words. 'And no more talking without permission,' he added. 'We've got to get you ready for your hearing…'

He pressed what looked like a light switch. The wall behind Mel split open along the lines of the cross and then slid and folded aside. The podium rolled away from under her feet but the clamps held her from falling as her toes wiggled clear of the ground. She twisted her head round. There was a much larger room behind her, but she could not make out any details because of the thing she was fastened to.

It was an upright black rectangular cast-iron frame taller than she was set in a base with a raised rim, rather like a large tray, the front section of which had been slotted under the podium. The inside of the frame was decorated with complicated metal scrollwork fittings. The clamps about her wrists and ankles extended forward from the scrollwork corners on short sliding arms. The frame was vertical and the clamps had been opened wide and pushed into slots in the thin chart wall, their black rubber inner linings merging with the black marking on the wall.

'This is the Frame of Truth,' Colter said proudly. 'The basic design's over a century old but it's had some modern servomechanisms added. The most important thing you've got to remember is that it's a machine, and in Shackleswell girls serve machines.'

He and Mattock moved to the sides of the frame and cranked some handles. The arms holding the clamps retracted, pulling Mel with it until she hung spreadeagled within the frame. She twisted her head round wildly, moaning behind her gag. A little over midway up the frame were a pair of inward facing horizontal arms bearing upright wheel hubs fitted with eight black rubber paddle blades. Lower down were two lengths of cane on sprung mounts that held them horizontally across the inside of the frame. An inverted "Y" shaped arm jutting down from the middle of the frame top opposed a rod with a fluted bulbous cap rising at an angle up from the base of the device midway between its side posts. In front of it was a stouter rod ending in a fork mount like the front wheel of a bike. It was partly enclosed by a semicircle of clear plastic mudguard but instead of a wheel between the forks there was just a hub trailing a limp spray of rubber strips.

Mattock and Colter turned large wing nuts hidden in the scrollwork. These screwed the clamps outwards pulling Mel's arms and legs tight and wide as though she was frozen in the act of performing a star-jump. The pouting swell of her sex felt frighteningly exposed. Mel strained and squirmed but the clamps were unyielding and she fluttered within the frame like a butterfly trapped in a spider web.

The policemen adjusted the arms on which the pairs of paddle wheels were mounted. She could see they were powered by drive chains running through their hollow supporting arms connected to cogs on their hubs. Alternating blades were set at slight angles to the centreline of rotation so they would sweep through a wider target area. The wheels were positioned beside and a little below her breasts so that she felt the flats of the blades pressed against the undersides of her breasts. The canes were laid across the swell of her rump, one for each buttock, and then cocked back against their springs.

The "Y" arm pointing down from the top of the frame was a brace that clamped about the sides of her head. Rubber cups were screwed inwards to press against her temples, holding her head so she could not turn it aside. A curving strip of rubber, like a section cut from a ring, dangled from the ends of the head-brace arms on a pair of coil springs. Colter pulled out her ball gag and pushed the strip edgewise into her mouth where it was held there by the tension of the springs.

'You'll need that if the judge thinks you're not being truthful,' Colter said. 'We don't want you to bite through your tongue or crack a tooth, do we?'

Mel found she could not spit out the strip but it was thin enough to allow her to speak around. 'You…you don't have to punish me, just please let me go,' she begged pitifully as she fought back tears. 'I'm sorry if I broke any of your laws… I'll never come back again, I promise!'

'But we don't want you to go,' said Colter.

'This isn't about punishing you,' Mattock said, 'this is about saving you.'

They positioned the tip of the vertical rod against the crinkled mouth of her anus. It had a phallic black rubber head glistening with oil or grease. Mattock twisted it round and it screwed upward, forcing its way through her anal sphincter, parting it wide, and up into her rectum.

Mel gasped as it unnaturally penetrated her rear passage from outside to in. She had never had anything like it inside her before. Her cheeks were burning at the strange sensation. It felt frighteningly like it was going up her spine and would split her open! Yet at the same time the perverse stimulation was causing a warm wetness to seep through the folds of her sex and she could feel her clitoris swelling as if it was being pushed up from within. The policemen would see it rising. Mel screwed up her eyes in shame, wishing the earth would swallow her up. How could her body mock her like this?

The phallus stopped its advance, leaving her plugged tightly. Frantically she squeezed on the intruder with her anal ring in a vain attempt to force it back out.

Colter swung the front forked rod with its outer guard and lash thongs in towards the apex of her thighs, drawing out the thongs to ensure they would strike the mound of her exposed pudenda when they were spun and extended. When he was satisfied he locked it in place and then patted her sex. Instinctively Mel tried to pull away from his touch but the rod up her rear held her hips in place.

The policemen stepped back to admire their handiwork. Mel was shivering in fear and disbelief and tears were slowly running down her cheeks.

'Now that's how a girl should look going up before a judge,' said Mattock in satisfaction. 'Properly humbled with her arse stuffed and tits trembling.'

'Which is the way we like 'em in Shackleswell,' Colter agreed.

Mattock swung the TV screen out from the wall so that it hung just above the camera they had been using earlier. 'Now the judge will be able to see you and you'll be able to see him,' he said. 'He should be ready to hear your case shortly.'

'He can control all the functions of the frame remotely,' Colter told Mel. 'He'll use it to get the truth out of you. If you're smart you won't fight it...'

The big screen came to life. 'There, I said we wouldn't keep you waiting long,' said Mattock.

An image appeared of a greying, stern-faced man, dressed in imposing red robes and judicial wig. He was seated at a desk on which was visible the back of an open laptop.

'It's Judge Gouge,' Colter said to Mel. 'Don't speak until you're given permission, call him "Sir" and answer every question truthfully. That's very important...' He stepped forward into camera shot. 'This is Melanie Paget, My Lord,' he said formally. 'She was arrested earlier this morning in the town square by Constable Mattock and myself on a charge of vagrancy. Our report should be on your screen...'

'Yes, I have it here...' The judge consulted the laptop for a minute then looked up at Mel with a penetrating gaze that seemed to reach right through the screen. 'I see that you have refused to give any further details about yourself, girl. How did you come to be in Shackleswell without any means of support or an address that can be used to confirm your identity?'

His manner was perfectly measured and reasonable, as though it was just another day in court and she was an ordinary prisoner. Maybe it was normal for him to interrogate naked bound girls with rods up their backsides but how could she possibly be expected to reply sensibly in such circumstances?

'P… please… you can't do this to me…it's not right… ahhh!'

The judge had pressed a control on his laptop. The cocked canes poised behind Mel's bottom slashed across her buttocks with an audible hiss and crack of cane on flesh. She felt the impact of the blows ripple through her followed by stinging heat as if her bottom was on fire. She had never been caned before. Held fast by the rod up her rear she could not even ride the strokes. As her buttocks contracted she actually clenched it tighter inside her. Something about the perverse combination of pain, internal pressure and exposure made her pussy tingle and pulse. Mel sobbed in confusion and disbelief as hot tears burned in the corners of her eyes.

Anger and resentment, which had been numbed by the speed of events, now flickered within her. How dare they treat her like this! It was obscene, cruel and illegal. She heard a whir of some motor hidden in the fame base followed by clicks as the canes were re-cocked and struggled to contain herself. All her indignation and outrage counted for nothing against the raw power they had over her.

'That was a warning,' Gouge said sternly. 'Now you will answer my question fully and clearly and when you do you will be properly respectful.'

Mel sniffed and blinked away her tears. Although she was spreadeagled naked and impaled before him it seemed she had to pretend to be civil. It was madness! With an effort she said meekly: 'I live… lived in Shrewsbury, Sir. It doesn't matter exactly where because I've left home.'

'And you have no other residence?'

'No, Sir.'

'You're not in further education?'

'No yet, Sir. I was hitching to London. I thought I could get some work. A lorry driver said he could drop me here and I'd have better chances. I'd hardly ever heard of Shackleswell but it looked like a nice clean town. I was only here about ten minutes when these policemen stopped me and asked me who I was and where I'd come from. Because I didn't want to give my home address and didn't have any other address to give or much money they said I was a vagrant and that was against the law and they arrested me.'

'It is against the law in Shackleswell,' the judge confirmed. 'Here everybody has a productive occupation of some kind. We don't let any asset go to waste. Why did you leave home?'

That was a question she would not answer. Hastily she said: 'That's none of your business… awww… eeeehh…uuhhh!'

The paddle wheels on either side of her chest had spun into motion, turning in opposite directions and sending a torrent of rubber smacking into her breasts, striking their sides, undercurves and even obliquely across her nipples. As she shrieked and yelped her full globes heaved and shivered under their impact. She arched her back trying to lift them clear of the flailing paddles but there was no escape. The individual smacks merged into a continuous pattering rasp and her treacherously erect nipples were beaten down only to spring up again and again. As a scarlet blaze spread across her pale soft curves Mel writhed and strained within the frame, sobbing and biting down on the rubber strap between her teeth.

Yet even as the stinging blows fell she was achingly aware of Gouge, Colter and Mattock watching her breasts dance as though it was perfectly normal. Through her tears she saw they were enjoying the spectacle of her pain and degradation, compounding her shame and misery.

It ended as suddenly as it had begun. The wheels whirred to a stop and her pummelled breasts were allowed to rest naturally once more. Mel hung limply from her clamps, groaning and sobbing, her chest heaving. It felt as if her breasts were on fire while her sore nipples throbbed and pulsated. Her tears dripped onto their upper slopes, adding the sting of their salt to her abused flesh that burned and shimmered with pain. Shockingly she realised her pussy was also feeling hotter and wetter, though not from her tears. How could she be responding like this?

'Why did you leave home, girl?' Gouge repeated.

'Sorry... Sir... but that's... private,' Mel said feebly.

'As you must have realised by now you have nothing you can call private any more, not your body or your mind.' His finger hovered above the controls on his desk. 'I can make you tell me.'

'Lock me up for being a vagrant if you want, Sir, but that's ... a family matter.'

He hesitated. 'Ah... family. And what family do you have?'

'My mother and father... and my sister, Madelyn, Sir. Well... she's my stepsister, really, but we've lived together since we were very young.'

'Would you say you are a close family?'

Mel swallowed hard. There was so much meaning in that simple word: "close". 'Yes, Sir.'

'I see. And do any of them know where you are now?'

Mel said: 'No, Sir, I haven't called them yet,' before she realised she could have lied. But it was too late to take the words back. Now they knew she was alone and nobody would be coming to Shackleswell to look for her. They could do anything they wanted to her...

'Won't they be missing you by now?'

What a question to have to answer. Until a few days ago the response would have been easy and automatic. But now... 'I don't think so, Sir,' she said in a bleak whisper.

'Then something significant must have happened to drive you apart. Were they abusive to you or your sister in any way?'

The suggestion was shocking. 'Oh no, Sir. They were... they are perfect parents. We all went to church together. They loved us.'

'I see. You use the past tense when speaking of their love. Don't you think they love you any more? Is it something you did?'

Mel chewed on her strap and said nothing. That was something she could never tell anybody. The spring-loaded canes swished through the air and laid a fresh pair of stripes across her bottom. Mel winced, dizzy with pain and the perversely thrilling hot warmth seeping through her sex. She bit harder on her strap and shook her head.

'Suppose I said I would halve your sentence if you tell me exactly why you ran away from home,' Gouge said.

He was trying to take her to that dark place she did not want to think about. Why wouldn't he leave her alone! It was all too much. 'Do what you want but I'll never tell you!' she shouted. 'This is all mad and you're all sick perverts and you can go to....eeeeehh!'

The flail between her legs whirred into life and the thongs hissed through the air. They slapped and swiped across the helplessly exposed swell of her vulva, setting the plaint cleft mound shivering. Sharp, crisp smacks of leather striking flesh filled the room as they cut into the depths of her slot, pulling it open and smacking her delicate inner labia, licking about the mouth of her vagina and rasping across the nub of her clitoris.

Mel shrieked and bit down on the rubber strap between her teeth even as her pussy seemed to explode in searing pain. It was far worse than the canes on her bottom or the breast spanking. Her hips twisted wildly but impaled on the anal rod she could not escape the relentless hail of blows and only succeeded in churning the phallus with dark sensuality inside her rectum. The fear, pain and stimulation inside and out overwhelmed her. She lost control of her bladder and hot urine spurted from her cleft and was caught by the tips of the flailing lashes, splattering it across her thighs and belly and then up over her breasts and into her face. Only the guard about the wheel prevented it from being sprayed all over the room. That was why it was there. How many other girls had been driven to pee from pain like her? It cupped the flying droplets and channelled them in a trickle down into the base tray

Wetted by her discharge, the thongs cut even deeper into her flesh. Her pussy throbbed and burned, turning from pink to scarlet. Mel bawled uncontrollably, not only the pain but also the stark humiliation at disgracing herself so intimately before strangers. Surely her misery could not get any worse… except it did.

Through her agony she became aware of a single point of hardness that was standing out from her soft valley of elastic flesh as it was flattened and splayed by the rain of lash strokes. Her clitoris was standing up hard and proud, as though welcoming the pain. Every lash stroke drove it back into her soft depths only for it to spring back up again. There was no escape. She could not run away again. The terrible cock-like rod up her rectum held her in place, impaled and helpless.

Shame heaped upon misery as her loins filled with raw hot liquid arousal more intense than anything she had ever known. This proved how sick she was. What would she do? She could not stop it but they must never know. She was going to…

Mel screamed as she orgasmed like a breaking wave that rolled on and on until welcome darkness enfolded her.

When Mel recovered her senses the lashes had stopped beating her pubes. For a moment she thought she been trapped in a terrible dream. Then she realised her aching, tingling, burning body still hung within in the Frame of Truth. Had she fainted from the pain or the intensity of her orgasm? No, that would be crazy. It was the shock of both together.

Sweat, tears, urine and orgasmic juices stained her breasts, stomach and thighs, yet she had a strange sensation of perfect ease and balm. She opened her crusted eyes. Colter and Mattock were wiping her down with damp cloths. The strap was pulled from between her teeth and the spout of a water bottle was pushed between her lips. She drank from it automatically.

Could they tell what she had done?

'Look at this,' Colter said to Mattock as he wiped a cloth through the sore lips of her pussy to reveal a shiny trail. 'She juiced herself real good.'

'A natural-born slut,' Mattock agreed.

Mel whimpered. How could her body have betrayed her like this? Was she abnormal? She thought of that final dark secret which stabbed her heart even as she hugged it to her. Perhaps she was. She had revealed everything else to her captors except that. Now it was all she had left to call her own…

On the screen Judge Gouge banged his gavel and Colter slapped Mel's cheeks to get her attention. 'Look at the judge…'

'Melanie Paget, apparently you would prefer to suffer rather than confess the truth. However, I have learned enough to make a judgement,' Gouge said. 'For the crime of vagrancy I sentence you to an indeterminate period of service in the city of Shackleswell, according to our rules and statutes. You will be trained to perform this service at Gryndstone School. During your service life you will be referred to by the part name of...' he consulted his laptop '... Spring 157, with which you will be marked. Repeat that designation.'

'Spring 157,' Mel replied feebly.

The desktop printer came on, spilling out a sheaf of papers and a pink self-adhesive label. Colter took them and held up the label for Mel to see. It read: SPRING 157 in bold type. He peeled off the backing and stuck it across her forehead.

Now she was a labelled prisoner.

'That is your sole identification from now on and replaces your former name which you will no longer use,' Gouge continued. 'You will remain naked during service periods unless permitted clothing by your masters. You will be controlled and restrained according to the requirements of your assigned function. You will be available for citizens to use for their sexual pleasure as they wish within the legal limits. Any failure to perform to your utmost or disobedience will be punished according to the standard scale of discipline. Do you understand?'

Melanie was still trying to gather her thoughts and his words seemed unreal. 'Yes... no. You're sentencing me to be a... sex slave?'

'That is a very crude word for what you are now, 157,' said Gouge. 'Instead of throwing your life away you will become a productive part of this town: a cog of flesh within its social and commercial machinery.' He addressed Colter and Mattock. 'Take this unit to Gryndstone School.' He rapped his gavel again. 'My judgement is concluded.'

The screen went dark.

CHAPTER TWO

Mel hung trembling in the Frame of Truth, gazing blankly at the dead screen. Her breasts, bottom and groin simmered and stung while her anus ached from clenching the rod inside her. The label bearing her new name felt strange and tight across her forehead. Yet her physical discomforts paled before the turmoil in her mind. Part of her wanted to rage and scream at what she had suffered but fear and shock held it in check. She could not accept this perverted new reality into which she had been plunged. It was utterly beyond anything she had experienced before and she had never felt so wretched and confused.

She was shaken out of her daze by Colter slapping her cheek again.

'Listen to me, 157,' he said sternly. 'We'll be taking you to Gryndstone in a little while and they'll teach you how to serve properly, give pleasure and act respectfully. But your education in city ways starts here. Now you've been sentenced we can do what we like with you, do you understand?'

A cold hand seemed to close about her heart as she nodded mechanically.

'And what we'd like to do is screw you. Nothing strange about that. You're a pretty girl and we'd enjoy it. That's what you're for. Lots of other men in Shackleswell are going to be doing the same to you soon enough so there's no point putting it off. Actually we're doing you a favour and getting what you fear worst out of the way. You're frightened, right?' Mel nodded again. 'Well that's perfectly normal and breaking you in quickly will make everything that comes later a bit easier. It might hurt more but nothing will be as bad as your first time.

Trust me. We've had plenty of girls through here and we know how it works...'

They turned the Frame of Truth round, rotating it about some hidden pivot and Mel saw the room in which it rested properly for the first time. 'Welcome to our interrogation suite...'

It was a windowless room with several doors opening off it. Resting against the walls were racks, trestles and even what looked like folding gibbets. Between them were racks of straps, chains, lashes and an intimidating number of sex toys of every shape and size. Perhaps most sinister of all, in the middle of the room, was a solid black wooden table shaped like an "X" hung about its sides with heavy straps.

'You'll get used to being around this sort of equipment,' Mattock said. 'Shackleswell girls feel right at home here.'

Mel opened her mouth to protest but then realised it was pointless. What she felt no longer mattered. She was just a numbered slave. Even her name had been taken from her. A strange sense of hopeless resignation seemed to be enfolding her like a blanket and she wrapped herself in it with perverse relief. Yes, please, just do what you want to me! Just get it over with!

Mattock unfolded a waist-high trestle from the wall. It had a very narrow black vinyl padded top, almost like a thick plank on edge and four splayed legs fitted with heavy straps.

They unclamped Mel from the frame. She was too numb to resist and in any case her legs were so weak they had to half-carry her over to the trestle. 'Bend over, face down,' Colter commanded.

Mel rested her stomach along the trestle top and laid her arms and legs against the sides of its supporting struts. It pressed into her sternum while her breasts hung down on either side of its main beam. Her knees bent slightly and her hands did not touch the ground, while her head and bottom overhung the ends.

Colter and Mattock strapped her wrists and ankles to the sides of the legs and then added more straps across her elbows and thighs. An extra strap went over the small of her back, pressing her stomach down against the top edge. She was bound to the device so tightly she could only move her head and flex her fingers and toes.

There was a pair of weighted chains with crocodile-clip ends looped under the trestle top. These they clamped to her nipples, dragging them out into pink cones and making her wince.

They took off their uniform jackets, hanging them up beside the rack of lashes, then they peeled open their flies. There were no visible zips or buttons. Flaps of overlapping fabric opened down the front seam that was far deeper than a normal fly and ran back between their legs. The halves pulled wide, folding back neatly and exposing their genitals, which then slid easily through the triangular opening and hung freely in front of their trousers.

Mel shuddered as she saw their cocks were already swelling and rising in anticipation of that they were going to do to her. They were deliberately showing themselves off. She felt revolted but she could not take her eyes off their thick penises and heavy hairy testicles. They were the symbols of their absolute power over her: the power to penetrate her like swords of flesh. How much would it hurt to have them inside her?

'Better get used to the sight of these as well,' Mattock advised her, stroking his by now stiff penis. 'You'll be seeing plenty more of them in Shackleswell.'

From the rack of lashes they took down what looked like flyswatters with black rubber blades and swished them experimentally through the air.

Mel whimpered and tugged at her straps. 'Please don't beat me! I'll try to please you but don't hit me.' She was appalled at how craven she sounded.

'You learn that a bit of pain spices up the pleasure,' Colter said. 'These'll sting but they won't cut your skin. You'll have far worse in future so you might as well get a taste for it now. After the way you came on the Frame you can take it.'

It was true she had orgasmed. What did that say about her?

Colter moved round to stand behind Mel looking at her bottom raised in the air, at her splayed legs and exposed pubes. Reaching under the end of the trestle he drew out a pair of chains with sprung clamps on their ends. Winding them about the outside of her thighs he pinched her thick soft love-lips between thumb and forefinger and closed the clamps about them. Mel winced as they pulled tight, drawing her tender sex-lips wide and exposing her inner valley to his eyes and everything it contained. Her clitoris was swelling again. Why did it do that?

Meanwhile Mattock was standing in front of her and her wide eyes were following the bobbing of his penis head as though she was hypnotised. Attached to the front of the trestle by a length of fine chain was a rubber ring with two T-bars extending off opposite sides. Mattock took it up, pried her mouth open and pushed it between her teeth. The ring went under her tongue while the bars slid between her jaws, pushing them wide. The crosspieces nestled against the inside of her cheeks, holding the ring in place.

'Don't want you biting,' Mattock said. 'Ever given a man oral before?'

Numbly Mel shook her head.

'I've got a virgin hole here,' he remarked.

Colter had been feeling Mel's sex, sliding his stiff fingers further up inside her, thumbing her clitoris and making her shudder. The feeling she had on the frame was returning. How could she possibly respond the same way so soon?

'This has been used but she's tight,' Colter observed. 'I don't think this little cog's had the polish worn off her yet. She's as wet as a slut can get and her clit's up.'

'Told you she was a natural,' said Mattock. He took hold of Mel by her hair and pulled her head up, positioning the purple plum of his shaft before her face so she had to stare at its single slotted eye. 'You suck and lick this as hard as you can and when I come you swallow it all down, got that?'

They were giving her instructions on how she was to degrade herself! She nodded.

He rammed his shaft between her parted lips and the taste of a man filled Mel's mouth for the first time. At the same moment Colter took hold of her hips and forced his shaft into her vagina.

She was skewered between them, rocking with their thrusts, snatching breaths while being half choked by Mattock's cockhead while Colter's cock was pumping into her sore vagina. Mel had only had intercourse half a dozen times before and now she was taking two men inside her at once. She did not really know what she was doing only that the sooner they came the sooner it would be over. Clumsily she began to squeeze and suck on both shafts. It was a surprise to find she could suck with her vagina but it seemed to be happening.

Her world shrunk to encompass her bound body and the two men apparently trying to ram their straining penises as deep as possible inside her until they met in the middle. She closed her eyes, forgetting about the men and concentrated only on their cocks. They were like hard fleshy snakes, writhing and slithering and pounded away inside her.

The pumping motion set the trestle creaking. Chains jingled and her breasts began to bob and sway in heavy liquid motion. Slowly the weights hanging from her nipples began to swing in time, tugging on her tender flesh.

Then the men began to use their paddles. Colter swiped his blade across her haunches while Mattock attacked her breasts, beating them against the sides of the trestle beam. Her resilient flesh flattened and then sprang back. Her nipples chains danced a jig under her.

Mel almost choked on his shaft as she tried to cry out and she writhed and jerked at her straps. But her feelings meant nothing. Faster and faster the blows fell. She was like a horse being whipped along to the winning post. She was crying but she kept on sucking. It was all she could do. The blows hurt and yet did not hurt. It was unspeakably cruel to use her like this but it began not to matter because she knew there was a reward at the finish. The knot in her stomach was no longer fear but something equally primeval and as hard to control and it pulsed and grew until she felt she was going to burst.

Suddenly hot male seed was spouting in both her mouths and it was revolting and she was swallowing it down hungrily. Then a new starburst of pleasure exploded in her brain and tore through her straining body.

The flesh snakes went limp as she drained them of their desire and Mel sagged across the trestle. She was saturated with a pink mist of pleasure even as she was confused and sickened by what she had done. She felt the men resting their hands on her waist and buttocks as they recovered from their exertions. Mattock's softening cock was still lodged in her mouth while Colter's cock was still snug in her vagina. They were in no hurry to pull them out. Why should they be? Sperm and her juices began to dribble onto the padding of the trestle top.

After a minute Mel heard Colter sigh and say with some satisfaction: 'I think SPRING 157 is going to do fine in Shackleswell.'

'I think she will to,' Mattock agreed.

CHAPTER THREE

Ten minutes latter, with her head hung in shame, Mel stumbled after Mattock and Colter as they led her through to the back of the police station. The ball gag was back in her mouth, her wrists were strapped behind her back and a choke chain enclosed her neck in its warning grip. She was leashed like a dog and would go where her masters led her.

Mel's pussy ached, her breasts and bottom smarted, her thighs were slippery with their discharge and she could still taste Mattock's sperm in her mouth. Yet now the men were making nothing of it, passing casual remarks as though it was all perfectly normal to lead a naked, freshly-raped girl along by a chain down a corridor of their police station.

She wanted to hate them for what they had done to her, yet they had been so honest about it she felt even more confused instead. Was it possible they really did believe they had been cruel to be kind? The rules here were different. Had it all been perfectly legal and proper and was she the one out of step? A judge had passed a sentence upon her and she had been brought up to respect the law. But that could not make what they had done fundamentally right, only that in this city it was apparently permissible. And this was the place she was expected to serve in as a slave.

At some point Mel knew she would cry over what had been done to her that morning. It had been too strange and frightening and intense not to. But she would not do it in front of Colter and Mattock. It was possibly the last shred of control she had left over her life.

An outer doorway opened directly into the covered car stand. Mel cringed as a couple of uniformed officers strode past. They nodded at Colter and Mattock and glanced appreciatively at Mel but showed no surprise at the sight of her naked and leashed. God, they really were all part of it, she thought.

Colter and Mattock led her over to a plain estate car. They opened the rear hatch and Mel saw it contained a small, upright wire mesh cage. For a moment Mel thought it was for a police dog, then she realized it was just big enough to take her kneeling down.

Colter swung open the cage door, revealing it was floored with a strip of rubber matting. 'In you get, 157,' he said briskly.

With a lift under her bottom from Mattock, Mel scrambled over the tailgate and shuffled into the cage. Colter looped the end of her leash through the mesh and tied it off, then the door clanged shut behind her. They threw a fitted green plastic sheet over the cage to conceal her from outside view. It had narrow gauze slits let into it to let in air which also allowed her to see a little of her surroundings. The officers got in the front and drove off.

They passed along neat clean streets, parades of shops and some older buildings that might have been factories or mills. Mel gazed out at them in a daze. It had seemed such a nice town in the brief time she had to look around before she had been arrested. Everything was well maintained, there was no graffiti or litter and the people on the pavements appeared smartly dressed, if in rather conservative styles. It gave the impression of an old industrial town that had managed to preserve its heritage by finding some new source of income. With so many cities looking rundown nowadays that was an achievement. How could she have imagined what went on behind its respectable façade?

If only she had chosen to spend a little of her meagre funds on a coach ticket to London instead of trying to save money by hitching, Mel thought bitterly, maybe she would be there by now trying to find some work and a place to stay. It would not have been easy but at least she would not be in this living nightmare. The trouble was she had never had time to make any real plans. She had just wanted to get away and she had snatched up what she could after the moment when… no, she would not think about it.

Would her parents search for her? After what had happened perhaps they never wanted to see her again. Maddy would try to find her as soon as she could, Mel knew that, but how far would she get? Even if an official search was started for her and they found the truck driver who had given her a lift to Shackleswell, where would that get them? Apparently several local policemen plus at least one judge were part of the conspiracy. They would hardly admit to what they had done to her. Now she was being taken to a school for training slave girls. How far did this perversion spread? Who else in Shackleswell knew what was going on? Gouge had talked of her serving the town and citizens using her but did that mean those well-dressed people she could see out there? The whole town could not really be involved… could it?

They came to a quiet tree-line street on the edge of the suburbs. Mel glimpsed red brick walling, iron railings and an upright Victorian-style building with high windows and steep slate roofs. There was an arching sign over a set of black iron gates that read: GRYNDSTONE SCHOOL: Private. She really was being taken to a school, or at least what had once been a school.

The police car turned down a narrow road beside the school lined by a row of trees and a long high brick wall that presumably marked the boundary of the school grounds. At the bottom they turned again into a secluded mews. On one side was a cottage terrace while on the other, adjoining the school grounds, was what looked like a block of renovated stables or storehouses. There was an open-fronted carport let into the ground floor of one of the buildings and into this they reversed.

Unloading Mel from the back, the policemen led her over to a large plain green-wooden door in the side of the carport bearing the sign: THE OLD SCHOOL HOUSE: Deliveries. Set in the wall beside it was an intercom speaker. Colter pressed the call button and a female voice replied: 'Can I help you?'

'Constables Colter and Mattock, with SPRING 157.'

'Oh yes, we've been expecting her. Do come in…'

The door unlocked and they stepped into a short corridor with a second security door at the far end, which let them into a room with white-painted brick walls.

Behind a desk arrayed with computer and telephone sat a fortyish woman with her dark hair pinned up in a tight bun. There were two other green wooden doors, one in the end wall bracketed by a couple of barred pebble-glass windows letting in daylight while the other was a side door bearing the sign: PREPARATION ROOM. Aside from this there were the usual cabinets and shelves loaded with box files and it might have been any small office except for a couple of details. Beside the desk ceiling stanchions supported a rail a little above head height, from which hung a row of large hooks. From the end hook hung a leash chain like Mel's that encircled the neck of another naked, bound and ball-gagged girl.

She had a pretty face, firm nose, dark eyes and a wide sensuous mouth. Her tangle of dark curling hair and olive tinted skin suggested some Latin blood. Her figure was good with well-rounded breasts capped by large brown nipples, deep cleft buttocks and a pouting cleft peeping out from under thick dark curls. She glanced up briefly at Mel and her escort then turned her eyes aside in shame. Across her forehead was a pink label reading: CAM 031.

As they entered the woman behind the desk rose and came round from behind her desk, brushing down the skirt of a modest grey two-piece. She had a trim figure, a smooth intelligent face and clear grey eyes. 'Good afternoon, Constables,' she said meekly. 'How nice to see you again.'

'Good afternoon, Miss Trunnion,' Colter replied cheerfully. He hung Mel's leash chain over one of the ceiling hooks next to "CAM 031", looking her over appraisingly as he did so. 'Just waiting for number three, are you?'

'Yes, they're bringing her by prison van. She should be here very shortly.' Miss Trunnion was looking Mel up and down with frank interest, her eyes lingering on her breasts and pubes, not sparing her blushes. 'So this is SPRING 157. Well she looks pretty enough.'

'We've given her a road test,' Colter confided. 'Needs a little more tooling but I think she's got the right spirit.'

'I'd say she's a natural,' Mattock added.

'I'm sure she'll make a fine Gryndstone girl,' said Miss Trunnion.

'If you'd just sign for her,' Colter said, holding out a clipboard with a copy of the court papers fastened to it.

Miss Trunnion signed and Colter took the clipboard back. 'She's all yours.'

Mattock slapped Mel's bottom. 'See you around, girl. Good luck...'

The policemen left the way they had entered.

Miss Trunnion walked round Mel, appraising her from all angles, then stroked her cheek gently and smiled. 'It's all right, I know you're feeling confused and frightened right now. All outsiders do at first. Just get through the first week and you'll be surprised how natural it all begins to seem.'

The words were spoken in a kindly tone but Miss Trunnion's touch made Mel shiver. Even in this mad world she now found herself in she instinctively expected more sympathy from a woman, but she seemed to be the same as the others. What was she actually: a kind of school secretary? At a school that accepted new girls delivered naked and bound? How could she go along with the way the men were treating her?

Miss Trunnion lifted CAM 031's chin, turning her head so she looked Mel in the eye. 'I do hope you're going to be good friends. It's most important because you'll need to support each other over the next few weeks. It won't be easy but it's the only way to turn you into productive citizens.'

Mel saw "Cam" was looking just as confused and frightened as she felt. At least I'm not alone, Mel thought. She tried to smile back reassuringly around her gag.

The buzzer of the outer door intercom sounded.

'Ah, this will be your chain-sister now,' Miss Trunnion said.

Mel and Cam exchanged the same mute thought: *chain-sister*?

Miss Trunnion opened the door to admit two large men in dark blue overalls, gauntlets and crash helmets with neck guards. They were leading a naked black girl after them on the end of a choke chain leash.

On her forehead was a pink label that read: BOLT 184 framed by deep brown hair tied up in a ponytail. "Bolt" was slightly darker skinned and more sturdily built then "Cam" with broader shoulders, looking as though she might have been half Caribbean. She also looked extremely angry. Her cheeks were flushed and eyes wide and darting. Yet even her rage could not disguise her pretty, heart-shaped face with a slightly snubbed uptilted nose, arching dark eyebrows, deep brown eye and a full-lipped mouth. White teeth clenched on her ball gag. Her breasts were heavy and prominent, capped by large nipples with domelike areolae. Her buttocks were full and round, her hips wide and legs shapely but strong. A delta of jet-black curls crowned the apex of her thighs.

As she was dragged in, Bolt looked wildly about her, goggled for a moment at Mel and Cam, then began squirming and jerking at her leash and strapped wrists. Maybe it was futile but this show of resistance made Mel suddenly feel ashamed. How easily she had caved in to her captors and trotted after them like an obedient dog. At least Bolt was fighting back. Perhaps a black girl had more reason than she did to fear anything that resembled slavery.

'Afternoon, Miss Trunnion,' said one of the guards, looping the end of Bolt's leash over a hook next to Mel and leaving her to twist round on the chain. 'This one's going to need some firm handling. You'd better warn Mr Bradawl that she bites, given half a chance.'

Miss Trunnion said calmly: 'Thank you, Mr Ratchet. I'm sure we can deal with her.'

She signed another clipboard receipt for Bolt and the men departed. Again it was all done so matter-of-factly, Mel thought. How many girls before them had she handled like this? And what happened to them next?

Miss Trunnion smiled benignly at Bolt, who glared back at her. She was making angry gurgling noises about her gag and pulling on her leash even though Mel could see the links cutting into her flesh.

'Don't damage that pretty neck,' Miss Trunnion said. She reached out to stroke her cheek but Bolt lunged at her. Miss Trunnion took a step back, shaking her head sadly. 'You can't possibly escape so why don't you just stand still and quiet like your chain-sisters? It'll be so much easier that way.'

Bolt made a growling nose and jerked on her chain again. Clearly she had no intention of making this easy for anybody.

Miss Trunnion went back to her desk and picked up the phone. 'Headmaster... yes, they're all here now waiting for you... thank you, I'll tell them.' She put the phone down and beamed at the captive girls. 'Headmaster Bradawl will be down in a few minutes to personally prepare you for schooling,' she announced. She said it as though they should feel honoured by his attentions.

Cam hung her head while Bolt glowered back at her defiantly.

'He knows how to handle your kind,' Miss Trunnion said to Bolt. 'You aren't the first who couldn't accept what's happened to her. They all learn what's good for them in the end.'

Five minutes later a man came in through the green door set between the barred windows.

He was heavily built in his late forties with greying hair and was dressed in old-fashioned teachers' mortarboard and flowing black gown. Hooked through a sort of holster clipped to his belt, like a gunslinger's pistol, was a crook-handled school cane. But this was not what drew Mel's astonished gaze. Between the folds of his robes his heavy penis and testicles hung freely on display in front of his trousers, which were tailored in the same way as Colter's and Mattock's.

Miss Trunnion had risen again and bobbed her head. 'Here they are, Headmaster.'

'Thank you, Miss Trunnion,' he said.

Bradawl walked round the three girls suspended from their leash chains, looking them over closely.

Cam was gazing at his genitals in blushing saucer-eyed disbelief while Bolt was gaping at them in disgust and contempt. He must know he was exposing himself before them and Miss Trunnion, yet she had said nothing, Mel thought. Policemen did it and now it seemed teachers did it. Here this must be normal. Normal for Shackleswell...

Suddenly Mel realised she had been staring and turned her eyes aside in fear and embarrassment.

Bradawl smiled. 'No, don't look away, 157, that's why it's on show. All teachers at Gryndstone display their manhoods and we are proud to do so. It reminds our pupils who are the masters here.' He addressed them all. 'I'm Oliver Bradawl. When permitted you will address me simply as "Headmaster". I run Gryndstone School and teach the industrial history of Shackleswell and gynaetics, which, though you will not know it, is the study of integrating female bodies with mechanical systems. I will oversee your education while you are pupils here. I will begin by making certain changes to your bodies so you can function more efficiently and outfit you as proper Gryndstone pupils...'

Bolt lunged against her chain and kicked viciously out at Bradawl's groin. He twisted to one side, caught hold of her heel and held her foot up high, leaving her wobbling helplessly on one leg.

'You bad girl!' Miss Trunnion exclaimed. 'Headmaster, I'm so sorry. Mr Ratchet said she was a biter.'

'That was spirited but foolish,' Bradawl told Bolt. 'It's done you no good and only left yourself vulnerable to punishment...'

With his free hand he unholstered his cane and swung it up under her raised leg so that it thwacked crisply into the soft swell of her nut-brown buttocks. He drew back and swung again, this time against the inner thigh of her standing leg, then up into the dark-haired swell of her sex. Bolt shrieked, gurgled, twisted and squirmed wildly, twirling about her neck chain, but she was unable to escape the swish and crack of the cane against her flesh.

After six strokes Bradawl let her leg drop. 'That is the punishment for disobedience in Gryndstone. Do not forget it.'

Dark welts were already rising across Bolt's buttocks and thighs and she looked wide-eyed, tear-stained and fearful. Perhaps she was temporarily subdued, Mel thought, but she did not look beaten.

Bradawl turned to at Mel and Cam. 'It is also the rule in Gryndstone that your chain-sisters share responsibility for your actions.' Before they could comprehend his meaning he swung his cane quickly, slashing it across the fronts of their thighs left and right and making them curl over and yelp in pain. 'Perhaps this will encourage you to see that your chain-sister behaves more sensibly in future.'

Turning aside from the string of three now damp-eyed girls, Bradawl said to Miss Trunnion: 'I'll take the first one in for adjustment and see if I can put a little iron into her soul.'

Miss Trunnion unhooked Cam's leash from its hook and handed it to Bradawl, who led her through into the Preparation Room. Mel saw a flash of white tiles and heard a faint whimper from Cam and then the door closed behind them.

At times during the next twenty minutes Mel thought she heard machinery running and muffled yelps of pain coming from behind the Preparation Room door. It was unpleasantly like being in a dentist's waiting room while waiting your turn. By her side Bolt was also listening. Instead of showing sympathy, however, she glowered angrily and shuffled her feet, looking about the room as though searching for some means of escape. This show of defiance was all very well, Mel thought, but she could have shown a little more concern for others.

After one particularly piercing yelp penetrated the door Miss Trunnion looked up from her keyboard and screen and said: 'It only hurts for a few seconds,' which Mel did not find very reassuring.

Finally the Preparation Room door opened once more and Bradawl emerged. He was now in rolled shirtsleeves and wearing a red rubberised apron and was leading Cam on a leash behind him. She was red-eyed, trembling and walked awkwardly. As he hooked the end of her leash back up and she lifted her head Mel gulped as she saw what he had done to her.

The least of it was the schoolgirl flat black shoes and white ankle socks she now wore and the pink and grey-striped tie that hung between her breasts. Then there were the heavy metal cuffs encircling her wrists and ankles and the metal collar with inset tether rings locked about her neck. Where she had a label stuck on her forehead "CAM 031" was now stamped in bold black type directly onto her skin. The same characters were also emblazoned across the upper slopes of her buttocks above their cleavage and on her pubic mound just above the apex of her cleft. All her pubic hair had been neatly shaven off. Worst of all, however, were the large silver rings that now deeply pierced both her brown nipples and both pairs of her labial lips.

When Bradawl had said he'd put iron into Cam he'd meant it literally...

'Why, she looks beautiful, Headmaster,' Miss Trunnion exclaimed, even as Bolt growled in rage beside Mel.

'Yes, she does,' Bradawl agreed. 'Now who's next?'

As Mel gazed into Cam's dazed and pain-filled eyes, Miss Trunnion unhooked her leash and handed it to Bradawl.

The Preparation Room was lit by more barred pebble-glass windows and lined with white tiles, cupboards and glass cabinets filled with many different boxes and jars and unidentifiable glittering devices, and a small workbench. In the centre of the room was a large black vinyl medical examination couch fitted with gynaecological stirrups. What made Mel shiver was the sight of the many thick restraining straps dangling from its sides.

Bradawl shut the door and looked Mel in the eye with a masterful gaze. 'Are you going to give me any trouble?'

Mel shook her head. At that moment she was too dazed to think about resisting.

'Good. It's not a sign of weakness to accept the inevitable and surrender yourself to your fate with dignity, you know, though I suspect Bolt 184 would disagree. Now let's have a proper look at you…'

He lifted her chin. 'A nice fresh-looking little cog,' he observed. He cupped and squeezed Mel's breasts casually, making her wince. 'A fine pair of breasts with good, thick, hard nipples. Don't worry, girl, that's perfectly natural.' He squatted down and fingered her pubes, making Mel shudder. 'Full, thick and pliant labia with plenty of flesh to hold a ring firm.'

Mel had hung her head in shame as they examined her, blinking tears from her eyes. He was handling her as if she was a dumb animal in an auction

'There will be some pain. Do you need to pee first?'

She shook her head.

'Right, bend her over the couch so I can stamp your haunches…'

Trembling, Mel forward over foot of the couch between the spread stirrup frames and lay face down fearful and shivering. She could smell female scent impregnating the vinyl. How many more girls had lain here before her? She twisted her head round. Bradawl was fitting large rubber type letters into a set of three different sized holders. They all read "SPRING 157" in reverse.

Bradawl swabbed a strip of skin across the top of her haunches just above the cleft of her buttocks with some sort of spirit that left it cool and dry. Then he inked and pressed the largest of the printing blocks against her. Mel flinched but she felt only the cool firm pressure of the stamp.

'This is indelible ink, 157,' Bradawl explained. 'I'll retouch it every month or so.' He pulled the block away and examined the result. 'A neat impression. Anybody using your rear can read that when they have you.'

He used an electric hairdryer to dry the mark to prevent smudging. Then he said: 'Right, let's get you strapped down properly...'

Sick with mounting fear, Mel turned and laid herself across the couch on her back so that her head went between the jaws of the vice, which Bradawl screwed tight. A thick rubber bit attached to the vice plates replaced her ball gag. With her tongue Mel could feel deep tooth marks indenting the rubber. Heavy straps went across her chest above and below her breasts, and her hips. Freeing her wrists he pulled her arms down to her sides and strapped them at the wrists and elbows. Bradawl spread her legs wide and slid them into the moulded knee and calf supports, securing them with straps across her thighs and ankles. Now her legs were drawn up and bent with her thighs wide open, showing her most intimate private parts. Except that she had no "private parts" now, she realised. Her body was open for all to see...and worse.

With her feet hanging in air out of the ends of the stirrups and her sex gaping wide Bradawl measured her feet. From a cupboard he brought out a pair of white ankle socks and simple black school-style shoes with single straps and low square heels. When he was sure of the fit he used a hammer and punches to stamp her part name and number into the straps.

'You are responsible for keeping them clean and polished,' Bradawl told her.

With her feet so modestly covered the rest of her looked even more exposed. Bradawl then set to work removing her pubic hair, clipping her honey-tinted bush short with scissors and then applying hot wax strips that he ripped off her mound, pulling out her stubble by the roots and making her yelp and clamp down on her bit. He finished the procedure by applying a cream that stung horribly.

'That'll inhibit any regrowth for a couple of months,' Bradawl said. 'Meanwhile you'll stay smooth as a peach.'

Mel blinked back tears. Her bare vulva now felt doubly naked and exposed.

He swabbed down her forehead and newly depilated sex with more sprit, then carefully applied the second smaller bowed type block he had prepared to her forehead. The third, with the name set above the number, he pressed to the mound of her pubes above the apex of her cleft. In a hand mirror he showed her the results. Mel shuddered. She now had an identification mark where she had previously had pubic hair. Anybody looking her in the face could see her new name and number printed neatly across her forehead.

'You're beginning to look like a proper flesh cog, 157,' Bradawl assured her, patting her head as you would a dog. 'Now we've got to get a bit of iron into you. These will help you function more efficiently with any machine you are assigned to operate.'

He brought over a tray of equipment and set it on a stand by the couch. Mel swivelled her eyes round as far as her head clamp would allow and saw an array of small shiny steel devices, some with clamps and some with needle tips of different shapes and sizes, together with plastic ampoules, cotton swabs and four shining silver rings. She began to whimper and strain at her straps.

'Hold still, 157,' Bradawl told her sternly. 'You don't want to make a mess of this, do you?'

Mel froze in horror.

He used disinfectant swabs to clean her nipples and pubic lips and then clamped a tong-like device to her right nipple. Its jaws had aligned slots in their centres. Under its pressure her nipple started to go numb. Bradawl smiled down at her frightened face.

'I'll fit you with standard labial and nipple locks to start with,' he said, holding up a slender padlock with ring-like hoop. 'They work on a common key. That way they can easily be swapped for other fittings as required.'

He took up a thick short needle on a handle with a guide flange that engaged with the jaws of the clamp. The needle was coated in a fine translucent film.

'Years ago we had to wait a couple of weeks for piercings to heal before we fitted full-sized rings. Now the bodkins leave bioplastic sheathes coated with local anaesthetic coagulant inside you. They seal the sides of the fistulas so you can be ringed and used right away. There'll be a few drops of blood but not much. The sheath dissolves when you're healed. Now you bite down as hard as you like on your bit because this is going to hurt a little…'

Mel shrieked as the cold steel lanced through her nipple while hot tears filled her eyes. As if in sympathy her left nipple pulsed with blood so hard it hurt.

Bradawl deftly slid the end of the padlock ring back through the tiny passage as the bodkin withdrew and clicked it shut. The padlock hung from her burning nipple against her trembling breast. By the time he had repeated the process for Mel's left nipple she was crying steadily. A little blood leaked from the incisions that he quickly swabbed up.

He used a curved needle for the thick flesh of her outer labia, aligning it with the holes he had bored through her shiny pink inner lips just above the mouth of her vaginal passage. Mel shrieked and strained so hard the couch shook but Bradawl took no notice. The ring padlocks threaded through her nether lips were a little larger than those in her nipples. They glinted against the flushed pink of her abused vulva like the handles of doors on the entrance to her interior.

Bradawl dabbed away a few last drops of blood and then stood back to admire Mel's trembling body in which flesh and steel were now inextricably joined.

'You look fine,' he assured her.

By now Mel was so exhausted from repeated highs of shock, pain and fear that she simply wanted to crawl into a warm dark hole, curl up and sleep and find when she woke that this had all been a terrible dream. However, the Headmaster was not finished with her yet.

He measured Mel's ankles and wrists and then from a cabinet of restraints selected two pairs of steel cuffs with convex sides, hinged in half, with inner lining of black rubber. Recesses had been cut in the middle of the outside face of each half. Across one recess was welded a curved bar about which a shackle could be locked. From the other recess protruded a sprung bolt snap hook, such as might be used to secure a dog leash.

Freeing her wrist and ankle straps, Bradawl snapped the cuffs in place, locking them with slender keys. They felt very heavy. The snap hooks were now set facing each other on the inside of the cuffs.

Bradawl brought her wrists together in front of her so that the cuffs clicked together and then he twisted. The bolt snaps engaged, securing her wrists. 'One way locking,' he said. Taking a slender key hanging on a belt chain he inserted it in a small hole in the side of one of the cuffs. The bolt withdrew and he pulled them apart. He made the same test on her ankles. Now she could be cuffed at any time according to the whim of those around her, or else secured to some other chain.

'A common key,' he said, holding it up for Mel to see. 'Everybody in Shackleswell carries them.'

He put a tape measure round Mel's neck and then selected a steel hoop collar, also rubber lined. It was hinged at the back and had a ring the size of those in her labia hanging from the front. Like the cuffs, smaller semicircles of thinner rod were welded across recesses cut out of the sides while the rear hinge pin had been formed into a vertical "D" ring.

Bradawl worked over it for a few moments at the bench with a small power tool and then came back to Mel. She saw: SPRING 157 had been engraved along its outer sides. He freed her head from the vice and snapped the collar shut about her neck. It felt cold and heavy.

From a box he brought out what looked like the knot and tail of a pink and grey-striped school tie without a collar loop.

'This is the Gryndstone school tie,' he told her. 'The colours represent iron and flesh. Wear it with pride.'

The large pre-formed knot slid over her front collar ring so that it protruded out from under it and hung over the tail of the tie. Popstuds secured the upper end of the knot to her collar. The tie hung between her bare breasts with its point stopping short of her navel.

'Now you're beginning to look like a proper Gryndstone schoolgirl.'

Next Bradawl took up a small electronic box with a lead and jack plug that he plugged into a socket in her collar. 'You'll learn the proper way to converse with your masters in lesson times but the collar will teach you what is prohibited twenty-four hours a day.' He pulled the bit from her mouth and held up a small card in front of her. It was printed with a list of two-dozen of the most common and much overused expletives and obscenities. 'Read them aloud as though you mean them,' he told her.

Too fearful to ask why, Mel obeyed. Bradawl had her repeat the list three times then he unplugged the control box. 'Now try again.'

'Fuc – awww!'

As she had started to shape the word contacts into the front of the collar protruding through the rubber lining had stung her throat with a short sharp electric shock, causing her larynx clench up and stifling the rest of the expletive.

'There's a sensor and language chip built into your collar linked to a power cell and capacitor,' Bradawl explained as she blinked back tears. 'It's now programmed to recognise the words on the list as you pronounce them and give you a warning. Before we had to use whips and tongue clamps but after a few weeks in your collar you won't even think about using those words ever again. Shackleswell girls don't foul their mouths with bad language. We have better uses for them.'

Even though she rarely swore, Mel felt the completeness of their control over her had gone up another step. From now on, even when she was able to use her mouth her words would be censored.

Bradawl had a length of chain in his hand and clipped it to the collar ring. He undid her straps and gave her new leash a tug. 'Get up, 157.'

She had no choice but to obey. Choice had been taken from her. Awkwardly Mel climbed down from the couch. She was frightened to bring her thighs together for fear of disturbing the padlock rings, which felt enormous and unnatural as they hung in the throbbing sockets pierced through her flesh. What they would have felt like without the protective sheaths and anaesthetic she could not imagine. As she moved they clinked together faintly. Her nipples pulsed about their own rings that swung with the motion of her breasts. They were standing up harder than she had ever known, almost as though they were proud to display them. Her body was such a traitor to her.

'Head up, feet apart and hands behind your neck, 157,' Bradawl ordered.

Mel obeyed. Bradawl circled round her toying with her new rings and stroking the letters and numbers stamped on her body. What must she look like in her neat white socks and school shoes? She closed her eyes, bit her lip, and shivered with every touch, acutely aware of the ring locks hanging free from her pudenda, tugging on her sex lips, the cold weight on her nipples, the absurd tie hanging between her breasts and the hard heavy ring about her neck.

'I think you'll be a credit to the school,' he declared.

He cuffed her wrists behind her back, popped the gag ball back in her mouth and led her out into the office where he hooked her leash up beside Cam's. Cam flashed Mel a shy glance of commiseration. Bolt jerked against her chain and swayed threateningly.

Bradawl eyed Bolt thoughtfully. 'Miss Trunnion, perhaps you would assist me with preparing our last pupil.'

'Certainly, Headmaster,' Miss Trunnion said.

Bolt was in the Preparation Room for nearly half an hour. Through the door Mel and Cam heard many muffled grunts, squeals of pain and Bradawl's voice snapping out commands to Miss Trunnion. Clearly Bolt was not cooperating. During the last ten minutes they were also distracted by a rising swell of excited voices from outside the pebbled windows. It reminded Mel of the sounds of a school playground. Well, that was logical enough, but who was out there and what were they doing?

When Bradawl finally emerged leading Bolt on her leash, he was robed and wearing his mortarboard once more. She was fighting back tears and trying to look hard and defiant. However like Mel and Cam she was now shaven, stamped, ringed and cuffed, with a Gryndstone tie hanging between her breasts and schoolgirl socks and shoes on. Following on behind her Miss Trunnion looked flushed and gazed at Bolt in open disapproval.

'At least you look like a Gryndstone girl now,' Bradawl was saying to Bolt. 'The rest will come in time. The school is a machine and it will mould and plane and grind you down until you are fit to serve.'

Mel shuddered.

'Now I'm going to link you three together in what's called a coffle,' he said.

With short lengths of chain Bradawl linked the front of Cam's collar and the back of Mel's, then he strung a length from the front of her collar to the back of Bolt's. However, instead of clipping the last leash length to the front of Bolt's collar he stooped and clipped the snaplink through her new pussy rings.

'If you had been better behaved this would have been clipped to your collar,' he told her.

Bolt growled and kicked out. But his firm hold on the chain brought her up short with a yelp as her brown labial lips were yanked into peaks by their shiny rings.

Bradawl pulled out his cane. 'Do you want to know what a thrashing on a freshly ringed vulva feels like?' he asked her.

Briefly Bolt's anger subsided to a simmering resentment. Bradawl freed Mel and Cam from their ceiling chains and took up the leash fastened to Bolt's pussy rings. He looked them over. 'Now you're fit to meet your fellow pupils,' he declared.

CHAPTER FOUR

Bradawl led Mel, Bolt and Cam blinking through the green door and into the summer sunlight. The chatter of voices swelled and enveloped them.

The back walls of the mews terrace formed the bottom end of a high-walled playground of black asphalt, marked out with various games courts in different coloured chalk lines. The green door was one of three that from this side looked as if they might have been converted from old stables or storehouses. At the top of the playground was the back of the school building Mel had seen from the road. It had a couple of wings embracing the top end of the playground.

The source of the excited voices was also now explained.

In the playground a few dozen naked, collared, tied and ringed girls, watched over by more black-robed, cane-carrying and cock-flashing teachers were spread out about a court. They were cheering on two teams of six female players, equally naked, who were passing a yellow inflatable ring between them in an effort to throw it over large angled phalluses that took the place of the hoops on netball posts at each end. However, the girls were not using their hands to pass and throw the hoop because they were cuffed behind their backs. The roots of half metre long inflatable phalluses of red or blue plastic had been plugged into their vaginas in some way and secured in place with their labial rings. They jutted at an angle up from their loins where they bobbed and swayed as they moved. They were stabilised to a degree by elastic cords connecting the middle of the shafts to the girls' nipple rings.

As they scampered about trying to pass or intercept the ring, breasts and phalluses sometimes bounced in rhythm and sometimes in opposition, jerking on their nipples. With the hoop hanging on her phallus one girl attempted to score. She spread her legs, bent over and then straightened up quickly, flipping the ring off the end of the phallus and sending it over the heads of the defending players. Her breasts were stretching out into points and then snapped back into heaving globes as the tension on the cords was released.

Both players and spectators seemed oblivious to the perversity of their situation and were participating with all the excitement and involvement of a normal team game, heedless of the exposure of their naked bodies. Mel's eyes passed across the assortment of multi-tinted flesh on display, much of it sheened with sweat. Almost all were girls of about her age. They held hands, had their arms about each other or were even cupping their partners' bottoms. Mel found herself gaping at vari-coloured and different sized nipples, bare pouting clefts, jiggling buttocks and even the dark flashes of anal mouths as players bent over. It was literally a school for enslaved girls. It was so sick and yet she could not help staring. She squirmed awkwardly and rubbed her thighs together.

Bradawl tugged on the chain clipped to Bolt's labial rings and with a yelp she followed after him, dragging Mel and Cam along in her wake with their newly ringed breasts jiggling as they stumbled to catch up.

As Bradawl led them along the side of the playground Mel cringed in sudden acute embarrassment. She was naked outdoors in a place that recalled childhood bad dreams of shameful exposure before her friends. Now she was being doubly humiliated for real, far beyond her worst nightmares. However, the spectators and players did not give them a second glance.

'You'll get plenty of exercise in one form or another while you're with us,' Bradawl remarked. 'You have to be fit to be a cog in Shackleswell. *Mens sana in corpore sano:* A healthy mind in a healthy body.'

Mel blinked incredulously. They called this healthy?

She saw one of the masters, whose cock had risen into erection, come up behind one of the girl spectators, take her by the collar, bend her forward and enter her without ceremony from behind. Had he gone up her rear? It had been so quick Mel was not sure. The girl braced herself against his thrusts with her hands on her knees while both continued to watch the game. The girls about her hardly glanced round as she was sodomized.

Bradawl led them up to the rear entrance of the school. Above it was what had to be a coat of arms. On a shield of blue was an embossed image highlighted in gold. It showed a naked woman chained spreadeagled within the ring formed by a huge cogwheel. On a scroll beneath it was a motto in Latin: "*Ferrum quod viscus iunctus.*"

'That's the motto of Shackleswell,' Bradawl said. 'It represents the union of body and machine. It means: "Iron and flesh joined."'

Mel's ringed nipples throbbed in sympathy.

Bradawl led them inside and along a high echoing institutional corridor to a door marked: *Classroom 1.* Within was a lofty room with pebble-glass windows. A couple of large store cupboards rested against the walls. There was a large teacher's desk, bare except for a laptop. Facing the desk were a row of three chairs of odd design. On the wall behind it was a large interactive whiteboard.

Bradawl began unhooking them from their coffle and sitting them on the chairs. When she saw the fittings Bolt shied away and received another couple of warning flicks from Bradawl's cane.

The chairs were of heavy plywood and tubular metal. They had wooden backrests and armrests but only half a seat. A triangular section had been cut out of the front of each. In the middle of the small padded ledge at the back to support their buttocks rose black rubber dildos with bulbous heads and slender tapering necks. The girls groaned as they were made to sit on them, driving them up into their rectums with little pops as their anal rings swallowed them up, closing with disturbing relief about their narrower roots. Bolt snivelled as she sat down and Mel wondered how much it hurt to sit on her sore bottom with her anus was plugged. Cam was trembling as her own weight forced the dildo up inside her while Mel felt sick as she was impaled on her chair. There seemed to be no end to the ingenuity of these people when it came to restraining and humiliating young women.

Snap hooks on the chair arms and legs clicked into their cuffs. Once they were seated, additional broad black rubber straps went across their necks, waists and thighs, holding the girls firmly in place. The sponge ball gags were replaced by heavier rubber bits, the ends of which were hooked to elastic cords fastened to the backs of the chairs. The tension not only held them firmly in their mouths but also pulled the girls' heads straight if they tried to twist them to one side.

Extending in loops from the backrest of each chair over their shoulders was a pair of crocodile clips on coiled electric wires. These were clipped to their nipple rings. Mel shivered at the threat they carried. How could they do this to them? Yet why were her nipples still hard? She looked slyly sideways and saw Cam's were also standing up and Bolt's were even bigger, her areolae bulging into domes about her nipple heads. Was it impossible to get them down once they had been ringed?

As the front legs of the chairs were set wider that the back this reduced the seats to little more than angled wooden padded ledges that only supported their thighs if they splayed them wide. This left the pouting swell of their vulvas exposed and vulnerable. This was accentuated by the short elastic cords bolted under the side ledges, the ends of which Hawk hooked to their labial rings, pulling their sex lips wide and exposing their tender inner valleys. Below their stretched and gaping pussies was a frame that supported a plastic bucket. From under the rear of the seat was a bracket on which was mounted a slender vibrator pointing vertically upward at the open mouths of their sexes.

By then Mel would have denied anything could further deepen her sense of shameful exposure and despair, but she was wrong. Small LED lights came on about the cutaway rim of the seat illuminating her groin. Forcing her head down she saw there was a tiny camera lens set in the front of seat staring up into her peeled-wide vulva.

When they were secured Bradawl took up his position behind the desk so that their gaping sexes were facing him and they could see his naked cock. He touched a key on the laptop and the screen behind him came to life. It was split into three sections, each one showing a close-up of one of their pussies as seen through the mini-cameras on their chairs. The rings piercing them were as big as dinner plates and the numbers and letters stamped on their mounds stood out like shop signs. The tiny apertures of their urethras were clearly visible while the crinkled mouths of their vaginas looked as though they could climb through them. The fleshy hoods of their clitorises were big enough to wear and looked suspiciously swollen. Below the swell of their vulvas they could see their anal mouths clenched about the bases of the plugs that impaled them. At the bottom of the screens were the heads of the vibrators.

They snivelled and groaned, squirming in their bonds in shame as they instinctively tried to close their legs. None of them had ever seen their most intimate parts displayed like this before, like fleshy orchid flowers. Mel felt an additional blush of shame as she found her eyes lingering on the sexes of the other two. Bolt's dark cleft was a little longer, she noticed, while Cam's pouted a little more.

Bradawl spoke. 'Gryndstone is Shackleswell's school for lost girls, for that is what you are at the moment: lost, worthless, rubbish.' He indicated the images of their genitals on the screen. 'Right now those are the most interesting and useful parts of you. They can be used to give pleasure, as storage devices, anchoring sockets and, by the careful application of stimulation, a means by which you can be controlled. At Gryndstone we will teach you to use them and the rest of your bodies properly and productively. You will not graduate until you are all fit to live up to the new names you now bear and take your places as components of the greatest machine there is: Shackleswell itself!

'I shall supervise you schooling and help teach you how to become fully functional girlcogs. The three of you will train, study, eat and sleep together as a unit. You will learn proper manners and deportment, how to work together efficiently, to give pleasure and above all...' he glared at Bolt, '... you will learn how to obey without question. When you leave Gryndstone you shall be fit to serve in any capacity in Shackleswell.

'Each of you has come here by different means and for different reasons. Those reasons you may wish to keep to yourselves for now, as do most of our girls, because they often involve personal hurt or shame, but there will come a time when you will have to face them.'

The three of them were still for a moment. We all have secrets, Mel thought.

'The means, however, are more general,' Bradawl continued smoothly. 'Through agents countrywide we run the Shackleswell Project, which is a re-education and rehabilitation programme for young female offenders. Some think it is a soft alternative to prison and assume we are bunch of naïve do-gooders. As you can see this is not the case.'

Mel saw Bolt stiffen in her chair.

'A variation of this programme is also offered for those who have had problems and setbacks in their lives and who are looking for a fresh start. Of course they also are destined for Gryndstone.'

Now Cam turned her head aside.

'Then there are those who are simply escaping from something without any clear destination. We have an understanding with certain commercial drivers to look out for runaways who fit our criteria and bring them here.'

Mel sagged. That was how it happened. The lorry driver had seemed so sympathetic she had mentioned she had family problems and admitted she was heading for London with no plans. It had not been chance the local police were waiting to arrest her on a trumped-up charge. She had been so naïve…

'You may be wondering how long we can hold you here. The answer is as long as we wish and you require. We will make arrangements for you to send messages to friends or families assuring them you are well, so no alarm will be raised. We also have countrywide contacts in influential positions who support our work and record of success turning wild girls into respectable citizens. Local authorities are glad to save themselves the time, money and aggravation involved in caring for troublesome girls. As long as certain paperwork is correctly filed they'll happily forget they exist. So you see nobody is going to rescue you from Shackleswell. Perhaps you don't deserve to be rescued.

'You are all in your varied ways victims of cowardice and failure to face your problems or try to improve your circumstances. Many other girls of your age have suffered as you have and they do not all end up where you are now. Your worst crime is that you've given up on yourselves! We're the only people left to care about you because we see you as a valuable resource going to waste. Therefore, since you have forfeited your right to self-determination, we have assumed it for you. We have the means to mould you into better, more useful, civilized, beings, both mentally and physically. Some girls come to us who have been abusing their bodies with junk food, drugs, drink and tobacco. All that stops here. You, like they, will live healthy lives and put your bodies to a better use. You will learn how to become the well-oiled cogs of society and not grit in its bearings. We shall give you a sense of purpose and pride in yourselves. Your training will be hard but the method is proven. We've had plenty of opportunity to refine it. Shackleswell has been taking in and correcting wayward girls for over a hundred and fifty years. You might say our town was built on the bodies of young women...'

Bradawl tapped his laptop and the image on the screen changed to show a stark black and white photograph of a stern-faced man with mutton-chop side-whiskers and a stiff white collar.

'This is William Samuel Rowland: 1819 to 1884,' Bradawl said. 'He was a Victorian inventor and freethinker who built much of Shackleswell and its industry so successfully that for a short time during the mid Nineteenth Century...' he paused and quickly touched a key on his laptop.

Mel's body arched against its straps as shocks stabbed through her nipples like hot needles, turning them into beacons of pain that radiated electric fire through her breasts. She bit down on the bar of rubber filling her mouth as a shameful wail of pain was forced out of her. Her hands clenched, driving her nails into her palms, and her creamy breasts shivered violently. On either side of her Bolt and Cam were suffering the same agonies. She heard a hissing sound. Cam was peeing into her bucket. The pain ceased abruptly and Mel sagged in her bonds, blinking tears from her eyes while her nipples throbbed and tingled. Saliva and teardrops ran down her chin and dripped onto the upper slopes of her heaving breasts.

'You may have found history lectures boring in the past, Bolt 184,' Bradawl said severely, 'but you will pay attention to this one and not look away again. As I have already made clear, disobedience, inattention or poor performance from any one of you brings down punishment upon you all. Do you understand?'

They all nodded miserably, although Bolt did so only with an effort.

Bradawl resumed his lecture with their eyes now glued to the screen. 'As I was saying, during the Nineteenth Century Shackleswell rivalled Sheffield in the production of industrial machine parts, for which it won the nickname "Irontown"...'

The images on the screen changed to show stages in the growth of Shackleswell with factories springing up, and houses and roads spreading out from its centre. As they flashed before them Bradawl touched another key on his laptop and Mel felt the vibrator head rising up in its mount and begin to slide through her gaping sex, stroking her clitoris as it pulsed and buzzed softly. From the squirms the other two were making it seems they were feeling the same thing. What sort of game was this?

'Rowland embodied both radical thinking and conservative and, by modern standards, highly chauvinistic ideals,' Bradawl said. 'In common with most

Victorians he believed men were inherently superior to women. It was how he applied such beliefs to his business plans that made him unique. He was concerned about the number of men had been killed fighting in foreign wars and feared what would happen to his remaining workers if another war depleted their numbers further. He needed a stable workforce he could rely on.

'He also hated to see any resource go to waste, such as potential workers being unproductively locked in jail for minor crimes. These he blamed partly on poor social conditions but mostly on an excess of drink and frustrated sexual desire. If the intake of one could be diminished and the other more easily satisfied, he reasoned, this would lead to a stable society and a contented and more productive workforce. Pub opening hours in what was virtually his own town could be controlled and prostitutes could always be hired, however, he hated the squalid nature of the profession. He believed sexual activity could be regulated and controlled by more orderly and rational methods.

'Rowland began a series of experiments that would solve all his problems. He demonstrated that on the small scale and over relatively short distances, the human body was a very flexible, efficient and non-polluting power source when coupled with suitable mechanical systems. He also discovered that though they were physically weaker than men, females were easier to train to function in this way, as long as they were properly prepared mentally and physically. Rowland did not approve of corsets, believing they damaged female health and decided their figures, strength and endurance could be improved and maintained by proper exercise and a healthy diet. Any clothing might catch in machines so it was removed. For the same reason the hair on their heads was kept short or tied back while their pubic hair was completely removed. A naked body could be more easily assessed for its health, simplified punishment if it was required and also helped keep women in a proper mental state of submission and obedience.

'Gradually he developed a system of manufacturing and distribution based upon girl-powered and operated machines. He called these girls: "gynaetomatons" or "gynatons" for short, meaning a woman who performed actions mechanically and precisely as required. They could be use to power many different devices...'

A new picture appeared showing Rowland seated in a light cane chair that rode upon a box frame with a single tiller-controlled wire-spoked steering wheel at the front and two larger drive wheels at the back. Sandwiched between the upper and lower faces of the frame were two naked women. They lay side by side on their backs with their heads facing forward and were held in place by heavy buckled straps about their necks, waists and arms. The framework was just deep enough to contain them except for their crooked knees that rose up through slots in the frame behind the driver's seat. Their feet were strapped to pedals connected to the axle of the rear wheels. Their breasts protruded through smaller padded slots in the frame on either side of Rowland's feet.

Mel felt the vibrator purr a little more strongly against her by now wet slot. Despite her fear and confusion she felt her clitoris pulsing in response. Stifled groans from the other girls suggested they were experiencing the same sensations, but they kept their eyes fixed on the screen.

'The Twin-Gynaton-powered Gentleman's Tricycle,' Bradawl said. 'A very efficient device to use about town.'

Images of the bizarre vehicle from different angles appeared on the screen. Mel saw how the girls were controlled. Rowland's feet rested on a sandwich of two light wooden boards linked by coil springs and hinge down one side. The lower board rested at an angle against the girls' breasts where it was studded with small pyramidal metal spikes. A closer view of the middle of the board showed a small pair of metal balls on arms set on a vertical shaft with a lever linking it to the underside of the footboards.

'This is a simple form of accelerator,' Bradawl explained. 'As the driver pressed his feet down, pushing the spikes onto their breasts, the girls were encouraged to pedal faster. The device carrying the twin balls is based upon Watt's conical pendulum governor and was turned by a shaft driven by the rear axle. As it spun faster it pushed back on the lower board, compressing the springs and easing the pressure of the studs on their breasts. It was one of many such systems that rewarded effort and obedience from gynatons.'

The imaged changed to show the girls' groins. Rods from the rear axle ran up between their legs to ribbed balls pressing into their vulvas. The vibrator buzzing away in Mel's own groin speeded up again and she knew she was making it wet with her juices.

'As you can see they were also directly rewarded for their exertions by sexual stimulation. Unlike many of his contemporaries, some of whom denied the female orgasm existed and were ignorant of the function of the clitoris, Rowland recognised the reality of female sexual arousal and developed a system of punishments and rewards using its power. He proved that suitable women could be conditioned to accept intimately merging with machines once their guilt about their responses was removed. The earlier they could be initiated into this process the better, of course...'

A new image had Rowland inspecting a row of naked and chained young women. Then they were shown being exercised on treadmills and squatting down on pistons lodged inside their rectums or vaginas to operate hydraulic pumps. Mel clenched about her anal plug in sympathy.

'Rowland found a source of young female labour in prisons, offering to take suitable girls off their hands to serve in his factories. Hard work and corrective discipline were a punishment for whatever crimes they had committed and also a means of re-education. The stimulation they experienced enhancing their sexual responses and conditioning to obedience also made them ideal as a means of keeping the passions of his male workers satisfied. You may think this was cruel but life as a well-fed and exercised gynaton, encouraged to enjoy the pleasures of sex in a controlled and safe environment, was preferable to prison or even living freely in a city slum. At the end of their period of service gynatons also made capable and obedient wives.'

A new image appeared showing a naked girl strapped spreadeagled to a table with her legs supported in the air by heavy metal rods and braces in the act of being pierced. A series of close-ups showed variously sized rings, rods and chains being strung through the girl's nipples and labia that were used to fasten her to various stanchions, levers and wheels.

'It was discovered that piercings, apart from making girls easier to confine and control, when used to physically link them with the devices they were operating, gave them more satisfaction, both physically and emotionally. As we would put it now, it made gynatons feel empowered.'

Mel shivered at the sight even as her vibrator buzzed a little harder, rubbing up and down through her sex.

'With increasing use of electric signals to sequence their actions while the gynatons provided fine control and dexterity, Rowland developed a version of a mechanical assembly line years before computer-controlled industrial robots. After his death these were developed even further...'

A grainy and slightly jerky black and white film appeared on the screen showing a row of naked woman chained to a production line carrying large but unidentifiable mechanisms. The girls had wires and contacts strapped to their bodies, especially their arms and backs. Other wires burrowed up their anuses and were clipped to their labia rings. They moved with metronomic precision, deftly adding components to the devices as they passed along the line in front of them.

'Maintaining a steady rate of production was rewarded by the usual stimulus,' Bradawl said, as the film showed close-ups of smiling faces shyly glancing at the camera. 'During wartime Shackleswell girls performed valuable work maintaining supplies of precision military equipment. Not that visiting dignitaries knew the truth about our true methods, of course...' A slightly better quality film showed a party of men in hats and stiff collars inspecting a busy machine shop staffed exclusively by women all respectably dressed in overalls. When the visitors had gone a foreman blew a whistle and all the girls shed their clothes, giggling and laughing to reveal their collars and piercings by which they were once more chained back to their benches.

'Although modern advanced mechanisation and computer technology has rendered some of the work done by gynatons obsolete, there are certain labour-intensive jobs they can perform and their training still serves a valuable social purpose. The demand for their sexual services has actually grown and is now used to augment the income of the town. In recent years, with growing concerns about social problems, a fragmenting population, pollution and the environment, Rowland's ideas and principles have become even more relevant... as you are even now discovering.'

The split screen images of their pubes appeared on the screen once more, showing the vibrators sliding up and down through their by now streaming sex valleys. Mel realised how very wet and hot she was and how her clit was as hard and pulsing as her nipples. She could actually hear her juices dripping into the bucket and could smell their arousal filling the air. Between the images, her sense of exposure, the vibrator and the piercings it had been impossible not to respond. She hated herself for doing so but she could not help it. Twisting her head round she saw Bolt and Cam were in the same state, squirming in their chairs, angry yet desperate, their eyes hollow with helpless need.

'In Gryndstone we control what happens to our girls' bodies,' Bradawl said, tapping more keys on his laptop. 'Including when and how they are penetrated...'

The angle at which the vibrators were moving tipped back from the vertical. The pumping heads found the mouths of their vaginas and plunged up into them. The three girls' eyes bulged as both their passages were filled. Then the anal plugs began to vibrate and the nipple cables began to deliver tiny teasing shocks. Mel was moaning and trembling helplessly, feeling the liquid heat filling her loins. How could she possibly be about to come for the third time in as many hours?

'We control what pain or pleasure you experience from now on,' Bradawl said as he watched them squirming in their seats. 'For healthy young females it can be considerable. Rowland investigated your capacity for multiple orgasms in great detail and also the means to initiate them, even in unwilling subjects. You may hate the process now but you will learn that only in Shackleswell will you find such intense pleasure and the freedom to enjoy it without guilt...'

Mel did not hear any more because at that moment she came yet again and even as she wanted to deny it she knew it was the most terrible and wonderful thing she had ever felt.

CHAPTER FIVE

Mel, Cam 031 and Bolt 184 sat hunched up against the sides of the cage that was apparently to be their sleeping quarters during the time they spent in Gryndstone. Evening light filtered in through narrow, high, barred windows. It shone on the tears streaming down their faces.

The cage was part of a double back-to-back row inside one of the wings of the school. They were essentially brick pens with metal barred front walls and ceilings, just high enough to sit upright in but too low to stand. Each had a single low gate set in the front wall just large enough for a girl to crawl through on her hands and knees. The floor area was about the size of a king-sized mattress, which was what it was covered with. There were three pillows and three blankets. Let into the outer bars low down on one side of the door was an opening sufficient for a squatting girl to push her hips through. It was covered on the outside of the bars by a projecting mesh canopy with an open bottom that enclosed the rim a waste bucket. Beside it was a toilet roll holder. Hooked into the bars on the other side was a paper tissue dispenser, with a small wire wastepaper basket hung underneath it and a water bottle with a peculiar spout that all of them had so far ignored. On one wall was a row of hooks for their shoes, socks and ties

Except for their sobs of misery the dormitory was silent and empty. The rest of the school was dining or at play. Perhaps it would have been better if they had company instead of being alone with their thoughts without the fear of a cane or cock to distract them. Once their tears started Mel found there was nothing she could do to stop them and she was too tired to try. They had to come sometime and the flow would only cease when she was completely drained. It must be the same for her new companions. Though she did not know what they had personally endured before she met them, they must have reached their emotional limits many hours ago. Bradawl had then pushed them over the brink and now had come the inevitable response. Gryndstone was already living up to its name...

Bradawl had allowed them to remain slumped limply in their chairs of pain and pleasure for a minute to recover from their enforced collective orgasm. Then he pressed a key on his laptop and warning jolts of electricity stung their nipples, jerking them back into unwilling attention.

'Gryndstone teaches six subjects over a six-day week with Sunday as a rest day,' he continued. 'You will normally receive a lesson in each subject every day. There is Physical Education to improve your fitness and stamina. Deportment and Self-Knowledge trains you to present yourself properly and confidently. In Domestic Skills you will learn how to clean, fetch and carry while restrained. Sexual Techniques will teach you to satisfy your masters in any way required. Mechanical Interface will prepare you for merging your bodies with machines. Finally, Obedience classes are self-explanatory.'

'Your timetable and other notices are displayed on the board outside the main hall. You are responsible for checking them. Bells will signal the beginning and end of lessons. The day begins with morning exercise, followed by breakfast, ablutions and school assembly. Then comes your first two lessons. There is a short break followed by two more lessons before lunch. There is an afternoon break and the final two lessons of the day. Then there is evening meal, recreation and bed.

'Apart from regular lessons you will undergo practical training days in town. Your progress will be continually assessed and you must achieve satisfactory grades in all subjects to graduate, however you cannot leave Gryndstone until you also are ready to confess the failings of your past life. You do this in assembly before your teachers and fellow pupils. Simply inform a teacher when you are ready to confess, but I warn you not make the choice lightly. You may think what you have already experienced has been hard but that moment of public confession will be far worse, because you will be baring not simply your body but your heart and soul. None of you can graduate until all three of you have confessed. Then you will take up residence in one of the town slave houses closest to whatever job or service you are judged best suited for and begin your new life as a fully functional and productive gynaton.'

'Now I'll show you where you will eat and wash, then you can get some proper rest. Tomorrow will be far busier than today.'

It was only then that Mel realised how hungry and thirsty she was. How long was it since she last had a proper meal? Suddenly she felt ravenously hungry.

Bradawl linked their collars back into a coffle and then he freed them from the chairs one at a time. The anal plugs pulled out of their bottoms with shameful sucking pops. He bent their arms behind their backs and clipped their cuffed wrists together. When they were all on their feet he led them back out into the corridor.

The game in the playground seemed to have finished and there was a subdued bustle of activity throughout the school. As they passed other classrooms they heard the voices of teachers, the occasional meek replies of pupils, the creak and whir of unknown machines, the sounds of cane striking flesh and shrieks and whimpers of pain.

Bradawl led them through a door labelled: DINING HALL. Mel's cosy image of her old school dining hall was dashed from her mind as she saw what it contained.

Along the middle of the room were set out four identical long low racks. Each rack supported rows of inverted clear plastic flasks containing what looked like semi-liquidized food. The flasks were linked to an array of a dozen large black rubber phalluses, six on each side of the unit, angled upward as though in erection. Hanging under each phallus was a bold laminated label bearing a part name and number. There was a broad wooden step running down each side of the unit with a foam rubber kneeling mat set out in front of each phallus. The mats had slots in their middles through which protruded the upper half of a wheel. Cast into its rubber rim were numerous prongs, ribs and knobs, all shiny with grease.

'Tonight you will eat alone but from tomorrow you'll be using these facilities with the rest of the school,' Bradawl explained. 'You will always eat from the same dispenser so we can monitor your nutritional intake.' He led them to the end of one row where they saw their own names and numbers hanging on three adjacent phalluses. 'The flasks contain a nutritionally balanced diet comprising a main meal and dessert, but you have to work to get them. Kneel down...'

Mel thought Bolt was going to lose her temper again at this fresh humiliation, but with a barely stifled groan she knelt on her mat, squatting over the wheel so that its projections nuzzle into her cleft. Mel and Cam did the same on either side of her. The slippery rubber fingers teased Mel's sore vulva. The phallus labelled SPRING 157 was now pointing right in her face. Though the rest of the moulding was lifelike, she saw it had an overlarge hole in its tip.

'To obtain food you have to rock back and forth to pump it out of the flasks and then suck it out of the dispenser spout,' Bradawl told them. 'Begin...'

With wretched sighs they clenched the wheels between their sore sex lips and began to ride their hips back and forth. At the same time they took the ends of the phalluses into their mouths and began to suck. The flasks bubbled and glopped and warm gobbets of food began to flow out of the phallus tips. It was a simple wholesome meal of potato and vegetable and actually tasted quite good. Even Bolt seemed to have put aside her anger for the moment and was gulping it down hungrily.

As they fed Bradawl said: 'Feeding also reinforces an important lesson all Gryndstone girls must learn: in Shackleswell the image of the penis represents the social hierarchy and your place in it. We are unashamedly a male-dominated society and the penis is the symbol of manhood and mastery. You bow down before it, suck upon it to give pleasure to your master and in return you receive sustenance from it, whether in the form of his sperm or food dispensed from its likeness. As both your most sensitive orifices are being stimulated to accept ingress, performing this service will in turn give you pleasure.'

He was quite openly admitting they were being conditioned to worship cock, Mel thought incredulously. A day ago such an idea would have disgusted her. Now, tired, hungry and helpless, she found the simple pleasure of consuming food combined with the gentle stimulation of her pussy perverse yet also weirdly satisfying. They're just rubber tubes shaped like cocks, she told herself. Sucking on this doesn't mean I'd do it to a man and like it. Of course she had done that once already that day, and come in the process.

The second flask contained apple and custard, which they gulped down with equal relish. The texture of the custard reminded Mel of Mattock's sperm slipping about inside her mouth. All right, but this tastes much better, she told herself.

When they were finished Bradawl led them through to a washroom of gleaming white tiles. It was not like anything Mel had seen before and again the phallic theme was evident.

The most normal things in the room were a row of washbasins interspersed with hanging rails of towels and shelves of hairbrushes, combs, electric hairdryers, hair ties and ribbons in the school colours, toothbrushes, soaps, shampoos and even bottles of perfume. To one side of this was a wall of open showers and on the other a row of open squat toilets. These were raised on a long plinth with steps leading up to them. An arrangement of bars and rods was set before them while mounted on the wall behind each of the drain holes were two black rubber phalluses, one above the other. The lower one jutted up at a sharp angle while the upper one was horizontal.

At the very centre of the room was a large swivel chair, separated from the bank of toilets by a short double arc of waist-high tubular metal railing, with the inner arc set a little higher than the outer. Anybody sitting in the chair could survey the whole room by simply turning round. Mel imagined it full of naked, showering, soapy, peeing chained girls with a teacher watching them. It was a voyeur's wet dream.

Sets of metal channels hung from sturdy-looking brackets on the ceiling. They ran in a continuous circuit round the room with side loops in front to the showers, towel rails and toilets. A few dozen long chains with ball runners engaged in the channels hung ready by the doorway.

'At Gryndstone you will learn the importance of personal hygiene,' Bradawl said. 'You exist to serve and your bodies will be kept ready to do so at all times.

Your hair and fingernails will be trimmed for you at regular intervals but you are responsible for your general cleanliness from day to day.' He clipped their collars to the overhead chains. 'Move round to the toilets,' he commanded.

They walked round to the toilets with their ceiling chains rattling along after them. There were strips of rubber matting set in the tiling on either side of the drain holes. In front of them two short polished posts supported a horizontal bar from the middle of which rose a vertical rod that forked into two arms each with a hook on the end. In an arc about the drain hole the spouts of water jets angled upward. There was a groove in the tiles from beneath the pairs of wall-mounted phalluses leading into the drain hole. The lower phallus jutted up at forty-five degrees almost from the base of the wall. Its shaft was quite slender and Mel could see it had a series of fine holes in their heads and sides, while the upper phallus appeared to have only one hole in its tip.

'You will be monitored every time you void your bladder or bowels to ensure you stay healthy,' Bradawl said. 'If you do not have a proper bowel movement at least once a day you will be purged. Like all gynaton toilets in Shackleswell you can use them even with your hands cuffed. Stand straddling the toilet facing outwards. Bend forward and hook your nipple rings over the actuator hooks. The arm will pivot down as you kneel on the pads and relieve yourselves.'

They all hesitated, confused and embarrassed.

'Gryndstone girls have no privacy anymore than animals do,' Bradawl said. 'You will do this or else…' he swished his cane through the air.

Blushing, the three of them climbed up the steps and stood as he had instructed. It took a moment for Mel to drop the nipple rings of her swaying breasts over the hooks on the forked arm. At least they had blunt tips but what was it all for anyway? Cam was managing with her smaller breasts more easily but Bolt was getting angry and impatient. Eventually they were all hooked up and gingerly knelt down on the pads. The forked arm pivoted with them against the resistance of some spring inside the mounting bar, tugging at their nipples and keeping their breasts raised. They knelt with their thighs wide straddling the toilet hole and exposing their groins once more to Bradawl's gaze. Was this why the toilets were set so high, Mel wondered? So they could be monitored each time they peed? It was so perverted.

'Void yourselves,' Bradawl said.

Mel screwed up her eyes and tried not to think of where she was. Her pee began to flow in fitful dribbles at first, then she groaned and pushed and her bowels opened. She heard hisses and plops from the other girls that indicated they had also overcome their personal shame. It was so degrading but they had no choice.

When they were done Bradawl said: 'Now pull back hard with you nipple rings…'

They did so, gritting their teeth as their tender nipples were stretched. The fork rods clicked and hard fine jets of water sprayed up at them from the spouts about the drain hole rim, washing their pussies and anuses clean. Mel gasped and giggled helplessly as the jets hissed and bubbled in her cleft and up into her front passage, finally washing away traces of Colter's sperm.

'Like any working parts a gynaton's vagina and anus must be regularly cleaned,' Bradawl continued as they squealed nervously. 'Her rectum especially needs careful maintenance. It must be empty at all times, greased and ready to take a securing plug, operating lever or a master's penis. To do this pull again…'

They did so. With a hiss the lower phalluses extended upwards, probing towards their bottoms.

'Let the flushing tools enter your rear passages...' Bradawl said.

Mel gritted her teeth as she felt the tip of the phallus pressing against her anus. At least after having just emptied her bowels her sphincter was relaxed and it slid easily up her. 'Work yourselves back and forward,' Bradawl said. Mel began to pump her hips, and warm water flowed through her out of the tip and side of the phallus. It filled her bowels, feeling disturbingly sensuous and making her shudder, then gushed back out of her bulging anus and down the drain hole. After half a minute of this Bradawl said: 'Pull again...' The phalluses retreated, sliding out of their thoroughly flushed rear passages.

'Now raise your bottoms and pull again...'

This time the upper phalluses extended from the wall.

'Take the upper dispensers into your rear passages,' he commanded. Miserably they obeyed. 'Work forward and back...' Mel rammed her bottom against the rod and felt it compress, pumping a spurt of something thick and greasy into her rectum. 'Now you are properly cleaned and lubricated,' Bradawl declared. 'Pull once more...' The lubricating spouts withdrew. 'Stand up, lean forward to unhook your nipple rings and step down.'

Mel did so, feeling strangely slippery inside. They lined up in front of Bradawl. He pointed to the arc of low rails. 'Bend over. I want to check you've cleaned yourselves properly...'

Now Mel understood the purpose of the railings. They were for displaying their most intimate parts to the master who sat in the chair for inspection. They were being treated like young children who could not be trusted to wipe their bottoms properly.

They bent over the rails facing outwards from the chair. The higher inner rail lifted their bottoms while their chests rested across the lower outer rails with their breasts dangling between them. There were hooks set in the underside of the outer rail. Bradawl passed a link of their ceiling chains near their collars over them, holding their heads down.

Bradawl flicked his cane across their bottoms. 'Spread your legs properly! You should not need to be told. Unless ordered otherwise always show yourselves off to the maximum. Do you understand?'

'Yes, Headmaster,' they said in chorus as they shuffled their legs wider until Mel's feet touched Cam's on one side and Bolt's on the other.

'Forget about shame. You have nothing to hide any more. Your bodies are no longer private, do you understand?'

'Yes, Headmaster.'

Bradawl went along the line of upturned bottoms, prying their buttock cheeks apart and examining the state of their anal mouths, which clenched nervously at his touch. He poked a stiff finger into their shy portals, ignoring their barely stifled whines and whimpers of misery at this new humiliation and withdrew it to see it was properly filmed with lubricant grease and no trace of excreta remained.

Twisting her head round, Mel saw Bradawl's cock was standing up stiffly. Playing with them was turning him on. It was perverted but then what could be more natural?

When Bradawl had finished his intimate inspection he nodded in approval. 'Good. Though you have not yet showered at least you are now usable as fleshcogs should be. Up until now you have probably thought of your bottom-holes as simple waste tubes for you bodies. Now you'll learn that they can serve more important functions. They can take rods and plugs inside them for the purposes of control or to operate machinery, but most of all they can give pleasure…'

As he spoke her took hold of Cam's hips and, without any warning, rammed his stiff penis into her rear.

She shrieked at this sudden painful penetration, jerking her head up against her collar chain, but she was of course quite helpless. Bradawl pulled out a little and then thrust into her again, jarring her hips against the railing. Mel saw tears drip from her eyes. Between grunts of effort Bradawl continued his lecture, almost as though he did not have his cock pumping within the rear passage of one of his students.

'Your bodies will soon adapt… with use and education… you will learn to take far larger objects inside you… yet we will ensure you do not lose this pleasant tightness…'

Abruptly Bradawl pulled his now glistening shaft out of Cam's frantically clenching bottom, leaving her stretched hole gaping wide, and stepped sideways to stand behind Mel. She felt his strong fingers pulling her buttock cheeks wide and then the pressure of his cockhead, still hot and slippery from being inside Cam's bottom, against her rear entrance. With a hard expert thrust he penetrated her, forcing her anal ring apart. She gasped as he filled and stretched her, careless of any pain.

She had a man's penis up her bum, pumping away inside her. Her eyes pricked with hot tears of pain and despair. The last of her virginities had been taken from her.

'You must be ready at all times to serve…' Bradawl grunted. 'That's why we send you to bed freshly greased… like any good tool that needs to be kept in working order… don't forget that's what you are now… tools of flesh…'

He pulled out of her, his shaft now straining with tension, leaving her suddenly aching and hollow, and stepped up behind Bolt.

Taking hold of her brown bottom and looking down on it approvingly, Bradawl said: 'I've been particularly looking forward to this moment. There's something very satisfying when a rebellious girl gets her comeuppance.' He gave her cheeks an open-palm slap that made Bolt wince. 'I have a partiality for girls' rears. I especially like a fine, well-rounded and fleshy bottom that shivers nicely when beaten, together with a deep dark bumhole. Is it as hot and tight in there as I imagined?'

Bolt yelped as he rammed his cock into her, driving her against the rails and making her heavy dangling breasts sway.

'Oh yes it is… highly satisfactory… you will give a great deal of pleasure to many men with this orifice.' Bolt's white teeth were clenched even as she sobbed with pain with every thrust into her entrails that Bradawl made. 'No matter how long you resist you will break in the end and you will remember this moment when you were mastered as nature intended.' With that he grunted and came inside Bolt as she sobbed and gasped in misery.

Bradawl rested for a minute against Bolt's trembling body, then withdrew from her abused rear. Her gaping, glistening, pitch-black anal ring slowly began to shrink and collapse inward and a trickle of white sperm appeared on its lip. Bradawl unhooked Mel and Cam from the rails and pushed them down onto their knees between Bolt's still spread legs, pressing their faces into her bottom. Mel was acutely aware of the heat and scent of her body.

He flicked his cane across their haunches. 'Lick it up, all of it.'

Too shocked to think of resisting, they obeyed, applying their trembling tongues to the sperm trickles now oozing out of Bolt's anus. It was the second time Mel had tasted men's sperm in a few hours. It was subtly different from Mattock's, or was that because she was lapping it up out of another girl's bottom? For a moment she felt sick but she forced herself to continue.

'This is another important lesson,' Bradawl told them. 'A master's sperm is never allowed to go to waste. One way or another it always ends up inside you. No, don't hesitate to put your tongues inside her. That's why she was cleaned out. There's nothing you can't do to each other now, however distasteful it may seem.'

Mel and Cam snivelled and slid their tongues about the rim of Bolt's anus. Mel's nose and cheek was pressed to Cam's and their breath mingled as they both tended to the most intimate part. A trickle of spent sperm ran down into the mouth of Bolt's cleft and Mel chased after it with her tongue. She found a heady-scented slippery fluid and realised it was Bolt's own lubrication. Had she been roused by her sodomy? She probably could not help it any more than Mel could. That didn't make it right but it was natural, wasn't it?

As they licked Bolt's rear clean, Bradawl went round to stand in front of Bolt. Lifting her head, he pushed his now semi-flaccid penis between her lips. 'While they see to you, you'll clean me.' He held his cane up. 'And make sure you do a good job, understand?'

Bolt sniffed and said in a miserable whisper: 'Yes, Headmaster.'

Miserably Bolt began to lick the cock that had just sodomized her. Could she taste herself on him, Mel thought? How sick would that be?

With his penis in Bolt's mouth, Bradawl said: 'You're chain-sisters now: a work unit or trigyn as Rowland called them. You will learn to cooperate and support each other in giving service, however intimate.'

After a minute he pulled his cleaned and revived member from between Bolt's lips and went round to inspect Mel and Cam's work on her rear. 'That's satisfactory. But you've all been soiled so get back on the podium and clean yourselves up again.'

He unhooked them and they climbed back onto the toilets and washed, flushed and greased themselves once more. When they were done he unclipped their cuffs and pointed to the showers and basins. 'Now wash yourself and clean your teeth. We want you mouths to be fresh as well.'

They slipped off their shoes, socks and ties and stepped into the shower pans.

Under the hot jets of water they soaped their bodies down, trying to wash away both literally and figuratively some of the traces of what had been down to them that day. It was a few minutes of luxurious freedom. Bolt, however, washed mechanically while hanging her head. Despite knowing she had largely brought it on herself, Mel felt a pang of sympathy for her. Bradawl had singled her out for special humiliation. She wanted to give her some words of comfort but she could not think what, and in any case was inhibited by Bradawl's presence.

For the first time Mel was able to handle the rings that she now wore pierced through her labia and nipples. The contrast between their hardness and her pliant flesh was striking, especially the mound of her depilated pubes, which was silky-soft. The piercings were still tender but she supposed it was amazing they did not hurt more, though she was acutely aware of their presence. She fingered her hard nipples, resisting the instinctive urge to try to pull the rings out. It would be stupid to damage herself further. For the moment she would simply have to accept they were there. Some people had similar things fitted as jewellery, of course, though they did it voluntarily. She tried to clean round them as delicately as she could.

The rounded inner faces of her collar and cuffs and the small degree to which she could slide them up or down meant she could soap and wash the skin under them.

She supposed this would also allow her to dry properly as well. At least she could keep clean. But that also meant there might be no reason to remove them for months, or even years.

She saw Cam rubbing at the part number stamped on her bare pubes, but the writing did not fade. Under cover of soaping herself, Mel rubbed her own pubes, forehead and upper slopes of her buttocks, but there was no trace of running ink. They were there until they faded naturally, except they would not be allowed to. They were as permanent as their masters cared to make them.

When they had showered they moved to the towels and basins. As she brushed her teeth she looked at herself in the mirror above the basin. It was not the Melanie Paget she knew but a naked girl with haunted eyes, a number on her forehead, a collar about her neck and slave rings in her nipples. She found towels and toothbrushes were already labelled with their part numbers. For a moment she wondered at the speed things had been arranged, then she understood. Whatever girl had turned up next would have been given that part name number by the judge and had it stamped on her. It was just a convenient label to identify her body and no more personal than her collar itself. Any girl might have taken her place as the latest part in the Shackleswell machine and be standing here looking at herself. She was simply a girlcog with a body to be maintained in good working order and a bottom to be used whenever a master wished.

Bradawl led them through to the other wing of the school.

'This is your recreation area,' he said. 'You are permitted to use it on rest days, after lessons and before bedtime.

The recreation room was surprising, unexpectedly colourful and well equipped. It was the same height as the other rooms in the school but within it had been divided into three horizontal levels accessed by short flights of metal frame stairs and entered via low doors framed by wired glass panels. The upper two floors were formed of a square lattice of wooden joists infilled with more heavy sheets of wired glass, so you could look right up through them from ground to ceiling. All levels were furnished with colourful pillows and beanbags. The lower level was lined with shelves of books and magazines, the middle one had a large flatscreen television and a rack of DVD's and the upper was fitted out with several games consoles. Bizarrely in a corner was a rack stacked with colourful double-ended dildos, plastic chains, sets of oversized toy handcuffs, soft rubber spanking paddles and gags. Would pupils really want to play with such things? Presumably they did.

It took Mel a few moments to realise that although there was enough headroom in each level to sit upright there was not enough to stand erect. To use it a girl would have to crawl in submissively on her hands and knees and essentially stay that way. Even when they were relaxing they would be reminded what they were.

Beyond the recreation room was the dormitory.

As Bradawl locked them into their bed cage, he said: 'You will have an early night tonight, as you will find you will need the extra rest. Tomorrow you will have an opportunity to socialize with the other girls. The three of you will sleep together as you do everything else while you're training. You will keep your cage neat and tidy at all times. The waste bucket is for peeing only. I'll see you tomorrow morning at school assembly…'

He hung their coffle chains on a hook by their cage and left, locking the dormitory door behind him.

They looked round their cage. The one thing that intruded into it was the spout of the water bottle hanging on the outer bars. It was yet another phallic black rubber spout dispenser. Even while they slept it would be there as a reminder of who their masters were. Bolt turned away from it and hunched miserably up in a corner. Mel and Cam did the same.

Alone with their thoughts and with no distractions, all the numerous wrenching shocks, humiliations, pain and violations of the day that had been held at bay until now caught up with them. First Cam, then Mel and finally Bolt began to sob and cry softly to themselves, rocking back and forth as all the heartache, fear and shame poured forth along with their tears.

An unknown time later Mel finally took a deep breath, groped for a tissue from the dispenser, wiped her eyes and blew her nose. They must get a lot of crying girls, she supposed. It seemed they had thought of everything. She was still desperately frightened and sick with worry, yet the tears had done their job and dulled her pain. She even felt a curious flash of pride that she was not feeling even worse after everything that she had endured, though she was not sure why. Maybe she was tougher than she thought.

After a little while Cam also took a tissue and tried to clean herself up, followed by Bolt. They looked at each other uncertainly through red-rimmed eyes. For the first time in hours they were free to speak but none seemed willing. They might as well still have been gagged, Mel thought. Was it out of shame for the humiliating intimacy they had been forced to share? Except none of what had been done to them was their fault. They must remember that. Somebody also had to break the ice.

'Look, let's forget these stupid labels we've got stamped on us,' Mel said, forcing a rueful smile. 'I'm

Mel. What are your real names and where do you come from?'

'What do you want to know, for?' Bolt asked suspiciously.

'I'm just trying to be friendly,' Mel said, taken aback. 'We've got to make the best of things. If we start with our names and where we come from...'

'Just fuc – aww... shut up about me!' Bolt said, wincing and clutching at her collar as it punished her for attempting to swear. 'I'll worry about me, right! It's none of your fuc – ughh... business! You don't need to know my name 'cos I'm getting out of here tomorrow! These pervy shi— ahhhs... aren't going to turn me into any fuc – ee... ing machine, right?'

'Yes, sorry,' Mel said, 'it's just that we're all stuck in here and we've got to get along...'

'So you can stick your tongues up my cun... ahhhh... again?'

Mel flinched in the face of the black girl's burning anger and reckless disregard for her own comfort. Didn't she ever ease off? 'The Headmaster made us do that. We didn't have any choice. None of us do.'

'Yes you do, you can shut the fu... fu... up about it! Just leave me alone!' Bolt threw her sodden tissue down, turned away and wrapped her arms about her head.

Recalling Bradawl's warning, Mel picked up the tissue and put it in the wastebasket. There was no need to invite further punishment.

For the first time Cam spoke up. 'She's right,' she said in small weary voice. 'Maybe it's easier not to talk about personal things. If my family ever found out what I did today they'd...' she trailed off, took in a deep shuddering breath and wiped her eyes again. 'So, maybe you should just call me Cam...' she looked down at her shaven pubes, twisting her head to read the number upside-down '… Cam 031.' She frowned. 'I know what a spring is and what a bolt is but not what a "cam" is.'

'Sorry, me neither,' Mel admitted.

'Well whatever it is, it's not me, so this must be happening to somebody else.' She bit her lip. 'Or maybe it's all some sick nightmare. Maybe it'll go away.'

'I wish it was to but I think it's real,' Mel said. 'I could never imagine anything like this.'

'Neither could I.'

'Will you two fu… effing shut up!' Bolt said.

They did. Neither of them had the energy or desire to fight with Bolt, so instead they pulled their blankets, also marked with their part numbers, about them and lay down.

Perhaps there was some advantage in having part names, Mel thought. Apart from making introductions simple those words and numbers stamped upon their flesh gave them something to hide behind. They were unreal identities to which all the terrible things were happening while allowing their real selves to hide away inside. Beneath their immediate physical shame lurked the deeper shame of what had brought them here. Bolt obviously had problems in her past and Cam seemed quietly despairing. Perhaps they were all frightened of exposing their secrets. Yes, it would be a hundred times easier for Mel to bare her body to strangers than her soul and all the guilt that weighed it down.

Mel must have dozed because an unknown time later she heard the patter of shoes and clink of chains and the rest of the school were marched into the dormitory, presumably coming through from the recreation room. They saw a few girls pass the front of their cage, accompanied by the robed forms of masters with their cocks and balls on intimidating display. With clanks and jingles the girls were locked away and the masters departed.

A soft buzz of conversation broke out from the cells. Girls were calling out to others in different cells by their part names: sprocket, bobbin, flange, spindle, pin and many others. Mel was not sure what they all meant and some sounded old-fashioned. Were they names Rowland had first thought up to give to his slave girl workers?

The ceiling lights, which must have been set on a timer, dimmed and faded. Gradually the chatter died away as the girls settled down, but the dormitory did not fall totally silent. From the darkness came the unmistakable sighs, grunts and soft gasps of lovemaking.

'I suppose it would be warmer if we shared our blankets and sort of cuddled up together,' Cam said suggested in a small voice.

'I'm no lesbian!' Bolt growled. 'You two keep away from me.'

They rolled up tighter alone in their blankets. It would have been warmer to huddle together, Mel thought, but that was clearly not an option if they wanted any chance of rest. She fingered her cuffs, collar and rings, trying to get used to their strangeness. Her nipples were still hard and her pussy was, well, moist. How could she sleep with all these things in and around her? How could she sleep after what had been done to her and not knowing what new perversions tomorrow might bring? How could she sleep after the terrible thing she herself had done?

Finally, however, exhaustion overcame her fears and sleep she did.

CHAPTER SIX

They were roused the next morning by the sound of a cane being run across the bars of their cage.

'Rise and shine, cogs,' a black robed teacher was calling out loudly. Mel saw his thick penis swaying as he strode past their cage and shuddered.

They pulled on their socks, shoes and ties and then waited to be taken out of their cages in groups of three. Long coffle chains were clipped onto their collars as they emerged from their cages crawling on their hands and knees.

'Stand straight and hands behind necks!' the command came and they obeyed.

'Now, keeping those knees high, march!'

They high-stepped through the outer door of the dormitory and into the playground. There was still a chill in the morning air that crinkled their nipples, but they soon warmed up. As they circled the playground in a multi-coloured parade of flesh, prancing like show-ponies, four teachers stood at the inside corners of their circuit urging them on with flicks of their canes across their bobbing bottoms or bouncing nipple-ringed breasts. At first Mel, Bolt and Cam found it hard to keep in step and kept jerking each other with their collar chains. Warning swipes from canes forced them to find a common rhythm.

With their hands clasped behind their necks, the swing of their hips and roll of their bottoms was exaggerated. This in turn caused their breasts, already lifted higher by their raised arms, to sway, jiggle and toss with greater force. The playground was filled with the slap of their shoes, the panting for breath, the swish and crack of cane on flesh and, delicately accompanying it all, the faint chiming of forty or so pairs of labial rings clinking together.

When they were warmed up they were arranged in rows and made to do star-jumps and then touch their toes with legs spread. Linked together each move had to be done in time with those of their chain mates. The teachers passed behind them as they dipped down, flicking their bottoms with canes to encourage greater effort or stroking and patting the hindquarters of those doing well. She actually heard a few words of praise being given out. Of course the teachers were happy. The further the girls bent over the more they exposed themselves to them. She could see right up the groin of the girl in front of her as she bent down, thrusting her taut buttocks into the air. The dark crinkled starburst of her anus seemed to wink at her as she ducked down while the cleft peach of her ringed vulva spread its lips invitingly...

Mel shuddered. What was this place doing to her?

They finished with ten press-ups each. With slave girls the rule was their nipples must touch the ground each time to count. The teachers walked amongst them as they strained to lift themselves saying: 'I want to see those nips touching, not just your rings.'

Larger breasted girls had no advantage. They were expected to flatten their breasts against the asphalt, digging their rings into their flesh.

When they were sweating and glowing from their exertions they pranced back into the school through the outer door of the dining hall. They found their assigned feeding cocks, mounted their activating wheels and began to suck and grind. Though their arms were not cuffed they did not touch the spouts or wheels. Breakfast was egg and bacon on toast. Again it was very traditional English fare. Was that in keeping with the perverted hyper-Victorian values of the town, Mel wondered? It was an effort to suck out the lumpier bits through the phallic spouts but it still tasted good. A strange scent

~ 87 ~

filled the air, mingling breakfast aromas with fresh sweat and the scent of over three-dozen young girls' pussies being gently aroused.

As they ate Mel realised the girls about her were engaging in quick whispered conversations in between mouthfuls. The presiding teachers must have been able to hear them but did nothing to stop it so it.

When they had finished eating they were marched into the washroom. Their collars were clipped to the overhead chains and they queued into a warm, close-packed fleshy line for the toilets. Though they all had their hands free Mel saw that the other girls still operated the controls by hooking their nipple rings onto the hooks of the actuator arm.

When it was their turn Mel found she was much less reluctant to squat down than the previous day. It was oddly easier with company and after being loosened up by their exercise they were very ready to empty themselves. Following the other girls' lead they presented their rears over the bars for inspection by the teacher sitting in the swivel chair monitoring the bathroom, but he only fingered their bottoms quickly and patted them on their way.

Even louder chatter and gossip flowed about them at the showers and basins and again the teacher did not seem to mind. Since they could easily have been ordered to be silent or gagged, obviously it was considered sensible to allow them this small freedom. Alone in the press of nubile and freshly scrubbed flesh, Cam, Mel and Bolt, still unsure of themselves, were silent.

Mel saw an Asian girl, apparently urged on by others around her, nervously step across to the teacher and say something of apparent importance to him. He nodded and she ran back to the others who hugged and kissed her. What was that about? What were the rules here?

Her confusion must have been clear on her face because as the three of them were brushing their teeth, a slim honey-blonde girl labelled WIRE 142, who was on the end of a chain of girls beside them, leaned across and said: 'Don't worry, I felt lost my first day here. You won't believe it now, but it does get easier.'

Bolt glowered at her suspiciously. Mel said quickly: 'Thanks.'

When they were all cleaned up, their arms were cuffed behind them and they were marched along the main corridor.

Mel had been too confused to take in the photographs and paintings that hung on the walls yesterday, but now they caught her eye. There were colour photos, older black and white images, sepia tones and oil paintings that clearly covered many decades. However, where a normal school might have pictures of former headmasters, group sittings of pupils in their sets and images of special school events, Gryndstone had such things as a black and white photo showing a pair of girls strapped into the open frame of a mechanism resembling a small train engine. There was a man in old-fashioned railway driver's overalls standing on a platform beside them and the girls were smiling out of the front of the engine at the camera. The caption read: *Gryndstone cogs: Contrate 214 and Piston 129 drawing the circle line train, 1958.*

What was that about?

There were other captions by the images that Mel glanced at as she passed. By a painting of a man with a moustache and a high stiff collar it said: *G. Tamper, Headmaster 1905 to 1921.* In the portrait a naked and chained girl was shown kneeling at his feet kissing his erection. He held the end of her leash in one hand and a cane in the other.

They entered what must have been the school's combined assembly and sports hall. It had a low stage at one end on which sat a row of chairs and a lectern. Hanging on the wall behind them was a large yellowing banner showing a pair of chained kneeling girls bearing on their shoulders a metal-framed panel on which was inscribed a paragraph written in flowing copperplate lettering large enough to read from the back of the hall. Various climbing frames, ropes and beams that ran out along channels in the ceiling were folded back against the walls. The floor of the hall had been laid out with small kneeling mats in groups of three. In the middle of each mat was set an upright dildo on a weighted base.

As the coffles of girls filed in they went to a set of mats and knelt down on them, impaling themselves on the dildos, then sat back on their heels, looking up at the stage where a couple of masters were already seated. One group of mats at the font of the hall was left unoccupied. A master led Mel, Bolt and Cam past these and to one side where their rear collar rings were clipped to the ends of long chains running up to a channel in the ceiling. The master remained standing beside them. Mel suddenly felt exposed and singled out and almost wished she were kneeling impaled with the rest.

Other masters took their place on the stage and then Bradawl entered. He took his place at the lectern and smiled benevolently down at them.

'Good morning, girls.'

'Good morning, Headmaster,' they all said.

'We shall begin with our school pledge.'

The girls recited the words on the banner. As they did so they began to rock their hips back and forth, gently working the dildos about inside them:

"We promise we shall be sound and
Hard-working cogs in the city machine.
We are strong, greased and fit for purpose.
We offer our orifices to whatever use
Or service our masters desire.
May iron and flesh unite within us."

Mel shivered. It was as if they were chanting a school song or assembly hymn. But then despite its perverse details, the setting, the gowns, canes and overawing attitude all combined to make her feel like it was her first day at a new school. Was that the idea? To make them feel as helpless as children again?

The recitation ended and Bradawl spoke again. 'Now, we have three new students to welcome. Please bring them out, Mr Hawk...'

Hawk turned to a rotary handle set on a box on the wall and began to crank it. The ceiling chains began to slide out along their channel, dragging the three of them along until they stood in the middle of the room facing the rest of the school.

'From the back left, welcome them in the proper Gryndstone manner.'

A chain of three girls at the back of the hall rose from their mats and walked up to Cam, Mel and Bolt. Smiling, one after another they kissed them on the lips, their ringed nipples and, going down on one knee, their pubic clefts. They walked back to their places as another group came up to take their place. Bolt flinched away as they kissed her, Cam looked confused while Mel felt a surge of unexpected warmth. The girls who kissed her were smiling and friendly. Wire 142 was amongst them and added a little wink as she kissed Mel. She had a momentary sense of the appeal of this strange distorted world and the dark fascination of being part of something bigger than she had ever imagined. It might be sick but at least these girls had a purpose set out for them whereas right now she had nothing.

When the whole school had welcomed them, Bradawl said: 'Very good. Put them in their places, please Mr Hawk...'

Mel, Bolt and Cam were freed from the chains and taken to the spare mats at the front where they gingerly lowered themselves onto the dildos. Mel saw the mats were also stamped with their part names. At least they were not the focus of attention any more.

'We also have a confession to witness this morning,' Bradawl continued.

There was an excited stir in the hall. Mel saw the girls looking round them, all the while jigging a little faster on their dildos.

'Mr Stapler, please bring Spool 113 forward.'

A master standing at the back of the hall detached the Asian girl Mel had seen in the washroom from her chain-sisters and led her forward. Meanwhile Hawk had run back the chains that had secured Mel and was now wheeling out a new device that had been folded up against the wall.

It was a rectangular wooden platform with two side posts a little over head-high mounted on each end. Each post had chains trailing from its inner face and a large glass tube running up its front, at the top of which was a domed bell. Sets of graduation marks were painted on posts beside the tubes. Resting inside the bottom of each tube was a short thick round-ended bar of metal fitted with ring washers. In the middle of the platform was the jacket of an upright iron pump with a short section of greased piston showing capped by a rubber dildo handle. Rubber pipes with brass fittings ran from the base of the pump to the bases of the glass tubes. There was an odd detail of the device Mel could not make sense of. Hanging in rows on the posts beside a second set of lighter chains were half a dozen metal latticework domes of assorted sizes.

Spool was positioned on the platform straddling the pump, so that the dildo handle slid up her vagina. Short rubber cords bolted to the upper rim of the pump jacket were clipped to her labial rings, holding her impaled. Her arms were pulled out sideways and her cuffs were hooked to the upper set of chains connected to the posts, leaving some slack on them. Her feet were spread and the lowest set of post chains were secured to her ankle cuffs.

Mel found it impossible not to stare at Spool as she was secured. Her skin was olive with the upstanding ringed nipples on her rounded breasts a few shades darker. She had a mane of jet-black fluffy hair tied back in a big ponytail. Her hips were slim and her thighs girlishly rounded. Her eyes were dark and bright and her oriental nose was neatly snubbed. Her shaven and ringed cleft was round-lipped and pouting. She looked nervous, excited and proud at the same time, almost glowing with a sense of inner resolve.

Now the masters selected a pair of the mesh domes that had puzzled Mel and fitted them over Spool's breasts, kneading and squeezing her pliant flesh until it were confined within cages of mesh like bizarre bra cups. Spool whimpered as her breasts were imprisoned and Mel winced as she saw that each junction of the lattice held a stubby metal spike pointing inwards. There were holes at the top of each dome through which her nipples were pulled by their rings. Slender integral curved bolts were slid across the tops of the domes and through the rings, securing them in place and preventing the cages from slipping off, even if the studs would have permitted it. Constrained and moulded by their cages, Spool's breasts now stood out with impossible pertness from her chest. The ends of the post chains were then clipped to her protruding nipple rings and her breasts were totally imprisoned, looking as though they were leashed to the frame. Flesh and iron merged, Mel thought darkly.

When she was secured, Hawk and Stapler took up positions in front and behind Spool with their canes ready.

'What do you have to confess, Spool 113?' Bradawl asked.

'That… I've been a bad girl, Headmaster,' she said, in a small but clear voice. 'I was lost, I gave up on myself, but now I'm found. I was a disappointment to my parents. I was disrespectful. I did not try hard enough at school or work. I did not listen to good advice. I got into bad company. I drank and used drugs. I was wasting my life. I've been a bad girl… please, Masters, punish me!'

'Do so,' Bradawl commanded.

Hawk and Stapler swung at Spool from front and rear, laying their canes across her smooth, rounded buttocks, caged breasts and stomach. Her delicate olive skin shivered as the canes cut into it, leaving long thin stripes behind. Spool writhed, jerked and gasped, making little yipping sounds as her eyes filled with tears. Some strokes caught the undersides of her breasts where her flesh bulged through the cage lattice, leaving stripes across their heavy swells even as they drove the internal spikes into her flesh. The blows caused her imprisoned globes to tremble and bounce unnaturally, rattling their chains. Spool was twisting and bucking within the frame, sobbing in pain but making no attempt to evade the strokes. The motion was churning the handle of the pump inside her and Mel could see the wetness on her thighs. As the cracks of cane on flesh rang out through the hall the rest of the girls rode their phalluses with increasing vigour. Their eyes were sparkling and Mel could hear a murmur of: 'Go on… do it, do it!'

How could they encourage the punishment of one of their own? Yet she found she was also jerking her own hips up and down as she squeezed on her dildo. It was impossible to remain still in the circumstances and she could not ignore the thing inside her. Now it began to feel as though she was sucking on a comforter, like a baby's dummy, and in turn it was growing warm and slick with her juices.

After a dozen strokes each the masters rested their arms. Spool's cane-striped body swayed in its chains, her chest rising and falling unsteadily. Tear splashes showed on her glossy bound breasts. Then she lifted her chin.

'But now I'm Spool 113,' she said clearly. 'I'm named after a useful thing: a reel for winding yarn, cord, wire or filmstrips. I've got a purpose… a function in life. I can give pleasure. My body has power. I'm strong…'

With that she squatted down hard on the pump, driving the handle deep inside herself. Air hissed through the pipes into the cylinders and the metal bars rose a little. Now Mel understood their function. They were the hammers needed to ring the bells. Spool was going to drive them up the tubes by air pressure, but it was not going to be easy. As she raised her hips air bled past the hammer bars and they began to sink once more. Spool squatted down again, pumping them back up again and a little higher.

Not only was it going to be hard work, each stroke caused her pain. Pulling up as high as she could yanked on the rubber cords that bound her labial rings to the pump jacket rim, stretching her love lips. Fluid from her vagina was trickling down the rubber phallus and helping to grease the piston shaft as it plunged up and down. Spool's breasts suffered even worse agony. With each down-thrust of her hips onto the pump the cages were jerked up and outwards by their chains, unnaturally twisting and stretching the globes of flesh imprisoned within them and gouging her flesh with their spikes.

Yet even though Spool gasped and whimpered she kept on pumping, forcing the air into the tubes faster than it escaped, driving the pistons higher in fits and starts. Hoe could she stand that much pain and humiliation and yet keep going?

All the girls in the hall were willing her on, chanting: 'Higher, higher!' even as they were bouncing on their own dildos. Mel found she was pumping along in sympathy with Spool, getting wetter and more excited, even though she hated what seemed to be self-inflicted torture. Cam and Bolt were also jerking and grinding their hips, their eyes wide with incredulity and disgust yet unable to look away, as if they were watching some great feat of endurance.

Closer and closer the cylinders came to the top of the tubes and the bells. The rest of the girls were jerking up and down on their dildos wildly, making their breasts jiggle, crying out: 'Yes, yes…'

Mel could not take her eyes off Spool who was sweating now with trickles running down between her swaying, jerking caged breasts It was desperately fascinating to watch her suffering and she could not deny to herself that there was a terrible beauty about seeing a pretty girl in pain. No, what was the matter with her? This was sick and evil. If ringing the bells would end it then that was what she wanted. She called out: 'Yes, so it, do it…' with the rest.

'Ding, ding!' the pumping cylinders jerked up out of the ends of the tubes and struck the bells.

Spool convulsed and collapsed over the pump with her hips jerking while the whole school cheered. Amongst the cries were moans and groans as several girls flopped about in the unashamed throws of their own orgasms.

On the platform the masters applauded while Mel felt a shiver as a small thrill of delight coursed through her. The moment it had passed guilt flooded in to take its place and she hung her head in shame. How could she react like this? She was so bad!

When they had recovered and the cruel mesh domes had been remove from Spool's breasts, the whole school filed up by coffles to congratulate her with more intimate kisses as she hung spreadeagled between her posts. Mel, Bolt and Cam could not avoid joining them.

Spool was red-eyed, tear-streaked, sweating but for some reason supremely happy. There were scratches and pinpricks of blood on her breasts from where the spikes had gouged her. Mel saw the girls ahead of her lovingly kissing these injuries before dipping their heads to her still-impaled pussy.

When it came her turn all Mel could think to say was: 'Congratulations,' which seemed both unbelievably inadequate and wildly inappropriate.

Spool seemed oblivious to her doubts. 'Thank you, thank you...' she said, beaming tearfully back at her like a newlywed bride.

Mel kissed Spool's sore hot breasts, tasting sweat and blood, then bent and gave the girl's pussy a token peck. It was wet with a heady spicy scent. With all that pain and effort she really had come.

But why had she put herself through such a physically and emotionally draining ordeal? To graduate from school so she could become a full-time slave? Just how strange was Shackleswell?

CHAPTER SEVEN

As she left the hall in the tide of perfumed female flesh, Mel felt a sudden absurd frisson of schoolgirl fear that she did not know what her next lesson was. However, as Bradawl had said, there was a timetable for each coffle pinned up in the anteroom together with a map of the school. The layout was simple enough and there were only seven classrooms. Other chains of girls were hurrying off to their respective classes and Mel and the other joined them. Mel had expected them to be led by masters but apparently they were trusted to find their own way to class. Cuffed and chained as they were there was really nowhere else they could go. Even then Bolt dragged her feet and Mel and Cam had to virtually haul her along.

'I always hated fu… flaming school,' Mel heard her mutter.

At least they had no books or kit to worry about. All they had to bring were their bodies. Still, she suspected it was going to be a long hard day…

Their first class was Deportment and Self-knowledge, taken by Master Puncheon.

There were only two coffles in it, Mel's and another containing three girls who looked only slightly less nervous than they did. Presumably they were also recent arrivals. One master to six girls, Mel thought sardonically: what an amazing pupil-teacher ratio. Apparently only slave girls deserved such a degree of attention.

Like Classroom 1, the room was largely open except for his desk. Various items of equipment were folded back against the walls, which were otherwise covered by charts showing slave girls in various formal poses and several full-length mirrors. It was floored by polished boards and scattered sheets of rubber matting.

Mel took in the basic facts that Puncheon was of stout build and had receding hair, but to her, seen from where she knelt in a row with the others on a mat before him, his most notable feature was his genitals. His pubic hair was slightly ginger, his balls were heavy and his penis thick, even at rest. His robes and black trousers acted as frames for them and it was impossible not to be constantly aware of them and look for any sign of arousal and what that might mean. It was the symbol of their mastery constantly displayed before their eyes.

'In this class I will teach you about your identity as gynatons and how to present yourself correctly, both to each other and your masters,' Puncheon said, standing before them with his cock bared while stroking his cane. 'These basic lessons will be repeated and reinforced until they become second nature. Only when you have passed all of them to my satisfaction will you be fit to graduate and take your place as fully functional girlcogs in Shackleswell.' He smiled in a not unkind manner. 'I know at the moment you are all feeling nervous and fearful. This must seem very strange to you, but that will pass when you gain confidence. Knowing how to present yourselves properly will help. All societies have rules about polite behaviour and Shackleswell is no exception.

'Kneeling as you are now is your default starting position, unless instructed or restrained otherwise. Sit at all times with your knees spread wide, straight backs, breasts pushed out and chins up. Display yourself proudly and never attempt to conceal any of your orifices. You are fine, well-made parts so you should show yourselves off to the best advantage.' Shyly they shuffled their legs a little wider and straightened up. Puncheon tickled their nipple rings with the tip of his cane to encourage them to lift them higher.

'Good, now, proper deportment also means you must show you know your place and recognise the power your masters have over you. In Shackleswell the symbol of that power is the male member. When you are sent out into the town you will bow or kneel and kiss the penis of any master you are introduced to, as long as it is exposed for the purpose. In school you will do the same whenever you enter a classroom or are taken into a coffle.' He pushed out his hips. 'Do that now...'

They got up and filed past him, dipping their heads to kiss his cock tip. And they expected her to do this every lesson, she thought queasily. She kissed the soft foreskin and felt the shaft twitch at the touch of her lips.

When they were done Puncheon said: 'Good, we shall practise that until it becomes automatic. Now you must also learn how to greet each other properly. When you graduate to the status of a serviceable gynatron you will be required to intermesh with sister units you have not met before. When permitted you will greet them all alike in this manner.' He freed their linking collar chains then said: 'Keeping in your trygyns, stand facing each other...'

The two sets of girls arranged themselves. Mel was opposite a slim brunette called Bobbin 195. She gave her a quick nervous smile even as her neat upturned crimson-tipped breasts trembled.

'Now tilt you heads to the right, open your mouths and kiss deeply, touching your tongues together. Do not hold back...'

Hesitantly they stepped against each other, their breasts flattening, and kissed. Bobbin's lips were full and wide and she tasted fresh and sweet.

'As you do press your nipples into hers,' Puncheon said. 'Feel her rings touch yours. They are the symbols of your mutual binding to the ideals of Shackleswell: iron and flesh joined. Share them.'

Bobbin's nipples were hard cones. Their rings clinked together. It felt odd but exciting. Mel's own nipples pulsed and stood up a little more.

Puncheon reached between the three pairs of bodies to judge the hardness of their nipples. 'Good, that's as it should be. You are healthy young females responding naturally to your situation. Arousal will make you more eager to serve…' There was a swish of his cane. 'But you can kiss better than that, Bolt 184. Use your tongue…' Out of the corner of her eye Mel saw Bolt reluctantly press closer to the girl she was kissing.

'Now move round to kiss a different girl,' Puncheon commanded.

Mel shuffled sideways to face a short busty blonde called Pin 048. She flashed Mel a quick bright "let's go for it" smile and kissed with playful passion. Her pale pneumatic globes pressed fluidly into Mel's, enveloping their rings in their soft folds.

The last of the other trigyn was a black girl called Axle 076. She had darker skin than Bolt's, long jet-black hair tied back in a ponytail and prominent flat-tipped nipples of glossy chocolate through which her rings showed up starkly. Her part numbers had been highlighted in silver ink for contrast against her skin, giving her the illusion of having silver pubic hair. Unlike Bolt she looked nervous and kissed clumsily but with an effort to please.

'Good,' said Puncheon. 'You will also practice that greeting until it becomes second nature. Now you'll learn that what you were no longer matters, only what you are now. That includes your old names…'

He had the six of them kneel in a row on mats in front of the mirrors with their hands still cuffed behind them. They straddled vibrators on flat heavy mounts that were controlled by Puncheon via a remote handset. Taped to the mirrors were cards with brief phrases printed on them in bold type that they had to repeat as they stared at their reflections that showed them in open-legged postures of submission.

'My name is Spring 157,' Mel chanted aloud. 'A spring is an elastic substance that can return to its normal shape after being bent, compressed or stretched. It can be used to reduce vibration or concussion, as a power source or actuator. It is a useful thing therefore I am useful. My name is Spring 157...'

The pulsing of the vibrator rose a little with each repetition. A wet patch was forming on the mat under her. It was shameful but apparently natural and she could not help it. From the smell in the room the other girls were reacting in the same way. A new definition came to her: A girlcog: the only machine that lubricates itself.

Beside her Cam was saying: 'My name is Cam 031. A cam is a specially shaped section of a revolving shaft or wheel bearing against it designed to impart a particular motion to a lever or other moving part. It is a useful thing therefore I am useful. My name is Cam 031...'

Mel supposed it was meant to be an elementary kind of mental conditioning to help them accept their new identities, but it was so unsubtle she could not believe it could work. Still they had at least found out what "cam" meant now.

On the other side of Mel, Bolt was reciting woodenly: 'My name is Bolt 184. A bolt is a sliding locking bar or a screw-threaded metal pin for holding component parts together. It is a useful thing therefore I am useful. My name is Bolt 184...'

The vibrators died inside them. Puncheon's cane hissed through the air as he laid it across the tops of their breasts, making them shiver. They yelped but held their positions. Bolt got an extra swipe.

'No, Bolt 184,' Puncheon said sharply. 'You must say it with more feeling. This is who you are now. It's important. If you can't care about that you can't care about yourself. Start again…'

Mel saw Bolt grit her teeth and feared to would say something stupid. Then she began: 'My name is Bolt 184. A bolt is…' with a little more expression, though it was clear to Mel that she did not mean it.

PE with Master Hawk was the next lesson and, apart from being naked and their teacher having his genitals on display at all times, some of it was not much different from PE lessons everywhere. They joined with other coffles to make up a group of a dozen girls and ran up and down the playground weaving about cones and throwing balls to each other. It only became perverse when Hawk got out the inflatable phalluses Mel had seen the previous day and plugged them into them. The phalluses bounced about in front of them, twisting their base plugs in their pussies and tugging on their nipples with their securing cords.

They had to run a relay up and down the playground passing hoops from one to the next. Seeing her bright plastic phallus butting up against Cam's as they struggled to transfer hoops was so absurd that Mel began to laugh half hysterically and some of the other girls did the same. It was probably the best way to relieve the tension they felt and Hawk did not punish them as long as they continued to try to pass the hoops on. Bolt however did not laugh with the rest. She was clearly a good runner but her stubborn attitude made her slow to respond. That got Mel and Cam more shared flicks of the cane on her behalf.

In they morning break they were allowed out into the playground for twenty minutes. They were in their coffles with their hands cuffed so activity was limited, but most were taking the opportunity to chatter about Spool's "confession" in assembly, clustering round the girl herself who was showing off her scored breasts. Mel wanted to learn more about that but she had more pressing matters to deal with first. As the playground filled with naked flesh Mel found a quiet corner and spoke to Bolt.

'Look, Bolt, I know you hate all this and just want to get out of here, but at least play along. It's hard enough as it is without us getting punished because you can't be bothered to put on an act.'

Bolt was only half-listening. Her eyes were darting round the playground as though looking for a way out, but the walls were high and unbroken and all that could be seen above them were trees and rooftops.

'They're not making me believe any of that sh... ahhh... rubbish. And my name's not "Bolt"!'

'Well, since you won't say what it really is we have to call you something. You can't exactly pretend it's not there with it written across your head and pussy.'

'We might as well accept them,' Cam said dismally. 'We're all going to be here for the rest of our lives. I might as well be dead to my parents anyway. What's it matter what I'm called? A cam is a specially shaped section of a revolving shaft...'

'Shut the fu... fug up!' Bolt said.

'I'm just saying it's not worth getting angry about. They'll do what they want with us and we can't stop them.'

Bolt looked at her with contempt. 'You gutless piece of p... pee! They've ground you down already.'

Mel stood between the two girls, shaking her head in despair. Bolt boiled with anger and resentment that got in the way of common sense while Cam was sinking into despair. If they had not all been chained together she would have walked away from them.

'Stop it, both of you!' she snapped. 'This place is enough to send anybody crazy but we can't start arguing amongst ourselves as well or they really will have won.' She looked at Bolt. 'Will you please try to keep your pride under control! We've got the message that you're hard, right, so you don't have to prove anything to us.'

'I'm not promising anything.'

Mel sighed and turned to Cam. 'Will you at least try not to give up on everything just yet? At least let's get through one whole day first.'

Cam looked at Bolt and then took in a deep breath. 'Sorry. You're right. I'll do my best.'

Mel had never considered the problems of fetching and carrying about the house when you did not have the use of your hands. They had in Shackleswell and had of course also developed many useful gadgets to allow cuffed girlcogs to perform basic tasks about the house. In Domestic Skills, under the tutelage of Mr Emery, they learned how to use some of them in a classroom fitted out with assorted items of furniture, kitchen and bathroom appliances.

The "Household Gynegripper" was a pair of spring-loaded rubber-lined clamps set on an S-shaped arm with a pair of rubber plugs on the other end that socketed into their vagina and anus and hooked into their labial rings. Squeezing on their vaginal plug operated the jaws, while clenching with their anus rotate them from horizontal to vertical. Light chains hooked to their nipple rings braced the gripper, so that it jutted out of them like a snake with gaping jaws, looking both obscene and comical.

'Concentrate on keeping a firm grip,' Mr Emery advised them as they tried to pick up plastic mugs from a table. 'You will speed up later. Then we will move on to picking up heavier objects such as books. This is useful practice for MI, where you will learn to integrate with far larger mechanisms. Use the sensitivity of your sexes to judge the balance and weight of the object…'

There was a muffled curse as Bolt dropped her mug. She got a swipe of the cane for clumsiness and two for attempted bad language. Mel and Cam got a flick each just for being her coffle-sisters.

They did better at polishing and dusting.

They held the plug ends of rag-dusters in their mouths and soft plastic tubes of liquid polish inserted in their vaginas. Hooks on the tube caps were fastened to their labia rings with the nozzles sticking out between them like tiny penises. They dipped their heads to bring the dusters down in front of their pussies and squeezed, spraying polish onto the cloth. Then they lifted their heads and set to polishing a set of shelves. It was hard on the neck muscles but otherwise simple enough and even Bolt was only warned once for being slapdash. Soon the scent of lavender polish mingled with their juices as they oozed down their warm thighs from around the slippery bottles plugged inside them.

Master Stapler took them for Sexual Techniques in a classroom fitted out with racks of hooks from which hung a greater variety of sex toys than Mel had ever seen before, ceiling chains, wall bars, chairs of peculiar design and padded trestles. A ring of six rubber mats had been laid out end to end on the floor. After kissing his cock when they entered the room as they had been taught they knelt in a row before him together with Bobbin, Pin and Axel once more.

'As gynatons your primary purpose is of course to please men sexually,' Stapler told them earnestly. 'You will learn how to satisfy the needs of male organs soon enough, but first you must become thoroughly familiar with every aspect of your own bodies and those of your sisters, with whom you are totally interchangeable.

Girlcogs are permitted to have no inhibitions with contact and intimacy of any nature with their own kind whatsoever. If you have never coupled with another female this is where you will learn how, lesbian sex is only one of the permutations you will have to learn. Think of yourselves as multi-purpose flesh tools that can be assembled and cross-linked in a huge variety of different ways. Your bodies have different nubs and orifices that can be used both for coupling with machines, men and each other. You must have no hesitation about using them for any of these purposes. Before giving pleasure every nipple, mouth, vulva and bottom hole of your sister cogs must be as familiar to you as your own.'

He pointed to Mel. 'Lie on you back on the mat with your legs spread,' he commanded.

Heart thudding, Mel obeyed. The other girls were lined up behind her head. The first one was Cam.

'You will crawl over every girl in the line ahead of you, kissing her lips, nipples and pubes, taking their rings into your mouths as you do so. The girl underneath will do the same to you. When you reach the end, lay down at the foot of the last girl in the line. When the last girl passes over you get up and work you way along the line again. Begin…'

Biting her lip, Cam knelt down with her head upside down over Mel's. Giving a despairing smile she bent and kissed her. Then she shuffled forward and gingerly kissed and sucked Mel's left nipple, taking the ring into her mouth. As she did so Mel caught the ring dangling from the brown nipple of Cam's right breast that hung under her like a ripe fruit and sucked and tongued it. She shivered, feeling her loins tingle.

With her hands cuffed behind her back, Cam had to slither across Mel's body to work her way along. Her flesh was warm and soft. Mel felt her tongue toy with her labial rings and then slide tentatively into her slot even as she reciprocated, burying her nose in Cam's warm, sex-scented wetness. It was bad, shameful and exciting at the same time.

'Taste each other properly,' Stapler said. 'Become familiar with her natural oil so that you will recognise it on any mechanical device you may both take inside you. That way you will work together more efficiently, knowing you are both parts of a greater whole.'

A flick of the cane made Cam move on, leaving Mel with her nose and mouth wet from her juices. Bolt took her place.

She scowled down at Mel as though daring to respond, bent down and gave her a brief peck on the lips, shuffled forward and licked her tongue quickly over her nipples.

Stapler's cane cracked across Bolt's bottom. 'Try harder!' he warned her. The cane swiped Mel's inner thigh. 'Encourage her.'

Mel sucked desperately on Bolt's big terracotta-tinted nipples, rolling the rings about with her tongue and feeling them swelling into her mouth. The girl was not unresponsive, she was just plain stubborn. Couldn't she see they had no choice?

In return Bolt nipped Mel's nipples angrily which made Mel wince but she did not stop sucking at Bolt's heavy teats. Bolt spat out Mel's nipples and slithered downwards. She had a lovely body and Mel found it impossible not to respond to it. Bolt's deep, smooth, pierced cleft appeared over her face and she pulled it down onto her by its rings even as Bolt nuzzled roughly into her cleft, going through the motions of kissing and sucking. It still felt good and her cleft began to fill with warm wetness.

'Move on,' Stapler said.

Bobbin, Pin and Axle followed, rubbing, kissing and sucking their way across her body with varying degrees of enthusiasm and skill. Each one was distinctly different in body scent and taste, but they were all parcels of warm, fresh female flesh and a thrill to touch.

Mel felt her natural inhibitions crumbling away in the face of her apparently equally natural desire. She had no choice, of course, but maybe she did not want one. Perhaps she had always had lesbian tendencies... who was she fooling, of course she must have! It was tough on girls like Bolt who had problems with that, but again she had no choice. It was not her responsibility. She could lose herself in such distractions and briefly forget her own troubles. Was she being bad or pragmatic?

When Axle passed over her Mel got up and looked entranced but impatiently into her dusky bottom cleft as she worked her way down Cam's body.

'Move on,' said Stapler and Mel crawled across Cam's prone body to take her place. By now her nipples and pussy were already wet from the attentions of all the girls that had gone before and her eyes were large with helpless wonder as they gazed up at Mel. Was she also being bad or pragmatic?

In a few minutes they had become a rolling, flipping, self-consuming caterpillar loop of three ever-changing girl pairs going around and around the ring of mats. Sweaty flesh slid more easily over sweaty flesh. After a few more warning flicks of the cane even Bolt appeared to be joining in, spreading their intimate traces between them over and over. They were dribbling freely on the matting in between and the scent of female arousal filled the air. Soon Mel was kissing lips that had already kissed every other girl's lips, nipples and pubes, including her own. They were becoming a single sex machine. She forgot about Stapler and who she was. Only the hot yielding flesh above or below her mattered.

Then the caterpillar was bucking and shuddering as orgasms spread like a contagion in rapid succession and the girls spent in each other's faces. With groans they collapsed onto each other and lay still.

'Well done,' said Stapler.

After a minute or two their euphoria faded and slowly shame and guilt returned as they realised what they had been made to do.

'Positions,' Stapler said.

They untangled themselves and formed up into a kneeling line. Their faces were wet with a cocktail of juices and they exchanged shy, embarrassed glances, except for Bolt whose lips pinched tight once more as a scowl returned to her brow.

Stapler noticed Bolt's expression and flicked his cane sharply across her breasts, making her flinch. 'I see one of you resents the pleasure you have been permitted to share. As Gryndstone girls you must learn to show joy and gratitude for whatever service you have performed, not disapproval.' Bolt still looked sullen. 'Very well, you've brought this upon yourself...'

Dragging Bolt forward by the hair Stapler positioned her kneeling on a mat with her face down and bottom up. Then he cuffed her wrists to the sides of her ankle cuffs. He swiped his cane across her thighs. 'Spread them wider, cog, I should not have to tell you that.' Miserably Bolt shuffled her knees wider, exposing the smooth cleft pout of her coffee-tinted vulva and the dark pit of her anus.

'Now this is the basic posture of sexual display and submission, offering up your orifices to whatever usage a master might plan for them. Today that is a lesson in pain and pleasure...'

He unhooked a pair of black rubber dildos from the wall and plugged them into Mel and Cam. The shafts jutted out at right angles to the double plug ends that fitted into their vaginas and anuses, made easier by the natural oil that still coated the first orifice and the grease that filled the second. A disk of rubber surrounded the base of the dildo shafts, pressing against their shaven pubic mounds. On the inside soft rubber fingers teased their clitorises, while its outer face glittered with stubby pointed metal studs. Their labial rings passed through horizontal slots in the disk and were held in place amongst the studs on the outside by small rubber pegs, securing the dildo in place.

Stapler pointed at Mel. 'Enter her!'

Mel shuffled forward on her knees and slid the head of the dildo into Bolt's cleft, watching her ringed lips spread wide in helpless fascination. She was actually penetrating another girl like a man. The resistance of her passage pushed the rubber prongs deeper into her own slot and she felt her clitoris stiffen. She stopped when the tips of the studs brushed the soft swell of Bolt's bottom cheeks and Bolt shuddered. Cam and the other girls were watching wide-eyed.

'As her cage sisters you must encourage her to give herself freely and wholeheartedly to her training without making sour faces. You both need that lesson driven home. I'm going to cane you until you come. The harder you ram into her the sooner that will be. I want to see those studs digging into her behind. Any marks you leave are her fault. Begin!'

Mel bit her lip. Despite her annoying attitude she did not want to hurt Bolt but she had no choice. Yet she had only orgasmed herself five minutes ago. This could take a painfully long time for both of them. Taking a deep breath she pulled back her hips and thrust the full length of the dildo into Bolt.

Bolt whimpered as her vagina was filled and the studs jabbed into her bottom, indenting her flesh. Mel gasped as the rubber fingers toyed with her clitoris. Stapler's cane swished across Mel's buttocks, making her yelp and ram the dildo harder against Bolt's rear, who then yelped in turn.

'Harder!' Stapler said.

Sobbing, Mel began to pump vigorously into Bolt's pussy, setting her breasts bobbing. She could not be gentle so she must get this over with as quickly as possible for both their sakes. But how long would it take her to work her way back to an orgasm?

Not long, it seemed. She could already feel the space between her vulva and the dildo disk getting hot and slippery with her juices. Her clit was swollen and hard, pressing against the kneading, stroking fingers. Stapler's cane slashed across the tops of her heaving breasts, leaving a red stripe behind. Mel gasped, but oddly the pain was not a distraction but a spur, heightening her senses. She could see Bolt's bottom getting redder. At least there was no blood but it must hurt. And she was causing that hurt and her own breasts and bottom were tingling. It was all so sick and perverted. How could she be doing this?

The pressure was mounting in her loins. Surely she could not come again so soon! The Headmaster had said Rowland had investigated making slave girls have multiple orgasms even when they were unwilling. Was this one of those times?

The answer came in a rush that tore through her body and burst in her brain. Oh… yes!

Stapler pulled Mel aside, her shiny dildo sliding out of Bolt's clinging vagina and she lay sprawled on the floor as Cam was put in her place before Bolt's blushing mottled bottom and gaping dripping pubes. Swipes of the cane across Cam's acorn-brown buttocks made her shuffle forward and ram her dildo into its unwilling socket.

Then the cane cracked across Cam's big nipples, making her breasts bounce. Sobbing, she began to pump away...

Bolt said nothing during lunch and Mel did not want to risk starting an argument in the feeding hall. Her bottom was flushed and mottled with stud marks. In the short break afterwards before afternoon lessons began Mel led them into a corner of the playground.

Bolt glared at them in contempt. 'You enjoyed screwing me!'

'No we didn't...' Cam began.

'Let's admit we did some of it,' Mel interjected. 'At least I came. And I'm sorry that doing it hurt you, but you asked for it. If we'd refused Stapler he could have got another girl to screw you or simply given you a thrashing. I think it was better this way. At least you got a little pleasure out of it.'

Bolt reddened. 'I did not!'

'I could see you were getting wet.'

'No fu... flaming way!'

'I'm sorry but you were,' Cam said, adding with a blush: 'I could smell you.'

Bolt bit her lip but did not try to deny it any further. 'That sort of thing gets you off, does it?' she countered instead.

'I think here it does,' Mel admitted. 'It's all simply too close and intimate to pretend. Face it, we're being manipulated by professionals. We all came on the mats, even you.' She added quickly: 'Of course that doesn't mean you were being weak or you're a closet lesbian, just that you couldn't help it. None of us can. But we can make it easier in some ways, like not paying for your bad attitude. You're still getting us into trouble. I know you're looking for a way to escape and that's fine, but meanwhile doesn't it make sense to pretend you're being ground down just a little? Maybe it'll put them of their guard and make escaping easier when you get the chance.'

'Besides, if you don't behave better and get good marks we'll never graduate,' Cam pointed out. 'Remember the Headmaster said it was all of us or none.'

'So what?' Bolt said. 'I don't care if I never graduate. It can't be worse out there than it is in here. If I show them what a rubbish slave I'd make for long enough maybe they'll give up on me.'

Mel sighed. She had to admire Bolt's courage, or at least stubbornness, but she thought of Shackleswell's hundred and fifty years of practice at breaking in girls like them. 'I don't think these people give up that easily.'

The Mechanical Interface classroom was filled with half a dozen strange devices of steel, glass, copper, rubber and brass. Some of them looked antique but all were gleaming and immaculately maintained. Mel, Cam and Bolt gaped at the array of beams, rods, pins and chains uncertainly, while Bobbin, Pin and Axle, who must have seen them before, looked stoically resigned, though they did cast quick glances of anticipation at certain machines. Their MI Master, Mr Vice, explained.

'In here you will learn how to become as one with machines. In this room your nipples, vaginas and rectums will be put to uses chosen not by nature but by men to serve their greater purpose. Flesh always yields to iron and you will mould your bodies and minds to the requirements of the machines. Serve them well and you will be rewarded, be negligent and you will be punished. That is the natural order in Shackleswell. You will be rotated about the training machines until you are thoroughly familiar with every one and have learned the basic principles of serving as Rowland always intended gynatons should. While you are in this room I do not want to hear a word spoken. The only sounds you are permitted to make, whether of pleasure or pain, must harmonise with the devices you are serving.'

One by one he took them off their collar chains, secured them to their mechanical masters, and explained their functions. In a few minutes the room was filled with the whir of gears, the hiss of water and air through pipes, the clink of chain and the muted gasps and sighs of girls in pain and pleasure.

Mel stood facing a disk-like metal panel rather like a huge clockface as high as she could stretch. Her ankles were chained to its baseplate and her wrists to the ends of a pair of pointers like clock hands. Electric bush contacts under the hands passed over a ring of silver contact studs on the face of the disk, completing a circuit. Silver chains trailing from the hands were clipped to her nipple rings. A rod extended out from the central axel of the machine about which the pointers pivoted. Mounted at a right angle on the end of this rod was a steel phallus, on which she was impaled.

The outer rim of the disk was studded with lamp lenses that lit up in a random sequence of pairs, one on each half of the clock face. If Mel moved the pointer tips round to match with the lamps quickly enough gears within the machine purred, transmitting its vibration through the central rod to the steel phallus. If she did not she got a shock through her nipples. Despite the occasional pain her thighs were soon slick with her juices tease out of her by the hum of a well-tended machine.

As Master Vice had promised, all their orifices were being used to the maximum.

To one side of Mel, Bolt was impaled on a different training device. She stood with hands cuffed behind her and ankles loosely chained astride a vertical lever on a universal mount. Its tip was double pronged and capped by rubber balls, which were lodged up her anus and vagina. As she twisted about the lever moved back and forth, left and right. These movements were conveyed by pivoting rods running under the base of the device to a sprung metal pointer on a hinged mount that hovered over a large horizontal drum turning slowly before her. The surface of the drum was studded with metal balls, blocks and strips, forming a kind of maze. By working the lever Bolt could steer the pointer between the obstacles. It was almost a like a crude mechanical predecessor of a video game, a challenge that seemed to appeal to her, despite the penalty for touching one of the obstacles with the pointer. This triggered one of a pair of spring mounted, solenoid activated canes positioned behind her to come swishing down across her buttocks.

Cam, her arms cuffed behind her, was straddling a long length of polished "I" beam raised on trestle legs. This served as a track for a couple of small chassis to run along whose wheels were spring-clamped to the sides and lower flange of the rail. One was wedged between her thighs and supported a vertical anal plug on which she was impaled. In front of that was a sprung arm that carried a larger ribbed rubber wheel with pronged side flanges that ran along the top of the rail. As Cam moved the long soft prongs, pressed inwards by a pair of angled plates, ran through the cleft of her vulva.

The second chassis carried a tray with splayed sides, like the load bucket of a miniature dumper truck. This ran along the track just in front of Cam and was connected to her by a pair of light rods clipped to her nipple rings. At one end of the track was a hopper mounted above the rail filled with large ball bearings. At the other end below the rail was the mouth of a narrow funnel that fed into a storage bin.

Cam pushed the truck under the hopper where it threw a switch to dispense a load of bearings. Then she shuffled backwards, pulling the laden car by her nipples, which drew them out into painful brown cones. As she did so the pronged rubber wheel teased her slot. When she reached the far end she had to position the truck over the mouth of the bin and then twist round, tugging on the nipple rods and distending her breasts, until the bucket of bearings tipped sideways and dumped its contents into the funnel of the bin. Covered by the rattle and rush of the balls she groaned from the pain of her twisted breasts. Then she righted the bucket and went back for another load. After half a dozen trips the rubber wheel turning in her cleft was shiny and the track glistened with her juices.

Bobbin and Pin, with arms cuffed behind their backs, sat astride the ends of what looked at first glance to be a children's seesaw that both pivoted up and down and rotated about its central mount. However the seats were simply padded hoops, leaving their genitals and bottom clefts bulging through them. Their ankles were linked to the beams of the seesaw by slack chains, allowing them to propel themselves round.

Arrayed in a ring under them were a hundred or more red and blue metal cones, like third-size traffic cones, set out in random stacks on a series of alternating red or blue spots. Their task was to sort the cones into matching colours and set them on the appropriate colour spots. Of course with their hands cuffed they could only move the cones about by impaling their rounded tops in their anus or vagina, gripping and lifting. Their task was made harder by their nipples being linked together by long light chains that passed through a freely rotating ring set on the central axis of the seesaw. If they did not coordinate their actions and bend or turn together they gave each other painful jerks that made their breasts jiggle.

The reward for their efforts came as more of the cones were stacked on their rightful colour spots. Their weight activated pressure plates that via hydraulic links caused slender arms to extend out from the ends of the seesaw beams across the seat hoops. The tips of the rods carried vibrating tips that buzzed as they swung the seesaw round and wiggled as they rocked up and down. The more cones they stacked the deeper the vibrating rods probed their clitorises. The floor under them became marked with a ring of drips. However the stimulation also caused their vaginas and even their anuses to become more slippery and they had to work harder to grip the cones. It became a race to finish before they became incapable of functioning and the strain showed on their faces.

Axle was working a pump, but naturally it was without using her hands, which were cuffed behind her back. She was squatting over the end of a horizontal lever secured within her by an anal plug and clips to her labial rings. The lever was coupled to a man-high iron pillar in front of her. On the top of the pillar was a water-cooler bottle filled with red-tinted water. A tube from the bottom of this bottle ran down to a plastic bucket with a clamp on the end that reduced the flow of water to a steady trickle. The bucket was supported clear of the floor by a pair of light chains that ran over pulley wheels set in the sides of the pillar and then along to hook onto Axle's nipple rings. The tension of the empty bucket alone drew them out into sharp points.

She could not bend forward to ease the strain on her nipple chains by resting the bucket on the ground because of an adjustable hinged rod extending from the pillar. This was clipped to the front ring of her collar and held her at a constant distance from the device.

The end of the pump extractor tube sat in the bottom of the bucket where it sucked the water out as long as Axle worked the pump lever, keeping the water level to a minimum. However the discharge tube ran up to the top of the pillar and fed back into the top of the water cooler bottle where the cycle began once again.

There was one reward for Axle's labours. A hinged sprung rod rose up at an angle from the base of the pillar and passed through a slot in the lever arm beneath Axle's chocolate-lipped cleft that was held open wide by the clips hooked to her labial rings. Mounted on the end of the rod was a dildo. Axle penetrated herself with every pump stroke.

After fifteen minutes on the machine Mel saw Axle orgasm, trembling and gasping and rolling up her eyes. She sagged limply on the lever arm for some moments until the trickle of water into the bucket drew her nipples and breasts out into dusky cones and she had to begin pumping once more.

Amid the naked, sweating, straining, thrusting bodies glistened in the light, Master Vice strode up and down, nodding in approval or flicking his cane across a tremulous breast or shivering buttock that needed encouragement. Gradually the smell of machine oil was diluted by the tang of spilt female juices.

When they were done, cloths on rubber plugs were pushed into their mouths and pussies and they were set to wiping and polishing up all the sweat drips and vaginal dribbles they had made until the devices gleamed once more.

The lesson had been driven home: it was a duty, pleasure and privilege to merge with a machine, but they would always be its servants.

Whereas in MI they had been treated as machine part, in Obedience, their last class of the day, they were treated virtually as dumb animals. It was held out on the playground under the command of Master Router.

'You are no use to Shackleswell if you cannot be relied upon to perform your assigned functions without hesitation,' he told them. 'Where would we be if a machine took time to decide whether to respond to the turn of a key or the press of a button? Therefore you must learn to obey immediately and without question any lawful command given to you. An unlawful command is one such as: "Flap your arms and fly like a bird," which is impossible, or: "Step off the side of a tall building," which is self-destructive. Those orders would never be given. But any command that is merely unpleasant, embarrassing or uncomfortable is lawful and must be obeyed without question, such as: "Put your right index finger up the bottom hole of the girl standing on your left." Do it!'

They jerked into dazed action. Mel twisted round and pushed her finger into Bolt's bottom even as she felt Cam's finger pushing through her anal sphincter. A few days ago it would have clamped up tight against such a sudden intrusion, but after the usage of the day it relaxed and let her in.

Axle was left without any girl on the left to put her finger up.

'Cam 031 is unoccupied,' Router said.

Tugging the others with her, Axle shuffled round and pushed her finger up Cam's rear. Now they stood in a naked ring in a school playground forming a daisy chain of hands thrust up bottom cracks. Mel could feel Bolt trembling with suppressed anger, squeezing with her anus as if trying to push Mel's finger out, even as the intimate heat of her body soaked into her.

Router walked round looking them over. Mel blushed as if she had been caught doing something childishly naughty.

'Keeping your fingers where they are, go to the bottom of the playground and come back,' he commanded.

Awkwardly, weaving and twirling round as they went,

they shuffled down to the bottom of the playground and then back up again. They must look so weird, Mel thought.

'Has anybody anything to say about what you have just done?' he asked.

Mel prayed that Bolt would not say something stupid but wisely they all kept silent.

'Good, because your opinion is irrelevant. Why a command is given and for what purpose is none of your concern. All that matters is that your master desires you to do something and you obey. Never forget that. Now, a basic skill of obedience lies in fetching and carrying…'

He commanded them to remove their fingers and then set them chasing thrown balls and bringing them back in their mouths like dogs, kneeling at Router's feet and dropping them into his hand. Then he had them carrying objects like wooden ten-pins with long necks with rounded caps. They did not use their hands but squatted and grasped them with their vaginal mouths, carrying them swinging between their thighs in an undignified duck-like waddle. Around and around the playground they went, alternating between their groups, passing the warm wet pins from vagina to vagina.

'Continue until I tell you to stop,' Router said.

It was not physically hard compared to what they had already been put through that day, though their well-used passages did ache after a while. It was mildly stimulating but not likely to lead to orgasm. It was an exercise in boring repetition and mindless compliance.

'Don't think, just react,' Router advised. 'Lose your mind in the joy of reflex obedience.'

This attitude did not appeal to Bolt and she earned them all a few more cane stripes for being sullen and slow to respond. Mel and Cam plodded doggedly onward until the last bell sounded, signalling the end of lessons for the day.

CHAPTER EIGHT

They were sent to the washroom to join the rest of the school. The ceiling chains were not used and there was no sense of urgency. Master Puncheon, sitting in the monitor's chair, was reading a book. Mel spent a long time under the shower trying to wash away not only dirt and sweat but also the memory of all the usage she had endured. She was sore, aching and drained both physically and emotionally, but at least she had survived her first day at Gryndstone.

By the time Mel finished drying herself she felt a little better. The other girls were breaking up into chattering groups and filing out of the washroom in a casual fashion. Some were even laughing. They must have suffered the same way her trigyn had yet they appeared so normal. How could they just switch off like that? Perhaps that was the trick.

Mel, Bolt and Cam hesitated, uncertain what was expected of them next. Then Mel saw Wire 142 leaving with her arms about a red-haired girl, stamped SPAR 075 and a brunet called BUSH 103. 'Hallo, um what do we do now?' she asked her.

'Whatever you want until lights out at ten, except when we're called in for tea,' Wire said. 'We're going to the rec room. By the way, these are the other thirds of my trigyn...'

'Hallo,' said Spar and Bush with friendly smiles. They came forward to embrace Mel, Cam and Bolt. Mel and Cam hugged gingerly back but Bolt shied away.

'I don't care what they make us do to each other in lessons, I'm no lezzy!' she said sharply.

Mel felt embarrassed while Spar and Bush looked hurt. Wire said: 'Sorry, it's just the way we do things here. It's all we've got to give each other. Well, maybe we'll see you in the rec room. By the way, have you checked the phone home list yet?'

'Oh, yes, thanks for reminding us,' said Mel.

They made their way along to the Hall notice board, feeling out of place as you did in any institution after regular hours and doubly so when naked. When they were out of earshot of Wire and her chain-sisters Mel said to Bolt: 'Did you have to be so rude? They were only trying to be friendly.'

'I've had enough fu...ing tits rubbed up against mine for one day!' Bolt said angrily.

'I think we've got the message,' said Cam.

The list said they were to report to Classroom 1.

They found Bradawl seated at his desk. A few other girls were crouched or sprawled about the room on mats chewing on pens as they composed letters and cards or speaking quietly into phones. Mel, Cam and Bolt went up to Bradawl's desk, remembering just in time to duck down into the open front and kiss his penis. Under his powerful gaze Mel and Cam stood before him meekly with their hands folded behind their backs while Bolt looked impassive.

'Well, what did you think of your first day at Gryndstone?' he asked.

Did he expect them to lie? Mel took a deep breath, choosing her words carefully. 'I think this is a cruel and perverted place, Headmaster.'

Bolt growled: 'This fu...ing collar won't let me say what I think... Headmaster.'

Cam just whimpered and clamped her lips shut.

Unexpectedly Bradawl smiled. 'You're feeling angry and resentful. That's perfectly normal. Don't worry, it'll pass.' He handed them phones labelled with their part names. 'These will record and playback voicemail only. You may file all your communications on them. You will record brief messages to whoever you think will be missing you, either family or close friends, telling them you are all right. You will explain you do not want to get into one to one conversations for obvious reasons and they should reply in the same way. After checking the content I'll pass them on to our representative in London, who will send them via your phones that he's monitoring. Their replies will be relayed back here in the same way. One exchange only tonight.'

Bolt gave her phone back. 'I'm not calling anybody and talking lies... Headmaster.'

'Honesty,' said Bradawl. 'An admirable virtue if practiced wisely. Then you are excused...'

Bolt left.

Lying on a mat Mel felt a brief flush of resentment at the thought of unknown people playing around with her phone, then realised ruefully that it was nothing compared to what they had already done to her body. She debated trying to hide some sort of clever coded SOS in her message, but she had no idea how. Perhaps the most important thing at this moment was to assure them she was all right. To her parents she said:

'This is just to let you know I'm OK. I'm so sorry for everything. Don't blame Maddy because I started it. I'll call again when I get myself sorted out. If you want to leave a message for me do it this way because I don't want to get into any more arguments, not after everything that's already been said. Maybe those things you called me were true but they still hurt! I still love you and hope you can forgive me but I think we all need some space and time apart right now.'

It was not any easy message to send but the next one was harder, especially as she could not say all she wanted knowing Bradawl would hear it first.

'Maddy, it's me. Don't worry I'm fine. I just had to get away because my being there only made things worse. Try not to feel too bad about the way Mum and Dad reacted. It just got out of hand. We all need some space to cool off. We'll work this out somehow. Maybe we'd better not talk in real time right now so voicemail me back. I want to hear your voice. Evenings are good for me. Whatever happens you know I love you.'

Mel and Cam handed their messages back to Bradawl, who listened to them to them on earphones so her family woes were not made public. At least it was one tiny shred of privacy they were still permitted, Mel thought.

Bradawl downloaded the messages into his pc and sent them off. 'First day calls usually receive quick replies,' he said. 'You may wish to wait.'

They sat in a corner.

'They're very well organized,' Cam said. 'I suppose by sending our messages from London nobody can trace them back here. Do you think they do the same kind of thing with letters?'

'Probably. If Bradawl's history lesson was true then they'd had a century and half practice at hiding kidnapped girls away.'

'I wasn't exactly kidnapped,' Cam said, 'but I know my family would freak out if they knew what they've done to me...' she faltered and bit her lip.

Mel hugged her awkwardly. 'I know.'

Bradawl was right. They both got replies back inside fifteen minutes.

Mel's father said: 'Your Mother was very worried about you. You should have called sooner. Of course we love you and want you back home, but first you must accept the seriousness of the terrible thing you did. You must repent fully so we can forgive you...'

Mel wished he had not used the word: "repent". It made it seem so cold, as though he was hiding his true feelings behind religious language. But then she supposed she had sinned.

Maddy said: 'God, I was so frightened you might have done something stupid! It's so good to hear your voice. Things are pretty bad here but I can't run off as well. I wish college started sooner then I'd have an excuse. Dad's gone all stiff and cold. I think Mum would like to say more but doesn't dare. Oh hell, we really screwed up…'

Mel played her messages over three times before she handed the phone back to Bradawl.

She and Cam walked back to the rec room. Cam was frowning in thought.

Mel did not want to pry but she felt she had say something. 'Everything ok?'

'Just… family things, you know,' Cam said

'I know.'

'And you?'

'The same. Family and… stuff. Still, Bolt's not had anybody to talk to. I suppose that must be even worse for her.'

'I suppose so.'

'Maybe we'd better see how she's doing.'

'Oh, do we have to?' Cam pleaded. 'I know it's sad that she's so screwed up, but it is a lot easier without her around getting us into trouble.'

'I know, but I think we've got to try. After all we're meant to be her "chain-sisters."'

'Except she's the one dragging us down!'

As they were peering inside the lowest level of the rec room looking for Bolt they saw Wire seated in a corner. She waved to them. Spar and Bush were in the other corner with their heads in magazines. Mel and Cam crawled over to Wire and lay down on a pile of cushions. As she sprawled out Mel found she could look up through the two glass panelled floors above her at kaleidoscope of bottoms flattened against the glass, dangling breasts and bared pouting pubes.

'I'm sorry about Bolt,' Mel said quickly.

'It's all right, we all took time settling in,' said Wire. 'Well, how did your first day go?'

'Bolt had... problems,' Cam admitted. 'And I felt... well, dirty hardly covers it.'

'I don't know how we got through it,' Mel admitted. 'If I'd ever dreamed of doing half those things they made us do today I'd have thought I'd be dead!' She frowned. 'Actually I should be freaking out right now. Why aren't we all going mad? I can't believe I'm even here talking about it like it was so... so ordinary!'

'Because here it is ordinary,' Wire said. 'Gryndstone is a school and we all have to go to lessons. It's what we all went through not so long ago, just with a twist. They've made learning how to be sex slaves no different from doing English or Des. Tec. You'll be amazed how quickly you can adjust. After a few weeks you'll even find some lessons a bit boring.'

Cam shook her head. 'I don't believe it. We can't keep having all those things stuck up us and being forced to come like that over and over. I ache so much! And we've got to do it all over again tomorrow! I can't do it...'

'Yes, you can,' Wire assured her. 'Every day it gets a littler easier. We all ache at first but our bodies keep coming back for more. You won't believe how often you can learn to come in one day with a little practice and with everybody doing the same thing all around you. After a while that becomes ordinary and normal as well. You even get competitive over it.'

'But it's all so cruel,' Cam protested. 'They're sadists!'

'No, that's the clever thing,' Wire said. 'I didn't believe it my first week, then I started to understand. Think how they could have made it so much worse for us.' She waved an arm about her. 'Instead they give us good food, time to recover in comfort, even TV and games. If they ran this place like a concentration camp 24/7 we'd have nothing to lose and try anything to escape. They don't want that. In a twisted way they're trying to make us feel as though we belong here.'

'Only as slaves,' Mel said. 'They're self-confessed male chauvinists!'

'Yeah, but I think it's more than that. You got the history lecture, right? They really believe they're saving us from ourselves.' Wire frowned. 'Maybe we need saving. None of us would be here if we were leading normal, happy, fulfilled lives, would we? That gives them an opening to turn us into something better.'

'Their personal sex machines!'

'But happy, well-adjusted sex machines,' Wire said. 'Which are respectable things to be in Shackleswell. You wait until you start your work experience days in town, then you'll see how what we learn here makes sense and fits in with local society. It may be perverted but it works.'

Her response surprised Mel. Wire sounded a well-educated girl and not the kind who would say such a thing. 'But who'd want to live like that?'

Wire shrugged. 'I really don't know anymore. I'd never imagined it would be me but now I'm not sure. You'd be safe, you'd have friends, you'd count for something and you wouldn't have to worry about where your next meal was coming from. For some girls those are better prospects than what they had before.'

Just then Mel became aware of a growing babble of voices from somewhere above them and looked up. A lot of breasts were bobbing and bottoms squirming across the glass floor of the top level. Then she heard a familiar angry voice rise above the mounting clamour: 'Give that fu… fu… thing back to me!'

'I think we've found Bolt,' Cam said.

The three of them scrambled out and up the stairs. On the top level they had to push their way through a crush of naked bodies to get to Bolt. She was kneeling in front of a game console wrestling breast to breast with another girl over possession of a hand controller.

'I had it first!' Bolt was shouting.

'But we always take turns,' the other girl protested.

'Slaves don't deserve fu… fugging turns!' Bolt shouted back.

'We still share and take turns amongst ourselves!'

'I haven't been ground down like the rest of you! Cowards should be used to having things taken away from them!'

Wire said urgently to Mel and Cam: 'You've go to stop this or we'll all be in trouble. You're her chain-sisters. You're meant to help her behave properly.'

'That's what we've been trying to do all day!' Mel and Cam pushed forward until they reached Bolt and together tried to pry the controller from her hands. 'Sorry, she hasn't adjusted yet,' Mel apologised to the other girl, who was marked CASTOR 126.

'Gerrrof me!' Bolt cried. 'It's mine!'

'What's going on here?'

Master Hawk was crouching down by the doorway, peering into the low room. Instantly all the girls ducked their heads and raised their bottoms submissively.

Hawk glared at the dishevelled forms of Bolt, Mel, Cam and Castor all clutching at the controller. 'Access to the rec room is a privilege. If you can't use its facilities in a civilised manner then you lose your rights to them.'

Wire spoke up quickly. 'Please, Master. It's just a new girl who needs to be taught a lesson about behaving politely. May we sort this out amongst ourselves?'

There were murmurs of agreement from the other girls.

Hawk considered for a moment and then nodded. 'You can use the washroom for an hour,' he said. He pointed at Bolt. 'But if she causes any more trouble the rec room is closed to all of you for a week.' Then he turned and left.

The huddled girls rose with sighs of relief all round. Then they turned to glare at Bolt.

'Sorry,' Wire said to Mel and Cam, 'but you're going to have to be punished along with Bolt. Trigyns have to take responsibility for each other. That's how it works.'

They closed in about them, caught hold of their arms and twisted them behind their backs, securing them with brightly coloured play cuffs from the toy racks. Then they led them out of the rec room. Bolt did not come quietly but she was outnumbered. For the first time Mel thought she looked genuinely scared.

Surrounded by two-dozen girls they were marched across the playground to the washroom. Mel saw some of them were carrying brightly coloured dildos, spreader bars and spanking paddles. Inside there was no master sitting on the central chair.

The girls led them across to the plinth of squat toilets, dragged them up the steps and bent them forward so their heads hung over the toilet holes. They spread their ankles and slid them under the mounting bars of the forked actuator arms that they pushed flat under them. Spreader bar cuffs went about their ankles, holding them in place. Ceiling chains were slid round the channels and the ends were wrapped about their cuffed wrists, which were pulled up into the air, bending their arms at the shoulders and forcing their shoulders still lower until their faces almost touched the rims of the drain holes.

Mel and Cam, although frightened, did not resist as they were secured. Bolt kicked and struggled against the girls holding her, choking out curses that were cut short by shocks from her collar as she was bent over. When they were secured with their bottoms facing outward, Wire moved round to stand against the back wall of the toilets where they could look up and see her and she could look out over the crowd of girls half-filling the room.

'We're here to punish Bolt 184 for being a general pain in the arse, being selfish and not sharing,' she announced.

There was a murmur of approval. Bobbin, looking troubled, quickly ran up the steps and whispered nervously in Wire's ear.

'And disrupting lessons for others by not trying hard enough in class,' Wire added, to more mutters of general agreement. 'As her chain-sisters, Spring 157 and Cam 031 are to share her punishment.'

'You sh... stinking cowards,' Bolt spat. 'Doing the master's work for them!'

'We're all in this together,' said Wire, squatting down and looking Bolt in the eye. 'Do what you want after you graduate but don't ruin school for us. You may not like it but it is teaching us what we've got to know to live in Shackleswell. Don't treat us with contempt.'

'Why fu... ing not, when you're learning how to be good cock-sucking slaves!' Bolt retorted.

'We're being realistic. This is not what we would have chosen but it is better than so many other things. For many of us it's all we've got. Afterwards at least we know we're going to belong in Shackleswell and we'll always have friends around us. That's important.'

'I don't f... ing need anybody! I'm getting out of here!'

'It doesn't look like it to me. All being a selfish loner has got you is more pain and humiliation that your chain-sisters have to share.'

Bolt twisted her head round to gaze at Mel and Cam dismissively. 'They just chained me up next to them yesterday. They're not any kind of sisters.'

'If you learn anything in Gryndstone it's that you always need your sisters. You can't live as close as we do without realizing that. Maybe this'll help you remember...' Wire took hold of Bolt's hair, opened her own thighs wide and peed full into her face.

Bolt shrieked and spluttered, screwing up her eyes against the stinging jet. When the last drips fell from Wire's slot she moved aside and another girl took her place.

Other girls were already squatting down in front of Mel and Cam. Streams of hot urine were sent spurting from the depths of silver-ringed lovemouths over their faces and into their hair.

Meanwhile other girls queued up to take advantage of their upturned bottoms and spread thighs to spank or penetrate them. Rubber paddles smacked and cracked, sending flashy shivers through their buttocks until they were glowing red. They did not cut the skin but they stung fiercely. Halves of double-ended dildos were thrust up into excited vaginas. They were moulded in plaint jelly-plastic and curved like bananas with a bristle of soft prongs on the inside middle of the curve and two mushroom-like plugs projecting from each side. These popped through labial rings, holding them inside the user. Eagerly the girls took their places on the steps behind Bolt, Mel or Cam and thrust the thick coloured phalluses into whatever nervously clenching anus or vagina as they wished. The pliancy of the dildos did not damage their passages but the force with which they were rammed into them made their holes distend and bulge painfully.

Assailed from every side, drenched in girl pee, they could only sob and shiver and groan in pain and shame. During the next hour every girl in the school called into the washroom to vent her displeasure and empty her bladder. It was a miserable degrading punishment, as it was intended.

Yet at some point as the degradation was piled upon her, Mel found the pressure building inside her and she had a brief shuddering orgasm. Through her misery she thought: how sick was that? What am I?

Finally, drained of their displeasure, their classmates uncuffed them and left them sprawled on the toilet plinth tiles, smarting, bruised and dripping with urine.

The last to leave were Wire and Bobbin. 'Sorry,' Bobbin said.

'No hard feelings,' Wire added. 'Better than a beating from the Masters.'

After a minute Cam levered herself feebly upright, clutching her sore vagina, her hair sodden and face wet with pee.

'You stupid, stupid girl!' she sobbed at Bolt. 'See where being hard gets you? From now on just keep away from me. And don't ever try tell me what to do again.'

That night Cam slept curled up in Mel's arms with her back to Bolt. Bolt huddled up on the other side of the mattress and said nothing. Mel had to admit it was a lot friendlier and warmer that way.

CHAPTER NINE

Mel, Cam and Bolt were all incredibly sore the next day, both inside and out, which made lessons even harder. The schoolmasters must have known what had happened but made no mention of it and somehow they survived without incurring further punishment. Bolt at least seemed to have been temporarily subdued by the wrath of her peers, which almost made their suffering worthwhile.

Despite the washroom incident Mel and Cam found the other girls friendly enough. They did not seem to hold any personal grudges against them once the point had been made. Clearly they sympathised with their problems with Bolt. Perhaps their suffering had had served its purpose because Bolt was now largely ignoring everybody else and they ignored her, except when lessons forced them into intimate contact.

Mel was worried that Bolt would lose control again, but she participated in the lessons just enthusiastically enough to avoid further punishment from the teachers and further warnings from the pupils while making it clear the contempt in which she held the masters and other girls for cooperating with "the enemy", as she regarded their masters. However Mel could not imagine her being allowed to graduate as a star pupil, which meant neither could she or Cam. It seemed that Bolt was now, after open insubordination had proven too painful, determined to make her point by trying to wear down the patience of their masters in the stubborn belief that they would actually give up on her. Mel was sure they would not be tricked so easily.

With the problem of Bolt at least temporarily under control the most surprising thing for Mel was how quickly life in Gryndstone became routine, just as Wire said it would. The staff behaved as though lessons in sexual submission, blind obedience and mechanical violation were perfectly normal and natural, and isolated from the rest of the world as the girls were it was easy to get drawn into that illusion. In a strange way it made it all tolerable. It was just what you did at school.

Daily they were made to perform acts that only a short while ago Mel would have called obscene, degrading and were undeniably often painful. Yet they were treated matter-of-factly as part of ordinary school lessons and were certainly easier to master than quadratic equations. All they had to do was surrender their pride and dignity and let their instincts take over. It helped that there were others to share their pain and frustration, reinforcing the bond of a chain sisterhood between them. They could complain to each other afterward how stretched their rectums felt after being impaled by a particularly large dildo or how sore their nipples were from tugging their rings on machine hooks. It was both mundane and unreal.

Of course it was not always a rubber or metal phallus. At least once a day one of the teachers had intercourse with them. They had to accept that a man with a stiff cock jutting out in front of him had every right to push it into whatever orifice he chose and it was their duty to satisfy him. With by now well-exercised passages they could accommodate the size easily enough, but it was the mental attitude that was a challenge. It was no use going cold and behaving mechanically. That was punished. They had to learn to feel passion and believe it was vital they drained every cock put inside them. It had its advantages. Even synthetic passion made them lubricate copiously and so made penetration more comfortable. After a while it became hard to tell the difference between that and genuine arousal. For gynatons, Mel suspected, that was a normal state of mind.

This led to the matter of orgasms. Mel could not decide whether they were compensations or curses.

She was soon having three or four a day during lessons and growing in intensity, which was treated within the walls of Gryndstone as perfectly normal. After all, as was made clear to them, that was just how healthy gynatons were expected to respond to restraint and sexual stimulation, whether it be with a real penis or a rubber one. On the positive side at least for a few seconds they blotted every other care from her mind. Even Bolt had them, though she made it clear as soon as possible afterward that she resented the experience. Other girls seemed to accept them and even boast about them. If you felt no guilt, then why not? Mel had not quite reached that stage yet.

Mel was unsure whether the increase in her sex drive was due to their perverted training, or being constantly naked amongst other naked girls with her nipples and vulva continually stimulated by their piercing rings. That at least would be understandable. It was more worrying to think it might also be in her nature.

The easiest transition Mel made was accepting lesbianism as an integral part of everyday life at Gryndstone. That it involved perverse and intimate sex with strangers had been the hardest adjustment, but once she got to know the girls it became less shameful and even at times fun. There was her own personal sense of guilt and disloyalty to overcome but she simply had no choice and knew that weighing herself down with more emotional baggage would be stupid.

Girls had always accepted such intimacy more readily than men and most of them seemed to cope. It was just something they did in class. Of course many of them did it out of lessons as well. They needed some safety valve in their enclosed world and this was the most natural one, though not yet for Mel. At night she and Cam continued to sleep in each other's arms but they had not made love, possibly because by then they were simply too exhausted.

Her strange new lifestyle was at odds with the messages from home that brought her back to reality and the dark guilt she felt.

Her parents kept asking her to admit what a terrible thing she had done.

The trouble was she could not do that either. She could not take back what had happened and part of her did not want to, despite the anguish it had caused those she loved. Maddy just wanted to be close to her again.

'I understand why it's not a good idea for you to come back home but can we meet somewhere else?' she asked plaintively.

How could Mel explain she was a chained sex-slave in training and her masters probably would not allow family visits? She managed to construct a plausible excuse.

'If dad found out we were meeting secretly you know what he'd think. Let's just be patient and keep going the way we are. Don't worry, I'm eating regularly and getting plenty of exercise...'

Perhaps it was easier to face perverted life in Gryndstone than contemplate trying to put her personal life back together in the "real" world. She was physically safer than she would have been living in some rundown part of London, as long as you accepted living as a sex slave as "safer." Was that why her heart was not in trying to escape? If she had been given a chance then instinct would have driven her to make the attempt, but she did not have the urge to try to search for a way out like Bolt, who was always looking for some weakness in school security. She supposed being trained as a sex slave was a good excuse for not getting about so much, but did it mask an unpalatable truth? If she waited long enough, would she ever be able to muster the will to escape? Was life in Gryndstone taking her over?

They saw fresh batches of frightened girls come into the school and they were not the new girls any more. They mastered the routine. In a week life seemed almost tolerable. Mel began to wonder if as Wire had said, for some girls there who had endured tougher lives than she had, perhaps slavery in Shackleswell did not seem such a bad option. They had been enslaved and yet they were the focus of so much attention they felt in a strange way important. Except of course that it was morally obscene and completely wrong, as Mel had to keep reminding herself.

There were more confessions in school assembly. Mel could not imagine Bolt putting herself through that. Would Cam do it? What would she herself have to confess? No, she could not do that.

Trigyns also graduated. They were called up to the front by Bradawl, their school ties were removed and small medallions were hung on their collars in their place. They kissed all the teachers' cocks and thanked them. The girls seemed excited to be going as though they had just won golden tickets to wonderful jobs. At break Bradawl led them through the playground, hugging and kissing the other girls on the way. Then they went through the door of Miss Trunnion's office and that was the last they saw of them.

Then came Mel's second Sunday at Gryndstone.

Sundays were rest days after morning exercise and assembly where sore passages could recover from relentless penetration. The first Sunday had been wet and Mel and the other girls had spent most of the day lounging about the rec room watching films. This Sunday, however, dawned bright and clear.

Sunday assembly was more like a church service and Miss Trunnion joined the Masters on the stage.

As the girls knelt impaled on their mats Bradawl read out an excerpt from W.S.Rowland's private research notes, such as details of how he had learned to control a particular girl he was experimenting on through inducing multiple orgasms. It was treated as if it was an uplifting passage from the Bible. Perhaps to Gryndstone girls that was what it was intended to be. It was certainly the rulebook of their life.

This second Sunday Bradawl said: 'As it's such a fine day we shall have a school outing to Rowland Park.'

The assembled girls greeted this news with great excitement, suggesting many had been on such trips before. Mel felt a thrill herself. For the first time they would be getting out of school.

Packed lunches were handed out in small light backpacks together with rolled foam rubber ground sheets that they could string across their shoulders. A couple of girls were also laden with bags of inflatable balls, Frisbees and a rounders set. The masters then went round cuffing the girls' hands behind them and then hooking red ball gags strung on elastic cords onto the side rings of their collars.

'There will be no eating or talking while you are on the train,' Bradawl said. 'In the park you will be in your school uniform in public so you will behave as befits Gryndstone girls.'

Mel exchanged bemused glance with Cam and even Bolt did not try to disguise her puzzlement. She had imagined he had meant some sort of private park. How publicly could they possibly be displayed in what passed for Gryndstone uniforms? Also what train was he talking about?

While they were being kitted out, Bradawl, Hawk and Puncheon removed their robes and replaced their mortarboards with straw boaters. They also closed up their tailored trouser flaps, concealing their genitals. After days of staring at their members in varied states of arousal it was almost a shock not to find them there.

Led by the three teachers and with Miss Trunnion wearing a summer frock, in attendance, the girls were marched down the playground in their coffles and through a green door at the other end of the terrace from the office entrance. Mel recalled seeing coffles of girls being escorted through the doors on a few occasions but she had never asked what lay inside.

Within was a plain square brick room with small barred windows. In the middle was the housing, winding wheels and gates for a goods elevator that vanished into the depths. A wooden platform running on rails up the shaft served as the lift itself. The walls of the room were lined with four chimneybreasts with large open hearths but no grates. Mel could feel a draft blowing through them.

Round the central well, enclosed by mesh panels, wound a square spiral of wooden stairs. They clattered down these flights of stairs for several turns until they came to the bottom. Here the stairs opened onto what looked like a small underground station lit by electric laps. It was set on a side loop off a straight mainline, as though it was a halt to allow fast through trains to bypass slower stopping trains. There was a sign on the wall that read: GRYNDSTONE HALT. Mounted on the far wall of the main track was another sign: CIRCLE LINE

It seemed Gryndstone had its own underground train station.

As they were led closer to the platform edge Mel saw the rails running through the station were of a very narrow gauge. After the loop rejoined the main line at sets of points at either end of the station it vanished into the mouths of tunnels too low to stand upright in and far too small to take regular underground trains. There was no sign of electric power rails, yet all the brickwork looked soot free and the air was fresh. What sort of trains could run along such lines?

Bradawl consulted his watch. 'It should be along very shortly,' he announced.

As if on cue there came the sound of wheels rattling along the track, slowing as they got closer. A low-slung train pulled off the main line onto the platform loop and the driver drew it to a smooth halt.

It was pulling five low, lightweight, open carriages. Four had simple metal lattice frame sides and reminded Mel of cattle trucks while the fifth, just behind the engine, had solid sides and was fitted with three rows of comfortable double seats. The four trucks were floored with sponge rubber matting and had each had two rows of six phalluses rising vertically up from the floor, rather like the ones they squatted on in assembly. The frame sides were also hung with chains and fastening rings. In the last carriage a guard with peaked cap, flag and whistle, rode on a small fold-down seat. There was no problem guessing which carriages they would be travelling in.

However it was not the carriages that riveted Mel's attention, it was the driving engine. It was not electrically powered.

Two naked girls with strong thighs and firm buttocks lay side by side and face down imprisoned within a cylindrical metal frame reminiscent of the boiler section of an old-fashioned steam engine, which rested on four rail wheels, the front pair smaller than the rear. Their arms were stretched out in front of them and cuffed to the frame that carried buffers and lamps. Padded trays to which they were firmly strapped supported their chests and stomachs. Their legs were cuffed to sets of bicycle-like pedals and gears that were connected to the rear set of larger drive wheels.

Behind them sat the driver in an open cab above the rear drive wheels so that he could look over the top of the front section containing the two girls. He had some simple controls in front of him that connected to the wheel, gears and his living pistons in ways Mel could not make out, but the upturned buttocks of the two girls were bright pink.

Suddenly the photo on the school wall made sense and the scope of Shackleswell's secret world made a quantum leap in scale and audacity in Mel's mind. These people actually had a miniature railway line under their city with slave-girl powered engines carrying more slave girls as goods. Of course Wire could probably have told her about it, but obviously Mel had never asked. Why should she? It was staggering.

The guard assisted the teachers in loading almost forty naked girls onto his train as if he did it every day, which obviously he did. They simply squatted down impaling themselves in tight double rows in the cattle wagons and their coffle chains were clipped to the sides. Then the teachers took their seats up front.

The guard blew his whistle and waved his flag and the train began to move off, slowly at first but picking up speed steadily. It clicked over the points and rejoined the main line. Could two girls pull so much weight? Evidently they could with the help of gears and level rails. They plunged into the tunnel, which was illuminated at intervals by electric lamps, and sped along in almost perfect silence with only the occasional rattle of couplings and steady burr of metal wheels on rail.

Mel's training in MI began to assert itself. She could feel the slight vibration of the wheels and the click of joints and points transmitted up inside her by her phallus. This was what it felt like to be connected to a real moving machine. It was insidiously arousing.

Twisting her head round Mel saw the tunnel walls speeding past her were of painted brick, not prefabricated concrete sections. They were clean and well maintained but looked old. When had they been built? Had the girl engines been designed to fit through them, or had they been made to take their unique engines? Had Rowland himself planned the system?

After a few minutes the train emerged from the tunnel to pass through another station. The sign over the platform read: THE MILLHOUSE. Here a shorter girl-powered train was standing in the siding with slave girls supervised by an overseer unloading trolleys of boxes and cartons off flat wagons. A goods train?

Soon the tunnel widened to accommodate a second line running in parallel to theirs. Another girl-powered train went past in the opposite direction. This one carried no goods but drew three passenger carriages. Mel saw the sweating faces of the girls powering the train and the rings of their dangling breasts threaded through by a horizontal rod linking them to the frame of the engine. She also glimpsed the ordinary carefree faces of their passengers as they sped by. To them it seemed riding on a train pulled by slave girls was just normal everyday life.

They passed through a larger station called: GIN STREET JUNCTION, which seemed to be an interchange with another line. Old names like that suggested the network had been around for some time. How big was it? This was a Sunday and it seemed quite busy. Presumably it would be even more so through the week. They were running on the "circle line" so how many more lines were there? No reason why they did not serve the whole City.

The train begin to slow. It clicked over some points and pulled up at a station called: ROWLAND PARK, which boasted two loops of platform track. Another girl-train was already standing at the station disembarking a dozen people, including a party of three middle-aged couples leading a naked slave girl with a large picnic hamper strapped to her back. Was this what Bradawl had meant by being in public? The couples looked the gaggle of naked schoolgirls over with unabashed interest and Mel felt a sudden shy blush coming on. They were the first strangers to see them for nearly two weeks.

The coffles of girls were disembarked and climbed a spiral of stone stairs back up to ground level. They emerged from a low square building into warm bright sunshine. About them were rolling lawns, stands of trees, fountains, benches, statues and flowerbeds crisscrossed by loops and sweeps of gravel paths. There were people out walking or jogging and some had already laid out rugs and picnic cloths on the grass. Amongst the clothed bodies were flashes of bare flesh and the glint of cuffs and collars.

Mel shivered, acutely aware of being naked and exposed in the open before strange eyes. Suddenly the school playground seemed a very cosy place.

As he led the school party along one of the broader pathways Bradawl explained: 'Rowland Park is only open to gynaton-using Shackleswell citizens. As you can see many bring their own girls here for exercise.' They passed a group of slave girls throwing a beach ball about apparently unsupervised. 'The park has a secure perimeter so gynatons can be allowed to run free within its bounds.'

Mel saw Bolt staring at the girls with sudden interest.

'Many sporting and cultural events involving gynatons are also held here,' Bradawl continued, pointing to a bandstand nestling between the trees and what looked like a small open-air theatre. 'In many ways it is the true social and cultural hub of the city. It was intended as the prototype of similar parks Rowland hoped would be founded in towns across the country as others took up his eminently logical theory of gynaetics. Alas, this was not to be.'

Mel tried to imagine the whole country run on Rowland's principles and felt dizzy at the thought. It was crazy and yet, just suppose enough influential Victorians had taken his ideas up. They had been known believe some pretty weird things. Might this scene have become normal countrywide?

'This is the centre of the park and where we shall all meet again this afternoon,' Bradawl said.

They had reached a spot where half a dozen paths met at a circle of gravel that surrounded a substantial monument. It was like a six-sided market cross with a small clock tower on its roof and drinking fountains mounted on the inside of the pillars. Raised on a plinth under the middle of the cross was a bronze statue of W.S.Rowland depicted seated on another of his girl-powered machines. It resembled an old-fashioned penny-farthing bike except that the huge front wheel had been expanded sideways to form an oblate cage in which a naked girl was running round hunched over like a hamster.

As they got closer Mel saw the drinking fountains were of course fitted with phallic spouts. Below them were low wide bronze pans shaped a little like water-lily leaves with another fountain playing across them, the function of which Mel could not at first work out. Then she saw a slave girl run into the cross, squat down over one of the pans and pee gratefully and copiously. The small fountain playing over it washed her groin as she relieved herself. When she was done she unconcernedly shook the drips off her pubes and scampered away again.

They were alfresco pee pans that gynatons had to use like dogs, Mel realised. How very natural that they should relieve themselves under the gaze of Rowland's cold bronze eyes. No doubt that was how he would have wanted it.

The Gryndstone girls were ungagged and uncuffed. Bradawl pointed to the clock tower. 'Listen for the chimes through the day. You will all be back here by four o'clock,' he told them. 'In the meantime enjoy the park and have fun...'

The girls chattered excitedly as they broke up into smaller groups. Some took play items from the sports bag. In a few minutes they had spread out along the paths and between the trees.

Mel and Cam looked about them, momentarily at a loss. Suddenly they had hours of virtual freedom on their hands and did not know what to do with them. Nearly two weeks of rigid routine and confinement in the school grounds made it hard to plan for roaming about at will. Yet the teachers were no longer paying them any attention and were carrying the hamper off across the grass in search of a picnic spot. It seemed they really were free to go where they wished, as long as it was within the park. Hesitantly Cam picked a Frisbee out of the bag. 'Maybe we can play with this?' she asked.

Bolt, however, had a determined look on her face. She set off briskly along one of the broader pathways. Mel and Cam exchanged worried glances and hurried after her.

'You're not going to do anything silly, are you?' Cam asked.

'I'm just going to look around,' Bolt replied noncommittally. 'No harm in that, is there?'

'Would this looking round have anything to do with trying to find places where you could climb a wall or slip out through a gate?' Mel asked.

'Bradawl said we should have fun. This is what gives me fun. You don't have to come.'

'You don't really think you'll just be able to walk out of here, do you?' Cam asked. 'The Headmaster said it had a secure perimeter.'

'Then there's no harm in me looking, is there?' Bolt countered.

After a few minutes becoming used to seeing so many strangers around them, Mel decided it was curiously liberating walking around naked in such surroundings on warm day. Of course people looked at them as they passed, which was natural and even a little exciting, because as naked schoolgirls went they were pretty hot. However nobody was stopping them going where they wished. They were enjoying a kind of freedom.

Cam seemed to have the same feelings. 'This is actually quite nice.' She glanced at Bolt's set expression. 'Please don't spoil it.'

They came to a junction with another path. Crossing in front of them was something that stopped them short.

An elderly man was seated in a lightweight wire-mesh chair slung between two wire-spoked wheels a metre across. Slender shafts curved up from their axel to hitch onto the harness of the ponygirl pulling him along.

The harness bound her naked body tightly, with straps about her waist and crossing between her breasts. A narrower strap ran down into her bare pussy cleft where it was threaded through her labial rings, passed between her thighs and emerged from the cleavage of her taut buttocks. Above this a fake ponytail jutted out from the base of her spine. Her arms were bent at the elbows by linked cuffs between her wrists and upper arms while her hands were balled up inside fake rubber hooves, making it look as though she was pawing the air. Similar hooves enclosed her toes and the balls of her feet, which ankle braces forced her to run upon. A web of bridle straps, rings and buckles enclosed her face and blinkers shielded her eyes. A bobbing white plume was fastened to the strap that went across her forehead. Her hair, which was long and silvery, had been pulled through a ring in her bridle and hung down the supple curve of her back. The ends of reins were clipped to her nipple rings and passed up through rings extending from the sides of her collar, where they ran down over her shoulders to her driver's right hand. In his left he held a long carriage whip. Her bottom showed the pink stripes of its cuts,

They watched her trot away along the path in silence. Then Bolt said: 'You want to know why I'm trying to escape. That's why. Do you want to end up like that?'

Mel could think of no reply. The pony girl had looked achingly beautiful in her way but of course it had to be wrong. It was somehow more blatant than the girl-powered trains. They at least were practical in their way. The pony girl was being driven about primarily for show, to be displayed as a man's possession. Perhaps there was a self-indulgent side to Shackleswell life at odds with Rowland's logical mechanistic system of slavery. It went to show how little they really knew about the city.

They reached the edge of the park. Behind a screen of trees they saw a high brick boundary wall stretching away to the left and right. Close to was a gateway through which a steady stream of visitors was filing into the park. Mel, Bolt and Cam moved closer. There was a double set of large solid offset gates that meant you could not see directly in or out. The people entering had to then pass through turnstiles under the watchful gaze of men in blue uniforms who were presumably park wardens.

In such circumstances security was very simple. Free people wore clothes and did not have part names stamped on their foreheads or collars round their necks or cuffs on their wrists. Slave girls tended to stand out in a crowd.

'I don't think we can just walk out of here,' Cam said.

'And those walls look pretty high,' Mel observed.

They watched the flow of visitors for several minutes while Bolt scowled at the vigilant wardens. Then a couple of young woman amongst the incoming stream caught Mel's eye. They were identically dressed in grey thigh-length belted raincoats, ankle boots, scarves around their necks and headbands across their foreheads holding back their hair. They carried a picnic bag between them. As they passed through the turnstiles they showed something hung about their necks to the warden who nodded and waved them on.

The two women walked a little way from the gate then stopped not far from the watching girls and put down their bag. Unbelting their coats they stripped them off gratefully. Underneath they were naked. They had rings through their nipples and bare labia, which were stamped with part names. Cuffs on their wrists had charm chains threaded through their securing rings. They pulled off their headbands, exposing the print of part names and unwound their scarves revealing slave collars. Casually slinging their coats over their shoulders they took up their bag again and carried on through the trees.

Mel, Cam and Bolt gaped at them and then each other in astonishment. Had they just seen apparently free people turn themselves into slave girls?

United in confusion they followed the women through the trees until they found them laying out rugs on a grassy slope. By now they had pulled off their boots revealing cuffed ankles.

Mel felt absurdly nervous but she had to know what was going on. 'Excuse me, but are you really gynatons?'

The pair smiled up at them in good-natured amusement. The names on their foreheads were CHAIN 041 and SPINDLE 220. At least part stamps made introductions simple.

'Well don't we look like gynatons?' said Chain. 'Just like you're obviously Gryndstone girls.'

'Does Mr Hawk still teach PE?' Spindle asked.

'Er… yes,' said Cam.

'Has he had you yet? He's huge!'

Bolt was not going to be sidetracked. 'You look like slaves now, but you came in dressed like ordinary people.'

'Well we don't walk the streets bare-assed,' Chain said. 'There are sometimes visitors in the town who wouldn't understand.'

'Actually it's a pain because wearing clothes isn't very comfortable after a few years of going round stripped,' Spindle confided.

'But today's our day off and the weather was good we thought we'd come here.'

'You have days off!' Bolt exclaimed in disbelief.

The pair looked surprised. 'Of course,' Spindle said. 'Every gynaton needs time for rest and recreation. We wouldn't work very efficiently otherwise.'

'So you're just allowed to walk out?' Bolt said, still sounding suspicious.

Chain lifted what looked a small medallion that was clipped to the front of her collar. It had the current date and a code number stamped on it. 'We have to carry day passes from our master, of course, but as long as we have these we can go where we like.'

'We're going to see a film later,' Spindle added.

'How are you going to get in to see a film?' Bolt asked. 'Don't tell me you get pocket money as well?'

'Well, we have gyntokens,' Chain said, dipping her hand into the pocket of her coat lying beside her and bringing out a couple of what looked like bronze coins the size of commemorative crowns. 'These are as good as money for us. Every business in Shackleswell accepts them.'

'And if you want more you can always offer a screw,' Spindle added with a grin.

A true slave economy, Mel thought.

'But why don't you just run away?' Bolt asked.

The pair looked bemused. 'Where would we want to run to?'

An hour later Mel, Cam and Bolt were lying on their groundsheets in a small sunlit hollow in a corner of the park backed by a stand of trees eating their packed lunches. It was nice to laze in the warm sun and simply do nothing, Mel thought. Gynatons did need their R&R.

It was a novelty in itself to eat food with their hands and not suck it through a phallic-shaped feeding tube, although they could not help noticing there was a certain phallic theme to their meal. Each lunch bag contained fruit juices in tubular foil packs, large cooked vegetarian sausages, bridge rolls, gherkins and a banana. There was also a tub of creamy dip with large thick carrots.

Bolt sprawled on her stomach eating mechanically, still deep in thought following their conversation with Chain and Spindle that had revealed that slave life in Shackleswell was far more complicated than they had imagined. At least it had diverted her from trying to find some weak spot in the park perimeter, for which Mel was grateful. Cam and Mel lay on their backs with their dip pots nestled between their breasts crunching carrots.

'Do you think this is all part of our conditioning?' Cam said unexpectedly, as she licked the cream off her carrot suggestively.

Mel turned to look at her. 'What do you mean?'

'Giving us days off like this, allowing us a bit of freedom in a nice park, a little luxury like the rec room.

Is it all designed to make being turned into a slave just bearable so we accept it and don't make trouble?'

Mel shrugged. 'It might be. Or it might simply be a sensible way of keeping slaves happy and healthy. Both possibly. Same thing in the end.'

'But do they really care for us? Can you have humanitarian slave owners?

'Maybe you can in Shackleswell. If you believe their reasoning that we really are sort of inferior animals who need looking after for our own good. By those standards they probably think they are being kind to us.'

'Chain and Spindle seemed pretty happy.'

'They did,' Mel admitted.

'Brainwashed,' Bolt said bluntly.

'I think it has to be more than that,' Mel said. 'This town, this whole way of life, couldn't have lasted so long without finding some sort of balance that keeps the girls genuinely contented, that gives them some something back for what they've given up.'

Cam nodded and then frowned. 'But… is it right?'

Mel did not have a chance to answer because just then a drawling male voice said loudly: 'Well, what do we have here? A trigyn of pretty Gryndstone schoolgirls having a picnic all on their own in the woods?'

Caught by surprise, Mel, Cam and Bolt rolled over onto their knees, spilling their food onto the grass.

Three young men in coloured shirts with rolled-up sleeves, white flannel trousers and straw boaters were looking down at them. Instinctively the girls lowered their heads to the grass and raised their bottoms submissively as they had been taught in D&SK.

'Good afternoon, Masters,' they said meekly.

The young men, actually hardly more than boys Mel realised and certainly no older than they were themselves, walked round them and looking into their upturned bottoms. Mel saw the bulges in the front of their trousers, which had tailored flaps like their teachers', growing by the second. She felt her stomach knot in anticipation while her pussy clenched. She knew what was coming.

'Lazing around stuffing themselves, I see,' said the one in the lime green shirt, grinning hugely.

'I'm not sure if that's allowed,' said his companion in pink mischievously.

'Aren't we the ones meant to stuff their kind?' said Yellow, making a feeble joke as he tried to sound assured.

They're beginners like us, Mel thought.

'Do you think you've got something to stuff them with?' Green wondered.

'Oh, I've got something good,' said Pink, pushing his hips forward.

'They've got to let us do this, right?' Yellow asked anxiously.

'They've got to do whatever we tell them,' said Green. 'They've got to obey free men. That's what they teach them at school.'

'But they don't belong to us…'

'If they belong to the school they belong to everybody. They've got no day pass fobs so they're not protected.' He looked down at the girls sternly. 'Put your arms behind your backs,' he commanded.

Mel, Cam and Bolt obeyed. It was true. They were Gryndstone schoolgirls. They were there to serve and obey.

'See. Now we have some fun…'

The boys clipped their wrist cuffs together. Pulling the girls' heads up by their hair they took up the red ball gags that had been dangling almost unnoticed on their collars all morning and pushed them into their mouths. Then they threw the girls down on their backs on their mats.

'Spread those legs wider, gyns,' Green said, kicking at their feet.

Automatically Mel, Cam and Bolt presented themselves as they had been taught at school, spreading their thighs wide and flat and bending their knees so they exposed their groins to the maximum. Their smooth ringed mounds stood out proudly between the big tendons of their thighs with their ringed clefts already beginning to part wide as they pulsed with newly stirred arousal.

'Oh... wow,' Yellow said.

The boys hesitated, licking their lips at the sight, suddenly seeming less assured than they had at first. Their manner was awkward and a little old-fashioned. Was that the style in Shackleswell? For all their outward show they were not experienced. How many girls had they had in their power like this before, Mel wondered.

However base animal instinct ensured they would not falter now. They pulled the flaps of their trousers wide, freeing slim, stiff young cocks that seemed to spring to attention. Then they practically threw themselves down on their captives, thrusting their straining penises wildly about, sliding their shafts through the girls' slots before finding the mouths of their vaginas.

Pink mounted Bolt while Green slid into Cam. Yellow shirt grasped Mel's hips and rammed his cock into her passage without any concern for her comfort. She expected nothing less.

After hardly more than a minute of frantic pounding into the girls' groins that set their breasts jiggling, the boys spilt their seed inside them in lusty spurts. Then one by one they sagged over their captives' sweaty bodies, panting and exultant, and lay still.

Mel squirmed under Yellow-shirt's weight as he lay with his head pillowed on her breasts, still squeezing on his softening cock with her sheath. She found her overriding emotion was not disgust but frustration. He'd come too quickly for her. She was turning into a real slut.

Gradually the boys stirred on their living flesh mattresses and looked at each other with sheepish triumph.

'That was incredible!' Yellow admitted. 'It was like… like she was sucking it out of me with her pussy. What about yours?' he asked Green.

'She was really hot and wet inside.' He turned to Pink who was lying on top of Bolt. 'What about yours?'

'Yeah, hot too, and look at the size of her nipples.' He tugged casually on Bolt's rings that were standing out on the swollen peaks of her breasts. Bolt's eyes bulged and she snivelled in pain.

Grinning hugely the boys realised they had the most perfect playthings at their mercy. They spent a minute slapping and squeezed the girls' breasts in delight, flicking and twisting their nipple rings and watching the girls' faces contort as they whimpered in pain.

'Don't they make funny noises?' Yellow said.

'Swap you for her next time?' Green suggested to Pink.

'Ughh! I'm not going in her hole now you've used it,' Oink said with a shudder.

'They've got other holes, you know,' Green pointed out. 'For a start they can suck us clean…'

The boys grinned at each other in renewed delight.

They swapped over girls and knelt across the chests of their new mounts so they could pull out their gags and push their sticky penises into their mouths for cleaning. Mel had Pink's shaft in hers and she tasted Bolt's juices on it as she sucked it clean. Just treat it like a feeding phallus, Mel thought.

Under their ministrations the boys' cocks swiftly revived and stiffened again as only young cocks could. In a few minutes they were grasping the girls by the hair and grinding their faces into their groins as they thrust clumsily into their throats.

'I'm going to…. come in her mouth…' Yellow gasped as he

'She'll swallow it down,' Oink groaned. 'They like the taste…'

The boys spouted again, nearly choking the girls in the process, but obediently they swallowed it down. It was instinctive. Sperm must not be wasted.

When the boys had recovered they climbed off their chests and pushed the gags back into the girls' mouths. Their cocks lolled semi-hard and shiny.

'That was… amazing,' Yellow panted. 'They just lap it up.'

'Can you do it once more?' Green panted. 'Then that'd mean we've done the set.'

'You mean up their bottom holes?' said Pink. 'I don't know.'

'Are they clean up there?' Yellow asked.

'Of course,' Green assured him. 'They're flushed out and greased several times a day. It's what their bum holes are made for.'

'But they're smaller than their pussy holes. Won't it hurt them?'

'What does that matter?'

Nothing, Mel thought.

They rolled the girls over onto their stomachs to survey their final goals. They handled them almost as though they were inanimate objects. They were not remotely interested in their feelings. All they were to them were pleasurable mute female bodies conveniently at their disposal.

Curiously they pulled their bottom cheeks wide to study the tightly puckered anuses deep in their buttock valleys. Sensitised by their anal training, their glistening orifices clenched and pouted at the boys under the stimulation from their curious fingering, much to their amusement.

'I know, before we use their bums we've got to spank them to make them open up properly,' Green said. 'It's what they expect.'

'But we didn't bring a cane,' Pink pointed out.

They found some dead twigs under the trees that they could bundle up into workable birch lashes. They pulled girls up onto their knees with their faces on the ground and bottoms raised and took turns moving between them and swiping the lashes across the posterior of their choice. They chuckled as they made them frantically bob and weave about. The twigs not only scored their shivering buttocks but their vulvas as they pouted from between their thighs, still leaking fluid from their first usage.

The moans of the girls and the scarlet blush spreading across their bottoms filled the boys with sadistic delight and renewed vigour. Their cocks, bobbing freely in front of their trousers, grew hard once more. Throwing their lashes aside they plunged into the welcoming hot tightness of their mounts

Mel found herself sighing with relief as Green's shaft slid up inside her rectum and she clenched on it gratefully. Better a cock up her rear than a stinging scratchy birch lashing any day, though the pain had its uses and now a little sodomy was what she needed to... ahhhh... she came at last.

When they were done and finally spent, the boys sagged across their mounts while they recovered.

'These three are well stuffed,' Green declared, lightly slapping Mel's bottom as she curled up limply under him dribbling about her gag. 'They've been bloody good rides.'

The other two murmured agreement, gazing down appreciatively at the sweaty bodies under them.

Reluctantly they withdrew their by now soft penises from their clenching anal rings, trailing sticky threads after them. Kneeling over the girls' heads they wiped their shafts clean on their hair and then tucked their members away.

Pink glanced over the girls' half eaten lunches. 'Maybe we should let them get back to feeding.'

'Or,' Green said with a grin, surveying the contents of the open lunchboxes and the girls' still upturned haunches, 'let's leave them properly stuffed, sort of something to remember us by.'

'Talking about remembering, don't forget the tokens,' said Pink.

'I know the rule,' Green said. 'They can have both at the same time.'

He took three slave tokens from his pocket and pushed one each into Mel, Cam and Bolt's still wet and distended vaginas. 'That is for your trouble,' he said slowly and formally.

Then the boys forced unpeeled bananas into their slots, pushing the tokens all the way up them until only the stalks showed between their lips. The girls groaned as their sore passages were so roughly plugged.

'Who eats gherkins?' Pink said, holding one up in disgust.

'Nobody,' Green agreed, 'but we can do something else with them.'

Green pried apart Mel's buttocks and forced the gherkin into her anus until the end vanished inside her and her sphincter closed about it. The others laughed, then did the same to Cam and Bolt.

Finally the boys stood up, dusting off their trousers and smiling down on the huddled, well-used and abused bodies of their prey whose orifices were bulging unnaturally with their parting gifts. The cowed girls looked back up at them tearfully with fear and pleading in their eyes and Mel saw the boys swell with the warm glow of satisfaction of a job well done.

'Um, have you got a cuff key to undo them?' Yellow asked.

'Oh bloody heck, no!' Green exclaimed. 'Never mind, they'll manage somehow. They're used to being bound up.' He patted Mel on the head. 'You were all nice and hot and juicy,' he said by way of praise.

The other boys did the same and then they strode off through the trees whistling jauntily.

Mel, Bolt and Cam lay still for a few minutes recovering their strength. Then they squirmed about awkwardly until they could use their cuffed hands to pull each other's gags out.

After what they had just been through ordinary women would have been in shock, having hysterics or screaming for the police about now, Mel thought. However if this day had proved anything it was that they were no longer ordinary women. They had been multiply violated but they were Gryndstone girls and they had different priorities.

'A banana, a gherkin and a big coin!' Cam said bitterly. 'Oww! The little b… beasts! And why shove a token up us anyway?'

'A sort of tip, I suppose,' said Mel. 'Compensation for our "trouble" he said. Maybe every slave that gets an unauthorised screwing on Sundays in the park gets them. Tradition probably.'

'What are we going to do now?' Cam asked plaintively. 'We can't get our cuffs undone without a key.'

'We pack up best we can and then find the teachers. We don't want to leave a mess behind.'

'It was such a lovely spot,' said Cam regretfully.

'It still is,' said Mel.

'It's just the people you meet that lowers the tone,' said Bolt.

Mel looked at her expecting some tirade about what had been done to them to follow, but that was it. Bolt had actually made a little joke about their ordeal.

'Well,' Mel chuckled, 'boys will be boys…'

They squatted down amongst the trees and managed to expel the remains of the bananas and gherkins, but the big tokens remained lodged high up inside them beyond the play of their internal muscles.

'We'll need our hands free to get these out,' said Mel.

With mouths and cuffed hands they managed to gather up their possessions. Then, walking in slight waddles to favour their sore orifices and ever sorer welted bottoms, they set out back towards the cross. Bolt slogged along beside them, seeming to be accepting everything with untypical stoicism. By the time they reached the masters sprawled about on the grass not far from the cross their inner thighs were wet with the oozing remains of the boys spent sperm.

'Excuse us, Headmaster,' Mel said plaintively. 'We've had a little trouble. Could you uncuff us please?'

They had to explain how it happened and Bradawl questioned them closely. Not if they had suffered, of course. 'Did they enjoy using you? Did you give satisfaction?'

'We think so, Headmaster. They said we were good rides.'

'And they properly compensated you.'

'Yes, Headmaster.'

'Then you performed as Gryndstone girls should. Well done indeed. Now clean yourselves up…'

They cooled their bottoms and washed their pussies clean in the pans under the cross beneath Rowland's stern gaze. With a lot of jiggling and probing they managed to recover the gyntokens.

'I suppose you could say we made a profit on the day,' Mel observed.

Back at school that evening Mel, Cam and Bolt had to tell the story several times to their fellow pupils who listened in rapt attention. Many had been on training days in town but none had yet faced an unplanned real-life situation. Their audience ohhed and ahed as the gory details were recounted, envied the fact that they had already earned themselves slave tokens and sympathised with their thrashed bottoms. But not a single one suggested that what the boys had done to them had been wrong. It was simply the Shackleswell way of life.

'You did great,' said Wire. 'We'll make Gryndstone girls out of you yet.'

That night as Cam lay curled up in Mel's arms she said: 'I was so frightened while they were having us. It wasn't like a lesson in school and it felt dangerous. They might have done anything to us. Yet at the same time it was a sort of thrill. Then afterwards when the Headmaster said we'd done well I felt proud.'

'Did you come when the boys were having you? I think that's important.'

'Oh, I did and it felt good.' Cam sighed. 'But it was actually wrong, wasn't it?'

'Yes, at least it would be more or less anywhere else outside Shackleswell.'

'So then why did I come? How can I enjoy something like that? What's this place doing to us?'

Unexpectedly Mel felt Bolt suddenly cuddling up to them, adding her blanket and body heat to theirs. It was the first time she had shown any inclination to sleep together like other girls did. Her body felt nice but this sudden turnabout was disturbing.

'What are you doing?' Mel asked nervously as she felt Bolt's arms slide round her.

'Being a proper sharing chain-sister, of course. That's what you wanted, right?'

'Um, well, yes.'

'You want to know what this place is doing to us?' Bolt said to Cam, a razor edge entering he voice. 'Well, it thinks it's grinding us down into little identical model slave girls, that's what. They're also so sure it works they think we'll all end up brainwashed like Chain and Spindle and won't have the guts to escape. But they're not getting me. You two want to graduate? Well after what I've seen today so do I. From now on we're going to be the hottest, most submissive trigyn in Gryndstone and we're going to graduate in record time. Then, when we're out of here and I get my first day off, I'm not going to any park, I'm just gone!'

CHAPTER TEN

The next day all the teachers clearly knew about the incident in the park. Mel, Cam and Bolt were made to relate the event in detail both in D&SK and SI as a practical demonstration of their training being tested in the real world. They were praised for behaving suitably submissively, giving satisfaction to their impromptu masters and acting sensibly afterwards. From being a problem trio they were suddenly the trigyn to emulate. Perhaps it was this incident that explained why the following day Mel, Bolt and Cam saw on the timetable that they were to report the Headmaster for their first work experience day.

They knelt before Bradawl in Classroom 1 for their briefing. Bolt was all wide-eyed interest as she appeared to hang on his every word. Secretly Mel found this new attitude almost as disturbing as Bolt's previous show of insolence, which at least had been genuine. It made life easier only as long as she was not found out. Mel just hoped Bradawl would take it at face value.

'After your fine behaviour in the park I think you're ready for the next phase of your education,' Bradawl said. 'There will two tests designed to introduce you to serving in close proximity to the general public. One will be in a utilitarian capacity and the other offering a pleasure service, and they will take place at Central Station. This will also enable you to become familiar with our underground system. Not only is it the means by which you will most often travel to your assigned duties after you graduate but it employs many gynatons directly in its service operations.

'I'll escort you today but next time you will be expected to find your own way there, report to a supervisor and then travel back at the end of the day. That's the usual gynaton way in Shackleswell.'

A town where slaves were expected to take themselves unescorted to and from their labours, Mel thought incredulously. At first glance it seemed crazy, yet it would be a saving on supervisor man-hours. However as a consequence it meant giving gynatons a degree of responsibility. She thought of Chain and Spindle in the park seeming so at ease and confident. Could you have empowered slaves or, bearing in mind the enclosed nature of the underground, was it merely an illusion of freedom?

Bradawl put them into a coffle, cuffed and gagged them, then led them across the playground and down the stairs to Gryndstone Halt.

Mel had been too distracted the other day to notice there was a map of Shackleswell's underground network posted up in the school station. It would have answered some of her questions. Now while they were waiting for their train Bradawl made them study it and the timetable beside it. If she didn't know any better she would have taken it for any normal underground network.

There were six main colour-coded lines with interchanges marked where they crossed and several shorter local lines. The circle that they were on formed a continuous loop about the city, while the others snaked in from the suburbs across the city and back out again. All these passed through Shackleswell Central.

'Station officials may check your collar numbers and pass fobs but serving gynatons always travel free so you will never need tickets,' he told them. 'You may use the whole network but note those red bars on the map marking interchange points to uncontrolled public areas where you might encounter outsiders. They are always clearly signed. You do not pass these points unless you are properly clothed. Suitable off-duty dress will be provided after you graduate.'

Mel saw Bolt prick up her ears.

Their girl-train arrived. It was not the passenger special that had taken them to the park but a regular goods service with a single seated passenger carriage, two low wagons with cartons on wheeled pallets and a truck for kneeling impaled slave girls.

Did slave girls count as goods or passengers, Mel wondered.

Mel, Bolt and Cam clambered into the truck and impaled themselves beside the half-dozen other girls already on board, while Bradawl sat up front. The train pulled smoothly away again.

They changed to the Northern Line at Gin Street Junction, which Mel now saw was a larger station than Gryndstone Halt and fully manned. Goods trolleys loaded with packages in transport were lined up along the platform, there was a station office and low wooden hutch-like structures arrayed along the length of the platform.

When a train pulled up, naked slave girls emerged from the hutches like rabbits. Long chains were fastened to their collars that looped up to a framework of channels suspended from the roof, like those in the school washroom, confining them to the platform area. They wore small peaked caps and solid but highly polished black working shoes, which contrasted strangely with their nudity. They scuttled about loading and unloading the goods trolleys under the watchful eyes of male porters.

A flight of stairs and a short tunnel took them to the Northern line, where they caught another train. This was more crowded than the previous one with two carriages of seated passengers.

As they sped through the tunnels Mel squirmed on the fresh phallus thrust up inside her, feeling the exciting vibration of the train. How many other girls before her had ridden on this same prong of rubber?

After three more stops the train emerged into some much larger, lofty and brightly lit structure, which seemed to be a hive of activity by comparison with the stations they had previously passed through. Rolling wheels, snaking carriages and snatched views of pumping girlish limbs flashed by. As they slowed down Mel saw a sign reading: SHACKLESWELL CENTRAL.

The station was roofed by a series of interlocking domes supported by heavy columns. What looked like daylight was reflected down through large bull's-eye like skylights set in the apex of each dome. By their light Mel saw lines emerging from an arc of tunnel mouths that fed into the station where they merged, branched and passed over each other in maze of points and diamond crossings. Low footbridges crossed the tracks and there were forests of coloured signals with semaphore arms, miniature versions of the ones real railways used, signal boxes, sheds and workshops. It was a complex large enough to serve an entire city and emphasised the scale and durability of Shackleswell's secret world.

Their train pulled up at a platform and immediately more slavegirl porters began unloading the trolleys, swaying breasts bobbing and ringed nipples sparkling.

To one side was what looked like a goods yard handling larger items of freight, some of which was being stacked in sheds and under awnings. Opposite this was the passenger terminus where people strode calmly on and off the trains without sparing their imprisoned human engines or naked porters a second glance. But then several of the passengers were also leading naked girls after them like dogs. This was just everyday life.

As Bradawl took charge of them again Mel gazed at the slave girls labouring about her. There were teams of them working across a dozen platforms, pushing and pulling goods about. There must have been forty or fifty of them visible in a single glance about the station. The parade of naked bottoms, swaying breasts and exposed pudenda was irresistible to the eye. They were all shaven, ringed, collared, cuffed and stamped as Mel and her companions. None appeared any younger than her or older than about thirty. They were of all colours and builds and from what she could see were at least outwardly fit and healthy. Their nudity as such was not the most surprising thing, however, Mel had got used to that by now. It was the sheer numbers of them combined with the workaday setting and their accessories that made it so bizarre.

Though otherwise naked, they were all wearing the tiny porter hats, thick gloves and heavy boots. The first impression was that they were there to accentuate their nudity in a kinky way, like a contrived photo-shoot in some glossy garage glamour calendar. Then she saw how they were sweating as they heaved crates and pushed the trolleys and cartons around. This was serious work involving heavy objects some with sharp edges so perhaps their minimal protective clothing was justified. At least they were being protected, or was it simply common sense pragmatism? This was true hard labour, genuine slavery, and the reality that lay beyond Gryndstone schoolgirl life. It jarred with the mental accommodations Mel had been making to rationalise Shackleswell's philosophy and for a few seconds she looked about her with a critical eye.

However well-protected the girls were, they were indisputably true slaves. No glamour calendar Mel could have imagined would have contrived the means by which their movements were controlled and limited to their particular working areas. In a way they too were confined to rails but much more intimately than their sisters at Gin

~ 167 ~

Street Junction. It was, Mel realized with a shiver, the sort of thing their MI lessons were preparing them for.

There were narrow recessed channels set into the platforms shaped into tracks and loops that ran between them and the sheds and workshops. Each slavegirl porter had a telescopic rod lodged up her anus with a short chain linking its upper end to a single padlock that was looped through her labial piercings. The base of the rod ended in a greased ball that ran smoothly through the recessed channel but was obviously too big to pull out past the narrower gap formed by the channel lips. These rods slid along just behind the girls' heels, expanding and contracting about some internal spring to accommodate their movements as they bent and stretched to load boxes. They hardly seemed aware of them as they went about their tasks, crossing junctions and turning round loops, but they confined their activities solely to the routes permitted to them and nowhere else.

The rods meant they could be left to work with minimal supervision and work they did. Their faces were shiny from their exertions and the tang of their sweat hung in the otherwise fresh air, together with the spicy scent of female arousal. Hours of physical activity with a plug up their rears and a padlock hanging from their pussies must be stimulating. Was that some compensation or a cruel torment? No, it was just the Shackleswell way.

Suddenly Mel felt overwhelmed by the scale of the place. This had to be wrong. She could not blame Bolt for wanting to escape. Maybe she would go with her if she got up the nerve. However for now none of them had any choice but to play the part of a servile slave girls.

Bradawl led them across the platform bridges to a small office set in one corner of the station signposted: GYNATON SUPERVISOR. Here they were introduced to a Mr Wimble, a comfortable middle-aged man in a dark blue uniform who beamed at them genially as they knelt with thighs submissively spread before his desk.

'Latest batch for road testing, eh, Mr Bradawl? Nice looking girls. Well, we're all ready for them.'

He led the way along the platforms to a waiting area. There was a small coffee shop, a newsagents, some dispensing machines and a door leading to the men's lavatories. There was a sign on the door saying: *Closed for Maintenance*. Wimble led them inside. Mel felt sudden absurd thrill of trespassing on forbidden territory. In the lobby between the outer and inner doors were three booths with curtained fronts. Inside each booth was a small rectangular upright cage with a gap in the top of its front face, protected by a curved grille. Mounted on the side of each cage was a box with a coin slot in it. A sign over the booths said simply: £2.00 ORAL.

Mel felt her stomach begin to knot.

'Here we are, our stand-up fast service booths,' Wimble said. 'All our toilets have them. A lot of men come in here for a little quick relief while they're waiting for a train. Of course we serve local passengers from the mainline station upstairs as well, so business it usually pretty brisk.

'Now today you'll be taking the place of three of our regular girls. You'll be locked in these cages, which as you can see have a gap large enough to pass your head through. Your duty is to give oral relief to any man who's paid his money and stands before you. That's simple enough, but there are a couple of things designed to keep you on your toes. Let's get you inside and you'll see for yourselves…'

The cages opened at the back so they could clamber in. Their arms were left cuffed behind them but their gags were pulled out. There was a thigh-deep well let into the floor of the cage with a funnel across its centre. They slid their legs down on either side of this so they could stand upright. Mel felt rubber padding under her feet. When the rear doors of the cages were shut they were pressed against the front bars. They ducked their heads through the round padded apertures let into the top front of the cages and found they were now at about groin height. The visor-like grilles hung in front of their faces and they were connected to the coin boxes by short rods.

There were two smaller gaps in the bars below their heads large enough for their breasts to hang through. They were rimed with thick rubber cuffs plugged into hoses than ran down into the floor. Wimble adjusted the cuffs for each of them until their breasts were snugly collared and bulged invitingly. Their school ties he pulled through the bars and hung prominently between them. Then he stood back so each of them could see him through the open fronts of their booths, though they could no longer see each other.

'When a man stands on the mat in front of you and puts his coins in the slot the grille flips up and stays there until he steps off again. The funnels between your legs are for peeing in and there's a drinking tube inside the visors. That way you can stay in there all day quite with no trouble. Rest against the bars if you want to take the weight off your feet.'

Mel supposed it was a better way of getting their heads down to cock level than forcing them to kneel for hours on end, but it would still be hard work.

'Now there are notices posted about the station advertising you're here but when a man walks through that door you must sell yourselves. Some men might come in and put their cock straight in your mouth because they know what they want, but the others who only came in for a pee you've got to entice and beg to use you. There's an incentive to have as many customers as you can per hour because the more men you serve the more comfortable you'll stay.

'That mat they stand on in front of the cages is a pressure plate connected to a two-way valve and a hydraulic header tank. The longer anybody stands on the plate or the more men that stand on it the more oil is pumped back into the tank. When there's no pressure the oil slowly flows back the other way into those cuffs about your breasts. They have inner tubes with metal pins on that are slowly pressed out through the outer layers and into your boobies. Actually they'll help because a little pain on a pretty face excites the customers.

'Well, that's about all. Oh, you'll get no other food while you're in the cages except sperm, so you make the most of it. Anything you want to add, Mr Bradawl?'

'Just try your best and maintain the school name. I'll be back to collect you at six o'clock tonight.'

Wimble went along the booths turning a key in the coin boxes. 'Now the valves are open. I'll take the sign off the door and you can get ready for your first customers.' He and Bradawl went out.

Mel imagined she could already feel the collars tightening about her breasts.

She heard Cam moan: 'How can I beg to suck a man off? It was easier with the boys in the park. They just did what they wanted. But asking for it…'

Mel realised that Cam was not outwardly revolted by the physical fact of what she had to do, she was worried that she would be too embarrassed to beg. Of course they'd been trained how to give proper oral pleasure in Sex Tec and they'd all practiced on Mr Stapler's cock. Yet what did that say about what Gryndstone was turning them into? Three caged girls in school ties pleading to fellate any man for a modest fee outside a gentlemen's lavatory. Was that sick prostitution or simple basic slave-economy business? No, it was just everyday life in Shackleswell.

Before Mel could find words of encouragement for Cam, Bolt said: 'Course you can beg. Anyway they'll love it if you act shy. You've got the right sort of face.'

It was not bad advice. Maybe it was just Bolt playing her part as a supportive chain-sister but it helped.

The door swung open and man strode in.

'Please master,' they said, 'oral for just two pounds…'

Mel did not really see any men for the rest of the day. With a few exceptions they were really just a progression of differently shaped and flavoured penises thrust into her mouth that she had to milk dry. Some said nothing and just put their coin in the slot and pushed their cocks at her mouth like she was simply part of the machine. Even when she got into conversation with others, which was clearly part of the excitement for some, she rarely took in any features.

'That's so big, Master! Please be gentle…'

He took her by the hair, pried her jaws wide and pushed the head of his shaft between her lips. 'You can take it, girl. One big swallow…'

She choked and gasped as he forced it down her.

'That's it, right to the hilt. Oh, are your eyes bulging? Do you want to breathe?'

Mel nodded frantically. He pulled out just enough for her to suck in some air round his shaft. 'Thank you, master,' she gasped pitifully.

He plunged into her until her eyes bulged again.

It was verging on cruelty and yet her pussy was dripping into her pee funnel.

A thin, nervous, spotty young man used her, fumbling the coin into the slot and then jabbing his slender cock into her mouth. She felt sorry for him and tried to make it as pleasurable as possible, rolling her eyes helplessly up at him with her best puppy desperate to please gaze. He came in frantic spurts that she licked up with a show of delight.

'Oh… that's so nice and sweet and hot, Master,' she said huskily.

He smiled with pitiful gratitude and then scuttled out. It was probably the highlight of his week.

'Across the balls and then up the shaft again…' the plump man who liked to direct her every move commanded. 'That's right… now under the foreskin… yes… uhh… Ready to catch it… ahhhh… splendid… yes, gobble it all down like a good girl.' He patted her head as she licked him clean. 'You've got a fine tongue on you.'

'Thank you, Master,' Mel said indistinctly.

'Good to see Gryndstone standards have not dropped. I must make a note of your part number. If you're ever on the market I'd put in a bid for you.'

'You're very kind, Master.'

How wonderful, Mel thought dizzily, he wants to buy me. Still that was high praise indeed from somebody who was clearly a fellatio connoisseur.

Hour in and hour out, Mel sucked, licked, lapped and tongued everything that was put in her mouth.

When there was a longer gap between customers and the cuffs about her breasts began to prick Mel found she had no shame left.

'Please let me suck you, Master! I really need a lovely hard cock in my mouth right now. Please, for the sake of my tits. They're nice, aren't they but there are pins sticking in them. Please make them go away. I'll drink it all down, really I will. You can push it right down my throat…'

From the booths on either side of her she heard Bolt and Cam making similar desperate promises. It was a very long day.

When the Headmaster finally came back for them they could hardly speak, their jaws ached, their throats were sore and they were slightly nauseous from swallowing so much sperm. Wimble counted the money in their coinboxes and declared they had done nearly as well as their regular girls, which was highly satisfactory for first timers. Bradawl led them home stiff-legged, exhausted and frustrated. It had been impossible not to get aroused in the presence of so many erections, but there had been no chance to orgasm. At least they were give ice cream for tea as a special treat.

They went to bed that night only able to converse in whispers. They had been both stimulated and drained and yet physically, except for their jaws, they had not been much exercised. In the dim red nightlight they huddled together restlessly, unable to sleep.

'Well, I suppose it wasn't so bad after the first twenty cocks,' Cam croaked and they all chucked.

'I think today we got a real taste of Shackleswell,' Mel said.

The others groaned.

Then Bolt said almost shyly: 'Actually, I brought something from the rec room. I was wondering if you might want to use them, as we're all a bit wired and didn't get off at all...'

From under the corner of the mattress she pulled out a pair of double-ended dildos.

'It's just an idea,' she added defensively. 'It's the sort of thing the other girls do. If you two don't want to...'

In the dim light Mel saw Bolt looking anxious. There was no need for her to put on an act for them. She sensed Bolt really wanted this. Maybe playing her new role had given her an excuse to soften up. It must have been tough being a hard bitch and ignoring everybody for so long. Whatever the motive the suggestion was tempting. Despite all the intimacies forced on them in lessons they had never made voluntary love. Suddenly that seemed absurd.

'I think it's a great idea,' Cam said. 'We deserve something just for us after sucking all those cocks.' She looked at Mel. 'If you do.'

'Oh yes. I don't know why we haven't done it before.'

'Because I'd have made you feel like pervs,' Bolt suggested, then added quickly: 'But now that's changed, right?' She took a deep breath and offered them dildos. 'You do what you want, but I could really do with a good hard screw.'

'I think we can manage that,' Mel said.

They took the dildos and fed the ends up into their wet and hungry sheaths, popping the securing lugs through their pussy rings. Then they embraced Bolt and kissed her on her lips, her swollen ringed nipples and hot pulsing sex. Bolt trembled but let them handle her between them. She was surrendering some of her hard independent pride to admit she wanted this.

They mounted her from front and rear, pushing their play cocks up her vagina and rectum until she was deeply, lovingly, plugged. Then the beast with three backs rolled ecstatically about the mattress in a happy frenzy of passionate coupling.

Whatever had gone before and whatever lay ahead things would be different between them from now on.

The quality of Mel's immediate social life might have been improving but relations with her distant family were getting more strained.

Her parents were replying less often to her messages, seemingly resigned to the fact that Mel was not coming back home soon. They informed her that they were telling family and friends that Mel had decided to take a year off before going to college to travel around and "find herself". Mel despaired that her parents seemed to be trying harder to cover up her shameful secret than rebuild their relationship with her.

Maddy replied to every mail but she was beginning to ask awkward questions.

'Why can't you tell me where you're staying? And what do you do? How are you earning a living…'

Mel hated sending back evasive or noncommittal replies, but she could hardly admit the reality of her life. 'Well actually I've just been sucking fifty men off in a secret underground station…'

After three more days of regular lessons Mel, Cam and Bolt went for their second work experience day at Shackleswell Central. Bradawl took them down to Gryndstone Halt platform chained in a coffle with fobs on their collars showing they were on day release from school. He reminded them of the train times and said he would be waiting for them that evening. The train pulled in and he saw them aboard and watched as it pulled away. Mel felt a strange thrill at being sent off unescorted. It was an adventure different to roaming about in the park. Chained together as they were they had no choice where they should go, but that did not seem to matter.

They arrived at the station on time and reported to Mr Wimble.

He rubbed his hands together. 'Now in Shackleswell we take pride in being a clean and tidy town and down here's no different. So today you're going to be helping to keep the station clean but not with mops and brooms. We use proper Rowland designed machines…'

Mel shuffled along the station platform cleaning diligently as she went. Between the legs of passing passengers she glimpsed Bolt and Cam working their assigned platforms in the same way.

The passengers milled around Mel as they headed for the stairs or ran for trains hardly giving her a second glance. She was just a naked gynaton doing her job. The only passengers who did look at her were what she now recognised as off-duty slave girls in their grey coats and boots, who smiled and sometimes showed a twinkle of pussy rings between their legs. They understood what she was feeling. A few days ago she might have sucked the cocks of some of the men passing her by and now she was on her hands and knees vacuuming up the dirt from their shoes and they probably did not recognise her. Did that make her anonymous or versatile?

Mel was now intimately conjoined with the Gynavac Mark 5, the latest version of one of Rowland's original domestic designs. Its mechanical parts bore a slight resemblance to an upright cylinder and hose-style vacuum that in the rest of the country trundled about on small wheels and was given a cartoonish face and a friendly name. This being Shackleswell the Gynavac did not need humanising and its living power source provided a real and far more expressive face.

Mel towed behind her its flattened upright drum mounted on a tripod of rubber wheels that was slim enough to fit between her splayed lower legs. Her ankle cuffs were clipped to levers extending down from the top of the drum that powered the bellows that created the suction. Strapped to her shins from knee to extended toe tips were padded boards, to the undersides of which were fastened a row of three narrow rubber wheels like inline skates with buffing cloth sidebars. This arrangement allowed her to shuffle her legs rapidly back and forth without moving the drum and so pump the bellows.

The brush hose extended from the lower front of the drum and was slung under her body, supported by sleeves hooked to her labial rings, stretching her lips.

Where the hose passed between her dangling breasts the supporting sleeve hooks were clipped to her nipple rings. The hose plugged into a short tube on the end of which was mounted the wide brush head. The upper end of the tube had a rubber ball cap that was plugged into Mel's mouth, also forming an effective gag. A sprung cord that hooked to the back ring of her collar counterbalanced the weight of the brush head. The other end of the cord was fastened to a short vertical bracing rod extending from the top of the drum.

Polishing cloths with rubber heels were strapped to Mel's hands, allowing her to pull herself and the gynavac along. It was hard work but it had its compensations. She towed the device by means of a horizontal bar fastened two-thirds the way up the forward face of the drum with an expanding rubber plug on the end that was sunk into her anus. This bar had a second lower curved arm the tip of which slipped between the distended lips her labia as they helped support the hose and rubbed against her clitoris. This arm transmitted the vibrations of the bellows as she pumped them with her legs to her own pulsating pleasure nub. It was a powerful incentive to work as hard as she could.

As she shuffled along mini orgasms coursed sweetly through her.

She was intimately merged with a machine and she was rewarded for her efforts in the most basic way possible. It felt good to be useful.

'Hi, Maddy. You wanted to know the sort of work I've been doing. Well today I did some cleaning in an underground station, which is more fun than it sounds…'

CHAPTER ELEVEN

With Bolt now eagerly pushing them along towards graduation they had something to look forward to, even a sense of a challenge, helping them overcome tests that stretched their minds and bodies. Weeks became a month and more. Despite the challenges of their assessments as time passed and their confidence and experience grew, the three of them began to feel that there was nothing they could not do, however painful and degrading. They were obstacles to be overcome with pride.

An odd feeling was growing in Mel that if she could just do this right it would have proved something important and help her straighten out her personal troubles, though she was not sure what or how. All she did know was that the collapse of a close family could scar you far more deeply than any lashing.

Mel was getting to know Bolt and Cam very well, but in a curious way. Her knowledge of their bodies due to forced and sometime now unforced physical intimacy was delightfully extensive. She could also anticipate their reactions to lessons, their opinions on TV or films they saw together, teachers and other details of the microcosm of the school world, but she only knew disconnected and inconsequential snippets about their personal lives before they came here. She still did not know their real names or those of any other pupils. However, Mel was in no position to criticise them. After that first day she had been doing exactly the same thing. It seemed that they had all erected a barrier between their past and present lives. Perhaps it is the only way to survive here because allowing their past in would only highlight the bizarre, shameful and degrading life they were living in Gryndstone. This disconnection made it tolerable. Perhaps that was half the idea of giving them new part names. Or was it simply as Wire had said that they were all flawed or damaged in some way? Shame might flow in reverse if past guilty secrets were revealed. That was what made the public confessions so moving and surprising...

'What do you have to confess, Wire 142?' Bradawl asked.

Wire was chained between the posts of the confession device, with the spiked domes clamped to her breasts, trembling but resolute. As the whole school looked on, their sexes sucking on their impaling phalluses in anticipation, Wire said: 'I had money and a good education and I screwed it up! I should have been grateful but I was spoilt and selfish. I let people down and abused my body in many ways. I was wasting my life. I've been bad. I deserve to be punished. Please punish me, Masters!'

The canes lashed out across her slender body and she screamed.

Later at break time out in the playground Mel kissed Wire's sore breasts again.

'I had no idea about your life,' Mel admitted. 'You've been, well, so friendly and helpful to us.'

Wire grinned ruefully. 'I'm glad you thought so. I'm the last in my trigyn to confess because I felt I had a lot of bad things to make up for. It was about the hardest thing I've ever done but I'm so glad I did. Maybe knowing other girls here have survived far worse helped straighten me out. Now I can start fresh being useful in Shackleswell. Our grades are good so we'll probably graduate tomorrow. I hope you'll all come along tonight to say goodbye properly.'

'Of course we will,' Mel assured her.

She looked at Mel searchingly. 'After the way you've all come on recently, are any of you going to be confessing soon?'

'Yeah, we've got to start thinking about that,' Bolt said after they had surrendered their places near Wire to other girls who wanted to congratulate her. 'We should start working on our confessions. Better space them out, though. It wouldn't look right going all at once.'

Cam chewed her lip. 'I was wondering about it. I'm frightened, but, yes, I think I can confess. It's probably what I need to do.'

'Great,' Bolt said. 'What about you, Spring?'

Mel gulped. The very thought of such a thing was so appalling that she had put it right out of her mind. Now the idea terrified her. How could she ever confess her sins?

'Don't look so miserable,' Bolt said. 'Just make something up that sounds good. That's what I'm going to do. My past is no business of anybody else, right?'

Mel blinked. The idea of lying in confession had never occurred to her.

That evening the girls said goodbye to Wire, Spar and Bush in proper gynaton fashion. They were in three adjacent bed cages, borrowed from their neighbours, waiting to receive guests with open legs. The visitors mounted them in turn and they had gentle "ring on ring" sex as their nipple and pussy rings chimed together. There was much rubbing and kissing leading to the gift of a small, intimate orgasm to remember them by.

It was as Mel coupled with Wire and their slippery sex lips slid through each other and their hard clitorises kissed, that she was suddenly overwhelmed by the realization of very normal this felt. Wire had been right about how adaptable they were, but could the process ever be reversed?

The next day Wire, Spar and Bush graduated. Mel felt a lump in her throat as they watched them being led down the playground by Bradawl. Of course they had promised to keep in touch but it was like seeing older students leave school and knowing they were moving up to take their place. It also meant she was one step closer to leaving herself.

'You've very fortunate,' Bradawl said as he prepared Mel, Cam and Bolt for their next work experience day.

They had already guessed this would be different from their previous outings. They were going to miss assembly so it had to be special.

'The Fillister family is one of the oldest in Shackleswell,' Bradawl continued. 'They've always supported this school and over the years they've taken many pupils for work experience on their estate. Today they're looking for a trigyn to serve as pets and pleasure companions. This will apparently involve a high degree of mechanical interface. I'm sure they'll have the latest systems so that will be very useful experience. I needn't say you are to be on your best behaviour.'

They did not travel to the Fillister's residence by anything as common as the underground. The family sent their own car that picked them up from the back of Miss Trunnion's office. It was a black 4 X 4 with tinted windows and was driven by a Mr Cleaver, a lean masterful man who introduced himself as the Fillester's gynaton keeper. Mel, Cam and Bolt raised their eyes in surprise above their gags. They actually had a special keeper for slave girls! This also clearly impressed Miss Trunnion, who came close to simpering over Cleaver.

In the back of the big car were three slave cages into which Mel, Bolt and Cam were loaded. Twenty minute's drive took them out of town and into the countryside where the Fillister's estate lay. Mel could not see much through the slots in her cage cover except for flashes of high walls, security gates and a long driveway winding through landscaped gardens.

They were unloaded at the side of an imposing Georgian country house that overawed them far more than the prospect of sucking cocks all day in the station. Beside the house was an old stable block and it was into this that Cleaver led them. Inside the walls were still hung with bridles and gleaming sets of buckled harness, but they were not designed to fit horses. There were also several gynaton-powered machines, but it was the three strange coloured rubber costumes, one red, one yellow and one blue, laid out a big table in the centre of the room that drew their eyes.

Cleaver lined the girls up before him and then spoke earnestly. 'You're going to be Old Mr Fillister's toys for the day while the family are out. Only he's not what he was. He's getting a bit vague but he does like to have Gryndstone girls around him. They always make him happy. He used to be a school governor years ago. Just be patient and humour him and he'll be fine.'

It sounded to Mel as though their temporary master to be was going senile. This was not a reassuring prospect.

'Old Mr Fillister also likes dogs,' Cleaver added. 'So that's what you'll be today: pretty bitch-dogs to keep him amused.' He indicated some wooden steps resting against one end of the table. 'So up you get, bitches...'

As commanded they knelt or lay on their backs with legs in the air on the table while Cleaver dressed them in the tight rubber garments, which had been dusted with talc to slide over their skin. It was strange to feel fabric enclosing their bodies after weeks of almost total nudity even if it did not cover their most sensitive parts. There were thigh-length boots with wires extending from their inside top rims that clipped to their labial rings. There were shoulder-length gloves and tight basques that nipped in their waists, cupped and pushed up their breasts without covering them and braced their backs.

Wires from the tops of the basques were clipped to their nipple rings. Cleaver pulled matching bridles over their heads that had fake dog ears stuck on their sides. Straps went across the bridge of their noses, under their chins and across their mouths, where instead of a bit they supported stiff rubber coated wires that hooked into the side of their cheeks and supported the ring bases of soft pink rubber tongues that slipped over the ends of their own tongues and lolled out of their mouths.

The final touch was curving hollow rubber dog tails. These were mounted perpendicularly on one end of "U" shaped rubber-coated spring clips. The other end was slid up into their rectums and pinched through their flesh against the end with the tail on which now rose from the base of their spines. There were also springs inside the tails and the slightest movement of their hips set them bobbing. Finally every element of their costumes was linked together by a web of tight straps, pressing into their flesh.

Mel knew there was more to the costumes than met the eye. The boots had integral coil spring braces along the sides of their knees holding them bent at forty-five degrees and allowing only a small amount of flexibility. She could feel pins on the inside of the boot toecaps, warning them against standing upright. Their gloves ended in padded fingerless mittens and were braced by more hidden springs at the elbows. There were odd thickenings in tops of the gloves and boots, suggesting devices hidden inside them, and all, straps included, were studded inside with metal contacts.

When they were all dressed as pseudo-dogs, Cleaver ordered them to clamber down off the table, which they did awkwardly, edging down the steps. Lining them up on all fours with tails wagging he took up a radio control unit fitted with tiny joysticks and selector buttons matching the colours of their costumes.

'This stimulates your major muscle groups and controls you individually or all together. Just respond as feels natural…' He touched a control.

Their legs and arms twitched by themselves and Mel found herself shuffling forward side by side with Bolt and Cam. It was eerily like invisible strings were jerking her about and she whimpered and dribbled about her fake tongue while Bolt and Cam rolled their eyes fearfully. Her instinct was to fight it yet she knew that would be futile. It was only a subtler form of bondage and there was only one proper response for a gynaton: total surrender.

For a few minutes Cleaver sent them shuffling round the room to get use to the system. The tiny jolts of current that stimulated their muscles did not hurt much and it became easier as they let their reflexes take over. They learned fast, but then they had no choice. Soon they wheeling about, stopping and backing up, nuzzling into each other's bottoms and even cocking their legs against the walls. A jolt to the base of their tongues was a signal to bark. There was even a sequence of muscular twitches that prompted them to sit up on their haunches, pull their arms up under their breasts with paws handing limp and beg. They did not have to be told to whimper and roll their eyes as well. They still had their school ties on which made them look even stranger, but they were so far into fantasyland by now that hardly mattered. It was utterly degrading so of course Mel felt her pussy growing hot and slippery.

Cleaver lined them up in front of him again. 'Just keep thinking like bitches and you'll do fine. But if you're slow to obey or disobedient…' he touched another button.

Their nipple and labial rings became hammers in their flesh, sending a searing jolt of hard current through their bodies. They howled round their fake tongues as they convulsed and rolled up into balls of pain.

Then it was gone, leaving them trembling and shaking. Warning twitches sent them struggling tearfully back up onto all fours.

'So will you be good?' Cleaver asked.

They nodded and wagged their tails pathetically.

He steered them out of the stables and then along a path that led around the side of the house through a gate and onto a terrace. Here a breakfast table was laid out under an awning. Seated at it were a smart fortyish couple and a girl of about Mel's age with auburn hair who was dressed in riding boots and jodhpurs.

They were being waited on, as if it was the most natural thing in the world, by what Mel supposed you had to call a gynaton maid.

She wore a tiny frilly cap perched on the top of her head. Her mouth was occupied by a red ring gag that held her lips open in a perpetual mute "O" of surprise and readiness for oral penetration. She wore a French maid-style bib and tiny apron, except they were made of soft clear plastic that hid nothing of her naked body. Light silver chains linked her wrist cuffs to side rings set in the belt of her apron, which was padlocked in the small of her back. A short hobble chain joined her ankle cuffs, forcing her to take tiny steps on her high heels.

Cleaver brought Mel, Bolt and Cam up to the table and then had them sit up and beg.

'The Gryndstone girls, sir,' Cleaver reported.

The man and woman looked them over with reserved approval while the young girl exclaimed: 'They're pretty!'

'They'll do,' the man conceded. He frowned down at them. 'Now, we're going to be out for much of the day and my father needs his amusement, otherwise he worries. You be good bitches for him, understand?'

They nodded and panted and wagged their tails.

'Oh, can't I play with them?' the girl said petulantly.

'They're for Grandfather,' the woman reminded her. 'Anyway I thought you were going out riding with Tessa for the day?'

'She's getting boring. Why can't I play with them? Grandfather's only going to fall asleep and he won't remember afterwards anyway.'

'Don't talk about him like that, dear,' her mother chided gently.

'Well it's true!'

'Don't talk back to your mother!' her father snapped.

There was something in his tone that made the girl drop her eyes and murmur meekly: 'Sorry, Father.'

'All right,' the man said to Cleaver, 'take them down to the summerhouse.'

The summerhouse lay beyond the terrace wall and a little way down the low rise the house occupied. It was an airy structure with a veranda, a shingle roof and lapped wood walls looking out across the trees and gardens to a lake. Inside, facing the open double doors, a distinguished white-haired old man sat in a reclining chair with a blanket wrapped round his legs. On a large cushion beside him knelt a pretty blonde maid without a gag. She was holding a book from which she had been reading aloud. She was tethered by a long chain to the doorpost, beside which was also a slave drinking fountain and pee pan. More tethering rings and chains hung round the walls together with a small rack of lashes. By the chair was a table with a phone, a tray of ice soft drinks, fruit and sweet bowls, a pile of books and some medicine bottles. To one side was a large flatscreen television and sound system.

The maid, who had the part stamp: Cog 107, bowed her head to Cleaver.

The old man looked up vaguely and then his eyes fastened on Mel and the others. 'Oh, I say, what pretty gyndogs. And they're Gryndstone girls! I used to have a lot to do with the school you know.'

'Yes, Mr Fillister,' said Cleaver. 'Your son sent them down for you to try out.' He handed him the control box.

'Oh, that was good of him. Where is he?'

'He'll be down to see you later, Mr Fillister.'

The old man was stroking the control box. 'I used to have lots of fun with these when they first came out. You can make them do tricks...'

He began playing with the joysticks. Mel, Cam and Bolt jerked into life and began shuffling round the room barking and wagging their tails. The old man chortled with delight. Cleaver nodded to Cog and quietly slipped away.

Grandfather Fillister played with them for most of the morning. He managed to steer them head to tail so they tongued each other out. Then he had them fetching sticks and balls thrown by Cog. When they brought them back and sat up in begging postures by his chair he happily stoked and patted them, toying with their breasts. Mel had to steel herself not to flinch at the touch of his wrinkled hands as he pawed her over, yet she also felt sorry for him and did not begrudge any pleasure she could give. She supposed his infatuation with gynatons was natural if he had grown up with them, as several generations in Shackleswell must have done. He was simply reliving happy memories.

With spanking paddle in hand Fillister managed to swipe it across their upturned bottoms as they presented them to him. Half the time he hit their tails, making them whip and slap violently from side to side while churning the spring clip ends inside their rectums. The blows that did land on their buttocks hardly hurt and raised only a light blush, but they yelped and wiggled in a show of pain that seemed to please him.

His greatest delight, however, was seeing them pee, for which they had to make many trips to drinking fountain. He had them cocking legs and peeing against the veranda post and nearby trees, and then lying on their backs on the grass with their legs spread peeing into the air so the streams crossed in glittering arcs.

'Gyndog fountains,' he said happily. 'I once got a dozen of you in a row doing that. Amazing height you reached. Strong inner muscles, I suppose. Nearly squeezed the life out of my cock afterwards!'

At lunchtime a slave housemaid brought a tray of food down to the summerhouse and Cog helped Grandfather Fillister eat it. Soon afterwards he was snoring.

'He'll sleep for a few hours now,' Cog confided in a soft voice. 'You can get some rest now'

She fed them some grapes and chocolates and then Mel, Cam and Bolt sprawled on the grass in the sun, grinning at each other round their fake tongues. It had been a weird day but this was not so bad, Mel thought. It was disconcerting to be used as pure playthings. She'd rather have some real work to do. That felt natural. Did she really mean that?

She must have dozed because she was jerked awake by sharp words.

'Give me that! He's asleep and he'll never know and nor will my parents.'

The daughter of the house was standing over Cog, pulling the remote control box from her hands. She now dressed in a long loose summer dress and white sandals.

'Please, Mistress… Miss Samantha, they're old Mr Fillister's toys,' Cog said.

'How dare you speak to me like that!'

Samantha Fillister wrenched Cog's arms behind her and cuffed her wrists together. As Cog protested she took an apple from the fruit bowl and rammed it into her mouth, jamming it between her teeth. Then she shortened Cog's leash chain, pulling her over to the doorpost.

'Now you don't make a sound until I come back,' she warned her.

Using the control box Samantha steered Mel, Bolt and Cam away from the Summerhouse and down towards the lake. They had no choice but to shuffle along as fast as they could with their breasts swaying and jiggling. The twitches that drove their limbs were accompanied with brief stabs of the punishment setting that lanced through then nipples and pussies, making them yelp and stumble. Mel saw Bolt and Cam both looked fearful but there was nothing they could do.

There was a dense thicket of rhododendron bushes near the shore. Samantha drove them into this, pushing aside the low branches. At the heart of the thicket there was an open patch of ground floored by bare stamped earth. On it was spread an old rug. She's been planning this, Mel thought.

Samantha grinned down at the girls in triumph. 'You really are pretty gyndogs,' she said. 'You're wasted on Grandfather. Are you going to be good?' Her finger hovered over the pain button. They nodded quickly. 'Now let's play my game...'

She rolled her dress up to her waist. She was naked underneath. Her buttocks were nicely rounded and a sparse triangle of russet curls capped her neatly cleft mound. She laid on her back on the rug, bent her knees and spread her legs, exposing her groin to them. She worked the control box until Bolt was straddled over her with her head above Samantha's groin and her pubes over Samantha's head. Mel knelt with her face pressed into Bolt's pussy while at the end of the line Cam's face was nuzzling into Mel's pubes.

'Now you will all use your tongues on the pussy you have in front of you. If I don't think your trying hard enough you'll get a shock. When I press move the one at the front goes round to the back and you all move up one space. I want to feel all your tongues in me again and again and watch you pleasuring each other until I come. Then I'll think of a new game. Begin...'

Bolt dipped her head and thrust her extended tongue deep into Samantha's sex, even as Mel felt Cam slide her tongue into her. As Mel twisted her head to lap at Bolt's pussy she saw Samantha looking up in hungry fascination at the desperate cunnilingus taking just above her head.

So they shuffled around Samantha, alternately pleasuring her and themselves for her amusement. Quick stabs of electric pain that she inflicted on them with delighted laughter punished any slackness. Soon their nipples and labia were tingling, driving on their mounting arousal. They could not help this. By now it was quite instinctive. As the scent of flowing female juices filled the tiny glade one by one they came, dripping their discharge onto Samantha's face which she wiped up and licked in wonder.

At last Samantha bucked her own hips, grinding her pussy into Cam's face. Then she sank back, breathing heavily and rubbing her fingers through her wet slot.

'Oh... that was nice! You do have good tongues on you. I wish you belonged to me. Think of the fun could have. Now, next you're going to –'

'Miss Samantha!' came Cleaver's voice calling out the distance. 'Listen to me wherever you are. I have to return those gyndogs to your Grandfather. They're his toys, not yours. Your parents will be back soon and your father won't be happy if he hears you took them...'

Panic replaced dreamy delight on Samantha's face. Hurriedly she pulled her dress back down and scrambled to her feet, peering anxiously through the foliage. They heard Cleaver calling out again, but his voice was fainter. Samantha flipped the joysticks on the control box, setting the girls' legs shuffling into motion.

'Back to the summerhouse, quickly!'

She sent them plunging through the bushes careless of scratches. They burst out into the open facing the wrong direction. In a panic Samantha stabbed at the controls, but instead of steering them along the path she sent them shuffling wildly down the grassy bank towards the edge of the lake.

'No, no stop!' she screeched.

But they could not stop. They were prisoners of reflex and the commands flowing through their dog suits. Over the bank they went and splashed into the green water. It was only shallow but they could not stand up and the weight of their cuffs and collars was pulling them under. The contacts in their costumes began to short out, making them jerk uncontrollably. Bubbles swirled past Mel's head. She was drowning....

Then a strong hand caught her by the collar and hauled her out of the lake to flop coughing and spluttering on the bank beside Cam and Bolt's dripping forms. She blinked the water from her eyes to see Cleaver wade back up onto the bank and stand glaring sternly at a trembling Samantha.

'Your Father's not going to like this, Miss.'

It was an hour later back at the Summerhouse.

Mel, Bolt and Cam knelt to one side in a coffle, stripped of their now useless gyndog costumes. Samantha stood miserably before her father and mother. Upon their return Cleaver reported the incident and now Cog was explaining how Samantha had taken restrained her and taken the girls away. Fortunately she had managed to reach the table phone with her foot, chew through her apple gag and call Cleaver's stable phone.

'Is this true?' her father asked Samantha.

'Yes, Father, but I only wanted to borrow them…'

'Be quiet! I've heard enough.'

Samantha bowed her head.

'She broke them.' Old Mr Fillister protested once again. 'They were my toys and she broke them.'

'Yes, Father,' his son said gently, 'and now she's going to be punished.'

Old Mr Fillister suddenly brightened. 'Oh… rosy bum time, is it?'

'Yes, Father.'

Samantha stifled a sob of fear.

'She was only playing with them, George,' her mother said. 'It was naughty but perfectly natural. If Cleaver hadn't panicked her no harm would have been done.'

'No, Mary,' her husband said. 'She disobeyed me and proved she was not fit to be in control of these girls. That's harm enough. You're always excusing her mistakes and because of that I've been too soft on her. Well, now she's going to get the punishment she deserves… and I think you'll share it with her.'

Samantha gasped while Mary Fillister went pale. 'No, George, you can't… not right now… I mean…' she stressed the next words: 'I'm still dressed for going out!'

'I know and it's your own fault. This is my right and duty. Now lift your skirts and bend over the rail, both of you!'

Miserably, mother and daughter turned and hitched up their skirts. Samantha's bottom Mel had already seen. Her mother's backside was of a similar build with slightly fleshier pale buttocks, but there was a thin metal strap running up from between her buttocks that joined a broader strap about her waist. A chastity belt?

They bent over the veranda balustrade, grasping the outside of the posts to brace themselves and presenting their bare bottoms to the rest of the company. George Fillister took out a key, inserted it in the slim lock in the small of his wife's back that joined the straps and pulled the belt off.

'Perhaps I should get one of these for Samantha to keep her under control as well,' he mused. Samantha whimpered.

Now Mary Fillister's pubic mound, covered in thicker ruddy curls than her daughter's, also pouted unwilling out at them from between shivering thighs.

Mel felt embarrassment at witnessing this private family shame but she could not look away.

'Mr Cleaver, please strap them down properly,' George said.

Cleaver bound the women's wrists to the posts and put more straps across their backs and about their ankles, pulling their legs apart.

From the rack George selected a lash and a spanking paddle, which he gave to Cleaver. 'If you would attend to my daughter. I want to see her rear burn and turn scarlet and I want to hear her scream.'

'Yes, Mr Fillister,' Cleaver said calmly, as though being asked to beat the naked bottom of his employer's daughter was nothing out of the ordinary. But then this was Shackleswell, Mel reminded herself.

The men took up positions of either side of the bound women and began to beat them. The pair of soft pale bottoms, so similar in form, shivered and jumped under the lash of thong and paddle, with ripples running across their hips and thighs. Anuses clenched at each blow and then gaped pitifully. The sweet crack of rubber on flesh filed the air.

Their pouting vulvas did not escape the punishment. As the blows compressed their buttock flesh they snacked into their tender nethermouths, stinging those most sensitive lips. In addition both George and Cleaver aimed a few strokes up into the women's groins, giving them a taste of the full force of a blow.

Mary Fillister controlled herself better, snivelling and moaning and clenching her teeth but not saying a word. Samantha however sobbed, screamed and begged for forgiveness at the top of her voice, promising to be a perfect daughter from now on if her father would only spare her this humiliation. In her extremis and clenched up with pain she even farted shamefully in between her pleadings. He took no notice, letting her bottom turn from pink to the blazing scarlet he had specified while tanning his wife's posterior to match.

Finally Samantha could control herself no longer. With a dreadful moan of the deepest shame a stream of pee burst from between her sore labia and hissed backwards hot and steaming, splashing across the wooden decking. As the dying drips of her impromptu fountain fell from her cleft she sagged across the balustrade in a dead faint.

Grandfather Fillister enthusiastically applauded her degrading display. 'Hah! That's the way we used to keep the girls in line in the old days!'

Back at school that evening, Mel, Cam and Bolt related their brief glimpse in to the lives of the spoilt, rich and over privileged to their fascinated fellow pupils.

Mel sent a mail to Maddy. 'Helped look after a rich old man today. He lives in a big house with fantastic grounds, including a lake. I even had time for a quick dip. He was nice but a bit dotty so I did my best to cheer him up. You could tell the family were in a bit of a mess and the daughter was a real handful. We're not the only people with problems so there's still hope...'

Maddy replied: 'Swims in lakes! I've been doing office cleaning which is so boring. It sounds like you've having more fun that I am...'

Was she having fun?

Later in bed the three of them talked it over.

'Gryndstone seems almost normal by comparison to all that,' Cam said.

Unexpectedly Bolt took some cheer from this revelation that the elite of local society were actually just as screwed up as their own families. 'They're no better than we are, except they've got the keys.'

'It shows that Shackleswell's a complicated place,' Mel agreed. 'But then what do you expect after a hundred and fifty years? Bits of it are still following on Rowland's practical ideals and others have got a bit, well, decadent.'

'Yeah, but which bit will we end up in?' Cam wondered. 'Maybe some of each won't be too bad, as long as our masters respect us for what we are. That's so important.'

CHAPTER TWELVE

Cam swayed between the confession platform's tethering posts, looking out at the assembled pupils. Mel's stomach knotted at the sight of her, so exposed, yet brave and beautiful.

'My family wanted me to stay in the family business and eventually marry one of my own people, but I knew better and didn't listen,' Cam said. 'I wanted to show them I could make it on my own. It went terribly wrong. Then somebody told me I could make money dancing in strip clubs, but it was horrible. Eventually I hit a club owner when he tried it on once too often and ran away, but I was too ashamed to go back home. I was on streets when a man from Shackleswell found me. Please punish me, I deserve it…'

The canes fell across her front and back.

'You were wonderful,' Mel said afterwards, hugging Cam while trying to avoid her sore breasts. 'How do you feel?'

'Better,' Cam said. 'Like a weight's lifted off my shoulders. It's frightening but so good to say it out loud like that.' She clutched their hands. 'You must do it as soon as you can. It's the only way. Then you can get on with your life.'

'As a slave? I don't think so,' Bolt interjected.

'It's better than having no life at all,' Cam insisted.

'After what you said about dancing in strip clubs being bad?'

'Somehow this is different,' Cam insisted. 'There's no guilt, we know the rules and we'd have friends. Anyway, will you?' she asked Mel.

'Maybe,' Mel said evasively. 'I've got to get my story right first.'

'It's got to be the truth or it won't count,' Cam said.

'It will be, most of it,' Mel promised.

She felt the pressure on her was rising. Their ever more frequent work experience trips into town were becoming welcome diversion from school routine and thoughts of her confession. That was like facing a final exam you could only pass by cheating.

Two days later Bradawl announced that they were to serve for a day in Spalling and Sons, the largest department store in the city. Again this was a prestigious assignment. Only the best people shopped there.

A Spalling's delivery van called for them bright and early and they were loaded inside. Mel hoped this second taste of exclusivity they were being treated to worked out better than the last one.

They were unloaded at Spalling's goods depot at the back of the imposing six-story mass of the store. From there they were led along winding back corridors to meet Mr Groover, head of customer care. He was a balding man in his fifties who actually wore a black tailcoat. He looked too superior to soil his hands with slave girls but he subjected them to a close examination, studying their faces, feeling their breasts and having them bend over his desk so he could probe up between their legs.

'You'll do,' he said at last, wiping his hands on a tissue. 'Plenty of physical variety which is good. We're always happy to help Gryndstone, of course, but we have our standards, you know. Only the best for Spalling's customers.'

Groover led them along to the back of the ladies fashion department, where he indicated a heavy door.

'Through there is the changing area exclusively for our gold key customers. While their wives are being fitted many gentlemen like to pass the time more pleasurably than by reading magazines. It's a mutually agreeable arrangement.'

Mel thought it sounded both old fashioned and perverse at the same time, like a lot of things in Shackleswell.

Mr Groover added delicately: 'Sometimes both partners come through or even occasionally ladies on their own. I trust you will have no trouble pleasing them?'

They shook their heads. Pleasing females was not a problem.

Groover introduced them to Harold, a desperately eager to please young man whose neck was too thin for his immaculate company collar and tie. He carried a bucket of sponges, clothes, douche tubes, a pee funnel and a grease gun and had the job of feeding and watering them and cleaning them up between customer visits.

They took them to the relief rooms. These were three small carefully lit cubicles with heavy padded doors and royal blue walls (the company logo colour) containing principally a bidet, a hand basin and a rape rack. This was a low bench the size of a kitchen table with an angled backboard resting on it with its lower edge so close to the front as to leave only a shelf-width between them. This ledge and the backboard were covered in deep blue vinyl padding to match the walls. The legs of the device extended upward to form sturdy head-high side posts linked by crossbars. It was of course amply fitted out with chains and straps together with a lightweight spanking paddle hung on a side post.

'Our customers may of course beat you in moderation,' Groover explained. 'The paddle is very light and will not do any serous damage. Harold has ice packs to reduce any excessive blush they might leave on you. When you are not in use a spyhole is open in the doors so our customers may select their preferred girl.'

Mel watched Cam being secured.

Groover and Harold sat her on the narrow padded ledge and laid her back against the rest. Groover pulled her legs out wide and up until her ankles were level with her shoulders, then he secured her ankle cuffs to chains hanging from the rack's front posts. Straps strung across from the rear posts were looped round the backs of her knees, holding them slightly bent and keeping her thighs from turning inwards. Her arms were pulled up and wide and her cuffs were clipped to chains bolted to the top corners of the backboard. There were lighter chains hanging on the sides of the board that Groover looped across and clipped to Cam's nipple rings. A second pair of chains fixed lower down on the sides of the board were strung across under the backs of her raised thighs and hooked to her labial rings, pulling her glistening lovemouth wide open in invitation. Finally Cam's red collar ball gag was replaced by one of Spalling blue. Their bondage was being colour co-ordinated.

Mini spotlights illuminated the rack and lit up Cam's chained and splayed body. With her legs pulled up and back tilted her parted vagina and anus was perfectly presented for penetration. Against the dark walls she seemed to glow. Cam's eyes met Mel's and she smiled around her gag. Ever since her confession she had seemed almost serene and now on top of that she looked incredibly screwable.

With Cam secured they moved along to the middle cubicle where Mel was chained to an identical rack in the same way. She felt her stomach flip as they pulled her legs wide, exposing her bare ringed pussy for all to see. Mel resisted just enough for them to work against her muscles. There was a guilty schoolgirl thrill in feeling she was being forced. They secured her and closed the door and Mel was alone.

Mel's thoughts drifted. She felt nervous anticipation but no real fear. Weeks of Gryndstone training had reduced what was to come almost to routine. In principle this was not so different from serving in the station, although the soundproofing was better so she could not hear Cam and Bolt or their customers. It was of course right at the other end of the social and comfort scale and at least this time she would not go short of cock and orgasms.

God, did she actually just think that?

Well she was strung out with her pussy chained wide facing the door a procession of strangers was going to walk through and she knew she looked bloody hot so of course they'd want her, which meant she'd also get off. It was natural.

Natural but wrong. She should not be gagging for it as well, that was crazy.

So why was her pussy already oozing with her cream?

Well that was just self-preservation and reflex, it didn't mean that what was being done to her, Cam, Bolt and all the other girls was not morally wrong.

Not in this city though. What about Chain and Spindle in the park? They seemed content, even happy.

So what, surely she wanted to escape from here and get back home?

Well yes… but back home to what?

Her first client was a large bored looking man who hung up his jacket, loosed his flies and jabbed his cock into her mechanically, hardly looking her in the eye. She found the backboard was sprung so his thrusts started her rocking back and forth, setting her breasts jiggling and tugging against their chains. There was a certain thrill in being used so casually, but the best thing was that he was obviously in no hurry to come so she was able to work up to her own climax. She rocked the rack as she orgasmed, almost sucking the sperm out of him. At least it wiped the bored look off his face. He pulled out of her, looking surprised and rather proud.

Harold slipped in a minute after he had left and carefully flushed Mel out and wiped her down, finishing by giving her a sip of water. She smiled her thanks, feeling almost as though she was being pampered. Harold would be wiping the bare pussies of naked bound slave girls all day. It was a hard job, Mel thought, but somebody had to do it.

The next man took up the spanking paddle and without preliminaries swiped it across her exposed groin and buttocks with crisp cracks. He swatted the open mouth of her sex, tormenting the hard nub of her clitoris. Her juices splattered across her belly and inner thighs and stained the paddle. He reached between her legs to beat her breasts, deliberately slapping them from side to side so they were jerked back by their nipple chains.

He did not put the paddle down until her eyes were bulging and wet with tears and she was writhing and straining at her chains, shamefully desperate to please him. Then he took her up her rear with almost brutal force, stretching her anus with his thrusts. He grasped hold of the loops of her nipple chains and used them like reins, hauling himself against her with them even as he drew out her trembling breasts into fat pink cones. He was delighting in her moans and yelps and her face screwed up in pain and the dribble round her gag dripping onto her breasts and Gryndstone tie.

You bastard! Mel screamed at him inside her head and then she came explosively and almost fainted with pleasure. Was she becoming a pain junkie, she thought as she hung limply in her rack? What would it be like to be owned by a man like him and used that way day after day?

After her abuser left Harold had to use his ice packs on her sore flesh and looked concerned and sympathetic. Mel decided he was actually a lot handsomer and nobler than she had at first thought.

Mel had her first couple. They were in their fifties, perhaps, with greying hair but otherwise appearing to be in good shape. Without a word she bent over in front of Mel and rolled up her skirt, presenting her bare bottom to her husband. A metal band ran up from between her buttocks. Another chastity belt. He unlocked it and pulled it open. Mel saw a pair of rubber phalluses pulling out of her anus and vagina. He took down the spanking paddle but he did not use it on Mel. As she slowly and skilfully tongued Mel he screwed his wife from behind, pausing only to swipe her bottom with the paddle. They were in no hurry and knew exactly what they were doing.

She was so submissive and skilled Mel recalled Bradawl's talk on their first day when he had said that after the end of their service gynatons made good wives. Was that still true? Was the woman tonguing her out an ex slave or was female submission simply the norm in male-dominated Shackleswell?

Whatever the truth they all came together and it felt good.

A lone woman in a two-piece business suit came in. She was slim and dark with bright intelligent eyes. She looked Mel up and down hungrily and nodded to herself.

She stood between Mel's spread legs, cupped and squeezed her breasts, then pulled out Mel's gag and kissed her passionately. When she pulled away she put a finger over Mel's lips to command silence. She went round to the back of the rack and worked a catch and the backboard flipped down flat. Groover had not told Mel it did that. It eased the ache in her hips.

The woman hitched up her skirt, clambered onto the now flat rack top and straddled Mel's head. Mel found her face nuzzling into a hot, sweet, scented peach of a vulva that sucked and slurped over her. At the same time she felt lips kissing her pussy. She tongued and lapped and sucked her pulsing lovemouth as passionately as she could. After the woman left Harold had to wipe spent juices from Mel's face and hair.

Mel was visited by another couple who were younger than the first pair. They stood in front of Mel and he pointed at the floor imperiously. His companion immediately knelt down. He freed his cock and screwed Mel while, with her face almost touching Mel's thigh, she watched her husband's cock intently as it pumped in and out of her vagina. After he had spent himself inside Mel he withdrew quickly and she pressed her lips against Mel's gaping sex and methodically sucked and licked up his sperm as it dribbled out of her.

When she was done she sat back on her heels, licking her lips and smiling up at him hopefully.

'All right, you can have the dress,' he said.

Finally they reached the end of the day. Mel heard Mr Groove's voice saying distantly: 'The store is closing now...'

Shortly afterwards Harold came into Mel's cubicle, looking red-faced and slightly furtive. Quickly he opened up his trousers and freed a slim semi-hard shaft that was still glistening with juices. As he positioned himself before Mel she smelt Cam's scent. He was going round screwing them before they were shipped off back to school. She clenched about his cock as he pumped desperately away inside her and did her best to make it as pleasurable as possible.

Presumably in Shackleswell this counted as one of the perks of the job.

'Hi, Maddy. I've been helping out with customer care in very high-class department store whose name I really can't mention. Just say that there is nothing they won't do to keep their customers happy...'

Maddy replied: 'It sounds like you're having such an interesting time! I should have run away, not you. Why can't I see you? I really don't think Dad will care now. I think he's pretending it never happened. We've been punished enough. I mean we are adults and we can make our own choices. And it's been nearly three months…'

Mel blinked. She'd been in Shackleswell nearly three months?

CHAPTER THIRTEEN

The Shackleswell Commercial Fellowship Society was hosting a dinner, celebrating fraternal links with other, very select, businesses around the country. It was held in a private suite in the city's smart new conference centre. Shortly speeches would be given, good food would be consumed and no doubt deals would be done. Before that of course fiddly little finger-food snacks were chewed and drinks were drunk standing up, which had to be served first...

A dozen naked Gryndstone girls were circulating the room serving the drinks and snacks in their own unique way. Locals would point them out to their guests and say proudly: 'That's how we train delinquent girls in this town.'

As a consequence several company bosses would no doubt see the benefits of moving their operations closer to Shackleswell. Gryndstone girls earned their keep in many ways.

Mel was carrying round glasses of champagne on a tray before her. Naturally she was not carrying it with her hands, which were cuffed behind her back. Like all the girls a little silver waitress cap on her head matched the silver bridle gag clamping her mouth shut. A crescent-moon tray was slung against her chest under her breasts, with the horns curving round the sides towards her armpits. It was held in place by a strap going round her back, a chain running up between her breasts to her collar, clips on the tray front hooked to her nipple rings and two light bracing rods supporting its front edge that ran up from her labia rings to which they were padlocked. She did not carry the tray so much as wear it. Loaded with gasses it was quite heavy and pulled on her nipples and labia, but then by now she expected nothing less.

Her breasts, which rested on the tray like pale pink jellies, had sponsors' advertising temporarily stencilled on them, as did her bottom. Many guests, when taking glasses from her tray, could not resist stroking and patting them, making her shiver. But then that was what they were there for.

She saw Cam through the crowd circulating with a tray of snacks. It was slung about her by similar means to Mel's tray, except that as its content was lighter it did not need the bracing rods. Instead her vulva was put to good use holding a metal cone hooked to her labial rings, which contained folded paper napkins.

Bolt carried a cylindrical wire basket slung between breasts. The top end was hooked to her collar ring and the sides were fastened to her breasts by adjustable metal hoops, causing them to bulge into attractive if painful brown fleshy balloons.

The basket held an inverted bottle of red wine, the weight of which was an incentive for her to plead mutely with guests to try the delights of red wine served at slavegirl body heat.

A transparent tube from the bottle was coiled about her waist and then down between her legs, guided by a projecting ring plugged into her anus, to enter a smaller reservoir bottle that filled her vaginal passage. Its spout protruded from between her sex lips and was held in place by hooks linked to her labial rings. The nozzle was fitted with a dispensing valve worked by a light vertical rod running back up across her stomach where it connected to a lever mounted on a horizontal bar clipped to her nipple rings. To get a drink a guest held his cup between Bolt's legs and worked the valve, twisting her nipples in the process, so that red wine at blood heat flowed from her pussy.

When the guests finally went in for their dinner the Gryndstone girls were stripped of their serving trays and arranged along the aside of the reception room bent over a long railing. This had been set out to display their schoolgirl bottoms to the guests when they departed. Large multicoloured plastic film letters were stuck on their buttocks, spelling out: A GIFT FROM SHACKLESWELL. Bunches of helium balloons were plugged into their anuses that bobbed and swayed above them. Silver foil cornucopias of wrapped sweets had been forced up their vaginas until they bulged, inviting dipping into their hot depths to retrieve them. It was a goodbye gift that guaranteed guests would leave in a good mood.

Mel had rested across the railing with her pussy bulging with treats and balloon hanging up out of her bottom for a good ten minutes before she realised she was accepting all this as perfectly natural. They were being submerged by the certainties and self-assurance of Shackleswell society. It was a methodical preparation for living a productive life after school as a working gynaton. Her future was being mapped out for her and she seemed helpless to do anything about it. Time was running out.

'Hi, Maddy. I've been doing some bar work, which is really tiring. All those loaded trays can really strain you if you're not carrying them properly. Maybe it has been long enough. I promise we'll meet sometime soon, but first I've got to get up the courage to move on...'

That night in bed Bolt asked Mel again: 'Come on, when are you going to confess? I don't want to go around being a living wine bottle any longer.'

Mel gulped. 'You go next. You're braver than me. No contest.'

'All right, I will. I'll do it tomorrow. I'll show you how it's done.'

'It's not as easy as you think,' Cam warned her.

Bolt stood chained between the posts of the confession machine with her head up. Her breasts squeezed painfully into the spiked cages stood out from her chest while her big ringed nipples pushed out of the cage crowns. There was a sheen of sweat on her brown skin, making her look in some strange exotic way polished.

From where Mel was riding her phallus Bolt looked proud and defiant. She's really going to do this, she thought.

'I've been stupid and I've done some dumb things,' Bolt said confidently. 'I was lost but now I'm found, right? I've got into some trouble in the past but now... now I've...'

She faltered, looking at all the expectant faces and biting her lip. Mel tensed. What was wrong?

Suddenly Bolt almost shouted: 'You want the truth? I never had a real family, right? I was in and out of foster homes. I was shi... shi... rubbish at school and got kicked out. There was this fire... On the streets I did drugs and I got arrested. A black girl screwing up just like you see on TV. I couldn't even be original! Then some do-gooder came along and told me about this Shackleswell project and I thought it was a soft option to jail. Never imagined it could be like this but that's me. I messed up again, right? Go on beat me for it! Yeah, I deserve it! Please...'

'Do it,' said Bradawl.

Bolt writhed under the blows, but she did not make a sound. When they finished she said: 'It's different now. That me's gone down the toilet. Call me Bolt. That holds things together. That's useful thing, right. I've got it together and I'm strong!'

Bolt squatted down on the dildo handle and pumped with frantic energy, not caring about the spiked cages dragging on her breasts, driving the striker bars up the glass tubes in great leaps. She rang the bells in a time that would probably never be beaten.

Later in the playground Bolt acknowledged the hugs and congratulations of the other girls with uncharacteristically muted pleasure.

'It all just came out' she admitted shamefaced to Cam and Mel. 'I couldn't fu…ing stop it!'

Mel kissed Bolt's sore breasts again and stroked her hair. 'Nobody's holding it against you. They understand. It was genuine, that's what counts. They recognize that because we're all flawed here.'

'But you know what I did, what I am?'

'You mean a pain in the behind? Mel grinned. 'We already knew that. No, seriously you were really amazingly brave. I don't think I could have admitted all that. I'm sorry for you.'

'Don't be sorry,' Bolt said firmly. 'I don't want pity, right? Just be lucky you haven't got all that baggage.'

Mel said nothing.

'But you do feel better now,' Cam suggested,

Bolt sighed. 'I suppose it was good to let it out. Yes, you were right, satisfied? Now let's graduate and get out of this fu… this damned place! It's all getting too bloody honest!'

The car showroom salesman was well into his sales pitch to his potential customer.

'Now this is a Shackleswell Eco Special 3GP,' he said smoothly, 'incorporating the latest in lightweight design and styling with traditional Rowland gyneatic engineering principles.'

The car was a compact three-door silver rear-engine teardrop. Its interior was simply fitted out with two light bucket seats. There was a manual gear stick, small steering wheel and a dashboard with very simple displays.

'It's an ideal about-town model and of course virtually silent and entirely emission free,' the salesman continued.

'How fast will it go?' the customer, a small neat man with large glasses.

'Mileage and top speed depend on your individual GP units. You can install your own or we can supply specially worked high-endurance units from our stock. Matching units come at a small extra charge. These are just demonstration models…'

He lifted the reach hatchback to expose the luggage tray over the engine and then raised that to open up the engine compartment itself. Within were the bowed backs of Cam, Mel and Bolt who were hunched over with their heads facing forward and their shoulder's touching. In front of their faces were the louvered openings of branching plastic ducting.

'Air ducted from the side vents to keep them cool,' the salesman explained. 'For servicing or changing units the engine frame easily disengages from the drive linkage and slides out like this…' He twisted a couple of handles and pulled. The light tubular frame the girls were mounted on slid smoothly out of the car. When their heads were clear of the compartment, bracing struts dropped down to support the end of the frame. In the base of the now virtually empty engine compartment were couplings to various control rods, a gearbox, a battery and dynamo.

The girls were strapped in postures like racing bikers, with their wrists chained to a single long bar in front of them and their feet cuffed to pedals that linked to gear chains. Tubes from plastic water bottles were slipped into the sides of their rubber ring-gagged mouths. Instead of saddles their stomachs rested on contoured pads strapped about their waists. This left their vulvas and bottom clefts exposed.

The salesman patted their rumps. 'They're also at a convenient height for giving relief if you temporarily remove their fittings,' he pointed out.

Insulated wires were plugged into their anuses and looped over to run into slots in the mounting frames.

'What are they?' the customer asked.

'Thermometers to monitor their temperature,' the salesman explained, tweaking the wires. 'The displays are on the dashboard. We wouldn't want them overheating.'

Rods with rubber pronged balls on their tips jutted up into their vulvas, which were held wide by coil springs hooked to their labial rings.

'Feedback rods from the gearbox,' the salesman said, fingering their sticky clefts. 'A steady rate of revs is most rewarding for them because it resonates in the rods. As you can see they're eager to be off. Virtually self-oiling. Sometimes you can get an orgasm every couple of miles.'

Under their groins were hung cupped funnels connected to a single large plastic waste bottle part filled with yellow fluid.

'Integral urine collection,' said the salesman. 'That way you can happily leave them in the car all day without them embarrassing you.'

Their dangling breasts were held steady by tensioning rods hooked to their nipple rings. Sliding up these rods were tubes controlled by spinning governors. On the tube ends resting just under their breasts were flat rubber rings studded with stubby metal pins.

'The accelerator unit,' the salesman explained. 'Pushing on the pedal raises the pads. They feel the pins in their breasts and pedal faster. This makes the governors speed up in turn and lowers them again.'

The customer took this all in with great interest. 'Can I take it for a test drive?'

'Of course, Sir,' said the salesman, sliding the living engine back into its compartment and closing the hatch again.

With only a soft purr of gears, the Eco Special 3GP rolled out of the showroom and onto the street. Inside the engine compartment, scented with a mixture of oil and female juices, Mel, Bolt and Cam pedalled harder to force the accelerator pins back out of their tender breast flesh.

They had been reduced to living engine components, Mel thought. Unlike a girl train they could not even see where they were going. It was inhuman slave labour! She had to get away from this perverted town! Then they reached a steady speed, the pronged balls begin to buzz in their clefts and Mel felt another orgasm coming on.

It was that evening, with her muscles still stiff from her exertions in the showroom, that Mel discovered Maddy had not replied to her last mail. So far she had responded to every one within an hour at the most. Concerned, Mel asked Bradawl if there were any delays on the system.

'It's working perfectly,' he assured her. 'The relay only takes seconds and we never deliberately hold back any messages either in or out.'

Of course there might be a perfectly normal explanation. Just in case she sent a mail to her parents. They had little to say over recent weeks but they should respond to this simple request. 'Can you please get Maddy to call me?'

Mel waited in the classroom until Bradawl relayed the reply. It was from her father and was short and terse: 'Maddy has gone away.'

Gone away where, Mel thought in despair? But even then she would call her. What was Maddy doing? Had she run out of patience with her parents or was she giving up on her? Now Mel became acutely aware of her isolation and confinement. Shut away in the school what could she do? This place was taking over her mind and sapping her will. She would have to get out of here. Whether she would have the nerve to try to escape or even just use a public phone she did not know, but it was a start.

That meant first she would have to confess.

CHAPTER FOURTEEN

The next morning it took all Mel's courage to step up to Mr Emery, who was washroom monitor, and say: 'Please Master, would you tell the Headmaster I wish to confess?'

He just nodded his head. 'I'll tell him, girl.'

Other girls who had heard hugged and kissed her. Cam looked happy while Bolt gave a thumb's up.

In assembly Mel felt sick and dizzy when her name was called out by Bradawl. Being chained to the confession machine seemed unreal and she hardly noticed the spikes of the breast cages digging into her soft flesh. All she was aware of was the sea of expectant faces staring at her.

But her secret was safe, she told herself over and over. She had defied the truth rack and Judge Gouge to keep it. Nobody in Shackleswell knew. She would just say she had a stupid family argument and ran away. She meant to go to London but ended up here...

'What do you have to confess, Spring 157?' Bradawl asked.

'I... I've been a bad girl. I had a stupid argument with my family and ran away and...'

She faltered. The truth wanted to come out. It was getting in the way of her life. There was only so long she could keep this bottled up inside her. If Shackleswell had taught her anything it was that all shame had its limits.

'No, it wasn't a stupid argument. I have a stepsister called Maddy.... that's short for Madelyn. We've lived together since we were young. We were the same age more or less and we even look quite alike. Strangers thought we were real twins. As we got older we used to compare how we were growing... standing together naked in front of a mirror. And then one day we just...

kissed… and touched and… Yes, we had sex! I screwed her and it was fantastic! And we did it again… and then our parents caught us. They're quite religious and they couldn't accept it. It was terrible. And that's why I ran away and ended up here!'

The girls were all gaping at her open-mouthed but it was said and done.

'I'm not sorry for loving Maddy that way, only for the hurt it caused. Please beat me!'

The pain of the cane lashes felt so sweet, blotting out her guilt, but they stopped far too soon. She had been hiding behind the pain and degradation she had suffered, but now she was naked in every sense of the word. The truth was out and she had bared her soul. What else could she say next? What was she sure of?

'I was lost but now I'm Spring 157,' Mel gasped. 'A spring is something elastic that can return to its normal shape after being bent, compressed or stretched. It can be used to reduce vibration, concussion, as a power source or actuator. It's a useful thing so I'm useful. I'm strong…'

Mel began to squat down on the pump impaled within in her. The chains tugged on her nipples and twisted the spiked cages into her breasts but she did not care. She had admitted the worst thing she had ever done. She was dribbling round the pump handle as it rammed into her then dragged on her pussy rings but nothing else could hurt her so deeply again. She could hear the girls urging her on as they pumped their own phalluses and that felt wonderful. They didn't hate her for what she had done! Here nothing was hidden…

The bells rang and she orgasmed and everybody cheered wildly.

While she hung limp and sweaty between the posts the girls filed up and kissed her.

'Now I understand,' Cam said.

'You had to go one better than me!' Bolt said gruffly but not unkindly.

She saw only understanding and compassion in the other girls' eyes. They accepted her. As Wire had said they were all damaged in someway. In this perverted city perhaps it was not such a sin.

Mel was freed from the confession machine. Her legs felt like rubber and Master Stapler had to hold her upright.

Bradawl said: 'As both Spring's chain-sisters have already made their confessions and all have achieved satisfactory grades in their classes, as well as having passed all their practical tests, I declare that this trigyn is fit to graduate from Gryndstone. They will leave this morning.'

A new murmur of surprise went up and Mel felt dizzy. They were graduating right now?

Bolt and Cam were called up to the front of the hall. Their ties were removed, their graduation medals were clipped in their places and Bradawl congratulated them. There was no sign of condemnation for what she had just admitted. They kissed the cocks of all the masters and thanked them for what they had done.

'You will have your chance to say goodbye to our graduates in first break,' Bradawl told the other pupils. 'Now off to your lessons.' The rest of the school filed out. He smiled at Mel, Bolt and Cam. 'You are free until then. You might want to visit the washroom first.'

It was strange to be wandering about out of class while the rest of the school was at work and even stranger to be without their ties. Mel felt undressed. In the deserted washroom Mel cooled her sore breasts. The stud marks seemed to be fading already and the cane stripes were hardly worth mentioning. They were nothing to a Gryndstone pupil, except that technically she was a Gryndstone pupil no longer. Bolt and Cam were clearly desperate to hear more about her private shame but were also hesitant to ask.

'It just happened between Maddy and me,' Mel volunteered. 'We knew it was wrong even if it was exactly illegal, but we couldn't help it. It just felt so good. Then our parents caught us. They couldn't take it. It was the worst thing that had ever happened to me. I felt I'd started it all so I ran.'

'That must have been terrible,' Cam said gently.

'But do you think it was wrong?' Mel asked, looking at each of them doubtfully. Suddenly their understanding was very important.

'After all my screw-ups who am I to judge?' Bolt said, then smiled. 'So maybe I wouldn't have said that before I came here, but now I know screwing another girl can be, well, pretty good, I can't say it's wrong. As long as nobody made you do it then the moral stuff's up to you and her.'

'But you can't ignore how it affects your family either,' Cam said. 'You know you're going to have to work that out eventually.'

'I know,' Mel said. 'It frightens me.'

'Some day I'm going to have to make my peace with my family as well,' Cam admitted. 'I think confessing is a start. Do you feel better now?'

'I think I do,' Mel admitted.

'I said this place was too honest,' said Bolt. 'Now let's really get out of here.'

'It's a shame we haven't time for proper goodbyes,' said Cam. 'I was looking forward to our ring on ring night.'

'They probably want to get us away before I mess up again,' said Bolt. 'Can't say I blame them. Anyway, it means we get out a day early.'

At break time Bradawl led them down the playground through a fleshy wall of ringed nipples and bare pubes as the other girls crowded round them. The wonderful warmth and smell of their perfumed bodies was almost overwhelming.

'Keep in touch,' Bobbin, Pin and Axle begged.

'We will,' Mel promised, feeling dangerously emotional and blinking back tears. Even Bolt looked a little dewy-eyed while Cam did not try to disguise her feelings. Hard nipples pressed into soft breasts as they hugged girls they had lived intimately closely with, strained and suffered beside and made love to on so many occasions. Even those fresh girls they hardly knew would be riding the same phalluses they had used in the weeks to come, which was a strange sort of continuity. Somehow it felt as though she had been at Gryndstone for years and not months. Perhaps it was the quantity and intensity of new experiences that mattered and not simply time that had passed. Mel knew Gryndstone had moulded and shaped her mind and body and her life would never be the same again.

They made their goodbyes and then passed through the green door at the bottom of the playground into Miss Trunnion's office.

'Here are our latest graduates, Miss Trunnion,' said Bradawl.

'Yes, Headmaster,' said Miss Trunnion, misty-eyed.

'Don't be sad, they must move on.'

'I know, Headmaster.'

Bradawl looked at Mel, Bolt and Cam. 'Whatever you do next I'm sure you're going to make Gryndstone proud of you. Only in Shackleswell will you enjoy the freedom to be what you are without shame, to serve with pride and suffer with joy. Here you will always be valued as parts of a greater whole, never forget that.'

'No, Headmaster,' they said together, then they all bent and kissed his cock one last time and said thank you, even Bolt.

Mel recalled how the three of them had first seen Bradawl in this office what seemed like a lifetime ago and how shocked she had been. Now she felt an absurd pang of loss at the thought of leaving his school.

Bradawl departed. Miss Trunnion sniffed and dabbed her eyes with a tissue and then said briskly: 'I have your street clothes here…'

She brought out hangers holding three sets of grey knee-length belted coats, ankle boots, scarves and headbands. Mel had no idea they were handed out to them so soon after graduating.

'Give me you shoes and try them on…'

They handed over their school shoes and took the coats and boots. It felt rather cloying and slightly scratchy to be wrapped in fabric, Mel thought, although her coat was softly lined. Oddly all the time she had been kept naked Mel realised she had not felt cold. No wonder Chain and Spindle had taken their coats off as soon as they got into the park.

She looked at Cam and Bolt who were hesitantly pulling on their coats. She'd never seen them dressed before, except in dog suits which hardly counted. Now the jiggle of their breasts, the hardness of their nipples and the excitement of their lovemouths was concealed. What a loss of self-expression that was. She would have to judge their mood by their faces alone.

'We do get a few strangers in town so keep your headbands and scarves on in public,' Miss Trunnion advised.

They covered their foreheads and collars. Now they were nameless as well.

Miss Trunnion handed them each a small purse. 'Here are five gyntokens each pocket money, plus the ones you were given in the park.'

She also had some pamphlets for them. 'This is the address of your gynhouse and guidebook and maps to the city to help you find your way. There's no hurry. You don't have to report until six. Now here's a guide to the gyncom message board service to keep you in touch with your friends. And this is a list of further education classes and courses you might be interested in after you've settled down.'

'Further education?' Mel asked.

'You can't be a serving gyn all you life,' Miss Trunnion said, sounding wistful. 'You have to prepare for the future, but don't let that worry you now. Right, that's you set up.'

Suddenly she came forward and hugged each of them. 'Sorry, but I feel like this every time girls graduate. Please visit us. We like to know how our old girls are getting on.'

Mel felt something hard under the older woman's blouse as she hugged her. Nipple rings? Of course, "Trunnion" was a mechanical term...

Miss Trunnion recovered herself and pressed the switch under her desk and the inner door to the mews unlocked.

'We walk out just like that?' Bolt asked in disbelief, looking from her to the door.

'Aren't we escorted?' Mel said.

'No, you just go by yourselves,' said Miss Trunnion. 'It's a nice day. Or you could go down to the station...'

'We'll walk,' Bolt said quickly.

'Goodbye and good luck...'

Hesitantly they walked out of the mews and up the lane beside the school wall until they reached the main road. Cars and people were passing by. Bolt was looking about her as though expecting trouble but nobody stopped them. It felt strange. This was not a closed park but the real world they had not set foot in for months. They could go left or right along the road. It was up to them what way they took. They could pretend the cuffs and collars under their coats were not there. This was freedom. It was a little frightening.

They walked along to stand in front of the school. It looked so innocent from the outside.

Bolt suddenly laughed. 'They just let us out! After all those chains and straps and bars it was as easy as that! They really believe we'll do as we're told! They're fu… ing crazy!' She scowled at the school then set off down the road. 'Come on, let's get away from here. I don't want to look at that place ever again.'

'Some of it wasn't so bad,' Cam said as they strode along.

'Oh, and what particular screw, caning or tit-pulling were you thinking of?' Bolt asked sarcastically

'I meant having friends around who accepted me… and making love to you in our cage.'

Bolt had to grin. 'So I'm great in bed. But apart from that?'

'Apart from that we did have some fantastic orgasms.'

Bolt did not respond. At the junction at the end of the road she studied her map.

'What are you doing?' Cam asked.

'Finding the shortest way out of this town. When I'm clear I'll find somebody who'll give me a lift and then I'm gone.'

'Back home?' Cam asked.

'Yeah, Northhampton. My home town, not this place.'

'I didn't know you lived in Northampton,' Mel said. 'After everything we've done together I don't really know anything about your pasts, either of you.'

'We've all heard our confessions,' Cam said. 'I think that's what really matters.'

Bolt pointed to the left. 'That's the way I'm going.' She looked at them and took a deep breath. 'You could come with me if you want. It might be… fun.'

Cam smiled but shook her head. 'I don't think so. I've still got to sort myself out. I might as well do it here as anywhere.'

'Don't you hate what they make us do?'

'I started off hating it but now I'm not sure. Maybe it's no worse then the things I did to myself and others without any help. Being here is safer than being on the streets. Maybe I need some discipline to keep me in line.'

Bolt looked genuinely sad. 'Have they ground you down? Made you into a proper gynaton?'

'Maybe they just uncovered what was already there. I didn't think much of myself before I came here. At least I now know I'm good for something. I'm useful. Don't worry, I'll be fine.'

Bolt looked at Mel. 'Spring?'

'I've got to find a public phone and talk to my parents or sister direct. I must find out what she's doing. Then… I don't know. A step at a time. Maybe I can visit home on a day off.'

'Have they got to you too?

'I don't feel brainwashed, but like Cam said, we keep having these amazing orgasms. Something must be working right and I want to know why. Some of it I hate but even that excites me at the same time, like being in a perverted adventure. I certainly feel more alive here than at anytime in my life… except perhaps making love to Maddy. Maybe I have got a masochistic streak. Anyway, I haven't got anywhere else to go. Will you be all right?'

'Me? I'll be fine. No trouble.'

They looked at each other awkwardly for a moment and then embraced and kissed passionately.

'Ok, so some of it was fun,' Bolt admitted huskily.

Reluctantly they pulled apart again.

'Keep checking with the school,' Bolt said. 'I'll send them a postcard: "Hi, Suckers!" See if they put that up on the notice board.'

Mel forced a smile. 'We will... goodbye... and good luck.'

They watched Bolt stride off until she was out of sight. 'So what do we do now?' Cam asked.

Mel swallowed a lump in her throat. 'I want to try to ring home, if you don't mind.'.

'I've nowhere better to go... and I don't want to lose my last friend,' Cam said.

Mel looked at her, fighting back tears once more. They kissed, only pulling apart when they remembered where they were.

They found a phone box, which being in Shackleswell was clean and in working order and Mel made some reverse charge calls. Her parent's answer phone was on and Maddy's phone was not picked up.

Mel was dispirited. Cam said: 'Let's go into town and see what we can get to eat and drink with our tokens. If we're going to be staying here we should have a look around. You can try phoning again later.'

They walked along tree-lined streets, past carefully renovated and restored factories.

'It's all very clean, isn't it?' Cam said.

'Do you think they have teams of gynatons out here at night scrubbing the streets?' Mel joked, then realised that might literally be true.

They found a pub that had a walled beer garden with seats under sunshades. Nervously they went in to the bar.

The barman clearly recognized them. Their standard costumes must have been like uniforms to a Shackleswell native. 'And what can I get a pretty pair of gyns like yourselves?' he asked with a grin.

He knew they were naked and ringed underneath their coats. However he served them cheerfully enough. A drink and a sandwich were a token each.

They sat outside eating and drinking slowly while trying to get used to this unnatural freedom. It was not even Sunday. They should be in lessons now...

'Do you suppose we'll get into trouble for letting Bolt run away?' Cam asked.

'We'll we weren't chained to her,' Mel said. 'Nobody's ever said anything about what to do if somebody escapes. They just assumed we'd all behave. We could always say we thought Bolt would meet us later.'

'I don't want to lie,' Cam said. 'At least Shackleswell is honest in the way it treats us. That's why we have the collars and chains. They don't expect us to like everything they do to us, just try our best to serve and...'

She was interrupted by the appearance of the barman by their table.

'Excuse me, girls. I know it's your day off but do you want to earn yourself a few extra tokens?' he asked. 'A couple of our regular games room gyns are off sick and we need some performers to fill in.'

'Doing what, Master?' Mel asked hesitantly.

He told them.

Mel blinked. They were not being commanded to obey, simply requested, as if their desires actually mattered. It was a choice. They had the power just to say no and walk away. That was real freedom and the idea that they would give up a few precious hours of it was laughable. She glanced at Cam and read the same understanding in her eyes.

'We'll do it, Master,' they said.

The huge dartboard hanging on the wall in the pub games room had the outline of a slave girl picked out in wire in between the normal radiating numbered grid lines. It portrayed her with her back to the board, her head up, her arms drawn out and wrists aligned with cuff hooks on the board rim. Her thighs were pulled up and bent back level with her hips and her knees were bent at right angles.

Mel fitted the outline perfectly, held in place by cuff hooks and narrow metal straps about her elbows, chest, waist, thighs and knees. Further support was given by a right-angled bar projecting from the middle of her board capped by a rubber plug that was lodged in her rectum. She was almost totally immobile and she strained against her bonds with a perverse thrill. A mesh guard over her face was her only protection. She was a living target. The darts themselves had fine short points projecting from rounded sticky pad heads, ensuring they did not penetrate deeply but still stuck to what they hit.

Contoured and numbered wire grids clipped tightly about Mel's breasts and groin delineated the target areas. Hooks in the grids pulled her labial rings wide, making the wet pink mouth of her sex gape. Numbered wire loops showed that a hit on her breasts scored twenty, her areolae twenty-five and her nipple crowns fifty, while her labia were worth twenty five points, her vaginal mouth, a natural bulls-eye, fifty and her clitoris sixty. That was of course the most exquisite agony.

The players were good and her most sensitive parts were their favoured targets. Mel wailed and slobbered about her gag as their darts feathered her breasts and groin. They only raised pinpricks of blood but the pain combined with her bondage aroused her until she was dripping onto the floor.

When a game was won the board was lowered and the winner claimed his prize between her gaping thighs. Mel was a target for darts and for the players' penises. Like any gynaton she was there to be penetrated one way or another. By then she was in desperate need and welcomed the hard shafts that filled her aching void and rammed her against the board.

Next to the dartboard was the skittle alley. Cam was suspended over the end as the target for a game of Bat and Skittle.

Her arms were stretched up and outward over her head by a spreader bar linking her wrists. It was hung by a pair of chains, allowing her to sway and twist a little if she struggled but bringing her back to rest facing the bowlers' end. More chains ran down from the ends of the spreader bar to her ankle cuffs, holding her splayed legs wide with her feet dangling just above the boards of the alley.

The single target skittle was a heavy tapering wooden teardrop with along neck that was thrust deep up her rectum so that it hung freely beneath her. Its neck was carved into half a dozen thick ribs, helping her anal ring clamp about it and hold it inside her. A pair of light chains stapled to the sides of the skittle ran up Cam's back and over her shoulders to clip onto her nipple rings.

The bat hung between her legs in front of the skittle. It was a flat round wooden paddle just brushing the floor with a long shaft that was plugged into Cam's vagina. Hooks screwed into its sides secured it to her pussy rings. The shaft was in two sections joined halfway up by a heavy coil spring, allowing it to flex when struck. She used it to protect the skittle and prevent it being knocked out of her anal grip.

The players stood at the end of the short alley and bowled down wooden balls at the skittle and Cam tried to deflect them with the bat. They could shift about the end of the lane trying to get a clear shot at the skittle while Cam twisted round in her chain to protect it. Every strike on the sprung paddle set it bouncing and shivering, twisting it against her labial rings while the upper end churned about and vibrated inside her vaginal sheath. Soon she was lubricating profusely, making the bat handle shiny and dripping onto the floor beneath her splayed legs, joining the stains left by numerous girls who had hung there before her.

When a ball got past her guard and struck the skittle it was more painful as it jarred inside her rectum. A hard blow would dislodge one of the ribs from her grasp and it would slip one notch out of her sphincter. Blow by blow it would be loosened from her until it dropped out of her rear. As the skittle toppled over it tugged on its chains that jerked her nipples upward. Her yelp of pain signalled the end of the game.

The successful bowler would of course claim his prize of her now unplugged rear as she hung swaying in her chains blinking back the tears.

In other words it was just a normal afternoon in a Shackleswell pub.

'We're a real pair of pain slut sex slaves,' Cam sighed a couple of hours later as they left the pub.

'We're gynatons,' Mel corrected her.

'Same thing?'

'Slaves don't get days off.'

A police car drew up by the side of the pavement and PC Colter leaned out of the driver's window. Beside him sat PC Mattock. Mel's stomach flipped.

'Found you, Spring 157,' Colter said with a grin. 'Get in, you're wanted back at the station.'

Mel gulped. 'Why, Master?'

'You'll see. On the way we'll pick up your chain-sister, Bolt 184. You as well, Cam 031.'

'We... don't know where Bolt is,' Cam said nervously.

'Oh, we know exactly where she is,' Colter said casually, 'she's doing a runner. Do you think those anti-swearing chips are all you've got in your collars? They've got locator beacons in there as well. Now you two come with us…'

With heavy hearts Mel and Cam climbed into the back of the police car and it drove off.

As they headed out of town Mel slumped in her seat. Bradawl had not been so naïve as Bolt had thought. They had never really been freed. It had all been an illusion. 'Will you be able to catch Bolt before she escapes, Masters?' she asked miserably.

'We're not trying to catch her,' said Mattock with a chuckle. 'A lot of new girls escape on the first free day they get and we let them. They need to get it out of their system. They either sneak back later and say nothing or report themselves, feeling guilty, so we give them a spanking to make them feel better.'

Mel's head spun as she tried to take this in. 'Then why are you going after her, Masters?'

'Because she's stopped trying to escape.'

'She's… stopped?' Cam said incredulously.

'Which means she'll probably need her chain-sisters for a bit of emotional support.'

Bolt was hunched over with her legs drawn up tight and her head resting on her knees, exposing the dark cleft of her shiny ringed pubes. She was sitting on a weathered outcrop of rock beside a narrow country track that wound up a hill overlooking Shackleswell. She hardly stirred as the police car drew up and Mel and Cam scrambled out and ran up to her.

'Are you all right?' Cam asked anxiously, stroking Bolt's hair.

'Has anybody hurt you?' Mel added.

Bolt raised her head, revealing confused, tear-stained eyes. 'I've got nowhere to go,' she said pitifully.

'You were going home to Northampton,' Mel said.

'That's not home… it's where I lived… but there's nobody there who wants me back. I've got… nothing!'

She and Cam sat down on either side of Bolt and hugged her gently.

Mel looked out over the city of Shackleswell, which stood there solid, purposeful and dominating. It was the first time she had seen it like this. Now she knew that slave girls served it at every level, from pubs to assembly rooms, in the streets and the underground. They were essential to its survival and they bound it together. The city machine was built on their sweat and suffering and sustained by their orgasms. The price of being part of it was the total surrender of their bodies to pain and humiliation and the reward was belonging intimately and completely to something greater than themselves that was both frightening and wonderful. She could not escape it now. None of them could.

'Then you'd better come home with us,' she told Bolt.

Bolt looked at them and then burst into tears.

CHAPTER FIFTEEN

Mel felt a cold shiver as the three of them were escorted into Shackleswell Central police station, recalling her first visit. As Colter and Mattock led them to the interrogation rooms her stomach began to churn in anticipation, even though she was a different person from the naïve innocent they had tortured those months before. Now she did not try to ignore that darkly thrilling frisson of fear but revelled in its grip because she knew it would make what followed more intense. What that said about her she no longer cared.

They entered the interrogation room. The truth rack stood in one corner with its impaler rod glistening as though it had been used recently. Mattock commanded Bolt and Cam to stop there as they took in its "X" frame central table, the sinister devices on the walls and the folded gibbet arms.

'Are you going to punish me for escaping, Master?' Bolt asked meekly.

'No, girl, not for escaping, but we will give you a good hiding for the trouble you caused us having to find your friends and bring you back.' He looked at Cam. 'And we'll give you a few licks for lying when you said you didn't know where she was.'

Cam bowed her head. 'Sorry, Master.'

'I'll get some of the off duty lads in to give you two a proper seeing to. Now get your coats off…'

Mel moved to join them but Colter took her arm. 'No, you come this way…'

He led Mel on through double security doors into a smaller side room. 'I want you to meet somebody we arrested earlier,' he said. 'She's just waiting to be taken to Gryndstone…'

He ushered Mel inside with a pat on her bottom and closed the door behind her. Within was a small bare cell with a naked girl dangling from the ceiling. Her wrists and ankles were strapped together and a chain pulled her arms up above her until she stood on her toes. Her blonde head hung over her chest. Lash stripes showed scarlet across her full breasts and thighs.

As Mel entered she lifted her head fearfully. Mel gave a choking gasp and sprang forward to embrace her.

It was Madelyn!

Mel did not know how long she hugged and kissed Maddy while brokenly poured out her words of love. Maddy squirmed in her embrace, kissing her passionately in return even as she wept with joy. Finally Mel recovered her composure sufficiently to pull back a little, wiping the tears from her own and Maddy's eyes.

'You've no idea how long I've wanted to do that again,' she said huskily.

'As long as I have,' Maddy sobbed.

'But how did you get here? I never told you where I was.'

'Somebody left a message on my phone saying you were in Shackleswell.'

'Who?'

'A man. I didn't recognise his voice and he didn't give a name, he just said he was... something strange... a "gynaeneticist", whatever that is.'

Now Mel understood. That was why they had graduated so quickly. Bradawl had set all this up. Maddy's disarrayed hair had been hanging across her forehead. Only now did Mel notice the official pink court label taped underneath. She brushed the hair aside. The label read: "SPRING 202." That could not be chance. Thank you, Headmaster, she thought silently.

'I only got here this morning,' Maddy continued,

'but before I could even begin looking for you these policemen said I was a vagrant and arrested me and I had to strip and there was this judge on a television and they used this machine and…'

'I know,' Mel assured her, 'I know just what they did to you because they did it to me months ago. But you'll get over it because you're stronger than you imagine. You'll bounce back.' She chuckled. 'After all, you're going to be a spring, like me…'

'But they said I'd have to go to some sort of school,' Maddy groaned. 'I don't understand. What's happening? What is this place?'

'This is Irontown,' Mel explained, feeling a strange thrill as she used the old name. 'It's where they bring women and machines together to do amazing things. You're going to Gryndstone school for lost girls to learn how it's done. There they'll train you and turn you into a gynaton which is … well, something just like this…'

She pulled off her clothing and stood naked before her stepsister, feeling relieved to be rid of its encumbrance.

Maddy goggled at Mel's name stamps, rings, cuffs and collar. 'What have they done to you?' she wailed.

'It's all right,' Mel assured her. 'I know you're frightened and some of it will hurt at first but you'll get used to it. This is like a uniform. It shows you're useful and you belong in Shackleswell, and I promise you do belong here. You won't believe how quickly it feels normal, then even better than normal. When you graduate, you'll understand. And I'll be waiting for you. Oh, and you must say thank you to Headmaster Bradawl from me. For bringing us together…'

She kissed Maddy again, forestalling any more questions. She would have to learn the rest for herself. This time their bare breasts pressed against each other and she felt the warmth of Maddy's naked flesh against her own, as it should be. Maddy's pubic hair tickled. She would soon lose that...

Colter came back in while they were still locked together and grinned. 'That's better. Can't have too many clothed girls around here. Right, time to put on a little show...'

He pulled Mel's arms round behind her and clipped her cuffs together. Then he freed Maddy's ankles, unhooked her from the ceiling chain and led her back into the interrogation room with Mel at her side. Maddy gasped.

Bolt and Cam were suspended from adjacent fold-out gibbets while Mattock and two other men in rolled-shirtsleeves and peel-back trousers were having fun with them.

Suspension bars were fastened by swivel links the ends of the gibbet arms. Bolt and Cam hung face down under them. Their arms were bent round behind them and stretched out straight with their cuffs chained to rings on the bar ends, pulling their shoulders back. Another chain was clipped to rings set in the fastening straps of rubber bit gags that stretched their mouths and kept their heads up. A vertical chain was hooked to a broad strap that went round their waists, supporting their torsos. Their legs were splayed and knees bent. Chains from the bar ends were clipped to their ankles and another pair of straps that went around the tops of their thighs. This left their groins wide open, bare ringed pussies exposed and bottoms invitingly upturned. Short chains ran from the rings in the backs of their gag straps to large rubber hooks, the curling tips of which had been slid up their rectums, making their anuses bulge.

Their heads were aligned towards each other so they could look into each other's faces. They were held in this position by long chains that linked their nipple rings. Mattock was hooking small lead weights over the middles of the chains, making their arcs more acute. The tension had stretched their nipples and drawn out their breasts into rounded cones.

As Mel and Maddy entered the two new men were standing between the girls' splayed thighs thrusting into their vaginas. With one hand they held the chains linking the girls gags and bottom hooks like reins to brace them against their thrusts, while in the other they had long-handled spanking paddles. These they were swinging up under the girls' bodies to smack into the taut under-swells of their chain-stretched breasts. Each thrust and smack made Bolt and Cam sway and twist in their harness, jerking on their nipple chains or making them sway painfully. Their cheeks were wet with tears, their bodies writhed in their harnesses and they yelped and moaned and dribbled about their gags, yet their eyes were unfocussed and half closed in slavish ecstasy.

Maddy whimpered in horror and turned her head aside.

'Don't worry,' Mel said softly, 'it's how they want to be treated.'

With grunts of satisfaction the men came inside Cam and Bolt even as they bucked and squirmed in their chains, helplessly surrendering to their own orgasmic rushes. Only when their struggles had subsided and they hung limply and servile once more, did the men pull their shafts out of their ravaged vaginas. The floor under their spread legs was dark with splashes of female juices and spent sperm.

'Now, anybody want to see hot stepsisters screw each other?' Colter asked. 'Don't worry, they're gagging for it.'

The others grinned and looked Mel and Maddy up and down with calculated interest. Though they dangled sweaty and beaten in their chains, Cam and Bolt were staring at them in growing wonder. Then Cam smiled at Mel around her gag.

Maddy rolled her eyes up and bit her lip in shame. Mel whispered: 'You know that's true. We don't have to pretend any more. Just let it happen. Even pain can feel good here…'

Colter laid Maddy on her back across the "X" table and dragged her legs wide. Maddy resisted feebly but could not prevent her ankles being strapped to its lower ends. Colter separated Maddy's wrists and pulled her arms apart, fastening them in the same way. As she looked at her sister spreadeagled, helpless and achingly vulnerable Mel trembled, thinking that it was the most desirable thing she had ever seen.

From the rack of canes and humiliation devices Mattock brought over a large double-ended dildo. 'She's got to have something to stick up her,' he said with a grin.

They slid one end of the dildo into Mel and secured its fastening to her pussy rings. Maddy's eyes went round with horror as she saw the huge thing sticking out of her stepsister's slot.

Colter positioned Mel at the apex of the wedge cut out of the table where Maddy's pouting sex overhung the edge. Maddy looked up at her trembling in fear and Mel smiled gently back. It's all right, she mouthed.

The men gathered round the table with Colter at its head as though supervising. The two shirtsleeved officers positioned themselves on either side of Maddy while Mattock stood behind Mel. They all held spanking paddles.

Colter said: 'The harder you screw her, the less we'll spank her tits, understand?'

Mel nodded. She understood.

She slid the tip of the dildo between Maddy's lovlips, seeing them part and stretch to accommodate it, seeing her eyes grow wide in fear and wonder. She wanted to slide it up her gently, knowing how tight her passage would be unlike her own trained sheath, but Mattock was impatient. He swiped his paddle across Mel's buttocks with stinging force, making her jerk her hips forward, ramming the dildo full length into Maddy.

Her lovely face contorted and she gave a whimper of pain.

This was a signal to the others to begin. The paddles fell across Maddy's breasts, making them flatten and spring back with fluid resilience. She writhed in he bonds and sobbed in pain

Mattock was spanking Mel's bottom, forcing her to thrust harder and harder, making Maddy's juices flow, seeing her lower stomach bulge as the big dildo filled her passage to capacity. It was almost as if she was moving inside her like a man. What a power to have! It was terrible seeing Maddy in true pain yet she knew it had to be done. The sooner she reached her crisis point and understood the happier she would be.

Maddy's abused breasts were going from pink to scarlet. The paddle blows were now batting them from side to side and they were rebounding and shivering resiliently like fleshy bells. Yet her nipples were standing up in hard peaks as proud as Mel's.

Then Colter twisted Maddy's head to one side and rammed his cock into her mouth. Despite her pain her lips clamped about his shaft as her cheeks bulged. The shirt-sleeved constables dropped their paddles and began rubbing their revived cocks across Maddy's burning breasts and throbbing scarlet nipples. Mattock took Mel by the hips and forced his shaft into her anus. Now he was connected through her body to her stepsister.

For a few seconds there was no sound but the men grunting as they strained to achieve their relief. Jets of sperm splattered across Maddy's simmering breasts, into her mouth and deep up inside Mel's rectum. Maddy convulsed and Mel saw wonder and pure pleasure wipe the pain from her face and knew with joy that she had tasted her first slavish orgasm.

Then Mel's hips bucked, she clenched the dildo and Mattock's cock and fireworks of raw delight exploded in her brain. Her reward had finally come.

Utterly spent Mel collapsed across Maddy's hot, sweaty, abused, lovely body. Her breasts flattened across her heaving chest and burning globes and their juices mingled and dripped together onto the floor.

Distantly Mel heard the men saying: 'That was good…' 'Naturals, both of them…' 'Think what they'd sell for as a pair…' 'Well, nobody would want to split them up, would they?'

Then she understood everything.

Irontown was only place in the country where she and Maddy would be applauded for what they had just done. Here they were valued for being lovers, not condemned. It was the only place they could ever be free to be what they were.

EPILOGUE

The train waited by the platform of Gryndstone Halt while the masters loaded two coffles of new girls on board.

Their rings felt heavy and new in their flesh and they were still nervous and frisky at being chained and naked. With gag-muffled squeaks and whimpers they squatted down and impaled themselves on the phalluses of the cattle truck. They were too fearful and excited to notice the two blonde girls who powered the engine of their train, or that a photograph of them hung outside their school assembly hall.

Within the engine frame Mel and Maddy lay prone, resting patiently in their cuffs and straps. Sweat sheened their bodies and their full, pale, tethered breasts hung cooling pleasantly below them. Their nipple rings were pierced and joined by a long rod bolted at each end to the engine frame. Through it they could feel transmitted the clatter of the wheels, the whirr of the gears and rattle of the couplings. They were as one with the engine and each other.

The guard blew his whistle. Their driver released the brakes and pushed the power lever forward. The ribbed speed control rods slid further up their rectums accompanied by the warning pricks on the fleshy curves of their buttocks from the spiked pads mounted behind them. Obediently Mel and Maddy began to pedal, their buttocks, thighs and calves bulging with effort as they overcame the inertia of the carriages and their living cargo.

Slowly at first but with steadily increasing speed the train pulled out of Gryndstone Halt powered solely by their straining bodies.

As they got up speed and the feedback governors spun faster the spikes pulled back. In their place the pronged balls in their clefts began to vibrate, bringing smiles to their lips as they were rewarded for their efforts. Drips fell happily from between their thighs onto the track rushing by below them. Once more Rowland's theories were proven as girls and machine merged into one.

Tomorrow Mel and Maddy had a day off and they would meet up with Cam and Bolt and make a happy foursome. But for now they were simply perfectly matched living engines serving their chosen purpose as they sped through the tunnels under Irontown.

THE END